The

DAY

TRIPPER

The

DAY

TRIPPER

a novel by

JAMES GOODHAND

mira

ISBN-13: 978-0-7783-6964-6

The Day Tripper

Mira
22 Adelaide St. West, 41st Floor
Toronto, Ontario M5H 4E3, Canada
BookClubbish.com

Printed in U.S.A.

For Vikki and Felix

PROLOGUE

Wind howls through the rafters. A hundred candle flames waver in response, sweet-smelling smoke coiling into the air. The floor flashes green and magenta as a shaft of sunlight darts through the stained glass. Symbolic, these people are probably thinking. It feels more like a taunt. In any case, it's hastily whipped away by the storm.

The organ falls silent as the vicar takes his place. Expression unbearably serious, as if there's any danger of the solemnity of this occasion being ignored. I follow his instruction for the congregation to stand, my legs like they belong to someone else. His eyes settle on me and soften.

I nod. *I'll be okay.*

My hands are near-translucent, aside from the tar stains on the index and middle fingers of my right. Whiskey sticks to my throat, together with something bitter, rough as sand.

Just get this done. It'll be over soon. You can get through this.

The booze hasn't helped; I'm still burned-through with grief. I rest my chin on my collarbone, gazing down at my charcoal suit. It's like there's nothing inside it, shoulders like a clothes hanger, as though I could look clean through myself if it wasn't for my ill-fitting jacket.

The doors at the rear of the church clank open. It is time.

The vicar's eyes meet mine again. A smile spreads across his face.

A rustle as best clothes turn rearward.

Like he's lived for this moment, the organist hits the one note of the introduction over and over. Wagner's "Bridal Chorus." All stops out.

"Congratulations, mate," says the guy next to me, dressed the same as me but otherwise unfamiliar. "Boy done good."

I can't turn around. Not yet. I have no idea who's walking toward me. All I know is that the one person in this world who I yearn for, it cannot possibly be.

SEPTEMBER 6, 1995 | AGE 20

Things Can Only Get Better

Her street looks like a TV commercial. I let the car coast and glance again at the beer mat in my lap. *44 Poplar Avenue*, it says in Holly's tipsy scribble—handwriting that could only belong to a trainee doctor. I stop over the driveway. We said three and it's barely five past. I feel early, uptight. Half past would've looked better.

The white town house is dazzling in the sun. A sash window rumbles open on the second floor and two women—her housemates, I guess—stare down at me, making no attempt to hide that they're sizing me up.

It's close to eighty degrees and my shirt is soaked against my back as I get out of the car. I nod an *all right* up at the window, try to guess the verdict, but their grins give nothing away.

Holly steps through the front door. There's the bolt of electricity in my chest, stopping me midstride. For a moment too long

we're both silent, sharing awkward smiles between two people
who saw each other naked for the first time when last together.
Four days ago now; we got wrecked on rum and Coke celebrating my birthday, ended up on her mate's sofa where too many
interruptions and a room that wouldn't stop spinning turned
the moment from intense to hilarious.

"You look—"

"Ridiculous?" Holly says, holding the hem of her tartan dress
and performing a twirl.

"Incredible."

"Digging the granny skirt? Thrift shop's finest…"

It really is a granny skirt, pleated with buttons up the front.
But she's wearing it pulled up over her chest, coupled with a
string of pearls bound round her wrist and what appear to be
kids' plastic sunnies. As with all her recycled ensembles, the
whole is a million times the sum of its parts.

"Shit, almost forgot," I say, darting back to the car. I've never
bought a girl flowers before, and I'm certain I'm making a dick
of myself as I extract the bunch from the back seat, slicing a
couple of heads clean off in the process.

"Wowzer!" Holly says. She peeks over her lime-green shades.
Her eyes swell, and I glance up to see one of her housemates
giving me a look that reads *fair play, mate.*

"Sorry. Bit cheesy, I know."

"Hardly," she says, fingers stroking the red and white heads.

I think of the woman in the florist's earlier, wonder why she
gave me that funny look and asked twice if I was sure when I
picked the crimson tulips and white roses. I have, it seems, got
this right at least.

"Water," Holly says. "Won't be a second."

I follow her up the steps as far as the open front door. The
house beyond is wall-less, sunny straight through. Even the escaping air smells expensive.

"Loving the car, baby," she says as she emerges minus the bouquet.

"Don't take the piss, you'll hurt her feelings."

"The color, though…"

"Heinz cream of tomato?"

"Delicious."

I jump in, and the old Mini groans on its suspension as Holly drapes herself across the hood. I think better of flicking the wipers on as she squidges her face against the windshield, making eyes at me and licking the glass. "Will you please just get in?" I say.

"So cool," she says, dropping into the passenger seat and wriggling to get comfortable.

"You can buy it if you like?"

"How could you?" Holly's glumly stroking the dashboard.

"She's in this week's *Exchange and Mart*. Yours for three hundred quid or very near offer." Until this morning there were signs in the window too, but they didn't survive the preparations for this afternoon: removal of some stubborn stains from the back seat, consideration of which tapes should and shouldn't be tossed about the place.

Holly's absently turning Green Day's *Dookie* over in her hands. "Liquidating assets for the next big step, yeah?"

"You got it."

"It's the right move, baby." She rubs a Converse against my calf as I spin the car around.

"Nice part of town, this," I say.

"You don't think it's a bit *lame* I'm back at my parents' place?"

"Not sure I'd say *lame*, exactly." We accelerate past Mercs nosing from driveways and razor-edged hedgerows. "What brought you back?"

She unwraps a fresh deck of Marlboro Lights. "It's twenty minutes on the tube to my hospital placement. My folks are in the States till New Year, place was empty anyway. Me and my girls thought we'd give squatting a go. It's very *now*."

"So I've heard." I tease two ciggies from her pack, blue clouds dispersing against the windshield as I light them at the same time. My hands are off the wheel. The old Mini straddles lanes, weaving around imperfections in the road like a runaway shopping trolley.

"Two years in halls was quite enough, thanks very much," Holly says through a giggle, her hands hovering toward the wheel. "You'll see, toy boy."

"Will you stop it with calling me that?" I'm grinning as I hold a finger up. "One year!"

"Nearer one and a half."

I laugh it off, but it needles me the way it always does when she says I'm her toy boy. She means no harm, but it's a reminder to feel inferior to her, in case it might've slipped my mind. The question is rarely far from my thoughts: *What is she doing with me?* She's twenty-one, expensively educated, halfway to a medicine degree. And style radiates off her like a perfume. I was a teenager till a few days ago, my long hair has more to do with hiding acne scars than looking like Kurt Cobain, and I can't imagine I'll be cool handing her *my* home address anytime soon.

"So where you whisking us away to?" Holly asks. She's kicked off her boots, feet resting on the dash.

"Nowhere really," I tell her, like I've given it no thought.

"So exciting," she says, screwing her face up.

We pick up the South Circular, the smell of tarmac and takeaways on the hot breeze. I steal a glance at her profile. Funny how you can picture someone all the time, and then find your imagination doesn't come close. The world beyond this car looks so ordinary, banal. My hands are clammy on the wheel.

"Weird, innit?" she says.

"What is?" Our eyes lock and we both laugh.

"*Us*. An actual *date*."

"Bit weird, maybe."

"*Nice* weird. Not sure I've ever really seen you by daylight." She makes a show of checking me out. "Probably still would, though."

"Why, thank you."

"Is this the first time we've even been sober together?"

I shrug. "Probably." I have a thirst all of a sudden to correct that fact.

We've known each other five weeks. It was an open-mike night at the Blue Moon, a dingy, low-ceilinged pub with platinum records and signed photos of rock royalty covering the walls, with a legendary history on the London music scene. I've spent nigh on every evening in there this past year—five nights a week behind the bar, the other two in front of it, sinking a little liquid courage before playing guitar and singing for whatever the punters drop in a pint glass. Together with laboring on a city development by day, it's been twelve months of sweat that means I'll start uni with some money in my pocket.

It was the sort of night to remind those of us who *perform* why we live for it: packed out, noisy but interested audience. Attention without scrutiny. I was third act on and four pints down—the perfect arrangement. The set I played was typical enough: some Counting Crows, Bowie's "The Man Who Sold the World," one Blur and one Oasis to split the crowd.

I asked if there were any requests, braced for my manager to shout his stock reply: "Would you mind playing somewhere else?" But instead it was a girl left of the stage with a mass of corkscrew hair and a business shirt that was buttoned wonky, collar slung over one shoulder, who called out. She asked if I knew any Buddy Holly. I asked if she was kidding, and she swore she wasn't—she'd later tell me how her dad was such a fan she'd been named after him. So I played "Everyday" and "Peggy Sue." No self-doubt to take the shiny edges off—performance of my life.

Our eyes never left each other's. Two hundred people turned invisible, irrelevant.

It's not that Holly's the first woman I met in my time at the Blue Moon. A handful of times I'd caught someone's eye as I played, enjoyed the unfair advantage gifted to someone who'll risk everything and bare themselves into a microphone. I'd sort a few free drinks from the bar, be loose enough to deliver a line just so. I'm not sure if it was the probability of sex when I left with someone on my arm that gave me the biggest kick, or the jealous gaze of other blokes following me out.

With Holly it was different. That first night, we drank and talked till long past closing. Every shift I worked from then on fizzed with life, my eyes forever flitting through crowds and to opening doors. When she did show, she'd stay after her St. Thomas's colleagues left, and in the low light of the closed pub, we'd talk about God and karma and Marmite versus Bovril and the futility of existence and who was likely to be better hung out of Major or Blair, till we were forced to go our separate ways into London's lonely small hours. Sometimes she'd linger on the goodbye, but it was four whole weeks before I kissed her.

I'm yet to shake the first-proper-date nerves as I swing the car into a parking bay.

"Are we there yet?" Holly says in a child's voice.

"Very nearly," I reply, dashing into the Victoria Wine we're parked outside. The shop simmers with that offie smell: soggy carpet and ciggies. I grab eight Stellas, two bottles of white wine, a bag of ice and a shiny bucket. What with buying flowers earlier, this spree nearly cleans me out of the cash I allocated for today. The guy at the till complains tonelessly about the heat as he bags my stuff with shaky hands, squinting eyes to the floor. I tell him to keep my last three quid. At the cash machine outside, I plunder some uni savings.

"Nice work," Holly says as I pass the shopping over. "What you having, though?"

I pull my collar high, make a show of sheepishly looking around us before cracking a beer open. The sound is like a wave crashing on an island paradise. Hiding beneath the dash, I vacuum up the foam and knock back a quarter of the can so quick it gives me brain freeze. I pass it to Holly.

She takes a swig as we hit the road again. "You're a bad man, Alex Dean."

I can smell the river on the fresh air that drifts through the car. The hit of booze loosens my bones; I'm inching toward being myself.

Staying Out for the Summer

I'm lying on the bench seat of the small boat with my hands behind my head. A tower of ash teeters on the ciggie between my teeth. My bare foot rests on the wheel, not that I'm looking where we're going.

"So peaceful," Holly says, trailing her fingers through the green water.

The sun is lower now and even hotter; I can almost hear my forehead sizzling. I pour some wine into my mouth, most of which trickles down to my ear.

"It all changes out west. Could be in the middle of the countryside." The Thames is a third of the width it was at the boatyard, waterside offices and flats replaced now by willows that dangle into the murky shallows.

"You'll be doing a lot more of this soon," Holly says. There's a hint of sorrow in her smile. I'm surprised by it.

"Getting pissed in the daytime?"

"Well, that too. But I mean this...*boating.*"

"Kinda goes with the Cambridge territory, I guess."

"Definitely."

"Well, as long as they run on batteries like this baby, I'll be just dandy." I slam the lever beside the wheel from Forward to Reverse repeatedly. The electric motor beneath us whines in protest, the water in our wake losing its composure.

Holly nods toward an approaching rowing boat. "This does feel a bit cheat-y."

I stand up and wave excessively at the passing couple. "Cracking day for it," I shout, wine slopping everywhere. Holly clings on as the boat sways.

They mutter a polite reply. Their oars gather pace all of a sudden.

"Too busy to even wave back, see?" I point out. "Let alone drink and smoke as well. This really is the only way to travel."

"As long as you don't want to be out more than three hours."

"Well, there is that." The guy at the hire place, Nige, was sternly adamant about the time limit, and the penalty should we run out of power and have to be towed back.

Holly grabs us another two beers, bucket running with condensation. "How long till you go, now?"

"Two weeks, give or take."

"You'll be fine," she says, detecting the wariness in my tone. "More than fine. *Awesome*, in fact. Just wait." She holds up her can and I tap mine to it.

"Sure."

"Best make the most of the time left. With me and all your other girls."

I smirk. "There are no *other* girls."

"Hmm. Alex Dean, rock and roller. One-woman man?"

Her words buoy my ego. I sink half the beer and light another two cigs from the dying embers of my last. "You're kind of the reason why I'm going at all."

She gazes suspiciously at me, jetting smoke diagonally skyward. "Pretty sure you got your Cambridge place long before you knew me."

"Having a place and actually taking it up—that's two different things."

She looks unconvinced.

"I was kind of struggling to imagine myself there. Before you."

It's true—the sort of truth that gets shaken loose once you've had a few. Holly was never surprised about Cambridge the way most people are. I never imagined I'd get a place, wouldn't have bothered applying without my maths teacher, Mrs. Watson, practically standing over me as I registered for college open days, and later when it was time to do the entry forms. She'd taught me for five years and swore I was *going places*. It's not that I'm especially clever or anything. But ever since I can remember, I've had this restlessness about wanting to *know* things. Sometimes it's almost a panic: so much to learn, too much for one lifetime.

Three days I was in Cambridge for the interview. I was certain it would be a waste of time. But as I watched those people who'll one day own the world breezing through the winter mist, and as I passed the small hours drinking warm beer in bright rooms with people my age but otherwise alien, it began to creep on me: the world got wider, fences I hadn't seen became visible, then fell. The voice that answered interview questions became less boringly recognizable as my own.

I got in. Surprise outweighed celebration, aside from Mrs. Watson, who bought me a fountain pen too nice to use. It was barely mentioned at home after the initial shock. Dad could be heard explaining how "they have to take a few kids from state comps."

"How d'you figure I've got anything to do with it?" Holly

says. She lies beside me, twizzling my hair. "This bright future of yours."

"Cause and effect, darling," I say, waving my cigarette around. "In fact, we had a very interesting chat about the whole *causality* subject at my interview."

"One event being responsible for another."

"Quite."

"So what am I, a cause or an effect?"

"In this instance, you are a *cause*."

"Must've blinked and missed it."

I turn and our faces are almost touching. "Meeting you was a…reminder."

"Right."

"The world is as wide as the chances that come our way. Take an opportunity, and it leads to more opportunity, and so on. The world opens up, like wings or…something."

"Profound." She laughs.

"Stop it, I'm trying to be *deep*," I say. "After I got that Cambridge place, my life was no different than before. Then I spent this last year working like a dog, scraping plaster off concrete all day, working the Blue Moon every night. Going home to the same old housing estate where I've spent my whole life. Back in the world I'm used to. No causes. No effects. Stagnant."

"The future is a consequence of the present."

"Exactly. And when the present is dull as anything… Started to wonder if I could do it. Couldn't *see* myself there anymore."

"That's silly."

"Sure. But then there was *you*. Great big cause that you are."

"Whatever. Really?"

"Christ, you save lives for a living."

"Not yet I don't. After a thirty-hour shift I'm more likely to be accidentally ending them."

"And you look like you've taken a wrong turn off a catwalk."

She slaps my arm. "Now I know you're ripping the piss."

"I'm really not. You make me want to…do better."

"You don't need me."

"Do I sound like a wanker?"

"A very charming one."

"That's something."

"Well, I'm glad to be of service." Her lips meet mine, hot and boozy. "I think we look rather good together."

I smirk, although a part of me is wondering if she means we *look good* in the way her recycled clothes do. Remarkable in part for their shitty origins.

"You'll miss me, though?" she says.

I'll miss her all right. But becoming the person I should be for her is more important than seeing her. "No chance," I tell her, winking like a twat.

"Still no thoughts on what you want to do after?"

"Be a success."

Holly rolls her eyes. "That again. *I want to be looked up to*," she says in a poor impression of my voice. "Nothing more specific yet?"

"I'll work it out." I haven't a clue. I *do* want to be looked up to—is that so bad? I want people to hear my name and think: *That guy's done all right for himself.*

"Alex," Holly says, surveying the scenery. "Not sure we're going anywhere."

"Now, let's not be having any of that chat."

"Not in the relationship sense. I mean more in the nautical way."

We are in the middle of the river, turned diagonally. "You may have a point."

Holly takes the controls. There's grumbling beneath us.

"Move aside," I say, before running through the exact same operations whilst she stares incredulously at me. "Bloody batteries," I shout with some comedic fist-shaking. "Looks like we're out here all night."

"Nige will be worried sick."

I snort into my beer. "Shit—*Nige!* What we gonna do about Nige?"

"Not so fast," Holly says. "Not sure this is a battery issue." She grabs hold of the blue rope tied to the side of the boat. It disappears into the water, taut as a guitar string. She tugs at it whilst operating the motor. Nothing gives.

"What's the score?" I ask, pulling on the rope too, a sudden compulsion to be taking control.

"All tangled up, babe. The mooring line's got wound round the prop by the looks." She leans over the back of the boat, arms stretched into the water. "Maybe we should've been paying a bit more attention."

"Mooring line? *Prop?* Are you in the navy or something?"

"It's just…boats."

"You know about boats?"

"Not really. Just, you know, Henley Regatta and shit." She starts giggling uncontrollably, likely to fall in any second. "You've got longer arms than me. You have a go."

I slip my shirt off my back, my belly seared pink. Holly sings that Etta James song from the Diet Coke advert, waving her beer and cigarette in approximate time to the beat.

"Maybe if I can undo this end from the cleat," she says.

"*Cleat,*" I echo, rolling my eyes.

"Stop making me laugh," she says, kicking my half-exposed arse.

"Can't get a decent grip on it," I say after a minute's fumbling.

"All under control." Holly kneels behind me, having unlashed the two oars from the side of the boat.

"Great."

"You put your feet up, baby," she says, snapping the metal rings to the side of the boat. "These things here, they're called rollocks." She eyeballs me, waiting on a response.

"Rollocks?"

"Yup."

"Useful to know."

Holly paddles an oar and we rotate gracefully, parallel with the banks once more. I take one of the oars from her and sweep it into the river. We are showered as the boat rocks dramatically.

"Let me guess, you've not done this before?" she says.

"Not really." I hope it looks like I don't care.

"Out the way, toy boy," she says. "I've got this covered."

I light a cig and lean uneasily on the wheel as we glide along the glassy surface. Holly's forehead glistens with sweat. Surely I'm the only guy she knows who'd take her on a boat and not be able to row the thing.

"Bollocks to this," I say, on my feet now. "Far too much like hard work." With a Chippendale's flourish, my jeans are off. Followed by my pants, for no reason other than a show of commitment to the task. Beyond the first few lukewarm inches, the water is soberingly cold on sunburnt skin. I sink like a stone before thrashing my way to the surface. The Thames tastes even greener than it looks.

"You are such a tit," Holly says, as I tread water behind the boat.

"Give it some power," I say after a couple of minutes fumbling with the propeller. A jetsam of shredded rope surfaces around me as the motor spools up.

Holly swings the boat in an arc till she's alongside me. We're on a slow curve in the river, and all around us is quiet. I stare up at her standing at the wheel. The blurred sun behind her stings my wet eyes. She checks twice that we're not overlooked, before tugging her repurposed old-lady skirt over her head. One arm covers her chest as she shuffles her knickers down her thighs. I look away till I hear her jump in.

"Not as warm as it looks?"

"It's perfect," she says, grinning at me as she smooths her hair back. We tread water in close proximity, brushing against each other more than is accidental. For twenty minutes we swim laps of the boat, shouting pleasantries to occasional passing watercraft.

Shielded by the boat, I float on my back, feel the sun on my palest parts. "Having fun?" I ask her.

She links her arm into mine and we float together like sleeping otters. "There is, in my experience, a particular type of man who, when presented with a body of water and an audience, can't resist stripping off and jumping in."

"That's a good thing, right?"

"Not usually, if I'm honest."

"Is this to do with the unflattering effects of cold water? Because my old chap's usually bigger than this. *Much* bigger."

"It's a rather deeper character observation, actually."

"Go on."

"Met a few in my time. Show them a pier or a swimming pool in winter and they're off. Not sure if it's the nudity or the demonstration of hardiness that does it for them."

"Maybe that's just the posh kids."

"Hmm. It's usually the self-styled *legends*, the *I can drink you under the table* types. *Last man standing.*" She prods me in the ribs. "Ringing any bells?"

"Not even slightly."

"Okay."

"You *are* in here too."

"So I am." She coils her leg around mine. Our naked bodies are pressed together, the veil of water between our skin hot now. "All the dickheads together."

"Not sure I'm quite the life and soul you imagine," I say, slightly surprised she's not yet seen through me.

She eyes me suspiciously. "It's okay. You have enough redeeming features."

Maybe she'd think I was lying if I told her how I was a loner for most of my school days. Might struggle to believe that my guitar skills and academic successes are owed to the need to fill the long days and nights and years hiding in my room. It was only in the reshuffle that occurs at the start of sixth form, aged sixteen, that I began to have any sort of social life. Parties, which scared the shit out of me initially, were easier after a few drinks. And the more I sank, the more popular I became. The more I was *included*. It took no more than a couple of very public passings-out and an inability to refuse a dare before I had people fooled: Alex Dean, party animal. Sure, those nights involved multiple trips to the bathroom to purge, clearing room for more booze, but the thought of being anything other than the last person to leave terrified me. What would they all say about me after I left? Easier to hang around, keep knocking the drinks back.

Holly clambers back into the boat, rolling over the side. Her fit of giggles robs her of strength, and she flops in like a caught fish. "It's my amazing grace that does it for you?" she says, peeping over the edge.

"Going so soon?"

"Not a bit of it." I swim alongside as she maneuvers the boat over to the bank. She ducks the overhanging branches, stopping beneath a canopy of greenery. She wraps my shirt around herself and ties what remains of the rope to a solid bough.

I'm showing my bright white arse to the suddenly busy river as I follow her, climbing through the boat and onto the bank. We only have to walk a few meters into the tall grass and the marshy ground beneath to be all but hidden from the world.

She lets my shirt drop to the ground. We've both been naked for the past half an hour but it feels different now. She smiles at me. Nervous, almost vulnerable. We are clammy with river water as we kiss. There is a weedy smell to our hair as I sweep it from our faces, but it's not off-putting. The earth is like warm clay on my back as we sink to the ground. Sunlight glints through the tree cover. An audience of meadow flowers arches around us, tiny heads of reds and whites.

The sex is slow. Time, I imagine, continues at its usual pace around us, but we are detached from it. The mud and the damp and the sweat between our bodies feel like a hot shower, washing me clean. Holly's lips are to my ear, her hot breath filling my head as, quietly, helplessly, we both come in perfect sync.

We lie there, her head on my shoulder, eyes wet against my skin. Sun skims the treetops, coloring us like an open fire as we float in that space between sleeping and waking. There have of course been women before her, if fewer than I'd like people to imagine: seven, present company excluded. But this is something so totally new. I couldn't be further from the hollowness, the urgency to leave, that ordinarily follow sex. This moment would normally be an ending, a job done.

"Sing to me," she whispers.

"Really?"

"Don't laugh. It's not silly."

"Maybe a bit."

She shrugs and tucks her head more tightly into my neck.

I tap my palms on her hot back in a familiar loose rhythm. "You know this is how they did the drums on the original recording?" I say. "Just Buddy Holly slapping out a rhythm on his knees by the mike."

I can hear the smile in her voice. "Less of the trivia, songbird."

Just like that first night at the Blue Moon, I sing "Everyday" to her, running through it twice before moving on to "Peggy Sue," and all the other songs in Buddy Holly's back catalog that I can remember enough words from.

I should feel ridiculous, but I don't. Instead, I'm brimming with a calm excitement, thinking of the life that lies ahead. Right now I have no doubts. Nothing about the future scares me. It actually glows with possibilities.

Head Over Feet

"Sits on the PTA of her kids' school," Holly says, side-eyeing behind the rim of her pint glass. "Writes bad poetry for the parish magazine. Likes baking bread. And Neil Sedaka. And angry anal."

"Blimey."

"Definitely votes Tory."

"Of course."

"Your go."

I look around at the tables and the crowds of drinkers. "Bloke in the…knitwear," I say, guiding her eyes.

"Oh, yes! Tell me about him."

"See the woman with him? They're definitely married?"

"Just not to each other?"

"Don't steal my lines."

"Voting intention?"

"Drives a Range Rover with a Friends of the Earth sticker in the window. New Labour was made for him."

"Here we go," Holly says, grinning. She strips the cellophane from yet another pack of cigs. "Knew it couldn't be long."

It's past ten now and we've been sitting at the riverside terrace of this bar since we returned the boat an hour and a half ago. Holly insisted on dealing with Nige alone. I've no idea what she said, but we escaped without his much-hyped penalty fee despite returning over an hour late. Back now where the Thames is wide and alive, music pumps from party cruisers, and the streetlights on the bank glow through the haze from a crowd in which no one is not smoking.

"This is the bit where you remind me of your Tony Blair suspicions," she says.

I grab a stuffed potato skin from the plate of mixed starters we ordered. We've been drinking and eating slowly since we arrived. It's not something I'm used to: no immediate thirst or hunger to be satisfied urgently. "I'm cool with him."

"Really?"

I grin. "Sure."

"Nothing to say about him being a Tory in disguise?" she asks. "No pining for a proper socialist? No analogies equating ever-growing economies with cancerous tumors? No observations that *The Man* is paying badly then lending cheaply so workers are in debt for what should've been theirs anyway?"

"You make me sound so...*sixth form*."

"Perish the thought."

"Fuck the Tories, though."

"There's something we *can* agree on," Holly says. "He'll do it, you know—finally get us shot of them. Who cares if he has to be all things to all men to do it?"

"One good thing, once you're earning big bucks you won't have to pay much tax with Blair in charge."

"*Big bucks,*" she echoes. "Because that's why I picked medicine."

"Tell your folks their money's safe."

"Oh, they are *total* converts."

"I'm surprised."

She sticks her tongue out at me. "Times are changing, baby. Can't you feel it?"

I smile. This is the point where I'd usually start ranting something hackneyed about seizing the means of production or suchlike. But my cynicism has been starved of air and can't be roused. I instead find myself agreeing with her. There *is* something in the air, energy like a brewing storm. This drunken crowd oozes it. Change. Flux. *Optimism.*

"One for the road?" I ask, the bell ringing for last orders inside the bar.

"Let's make it a quick one."

"Somewhere you need to be?"

"Come back to mine, yeah? Stay over, maybe?"

"Sure." Even after all that's gone on today, there's a fizz of nerves.

"Don't know about you but I'm ready for round two."

"See if I can get in the mood."

"Cheers. Appreciate it. Night's young—maybe a game of Scrabble as well?"

I'm nodding firmly. "Is it weird that I'm really excited about that too?"

"The best sort of weird."

I pat my pockets, a flash of panic calmed by finding my keys where I left them. "Worried they might have been for a swim."

"Can you remember where we left the car, though?"

"Let's hope so. Far too pissed for walking." I point toward the bar and turn.

"Don't be long, baby," she says, wide-eyed, sincere.

I'm still for a second. It's so alien, this feeling that nothing else in the world matters beyond this present moment, beyond her and me. I almost say it—would if the words weren't a foreign language to me. I could so easily tell her that I love her.

Live Forever

It's three-deep at the bar, and I get my order in seconds before they ring for time. I double up: a JD and Coke each and two beers to take with us. The lights are up and the music's gone quiet as I weave the tray through the punters. Standing in the doorway out to the terrace, I am disorientated. There must be fifty tables outside between here and the river and it's still packed out, darker and smokier than ever. I search the crowd but can't see Holly.

I negotiate my way down to the water's edge. She's maybe ten tables away, oblivious, a ciggie poised skyward in her fingers like she's posing for Vettriano. I smirk, enjoy my good fortune again.

"Excuse me, good gentlemen," I say to a group of four in my path, voice cocky with booze and lust. They shuffle over, not breaking from their conversation. The resulting gap between their circle and the edge of the path isn't wide enough—a careless elbow would send the tray of drinks into the river, possibly me with them.

"If you don't mind, guys?" I lay a palm on the forearm of the bloke with his back to me. Their circle opens out and he turns side-on, ushering me past. "Nice one," I say, glancing at him as I pass.

I look back at the ground. There's a delay in my brain processing who it is I'm walking past. There's a moment in which it seems that we'll just carry on, pretend like we don't know each other.

The air thickens. Time slows. I stop, a step past him. Look again. Razor-sharp short back and sides, hooded eyes, lopsided mouth. Preppy. It's a face I catch myself imagining sometimes, never for long. A waking nightmare. Not that my imagination does it justice. Not even close, I now realize.

His recognition of me unfolds in slow motion. Perhaps like me, alcohol has dulled his synapses, delayed the inevitable shift of mode.

Blake Benfield. There have been times in the past when just hearing that name in my head has stopped me dead, left me incapable.

How long since we last ran into each other? I was sixteen—best part of four years, then. Feels so recent. Our paths crossing has always been inevitable; we grew up barely a mile apart. He spat at me that last time, called me *faggot cunt*. The many times before that I'd just legged it, hidden from his fury and his hatred. But you get too old to do that.

This crowded place seems so quiet now. Like there's cotton wool stuffed in my ears. The two bottles tip over on my trembling tray, foam splattering to the ground. One rolls over the edge and shatters on the concrete. People turn.

How long have we stood here, him glaring at me, me unable to hold his stare? Saying nothing. A few seconds? Feels longer.

There's the smell of burned-out house in my nose. The sound of his whisper in my ears that I try to drown out.

Don't think about it. Do not think about that *day.*

Why do I shake? I'm a fucking grown man. Why am I shaking? He takes a half step closer to me.

I once told him I was sorry. It was years ago—when I was still a kid. I *was* sorry. Does he remember?

I spin around. Where's Holly? She must be watching this.

There's no more delay. There is, of course, nothing for me and this bloke to say to each other. We have ventured into each other's space, and that brings with it a remembering. And, as we always have, we must deal with that in our own way.

His knuckles graze my chin. I stumble backward and the tray falls to the ground. His swing is off, though; there is no pain. Not even surprise. We definitely have an audience now.

My response is pure instinct: palms raised, lean away. *Easy now.*

I don't want to fight this man. I want to go back thirty seconds, walk a different route, have this night back for myself.

Blake closes the gap, my weakness an invitation. His second punch crashes into my ear like a swinging girder. My brain slaps side to side in my skull. Vision sways. My head boils, a cool trickle from my eardrum.

Where is Holly? Panic grips. I can't just stand here and take this.

My eyes flit to our audience. He swings again, this time with his left. But I see it coming, dodge. He stumbles.

I drive my weight, shoulder first, into his ribs. He goes over, sprawled among the spilled drinks and shattered glass.

On all fours, he stares up at me. I'm perfectly positioned. I could kick him square in the face. End this right now. Why don't I do it? Why can't I bring myself to do it? I'd rather turn my back and cry than kick his head in.

He glares up at me. Why do I pity him? Why am I so uncomfortable towering over him like this? It's like the positions we've always held have been reversed. The power is mine.

I let him find his feet.

He's up and level with me again. He glares like a bloodthirsty dog, wipes his nose on the sleeve of his polo shirt. If we were alone, maybe I'd run. But with people watching, with *Holly* watching, that's no option.

My punch lands perfectly. His jaws scissor against each other. For a second his head floats, eyes rolling.

I realize my error too late. I should've followed up when I had the chance. One punch is only enough in the movies, everyone knows that. His hands are on the collar of my shirt, cloth tearing as he holds firm. His forehead slams into the bridge of my nose like a sledgehammer. My face is suddenly and totally numb. I drop to the ground. A ruby-red stain spreads fast through the jewels of broken glass around me.

He shouts above me. Every filthy word I've long come to expect. Something soft disperses against my head. Spit.

The neck of the Stella bottle I dropped lies on the ground. Inches away. Blood gurgles in my mouth as I take a deep breath. I launch like a sprinter. Leading with the dagger of green glass, I'm aiming straight at his face and closing fast.

Blake backs into a table, stumbles, hands slow to cover his face. His eyes widen, abject fear. But this is no time to be derailed.

I see it too late. No time to react. One of Blake's friends windmilling a table ashtray. The side of my skull cracks like thunder.

The ground feels like a cushion, drawing me in and bouncing me back. My vision finds enough order in time to see the sole of boot accelerating toward me, like a cartoon piano from the sky.

There is no pain. Just a sense of floating in space.

Time passes. More blows land.

The surface of the Thames billows like a black satin sheet as it rises toward me. There's no fear. Is that Holly I can hear calling my name? It's so distant, so hard to tell.

The river gathers me in like it's here to take care of me.

Cool water spears my lungs like sharpened icicles. I sink forever.

A low hum builds in my ears. Lights fades to nothing.

And I sleep.

NOVEMBER 30, 2010 | AGE 35

These Streets

My head throbs. It doesn't matter if I open or close my eyes, the pain worsens either way. My mouth is like dust. Joints and muscles lie seized.

Last night is a blank. I hate that. I look above me. Focusing is excruciating. The ceiling is browny cream, textured in spikes like a Christmas cake. An unshaded bulb swings in the draft, the filament shivering. It's *really* cold in here.

Where the fucking hell am I?

It even hurts to think. Something usually comes back by now after a serious session, even if the details have to be filled in later.

A cough gathers in my chest and rumbles its way out. I turn on my side, hacking and wheezing. It's all I can do not to puke. I sound ninety.

The room is small, barely twice the size of this single bed. Clothes cover the floor, black floorboards peeping through the mess here and there. I'm certain I've never clapped eyes on this shitty room before.

I raise myself to a half-sitting position, try to bundle my one flat pillow behind my aching back, but it's like a sheet of paper. There's a window behind me, sill covered with empties repurposed as ashtrays. The morning light—if it is still morning—is gray as smoke.

Why the hell am I fully dressed? These jeans and fleece, are they even mine? And why am I still so goddamned cold?

I dig a stiff tissue out of my pocket and blow my nose. It's the wrong shape, asymmetrical, twisted left. Massaging the knot of bone at the bridge switches a light on in my brain.

The fight. Blake Benfield.

The river. The *fucking* river.

How did I get here? Where is *here*?

Sometimes the recovery of a detail after a heavy night brings the whole lot flooding back—the edited highlights at least. But not so now. It feels so impossibly distant.

Who got me out of the river? I touch my face again. There's no tenderness, only unshaven skin. No blood on my hands. None on the pillow.

Surely my injuries needed attention? Was I *that* pissed? So wrecked that I only imagined the severity of my beating?

The pain I'm in is that of a brutal hangover. And there's a hollow ache in my bones. But nothing that suggests I got my head kicked in other than my nose, which feels misshapen and unfamiliar to my touch.

What the hell happened last night?

Holly. I jerk upright like I've been electrocuted, swing my feet onto the floor. I brace against the urge to vomit and eventually the bile retreats, leaving a hot trace down my esophagus.

Is this her place? I look around at the curtains that sag from the rail, clinging to the last remaining hooks. The tar-steeped net curtain beyond. The chest of drawers and its curling veneer. This *can't* be hers.

I have to steady myself against the walls and furniture as I lurch from the bed to the door. The corridor outside is almost in darkness, lined with maroon doors similar to the one I've emerged from. At the far end, daylight seeps from a half-open door. I can hear the tinkle of cutlery on china.

"Watcha?" the girl says as a I stand on the threshold.

"Morning," I say, forcing a smile. My voice is raspy and requires too much effort. It is alien, yet unquestionably my own.

"You look like I feel, mate," she says.

"Right. Sorry, this is…awkward."

"Why, what you done?" She's sitting on the edge of the kitchen worktop, wedging herself in place with a socked foot on the washing machine opposite. She shovels another mound of cereal into her mouth, bowl held under her chin. I'm trying not to stare, but I'm certain I've never met her before in my life. "Sugar Puffs?" she offers, glancing at the box next to her. "Well, *Super Honey Puffs* actually."

I raise a palm, the idea of food horrific. "I might have…how can I put this? I don't—"

"Spit it out, bruv."

"How did we get back here last night?"

"*We?* What's with the *we?*"

"Right. Sorry. How did *I* get here last night? Look, I've cocked up. I don't think I remember…your name?"

She holds her hand to her face in mock surprise. "Oh my days, Al."

"Sorry."

"Mate, that's a serious night you've had. Even by your standards. You're priceless sometimes." Her grinning expression implies this is a joke I should be in on too. *"I'm sorry but I don't remember your name,"* she says, an adequate impression of my gruff, wrecked voice.

"Did Holly bring me here? Was Holly here?"

"Don't know no Holly, mate."

"Who brought me here? Please?"

She stares at me deeper, like she's realized I'm not on a windup. She's younger than I thought, her youthful features at odds with how she speaks. Everything about her is slight: narrow face, tied-back hair, tiny frame that is lost in a fleecy tracksuit. What is *she* doing alone in a hole like this? I attempt a friendly smile.

"Kenzie," she says with a shudder of incredulity. "Just so we're clear."

"Cheers. Good to meet you, Kenzie."

"Give over, mate."

I back up a step, the need to vomit returning.

"Think you need a little something from your cupboard."

"Yes. Will do," I mumble, no idea what she means. But something strikes me as I look round the small kitchen—all the eye-level cupboards have hasps and padlocks on them. What's that about? Only one is unlocked and ajar; it is presumably where Kenzie took her lurid cereal box from.

My throat is dilating, mouth suddenly wet. "Bathroom," I say, looking along the dark corridor.

"For the best," Kenzie says.

"Where is it?"

"Shitting hell."

I thump a couple of closed doors but none give. "Kenzie!" I hiss. "Please?"

"How long have you lived here?" she says, stamping past me and kicking open a door at the top of a staircase.

"Lived?" The room is swimming as I stand, lost, staring at her.

"Mad," she says, walking away. "I won't tell the others, don't worry."

For ten minutes or more I lie fetal on the lino floor. The smell of piss is intense. Having purged the contents of my guts, I want to sleep. But there is too much pain. And too much confusion.

And it's *so* cold. A longing memory of yesterday returns, tugging my heart like it's a lost era: the boat, the hot sun. A tear tickles my face.

We were in the grips of a heat wave. Why is it *freezing*? Why are my arms sickly pale?

The basin creaks and gives a little as I grab the rim and draw myself up to standing. A face meets mine in the veined mirror. Yellowed eyeballs glare back at me. Wild. Petrified.

What the fuck?

I heave but there's nothing left to eject. Sweat beads on my forehead.

What's happened to me?

My skin is like a rubber mask, loose-fitting and closer to gray than any living thing should be. Burst blood vessels pepper my cheeks with color.

I squint. Deep lines beside my eyes fold into furrows.

There's a bang on the door. "Gonna be much longer, Al?" Kenzie says.

"Gimme a minute," I say, but I'm not sure any sound comes out.

"Places to be," she says. "So…if you wouldn't mind?"

Some sort of amnesia? Some crazy practical joke?

"How long have I been here?" I ask, opening the door to Kenzie. My attempt at a casual tone is hopeless—I sound as desperate as I feel.

"Not long enough to flush," she says, yanking the chain and shoving the window open.

"This house, I mean."

She looks at me with sad eyes. "Maybe you should get some rest, mate?"

"How long, Kenzie. Please?"

She shrugs. "Longer than me. You were here when I turned up. I didn't talk so much back then. You were kind to me."

"And that was…?"

"Four months-ish."

"Yes, of course," I say, rolling my eyes. "Sorry for asking. Won't trouble you further."

Kenzie shakes her head. "Well, if you don't mind, then?" She lowers the toilet seat.

I turn to leave. An icy gust whips by my neck from the opened window. I spin around. "What's the date?"

"Dunno. End of November."

The little sky I can see is frozen white, pregnant with snow.

"Want to know what year as well?" Kenzie asks with a smile.

I go to speak, tell her I'm perfectly aware it's '95, compelled to prove my sanity. To who, I wonder.

"2010," she says over me. "Just in case, yeah."

"Yup. Of course it is."

"No disrespect, bruv, but I'm about to piss myself here."

"It's really November?"

"Check for yourself—*Free-Ads* come through the door earlier."

"Right."

"You know, perfect if you're looking for *companionship with a larger lady, possibly more.*" She grins, like we've joked about this before.

I step into the corridor, more lost than ever.

"Alex," Kenzie calls. "Get yourself some rest, yeah. I'll be back later. I'll check in on you."

I Need a Dollar

I've been tearing my room apart for two hours straight when I hear the front door open. Male voices ascend the stairs. Instinct tells me to stash everything away.

I throw the guitar case back in the corner. It's covered in stickers, the biggest proclaiming *Tony Blair Is a War Criminal*. Upon opening it I almost didn't recognize my beloved Fender California. It's chipped and scratched and with excess string in a bird's nest round the pegs—it's had a hard time since I last gigged with it at the Blue Moon. What I assumed was a plectrum rattling inside the body turned out to be something else when I eventually shook it out through the sound hole—a padlock key. The kitchen cupboard it fitted yielded some unappetizing dried pasta, and a third of a bottle of sweet sherry. Is that what Kenzie meant about having something from my cupboard? She wasn't wrong—I'm no less confused than I was two hours ago, but I can think now the ache in my bones has eased. I always thought it was only fully-fledged alcoholics who need sherry to kick-start their day.

A heavy palm slaps the other side of my door. "Mr. Dean?" a creamy baritone booms, pure Swansea.

Fugue state. I read about it once—someone wakes up somewhere and time has passed since their last memory and they've got no clue how they ended up there. Or this is some cruel joke; surely that's most likely. There's a handful of pages in here from a newspaper called *The Metro*, and they're all dated 2010, just like the East London *Free-Ads* hanging from the letterbox. If someone's got it in for me, they've gone to a lot of trouble to keep me disorientated.

"Open up, Mr. Dean," the voice comes again. "There's a good chap."

I kick the clothes covering the floor to one side and hastily repack the chest of drawers. There's a wad of fivers I found bundled in socks, together with sixty quid in coins. I shove the notes in my pants, the bag of coins into the guitar case.

"Afternoon!" the man says with mock bonhomie as I release the deadlock on my door.

"Hi," I mumble, hanging on a clue as to how he knows me.

He scans the room. "Late in the year for spring cleaning."

"What can I do for you?" I say, oddly assertive; the last of the sherry lapping my system is working wonders.

"That's a laugh, old chap. Think we both know the answer to that."

I catch myself staring at the guy accompanying him who towers in the doorway. Mute and disinterested, he's damned near as tall and as wide as the threshold itself. A tattoo winds around his neck and reaches onto his cheek.

"My driver," clarifies the man.

"Right," I say, thinking better of asking why, if that's the case, he doesn't wait in the car.

"What have you got for me, then?"

"What *should* I have for you?"

"Don't get smart with me." He scratches at his short gray hair. The meathead driver looks at me for the first time.

"What do you want?"

"Do you think I own a portfolio of properties for the luxury of chasing scumbags like you for rent arrears?"

"I guess not."

"You guess right, Mr. Dean."

"What do I owe?"

"Didn't we have this very conversation less than forty-eight hours ago?"

I shrug.

"Two hundred and sixty smackers."

"Understood."

"Three twenty-five including this week. Why not be ahead of the game for once in your miserable life?"

In different circumstances I'd laugh right now. How can he be charging that for this dump?

"What have you got for me?"

I squirm slightly, feel the reassuring presence of the notes nestling against my privates.

"Bugger all?" he says.

I look at the floor and nod. I understand so little, but something tells me I should be holding on to the little money I do have.

"What's that? 'I'm very sorry, Mr. Hopkin, but I'm a feckless shit and I still don't have a pot to piss in.' *Well?*"

Lip service seems the safest way right now. "I'm sorry, Mr. Hopkin. I'll get it to you." Why does him treating me like scum make me feel like I *am* scum? Why do I feel I should apologize for ending up here, when I've had no choice in it?

He grabs my guitar case and shoves it into me so hard I almost go over onto the bed. "Twenty-four hours," he says.

"Got it."

"Well, run along, then." He glares at me, an outstretched arm directing me out of the room.

"Sorry, I…"

"Get out there. Make some dough. It's already getting dark."

"Yes, right."

"Busk!" he hisses, spit airborne. "That's what a *busker* does, isn't it? When you can be arsed. Sing for tuppence ha'penny?"

"I'm on it," I say, grabbing a puffer jacket and pair of health-hazard trainers from my unfamiliar floor-drobe.

"This time tomorrow," Mr. Hopkin booms as I follow him and his stooped assistant down the impossibly narrow stairs. "Or you'll be out on your ear. Mark my words, Mr. Dean."

Use Somebody

Seven tube stops and a short walk and I'm back at the river where Holly and I were last night. But it can't have been *last night*, can it? Mist rolls over the black water. My breath plumes white into the sharp air. People scurry, heads pulled low into heavy coats.

When I was here with Holly, there were tables and umbrellas stretching from the wine bar's glass frontage to the water's edge. It's an uncluttered tarmacked concourse now. The bar, whose name escapes me, is an expensive coffee shop today. I'm not sure why I spend so long inspecting the ground for evidence of the blood spilled here—I already know I'll find none.

What the fuck have you done to me, Blake Benfield?

The thought of him, the shape of his name, stirs the sickness again.

Had you not caused me enough grief already?

I take a seat on a concrete bench and lean my guitar case between my legs, this familiar if battered object offering a hint of comfort. I pull out my pack of cigs—I bought them an hour ago from the shop below the hovel I woke up in. "Eight quid," I mumble in disbelief.

I'm on my third when a kid sits down next to me.

"Not playing?" he asks, eyeing the guitar.

"Too cold," I grunt, no desire for a conversation.

"Not like you, old cuz." I turn and he winks at me. He's slight, his legs and arms so spindly they look absurdly long. A wisp of hair darkens his top lip. "Grow a pair, man," he says, grinning.

"Yeah, yeah."

"Ain't that what you always say to me when I'm moaning about the weather?"

I look down at my stained, calloused hands. They appear to have held a million cigs, and played a lot of guitar. "You know me, yeah?" I struggle to read his expression; a flash of anger perhaps. Or hurt, maybe. "Has someone put you up to this?" I ask.

"Is this a bad day?" He loads the phrase, like I have a history of them. "It's okay, man."

"What's my name?"

He jabs his tongue under his bottom lip, does a *mental* face at me. "What?"

I almost snigger at his show of disbelief; so blatant, so teenage. "My name."

"You wanna know your own name, Alex Dean?"

I feel an idiot and I can't bring myself to quiz him further. If he is part of some elaborate hoax, surely it'll become clear. "Sorry."

"You're James Dean's cooler brother."

"Right."

"Isn't that what you always say?" he asks.

"You know about James Dean?"

"Had to google him."

I nod, no idea what he's on about.

"Four sugars," he says, placing a cardboard cup between us. "You sweet-toothed fool."

"What is it?"

"Hot choccie, old cuz. What else?"

"For me?" I look at him again. Beneath his fluffy parka he's wearing a red sweatshirt and drainpipe trousers—school uniform.

"Drink up."

"That's kind. Why've you…"

"Just let your old mate Jazz take care of you for once, yeah?"

"Jazz?"

"What?"

I shake my head, take a slurp. It's divine. "You shouldn't—"

"My turn, old cuz. Overdue really, innit? Saw you sitting here. Not gonna earn nothing with your guitar hiding in there."

"I play here a lot?"

"What's up with you today, man?"

How I wish I knew. "A bit all over the place, you know?"

He noisily slurps his hot drink. "You'll be all right." He says it so bouncily that I almost believe him. "Wanna talk about it?"

"I'm cool," I lie. "So how often, would you say, do I…busk, here?"

"Most days, innit."

"*Right* here?"

"Is this like some test of my observation skills or something? Might wanna make the questions a bit tougher."

I stare into his kind eyes. "Look, mate… *Jazz*. I've had a hell of a twenty-four hours. Are you cool with just helping me out here?"

He nods, eager. "Most times you play here. Well, over there." He points at a woman ten meters away handing out Christian Aid leaflets. "Till they move you on." He grins like we're sharing a joke. "Then you come right back here. This place, it's *special* to you or something."

"I said that?"

"Once or twice." He snorts.

The hot chocolate warms me from the inside out and the steam beneath my nose smells of safety, of being in someone's care. It's enough, just briefly, for me to observe this present moment, pause the panic over what the hell's going on. "Thank you," I whisper to this generous young guy.

The dark is falling in now. A sheen of frost sparkles on untrodden ground. Sashes of Christmas lights glow on the opposite bank.

These people don't look quite right. Hair too short. Clothes too tight. Where are the retired gents in the their suits and hats and overcoats? Everyone, even the schoolkids, have mobile phones, and they are *tiny.*

Since my last memory, since the fight, has *time* really passed? What have I missed? What of Cambridge? What of *Holly*?

"You're better than you think you are," Jazz says from nowhere.

"Sorry?"

"I know about these days. When you, you know, can't… busk. Can't *play.*"

"I'm okay."

"You're well good. Everyone thinks so. Think you have to be reminded sometimes."

I smile. "That's kind of you."

He chuckles. "Like standing naked and letting people laugh at you."

"I say that, yeah?"

"You know you do."

"Sounds about right. Sounds bloody spot-on." I finish my drink and reach for my body-temperature cash. "Let me pay you back, yeah?"

"You don't owe me—"

"Get me next time," I say, peeling off a fiver and hoping that covers it.

"You always say that."

I rise to my feet, seized knees that are a fight to unfold.

"You should get going," I say to Jazz, like a responsible adult might. "Catch your death out here." I sound like a twat.

He stares blankly into the distance. "Yeah. Should be safe now."

"Safe?"

He shrugs. "You know…"

I give him what I hope is a reassuring smile.

"Where you headed?" he asks.

"Now, there's a question." It's been bugging me since I got here. Where do I go? Who do I see? Where do I find *answers*? I'm sure as hell not going back to that bedsit I woke up in. My parents' place, my *home*, is half an hour's bus ride from here. Maybe I should be checking myself into hospital, get to the bottom of what's going on in my head. But I don't feel compelled to do either of those things.

"You ever heard me talking about a girl called Holly?" I ask Jazz.

"Nah. She your girl?"

"I've never mentioned that name?"

"Don't ring a bell, old cuz."

"That's crazy."

"Why you talking to yourself?"

"Concentrating," I mumble.

"Bit weird."

"Poplar Avenue!" I snap, remembering what she wrote on the beer mat. "Thank Christ for that." I'm grinning with relief.

"You all right, man?"

"Maybe I will be," I tell him. "Any idea where's best to get a cab round here?"

Hard Times

My hand shakes as I go for the doorbell. The last time I stood on this porch, this house was so inviting, as if it was asking me to join the party. Today it's closed itself off to me, turned its back.

"Good evening," a smartly dressed man with a Polish accent says.

A warm draft sweeps over me from the bright hallway and my chest collapses. I'd been trying to ignore the chance that this is no longer Holly's family home.

"We don't buy at the door. I'm sorry." The man is softly spoken.

"Wrong house." I hold up a palm in apology but can't seem to walk away.

"Who are you looking for? Perhaps I can help?"

"Holly." I feel foolish uttering her name.

"Holly Chan?"

"Yes! Yes! You know her?"

"You're a friend of Holly's?"

"Does she…live here…still?"

"I'm Mr. Chan's PA. Perhaps you'd like to speak with him?"

"Holly's father?"

"He's on a call right now. Would you like to wait?"

"Sure. Yes. Please. I mean, he doesn't know me or anything…"

The guy smiles and opens the front door all the way. "He's a nice guy. He won't mind, not if it's about Holly."

He struts through the house like it's a catwalk, and I have to hurry to keep up. My heart jumps out of rhythm as we pass a portrait of Holly on the wall. She's in a mortarboard and gown, flanked by a parent on each side. "Graduation," I mumble. "Fuck-sake." I was with her *yesterday*. She was two years away from getting her degree.

"Five minutes, maybe," the guy says, guiding me to a leather sofa just off the vast kitchen. A log fire simmers and snaps in a grate next to me, and I offer my numb hands to the heat.

"You're very kind. Thank you."

On a sideboard across the room I spy a silver tray of decanters, cut crystal glittering under spotlights: whiskey, Cognac, Madeira, by the looks. The thirst assaults me. *Need* like I've barely known.

"Can I get you anything while you wait?" the PA asks. "A drink, maybe?"

"Well…"

"Tea? Coffee? Water?"

I am stony still as he hangs on an answer.

"Glass of wine, even?"

"Go on, then. Why not."

"Red? White?"

"You choose. Whatever's easiest."

Among the modern art *pieces* lining the walls, Holly's early life is well-documented: photo-calls at Disneyland, a caricature by a Paris street artist, her tending to a litter of stripy kittens, late teens and hiking up a rain-drenched mountainside. I've been scrutinizing the gallery and feeling a curious melancholy that I didn't know her as a child, when I hear hushed voices in the hallway. I upend my wineglass, savor the last drips. A thick red served warm, it deserved better than the two gulps I sank it in.

"Hello, hello?" a voice sings from across the room, jolly with a stateside twang.

I turn around. The likeness to Holly is unmissable, even if he is shorter than her and old enough to be her granddad. For a second he oozes style: crisp white shirt, hands slouched in pockets, Beatle boots pointing my way. But then his soft features twist and tense. His easy gaze becomes a glare. He straightens like there's an electric current through him.

I walk toward him, right hand outstretched. "Sorry to drop in like—"

"What the hell?"

"I was hoping I might—"

He jerks backward. "Stop!" he yells. "Stop right there!"

"Sorry, I—"

The color has drained from his cheeks. "Stefan!" he shouts. "Stefan. Here now, please!"

His PA appears like he's been beamed into the kitchen.

"Why did you let this man in my house?"

"I think I don't know this gentleman," Stefan says.

"I don't understand," I say. "I think maybe you've confused me with someone. I'm not here to make trouble."

Mr. Chan shakes his head at his PA. "This is Alex Dean!"

Stefan's hand reflexes to his mouth in shock. "I'm so sorry," he tells his boss. "Please. I didn't know it was him."

"How many times?" Holly's father says to me. He's edging backward with every step I take toward him. "How many times do we have to go through this?"

"I've never met you before. Not in my life."

"You need help, Alex."

"I just came to see Holly. That's all. Not here to cause grief."

He shakes his head. "Stefan, please?"

"I must ask you to leave," the PA says, too polite to be assertive.

"Why?" I snap. "Tell me why."

"Go!" Holly's father shouts, a rigid finger directing me back the way I came.

"I just need to see Holly," I whine. "Please. Just tell me where she is. I need her so badly right now."

"Leave!"

"Please, sir? I need to know where she is. And then I'll be gone."

"Call the police, Stefan."

"The police?" I say.

"Do I really have to remind you?" Holly's father hisses. "The injunction still stands, Alex. You set foot near me or my family, you get arrested."

Stefan talks hurriedly into a minuscule mobile phone.

"Why are you being like this?" I snap.

"They're sending a car," Stefan says, an admonishing glare fired my way.

"Your choice," Holly's father says.

"I mean no harm."

"You're prepared to risk yet another run-in with the law, are you?"

"*Another?*" I shake my head at him. "You've got me wrong."

He's silent, arms crossed.

"Holly wouldn't let you treat me like this," I tell him.

"How dare you!"

"Please?" I beg. I'm in his space now, and he's reversing, hyperalert. "Me and her, we're *close*. She talks about you. How you named her after Buddy Holly. I play his songs for her. Please, Mr. Chan. I'm not what you think."

"Never come here again," he says, marching toward me now, eyes wide and wild.

"This is crazy." Some instinct makes me back away from him, lets him frog-march me to the front door. Stefan swings it open, standing to attention like a hotel bellboy. There's a distant police siren. This is West London; surely it's not for me.

The porch steps are slippery with ice as I turn back. "Tell your daughter I came by. Please, Mr. Chan."

"Go to hell!" he yells. The door thumps closed.

I walk to the end of the avenue in a daze. My heart races as a police car speeds by with blue lights on but it doesn't turn in.

What does he think I've done?

I have nowhere to go, yet I walk with purpose.

Why won't he tell me where Holly is?

I want to hate the old man, but there's something to him that makes it impossible: the decency that radiated from him before he recognized me, the way his expression of anger seemed to be hurting *him*.

Who does he think I am?

Snow begins to fall. I could drop to the ground right now. Weep. Give up. Let the cold take me. But instead, I cross the main drag and let the warmth and low light of a pub suck me in. The place is both unfamiliar, and home.

As I stand at the bar, waiting on a pint, the worst of the panic retreats. The remainder of this cash is a life saver. No matter that I appear to have stumbled on London's only traditional pub with a no-smoking policy.

Five pints of Speckled Hen and a couple of Scotches to chase later, and I've hatched no plans, but I've found my mettle. I will work this out. I will *fix* this.

It's gone ten when, bursting, I weave my way to the toilets. I rest my forehead against the cold tiles above the urinal. I am exhausted. For an instant, my brain dares to relax. I close my eyes.

Sleep seizes its chance.

APRIL 4, 2019 | AGE 43

Lost Without You

A group of mopeds swarms toward me. Bright sunlight. Till a moment ago I was dreaming of Holly, so close I could smell her skin. I tried to fight the waking, to integrate the noise into the soundtrack, but it was futile. I sit bolt upright as the riders pass a meter from my ear and disappear up the road.

Back seat of a car. There's a duvet over me and I am, like yesterday morning, fully clothed. My spine spasms with pain as I attempt to rotate myself. Legs and feet fizzle as blood flow returns. There's a pouch of baccy wedged in the back of the driver's seat; I roll a cig with shaking fingers and crack the window open. The air is cool, damp, a whiff of greenery amid the petrochemical scent of city.

This car—a Ford, according to the steering wheel—is a family-sized hatchback with seat seams gashed open and a gear knob worn to tatters. And it is jam-packed: clothes and shoes piled in footwells, a towel drying over one seat, food packages and boxes of painkillers spilling from the open glove box. Wedged tight to the rear window is my guitar case. Most inexplicably, a length of garden hose lies loosely coiled across the front seats.

I find matches in the door bin, together with a toothbrush that's not seen water in a while. The smoke hits my lungs and I heave. Fling the door open. Little comes up, but the color is worrying.

Leaning against the car, I shiver in the coolness of the morning, but the rising sun is burning the mist away, hinting it might be a warm one. The car, blue and thick with grime, is parked on a rutted road lined with brambles and sun-bleached litter. Beyond a razor-wire fence, machinery comes to life on a building project. A pile driver joins the party, my head throbbing in time with its clanks.

How did I get here?

Last night seeps back into my brain. The row, the threat of police, the pub.

What after the pub?

The cash. I check my pockets. Check my pants.

Where's the money? No way I spent it all. I *wouldn't.*

I wrench free my guitar case: no sign of that sixty quid in coins. Tear through my bedding, check under seats and in every cubby. Nothing.

Have I been robbed? Stitched up while I was out of it?

I drop heavily onto the driver's seat, shoving the garden hose into the opposite footwell. Searching one last time, I flip the sun visors down.

The face that greets me in the small mirror is horrific. Waxy skin, like a dead body. Only it's too yellow to be dead. *Far* too yellow. My hair, which was largely still blond yesterday, is transparent, stuck limply to my head like wet spaghetti. My nose is a ball of blue. A vision of a knackered old boozer if ever I saw one.

I stumble out of the car, pat myself down again, noticing what I should've done minutes ago: these grubby clothes are not what I had on yesterday.

No way. No fucking way. Not *again*.

No memory of how I got here. No evidence of the cold snap, the snow that fell.

Another block of time—what—*gone*? Missing? *Forgotten*?

The panic and pacing and kicking of already dinked panels does nothing to ease the pain I'm in.

My knees drop to the dirt, hands grabbing my scalp. Today, I work this out.

I climb back behind the wheel. The key is in the ignition switch, left there all night it seems.

Home. My parents. The idea fills me with dread. But where else is there to go?

The car cranks over, but doesn't start. Three, four times I try. I'm about to pop the hood when I register the fuel gauge reading: needle off the bottom, warning light on.

No petrol. No cash. I'm unsurprised.

That yellow hosepipe catches my eye again. Enough, I reckon, to reach from exhaust pipe to side window. I grab it from the seat and hurl it into the undergrowth. The question assembles itself in my dulled brain: Might I never have made it through this last night had the car not run dry of petrol at a fortunate moment?

Among damp clothes and ruined shoes in the boot, I find an empty gallon can. In the absence of money, I grab my guitar case. Beyond the fence, a forklift driver eventually responds to my shouts and waves. The river, it turns out, is barely a mile from here.

River

People mill about with that good-humored energy that arrives with the first hot days after winter, eyes squinting, pale arms and calves freed. Twenty meters away, a preacher waves his Bible, promising fire and brimstone into his microphone. Perhaps I'm only the second most ridiculous figure on these banks.

My fingers are slow as I tweak the guitar into tune. I perch my backside on the edge of a low granite platform that wasn't here yesterday in the middle of the concourse. The wine bar that became a coffee shop is changed again: *Artisanal Chocolate*, it now advertises. I can't imagine I'm the only person who's ever sniggered at that.

It embarrasses me to leave the guitar case open next to me. What choice, though, do I have? If I was playing at the Blue Moon, how would I begin a set on a day like this? There's a certain vibrato from my shaky hands, and bum notes aplenty, but the intro of "Here Comes the Sun" rings through all the same. It's a balm on my ears, a sound that could not be more at odds with this unfathomable hell.

My voice is fucked. At first a tuneless whisper, it takes my whole chest to muster any sound at all. I'm whole tones flat and too hoarse to form half the words. People would surely be laughing at me, if only they were paying me any attention.

I've croaked my way through a second Beatles number without even a sympathetic penny to show for it when the preacher of doom marches over to me, leading with his Bible like a drawn sword. I brace for his judgment.

"Alex! Alex! What are you doing, my man?" His entire face grins.

"Skint," I mumble, shoving the case with my foot. "Flat broke."

"Who's gonna hear you, man?"

I think better of remarking that maybe they will, now I'm no longer being drowned out by promises of eternal life beside the Almighty.

"Where's your amp?" he asks.

"Yeah." What sort of idiot busks without an amp? "Must've left it in the car, I guess."

A warm laugh rolls out of him. "What we gonna do with you? You wanna use mine?"

"That'd be okay? You don't need—"

He wafts the Bible about. "Even the hardworking children of God are allowed a tea break."

"Thank you."

"Now get yourself up." He reaches out a hand so big it swallows mine. "You don't sit on the memorial, man. You know that, Alex. You of all people…"

"Memorial?" I spin around, take stock of the sculpture of chrome doves rising from this granite platform I've been sit-

ting on. And the bunch of flowers lying limp behind me. "Shit! Right."

"What's wrong with you today?" Again, the jolly laugh.

"Sorry." No wonder everyone's been ignoring me. What a fool I am.

Before I can move away, he comes at me, chest pushed forward. His solid arms wrap around me, his smooth cheek against mine. "I love you, brother."

The urge to break free is gone in an instant. Who is this man to me? Kindness comes in unexpected packages, I'm beginning to see.

Amped up, I don't have to work my voice so hard, and it takes on a bluesy lilt. I look over at the bench where I met that schoolboy Jazz—yesterday or *whenever*. He was dead right when he said how busking is like standing naked and letting people laugh at you. I am still largely ignored, but there are some smiles too. A semicircle forms when I play "Stand by Me," and they stay for more.

The self-consciousness doesn't last. I'm free for the first time since this nightmare began. I gaze along the Thames, think about the last time I sang: a few miles downriver, wild flowers tickling my bare skin, the girl I love in my arms. There's money in the case now, enough for fuel. But I play a little longer. Buddy Holly's "Everyday" ends the set.

It's Not Living if It's Not with You

This estate is just as it always was, aside from the alien-looking cars double-parked up our road. A few houses up, the 44 bus pulls over and school kids disembark, the sound like a perfect recording of when I was among their number.

I rap on the front door. The world shrinks, standing here. I'm on the edge of a place where my entire self is so often reduced to someone else's opinion of me.

"Bloody hell," Dad says.

He's taken the words out of my mouth. He looks so gaunt, so worn down. So *retired*. Does he look any older than I do, though? I'm not so sure. "Hi" is all I manage.

There's a delay in him shaking my outstretched hand, which he does limply. "Word gets round, I suppose."

"Word about what?"

"Coming in?"

The place is tidy, newly painted and recarpeted in the same colors it's always been. There's a calendar on the wall—the standard gift from the Chinese takeaway—and it's open on April 2019, same as the newspapers in the petrol station.

"Got some things I need to ask you guys," I tell Dad, following him to the kitchen.

"Here we go."

"Just some questions for you and Mum."

"Who is it, Colin?" I hear Mum call from the front room. My aching need to see her takes me by surprise.

"Don't go upsetting her, Alex." He looks me up and down. "You look a state, you know that? What's she going to think?"

"Things are kinda tricky right now."

He loudly tuts and fills the kettle. "Tea? And no, there isn't *something stronger*, before you ask."

"Tea's great."

"Well, go and make yourself known." He warms the pot. "But I mean it, Alex. Don't stress her." A familiar scowl is directed at me, a finger wagged.

When did I last see Mum? I'd got home at the crack of dawn and I ran into her getting ready for work. She had her arms full with boxes of homemade cream cakes—treats for the firefighters she cooks and cleans for. That was—what—a few mornings ago? But my memory seems to be stretching to fit this bizarre passage of time.

From the living room comes the sound of the Carpenters on the stereo, Mum's very own soundtrack. She was a singer herself once upon a time, spent a few seasons in the early seventies playing cruise ships. Karen Carpenter had always been her idol. It's a past she's talked about rarely, and only when Dad is well out of earshot. She is, apparently, where I *get it*.

The curtains are drawn against the sun, swaying softly in the breeze. The familiar opening to "Rainy Days and Mondays" plays.

Mum looks up from her armchair. It is the smile of someone who's made peace with their fate.

"Mum?"

She wriggles, pain twitching her face. Her slender arms are half-raised. "Come here. It's lovely to see you."

I nod, pretend I'm not fighting panic as I shuffle past the giant hospital bed where the sofa should be, dodging drip stands and gas cylinders. The table beside the wafer-thin telly is a mass of medications.

There's no weight to her touch, and I feel like I'm hugging thin air. I take the only available seat, a hard kitchen stool.

"Tell me what you've been doing," she says. Her brown eyes, the only thing unchanged about her, swell with interest.

"What's up, Mum? What is…it?"

She shrugs. "It came back again."

I want to ask *what* came back—I've never known her to have so much as a common cold. But I know the answer, really, and I can't bear to hear her say it.

"Thought I had it beat," she says.

I hold her hand. So fragile. "Good that you're at home."

"My choice," she says. "I've lived my life here. And I'll—"

"What's this?" I ask, unable to let her finish. I point at the ring binder in her lap, lined paper written in her loopy handwriting.

"Recipes." She smiles.

I'm about to register my surprise that she's turned her hand to writing a cookbook before realizing who it's being written for.

"Always imagined it would be me soldiering on alone, not your old dad."

"For sure."

"Still. Sixty-six. It's not *bad*, is it?"

I can't even reply.

"You're not looking after yourself, Alex."

"Don't worry about me. Please."

"I've been hoping you'd come," Mum says. "*He* said you

wouldn't." She points to the kitchen with her eyes, where out of sight the making of tea is producing a lot of banging noises.

"I'm gonna come every single day. You see if I don't."

She shakes her head—because she doesn't want the fuss, or because she doesn't believe me?

"I need you to know something," she says.

"Okay."

She looks sheepishly toward the kitchen. "I forgive you, Alex."

"I'm sorry?"

"I forgave you a long time ago. You must know that."

"Forgave me?"

She shudders, like I'm talking too loud. "We've both forgiven you." She whispers it, fearful eyes watching the door.

"For what?"

She squeezes my hand. "For *everything*, Alex."

It's clear the subject has to be changed when Dad arrives with the tray of tea. He perches on the high metal bed. We chat about people we've long known on the estate and about the weather, a veneer of polite conversation. Mum's head seems heavy on her neck. Every time I look at her, every word she says, is a knife through my heart. I'm too stunned to be sad.

"Alex has *something to ask us*," Dad says. He looks at Mum, expression saying *here we go again*.

"Money's a bit tight just now," Mum says. "I mean, maybe we…" She gazes at Dad, but he doesn't so much as blink.

"It's not money," I whine. "Why do you think I'm here for money?"

No reply.

"I need some help, that's all," I say. "I need to…fill in some blanks." It feels such a silly thing to say, but there's no reaction from them. "There are these *gaps* in my memory. *Big* gaps. Maybe I could just ask some things?"

"You're *forgetting* things?" Mum asks. "That doesn't sound good."

"Not a huge surprise," Dad mumbles.

"When did you guys last see me?"

They exchange glances. "Been a few months," Dad says.

"Just after Christmas," Mum says. "You popped over. It was… late."

Dad scoffs. "It'd be a wonder if you *did* remember that."

"And before that?" I ask.

"I don't know. What is this?"

"Please, Dad, just try to remember, yeah?"

"That day in the summer," Mum says. "When the hospital called?"

"Hospital?" I ask.

"Accident and Emergency. Don't think they knew who else to contact."

"Why was I there?"

"You'd had a fall. Maybe had a little too much to drink."

"Jesus." I am someone who has *falls*.

"More than a little too much," Dad adds.

"So you *see* me, yeah? I've been around since…" The question seems absurd. "You've seen me *consistently*, since I was, say, twenty?"

"Oh, love," Mum says sadly.

"Well, there've been some notable absences over that time frame, haven't there?" Dad says. "But one way or another, you're always *about*."

Mum glares at him and lays a hand on my knee. "You don't sound terribly well, Alex."

"Don't worry," I tell her. This information, scant though it is, confirms the one theory I've got: that my life has gone on uninterrupted for the past twenty-four years. I have been *present*. I just have no memory of it, of anything after that perfect day with Holly, of anything after the fight with Blake Benfield. Except, of course, I also remember yesterday, which itself was more than eight years ago. Wild.

"Maybe you should see someone?" Mum says.

"Do you remember an…*incident*? Back in '95? I got into a bit of a brawl. By the river?"

Mum looks into her lap.

"Hardly likely to forget it," Dad says. "Do we have to bring that up now?"

"You nearly died," Mum whispers. "Awful."

"Can we change the subject?" Dad says. I look at him, and he angrily mouths *don't upset her* at me.

"But I was okay?"

"You weren't breathing when they pulled you out. Intensive care for weeks," Mum says. "The worry!"

"Don't rake over this," Dad says, an order. I recognize the tone; I mess with him at my peril.

"You're shaking," Mum says to me. "When did you last eat, love?"

I shrug. God knows.

"You're wasting away." She looks up at Dad, who's on his feet now, arms folded. "We could get him something to eat, couldn't we? Just something simple, maybe? Wouldn't *hurt*."

Dad grunts and turns for the kitchen.

"Bless him," she says. "He's really trying—with the cooking and everything."

"Mum, there's something else."

She sighs, and it's clear she hasn't the energy for much more of this.

"What happened with Cambridge?" I hate myself for asking; such a trivial matter given the shape she's in.

"Cambridge?"

"Did I go? You know, take up my place? After I got out of hospital?"

"Gosh, yes, Cambridge."

"I didn't go?"

"It just sort of…fell off your radar, didn't it?"

"I got a place there, and I didn't take it?"

"Yes, yes," Mum says. "I remember."

"Why didn't I go?"

"I'm not sure you still fancied the idea. Not after your time in hospital." She pats my arm. "A long time ago, love."

We sit in silence. Fucking hell, I could use a drink.

Bruises

The Macmillan nurses are in with Mum, readying her for the night. I'm pacing the upstairs landing, although the immediate need to cry has retreated since I ate the toasted sandwich Dad made me.

My room is packed to the ceiling with junk; if my bed remains in here, it's long buried. I sidle in as far as I can. Daylight has faded to navy beyond the window. I gaze over the small back garden and the estate beyond, a hundred identical terraces and low-rise flat blocks: a familiar view, but it offers no comfort. This eight-foot-square room is where I spent so much of my early teens hidden away: learning songs on a charity shop guitar stuffed with socks, absorbed by homework and *New Scientist* magazines. No friends to leave the house for, only the crippling fear that came with the knowledge that somewhere out there was Blake Benfield. I'm nauseous at the memory, and grateful for the crowd I eventually fell in with in sixth form.

Stepping out of this now storeroom, I ease open the door to
Ross's bedroom. It's tidy and made up, that musty linen fragrance
of a rarely used spare room. In here, just as there are lining the
stair walls, are pictures of my successful younger brother, with
his beautiful wife and quartet of obnoxiously charming nieces
and nephews I know nothing of. The uninitiated would assume Ross to be an only child; I exist on these walls even less
than I do in my own memory. Certainly no mortarboard and
gown photo here.

No Cambridge. No Holly. No nothing. I think of that conversation we had in the boat, of cause and effect. This life I'm
experiencing is all *effect*. But what of the *cause*? What has led me
to *this*?

There must be a big box of cause, surely? Because I'm a cluster-
fuck of effects.

"Another on the way," Dad says, standing behind me in the
doorway.

I jump. "Didn't hear you come up the stairs."

"Due in the autumn. Another girl."

"You mean Ross? And…his wife."

Dad gazes at the wall of pictures. He is *actually* swollen with
pride, chest barreled forward. I doubt I'd recognize him in a
crowd looking like this.

"You've seen him recently?" I ask.

"He's in Australia, Alex. Can hardly *pop over*."

I stop myself remarking how that hasn't prevented them keeping his bed made up.

"Always in touch, though," he says, striking invisible dust
from the picture glass with his thumb.

"Of course," I mumble.

I was four when Ross came along. Dad understood my
brother. All Ross wanted to do was kick a ball, and if he got
upset, it was over simple things: hunger, falling over, getting in
scraps. He was the son Dad wanted: someone in his own image.

It was a role I never measured up to. My enthusiasm for having my head forever in a book rarely pleased him. For years, he dragged me to football training twice a week, where my disinterest and poor behavior would infuriate him. Silently simmering afterward, he'd sometimes punish me by repeatedly waking me after bedtime and switching on all the lights in my room. It would go on into the small hours, often on school nights.

Sure, there were times when Dad was okay with me too. He was cool and generous for a month or two when he got promoted to fleet manager. When his uncle left him enough money to buy this house off the council, things were good for weeks, and we mowed the lawn together for a bit and built a shed. During the Italia '90 World Cup we were best buddies, but when England lost in the semifinal, the air changed, and I was thrown out of the house for something or other.

"Cheers for the food," I say to Dad. "Good of you."

"Yeah, fine."

"I'm really sorry, about Mum."

"Yup."

"I want to help, Dad. What can I do to help?"

He shakes his head slowly.

"I really do," I say.

"A little late for that."

"Please let me fix that. If I've not been around, that's… unforgiveable. But I can change that right now."

"No, you're all right."

"Let me help. Look, I realize how awful this must all be. How hard this must be."

"Do you not see it, Alex?"

"See what?"

"All the stress you've caused her. All the *upset*…"

"What do you mean?"

His face is red with indignation. "Your mother. The cancer."

"What?"

"The stress, the misery."

"What are you saying, Dad? You're trying to tell me that I've…"

"These things make people *ill*. Eventually."

"You think this is…my fault?"

"You *don't*? Really?"

"No way, Dad. Bang out of—"

"You've no idea what your…*behavior* has done to her."

I step away from him across the landing. "No."

"Time to have a long hard look at yourself, boy."

"How can you—"

He raises a finger. "There is one person I hold responsible for this."

"No. Not having that. You can't be thinking that, Dad."

"I don't *think*, Alex. I *know*."

I recognize this tone. Arguing will do nothing. "That's not fucking fair," I whisper, slipping into the bathroom and bolting the door. The red-hot tears come, and for once it's like nothing's changed.

An hour passes, locked away with my tragic reflection. That hosepipe in the car this morning makes more sense than ever.

Mum's dozing when I creep downstairs to say my goodbyes. The Carpenters still playing: "Yesterday Once More," volume down low.

"Remember this song?" Mum whispers, groggy with pain relief.

"You used to sing me to sleep with it." I picture her in the twilight of my bedroom all those years ago, eyes shut like she was somewhere else, her voice carrying me away with her.

"I love you, Mum," I whisper into her warm, fine hair.

She smiles in slow motion. "Don't think you've ever said that," she says. "Not since you were tiny, anyway."

I hate myself a little more with the realization that she's right—what sort of arsehole never tells his mum he loves her?

I swear to her I'll be back tomorrow. Earlier I wondered if I might ask to stay the night, but the back seat of my shitty hatch-back is more inviting just now.

With Dad keeping his distance, I skulk a lap of the house before I leave. The drinks cabinet is locked. No wine or beer in the fridge. Not so much as some neglected sherry for trifles in the larder. It feels deliberate. Desperation begins to grip.

A short drive and I find an open corner shop. The balance of busking money buys me three cold ones. They barely touch the sides; the night ticks by slowly from the discomfort of the back seat. The sun is already on the rise when I eventually drift off.

AUGUST 11, 1999 | AGE 23

Erase/Rewind

I'm tacky with sweat. Shirt half-undone, only boxers on my lower half. I peel myself from this leather sofa and rub my aching head. Sunshine cuts through thin curtains. Another room I don't recognize. The telly's on quietly: a pop video of a gorgeous girl in school uniform and pigtails.

The air is muggy and I'm desperate for water. Two glasses beside me are empty, sticky with Coke and the nauseating smell of Jack Daniels. I pad across the floor into a bathroom and plug my mouth onto the cold tap. Breathless, I lean on the counter, feel myself plump up like a steeped raisin.

I raise my eyes, and in an instant I'm bolt upright. In the mirror, a skinny, rudely healthy man stares back at me. No wrinkles. Hair long and blond and wild. No jaundiced pallor today, just the kiss of the sun. I am a young man.

I *am* a young man.

Is this...*over*? Is this nightmare done with?

I massage my nose. It's as misshapen as ever. But no tenderness. The fight, the kicking I took from Blake Benfield, has to have been some time ago.

Perching on the edge of the bathtub, I take in my surroundings: Impulse body spray, overspilling makeup bag, bottle of Tommy Girl, iridescent thong kicked to the corner.

When I step back into the living room, a woman of about twenty is tidying empties and ashtrays. She's dressed in a baggy Gap T-shirt. She runs her fingers through a heap of blond hair.

"Morning," she says, sounding as hungover as I feel. "Coffee?"

I nod, suddenly aware of my lack of trousers. "Sure. Please."

Whilst she waits on the kettle, I sweep a curtain aside. The main road is two stories below and slow with rush hour traffic. There's a black cab, cars that don't look alien like they did *yesterday*, a distant green road sign pointing to Hackney. Unquestionably *London*.

I join the woman on the sofa, keeping to the opposite end. She passes me a mug, contents so black they're a mirror.

"Milk's off. Nice and strong, though."

"Thank you." Sour Nescafé scalds my throat, but it's welcome enough. I can't help myself staring at her tanned bare legs. She catches me and shuffles her T-shirt downward.

"Sorry, I don't remember much of...last night," I say.

She smirks. "Don't sweat it." She holds her mug close under her chin and rolls her eyes at the telly. "This song, man," she says, something called "Everybody's Free to Wear Sunscreen" now seeping through the speakers, the careworn yank's voice alien to me.

"Did we...?"

"Did we what?"

I steal another glance downward. Is she even wearing underwear? "You know. Did we...do...?"

"Get it on?"

"Yup. That."

"Is the idea so hideous?"

"No. No." She's an attractive woman. The idea would be nothing close to hideous, were it not for the fact that there's only one person I have any wish to be intimate with.

"Relax," she says. "After your initial enthusiastic flirting, you made it plenty clear that wasn't on your agenda."

"Right. Sorry."

She giggles. "Quit the apologies. What makes you think *I* was game?"

"Sorry."

She turns to face me at the other end of the sofa. "You really can't remember last night? Like, none of it?"

"Not a bit."

"Not even meeting us in the bar?"

"It's mad. I know."

"Wow. You should probably drink less."

"I'm sure you're right."

"We were out in Islington when we met you. Your mate Loz was getting friendly with my roomie." She gestures toward a slightly open door into a darkened bedroom. A snore rumbles beyond sight.

I nod. "That'd be Loz." He's someone I know from sixth form: great mate, bad influence.

"You and I sat here and had a few drinks with MTV up loud so we didn't have to listen to them smashing the granny out of each other. You crashed out. I buggered off to bed. Scandalous enough for you?"

"Shit. Okay."

"No need to look quite so relieved."

I sink half the scalding coffee in one hit. "I should be getting going," I tell her, not that I have any idea where to. "You reckon Loz'll be okay?"

"I think your wingman-ing duties are maybe over. He's a big boy. He'll find his own way home when he gets hungry."

I scoot round the floor, gathering up my jeans and shoes.

"Eclipse day, innit," she says, on her feet and opening a window wide. Warm air, sickly with diesel soot, rolls into the flat. "I swear the light already looks different. Is that my imagination or what?"

"Eclipse day?" I ask.

"Solar eclipse. Mate, where have you been?" She checks her watch. "Couple of hours' time."

"Right." It's an ideal opportunity to ask the question. "Remind me, what's the date?"

"August 11."

"Of course." It's not what I want to hear. The fight with Blake was September. This bizarre business is not done with. A chunk of time is still missing. I should check the year but can't bring myself to ask.

Pulling my jeans on, I find the wallet I've had since I was sixteen with twenty quid in. There's a crumpled pack of fags, and a small Nokia mobile phone.

"That bloody thing," she says.

I study it and try to disguise my fascination; I always swore I'd never have one.

"Ringing half the night after you crashed. Someone's missed you."

The screen glows green when I tap a key.

"Not bad news, I trust?" she says.

I shake my head as I look at the date. "Four years," I mumble. "Makes no sense. No fucking sense."

"You all right?"

The phone shakes in my fingers. "It says *Missed Calls*."

"It ain't kidding."

I stab at buttons and find myself lost in a maze of *menus*.

"New phone?" she says in response to my growing frustration. "Give it here." She navigates it expertly. "Popular boy."

"What is it?"

"*Six* missed calls, to be precise."

"Right."

"All from the same number." She passes it back to me. "Maybe flowers and chocolates would be the safest course of action."

I look again at the small screen.

Holly. She's been ringing half the night.

In thirty seconds flat, London's streets are beneath my feet again.

Beautiful Stranger

No ringing, straight to answerphone.

"Hey, it's Holly Chan. Here comes the beep."

I resist the desire to leave yet another message.

In a daze of bumped shoulders and mumbled apologies, I've walked clean through the city with this little phone glued to my face. Not that where I'm headed makes much sense—sure Holly was working at St. Thomas's hospital the last I knew, but now?

All the newspaper sellers advertise the same story: today's full solar eclipse. Already the daylight has dimmed and people break from their tunnel vision, look up occasionally instead.

I stop just off Fleet Street. This is the exact address where I spent six months laboring, saving for uni. It was a giant Erector set of steel beams then. Its polished facade of marble and smoked glass taunts me, reminds me I've been left behind.

What if she's not at work? I've got a little cash, maybe enough to get a cab to her parents' place. The idea fills me with dread. I try to persuade myself that her dad throwing me out is eleven years in the future. Twisted logic tells me that whatever he thinks I did that made him so mad probably hasn't happened yet. But I can't bring myself to *believe* these things. To *feel* them. Because they seem absurd.

I stab the green button. And I hear that recorded voice again. It's a sound that transports me to a perfect memory that is fading like an old photograph on a sunny wall. Why does it feel so long since I saw her? It's only been three days.

Where the hell do I find her?

By the time I reach the gardens at Embankment, it's twilight-dark. Little traffic flows; people stand still, looking to the heavens with dark glasses or disposable filters. I foolishly try to look but it's too bright; a floating crescent is etched purple on my eyeballs as I return my gaze to earth. I weave invisibly through the crowd on the lawns as this bizarre midmorning night takes hold.

"I wonder," a voice says behind my shoulder as I meander back onto the pavement beside the river.

I glance behind me, but the man stares into space. Is he talking to me?

He falls into step alongside me. "Can time be said to pass if nothing's happening?"

"I'm sorry?" I look again, and he gestures toward the immobile stargazers and the silently murky Thames.

"Time, that great unit of *change*," he says. "If nothing's happening, is time passing?"

I force a smile. "We're walking. And talking. So *something's* happening." I've never been any good at dismissing the approaches of lonely strangers.

"Very good, yes. Not to mention that great celestial event that you're ignoring."

"It hurts my eyes."

"Here," the man says, offering me the handheld welding mask he's carrying. "Works a treat."

I humor him, take a quick glance through the deep green glass. A rim of sunlight is seeping past the moon.

"Time is the moving image of reality," the man says. His tone is self-assured, enjoying its own profundity.

"Plato," I say, passing him back the mask.

"Indeed. Of course you know that."

I slow, turn and face him. He's a *big* man—several inches taller than me and the shape of a giant egg. "Do we know each other?" It sounds ruder than I intend, although my tone doesn't shake his smile.

"Tell me, what were you doing yesterday?"

There's a question. God alone knows what I was doing yesterday. "Look, I'm really sorry, but there's somewhere I need to be. I'm going to have to—"

"Where?" he asks.

"Sorry?"

"Where is it you need to be?" His voice is rich and confident, eyes twinkling with the enjoyment of toying with me. He reminds me of the dons at Cambridge when I was up for interview.

I fumble for an answer. "Well, I just need to—"

"Would it be impertinent to suggest that you don't *know* where you're going?"

I'm about to argue the toss, but he's right. Where *am* I going? I'm drifting in the direction of St. Thomas's hospital, but what the hell am I going to do when I get there? "Forgive me, I'm not sure I know who you are?"

He's not even remotely perplexed. "Paul H. Defrates," he says, holding a hand out. "*Dr.* Paul H. Defrates, but don't be cowed by the title."

"Alex," I say warily as I shake his hand—large but limp.

"I know." He appears smug about that, smile widening.

"Medical doctor?"

"Oh, no!" He tweaks the knot of his broad tie, making it even scruffier. "Not at all. Far from it." He doesn't elaborate.

It's dusky, quiet as the dead of night. We walk slowly.

"Forgive my asking again, Alex. What *were* you doing yesterday?"

"How come you want to know?"

"I mean you no harm. It's an innocent enough question."

I shrug. "I don't really…"

"I mean *your* yesterday. What were *you* doing the day before today?"

I stop moving. Who is this guy? What does he know? I try to read him, but he just stands there, hand in pocket, entirely sure of himself. His trousers and shirt are lightly stained here and there, his moccasins tattered; these details make him unintimidating.

"*When?* That's the question, really," he says. "*When* was your yesterday?" He swings his leg around and sets off again.

I hurry to keep up as we weave past a couple who are like statues. "What do you know? Stop, please. Do you know… something?"

"Of a fashion." He says it so casually.

"You know what's *happened* to me?"

He rocks his head as if to say *maybe*.

"What's going on?" I grab his arm. "Tell me. What the hell's going on?"

"How long's it been now?"

"This is…*day three.*"

"Early days," he says, faintly amused. "Feels longer, doesn't it?"

"Much." Holly, the boat, the night of the fight: it feels ages ago. "Do you know what this is all about? Tell me. Please."

"I don't have all the answers. I'm working on it, though."

"How do you know me? Know that I'm…"

"It's complicated. But don't worry yourself."

"Well, I'd like—"

"So many more important things to consider."

"How do I…get back?" I ask him, blocking his path now. "There's a way, right? There must be. How do I *escape* from this?"

My desperation doesn't faze him; the know-it-all's smirk goes nowhere. "It could be said that you *have* escaped."

"What does that mean? I don't know what that means."

"What is it you want?"

"My life back. September 1995." The saying of the words makes me ache for it.

The man nods. "Yes, yes. Of course."

"What happened to me?"

"Actually, I wonder if you might be able to tell *me* that. How did it begin?"

"Who are you?"

"Didn't we do introductions? Dr. P.H. Defrates. *Paul.*"

"I mean, why are you here?"

"Consider me an interested party. An expert of sorts."

"An expert in what?"

He bats the question away. "I'll help you any way I can, Alex. Trust me."

Right now, this rather smug, balding bloke appears to be my only hope. "How did you know to find me here? This is a massive city. How did you know I'd be exactly *here*?"

He holds up both palms. "Alex, please. These things, they'll become clear enough, but they are unimportant, really. Now, let me help you. You want my help?"

I shrug excessively. "I'd like any help I can get. Yes. Please."

"Well…"

"What do want me to tell you?"

"From the beginning?" he says.

I tell him about Blake Benfield, hitting the water, waking up in that vile bedsit with fifteen years gone and not a mark on me. The next day waking in the car. Then today.

Dr. Defrates doesn't flinch once. He asks for clarification on the precise dates, pulling a notepad from his pocket and licking the tiny pencil.

"This is impossible, right?" I say. "This is bullshit."

He looks to the sky, air noisily exiting his nostrils. "Here we are, Alex, on a small rock racing through the universe, currently in darkness because a trillion tons of floating moon has obscured our view of a raging gas fire ninety-three million miles away, itself also racing through this near-infinite universe." He grins. "And you're telling me that one man's consciousness being modestly de-tethered from the calendar is impossible?"

"What's going on with me, then? Do you know?"

"There'll be reasons. *You'll* have your reasons."

Like at daybreak, London is coming back to life now. I answer his questions about my medical history, my childhood, my mental health.

"This man you fought with," he asks. "This *Blake Benfield*. Who is he to you?"

"Long story." Not one I'm about to disclose to a stranger. Or anyone. "Does it matter?"

"Oh, just my curiosity. A man who feels strongly enough about you to beat you to a pulp and leave you to drown. Might be...*interesting*."

"It isn't."

"Very well."

"So how does this work?" I ask him, shifting the subject. I think of my conversation with Mum, about how I never made it to Cambridge, and the none-too-subtle hints of how deeply I've disappointed my parents. "When I...*land* on a date, it's like I've already lived everything up to that day. But *I* haven't lived that life. How does that...work?"

"Has the life that you're not aware of actually been *lived*, you mean?"

"Yes. That."

"Of course it has, Alex."

"My whole life already exists?"

"Yours, and mine, and everybody's." He moistens his smiling lips with his tongue. "We are all eternally surrounded by our own past and our own future."

I nod, keen for him to expand his point.

"The present is merely the conscious experience of a particular instant of one's existence."

"All right. But I'm pretty sure those instants should be *consciously experienced* in the right order."

Dr. Defrates sways his head side to side. "I'm not so sure of that. Not so sure at all."

"Really? Come on."

"I don't claim to hold all the answers."

"Tell me what you *do* know."

"Theories—that's all, Alex." He stops and gazes over the river. "You're familiar with Einstein's models of time and space?"

"The theory that all time exists, all at once."

"Quite. A big four-dimensional block in which all of space and all of time are sealed together."

"Sure."

"Like I say, we are all surrounded by our own past and future. *Haunted* by it, perhaps."

"So—what—I got my head kicked in and nearly drowned in the Thames, and I've become somehow...detached?"

Dr. Defrates grimaces. "Sort of, I suppose."

"And that means?"

He locks me in a patronizing stare. "Here's a little *what-if* for you, Alex. What if everybody experiences time randomly? It's just that their memory and conscious thoughts provide a grid—map references for everything—creating the *illusion* of one chronological, continuous existence."

"You think that's how it works?"

"Oh, it's only a theory."

"So the problem is me? My...*grid*? My *map*?"

"Perhaps. If the indexing system for your experiences went awry..."

"Things would seem to occur in the wrong order."

"Ends before beginnings." Dr. Defrates grins. "Imagine that!"

"Effects before causes?"

"Yes!" He gives an excited fist pump.

"Sounds completely nuts."

"One of many ideas of mine," he says, looking a touch crest-fallen. "Things are sure to become clearer. Be patient."

"So, what, I'm stuck like this? Doomed to never know what day's coming next?"

"I don't know, Alex. But I'll help you all I can."

"Please."

"You have my word. Trust me."

I nod. I *want* to trust him. What else do I have?

"The longer this goes on, the more we'll come to understand, I'm sure."

"What can I do?" I ask. "Please, tell me what I should be doing."

"Today is about making each other's acquaintance. I'm afraid I have no more I can offer you right at this juncture. But that will change, rest assured." He passes me a handwritten card. "Home and work addresses. You'll find me at one or the other. Always. You'll need to consign them to memory, of course."

I glance down. "You're a schoolteacher?"

"By day."

"Inner-city comprehensive. Wow. I imagine that's rewarding."

He grins. "No you don't."

"Yeah, you've got me there. I don't."

"It has its moments."

"When shall I come and find you?"

"Whenever there's something to discuss."

"You think I can beat this?"

"Tell me everything, and I'll not rest till I have the answers." He turns to walk away, raising a hand in a shimmering wave. "I shall see you...*later*."

"Or earlier," I reply.

He emits a jolly chuckle as he crosses the road. "You and I, Alex," he calls back to me, "we'll work well together."

At My Most Beautiful

I've never been in an airport lounge. But this place is what I imagine they look like. It doesn't look like a hospital cafeteria, that's for sure. I sit, self-consciously alone, among tables of chattering medics in lanyards and scrubs. I'd get myself a coffee if I wasn't quite so sick with nerves.

"I'm at work. What's so urgent?" Those were Holly's first words when she returned my many calls. I kept her long enough to find out where *work* is, and when she might spare me a moment of her time.

The taxi ride over cost me all my cash. Opened two months ago by the Queen, according to the plaque outside, this North London hospital is all turquoise glass and conditioned air.

I'm early for our meet. I fumble with my small phone. Tap in my old home phone number; it appears it takes more than a bang on the head and a near drowning to erase digits so burned into my memory.

Mum's just got off her shift at the fire station, she tells me. She's doing spaghetti Bolognese for her and Dad's tea. Her tomatoes aren't growing so well. Bloody slugs. Cracker on telly tonight—second part. It's a good one. She's energetic, "bright-eyed and bushy-tailed" is how she replies when I ask how she is. We chat about nothing, and also everything. If she can hear me tearing up, she doesn't say. What could I possibly be so sad about? Or so happy about?

"I love you, Mum," I tell her when the conversation has run its course.

"Don't think you've ever said that," she says. "Not since you were tiny, anyway." Exactly as she said yesterday. *My* yesterday.

"Never forget that I love you." I hold a napkin to my face, pretend to blow my nose, pray that no one's paying me any attention.

Fly Away

"Eclipse was *mental*, wasn't it?" Holly says. "Felt like a night shift in here." She sets a tray down on the table.

I'm struck dumb. I keep my hands beneath the table, fingertips so visibly shaking. She looks tired, harassed. Hair less kempt than I've seen it. Clothes professional, *reserved*. I swear I've never seen anything as beautiful as she is right now.

"They had the one you like," she says, passing me a foil-wrapped portion of soft cheese and some crackers. From beneath the cuff of her white coat, half a hummingbird is visible, tattooed on her wrist. It's new. Thinking of the four years of her I've missed knocks the wind from my chest. "I've got, like, fifteen minutes tops," she tells me. "Are you okay? You look…pale."

"Know any doctors?" It's a lame joke.

"Heavy night?" Her tone is disapproving.

I look down at the table. What *are* we to each other?

"Too busy to return my calls?" she asks.

"Sorry. Sorry." I open the pack of crackers, a lump in my throat at this simple kindness. "Lost my phone. Found it this morning, thank God." It kills me to lie to her, but what choice do I have? "Was everything...all right?"

"Good of you to ask." She whisks a sugar into her coffee, nearly knocking it over. "Awful shift, that's all. Wanted to debrief."

"Shit. I'm really sorry I missed you."

She shrugs, like my letting her down is no great surprise. "Lost a five-year-old. These things never get any easier."

"Wanna talk about it?"

"I'm cool today. Just would've been nicer not to have gone to bed alone. A *good-night* at least."

I could have spent the night with Holly. Instead I was playing wingman for a mate and sleeping on a stranger's sofa.

"Can I see you tonight instead?" I ask her, a wobble in my voice. I'm so desperate not to be *weird* with her, can't bear to waste these precious minutes. "Make it up?"

"Sure," she says. "I'm here till ten, though. You at the Blue Moon?"

I'm not about to play a gig if being with her is the alternative. "Nah, I'll blow them out."

Holly smiles over the rim of her cup—that wild-eyed expression she always reserved for my dicking about. "Now, is that the way to a successful pub management career?" she asks.

"Management?"

"Sorry, *assistant* pub management, then. Thought you were in the kitchen Wednesday nights?"

Bloody hell.

"I'll be free. Rest assured."

"Okay," she says, a twinkle in her eye that I'd trade everything in the world for.

"Nice place this," I say. "Swish..."

Holly laughs. "Who says *swish*?"

"Sorry. *Snazzy*."

She nearly spits her coffee out. "So it is. *Deluxe* no less."

"Swanky."

"Not going to tell me how it's a monument to New Labour excess?" she asks. "That we're taking our refreshments in the very embodiment of Tony Blair's ego?"

"It hadn't occurred to me."

"What have you done with Alex?"

"Not feeling very *political*."

"Oh, come on, not even going to ask me who's going to pick up the extortionate bill for such a piece of—" she does air quotation marks "—socially progressive willy waving?"

"I'm such a wanker, aren't I?"

She winks. "You're *my* wanker."

"Sorry about last night. For letting you down." The cracker I'm chewing sticks in my throat. Heat comes to my eyes.

Don't cry. For fuck's sake, don't cry.

"Baby," Holly says, grabbing my hand.

A tear rolls down my cheek and I slap it away like a wasp. "Sorry."

Two tables away, a guy keeps looking over. Dark eyes, chiseled chin, designer stubble. Stethoscope for his own lion's mane. His and Holly's eyes catch each other's and they swap a quick smile.

"Figured you must have been having too much fun at that bachelor pad of yours," she says. Again, the tone of someone tiring of my shit.

I need to know where I stand here. "Why don't you and I get a place?"

"I'm up for it. You know I am."

We're actually together. *Still.*

I want to punch the air. Perform a victory lap of this plush cafeteria. Give Dr. Dishy over there a high five.

"Just as soon as you get over your fixation with being on an equal financial footing as I am, maybe we can start looking?" Her tone tames my mood. This, it seems, is much discussed. "This is the eve of the twenty-first century, perhaps time to set aside your insecurities about being a *kept man*."

I could live with her. But I don't. I'm incredulous. But I'm also imagining her paying *my* share—how irrelevant I'd be rendered. "Sorry. I'm working on it," I tell her. I must be working on it, surely?

The guy's looking over again. She's pretending not to notice.

"Perhaps things would be different if I'd actually made it to uni." I feel compelled to muse the point out loud, remind Holly who I once was. Remind myself, maybe.

"Not mentioned that in a while," she says, expression sympathetic.

"It's been on my mind lately." I'm not kidding.

"It was your mind I fell in love with, Alex. And whether or not you have a first-class degree from Christ's College Cambridge makes no difference to that mind of yours whatsoever."

To know that she loves me, in spite of whatever's happened, leaves me weightless.

I gaze into her eyes and it's like no time has passed. "Do you remember that day," I ask her, "when we took a boat out on the river?"

"Didn't end so well."

"Yeah, but before the…fight. The day itself."

Her grin is wide. "Of course I do. One of my happiest memories. Almost *too* perfect."

You don't know the half of it.

She speaks quietly, cheeks flushed. "First time we ever…"

"How was it for you?"

"Shut up, you tit. You *know* how it was for me."

I speak quietly. "Fuck it off."

"What?"

"This. The rest of your shift."

She grins. "Those were the days."

"I'm serious."

"Find an overgrown riverbank? Relive our youth?" She sniggers, cheeks flushed by the daydream.

"Maybe." I'm not even thinking about sex, not really. Just of taking a walk, having her hand in mine. Take this summer afternoon for our own.

"You mean it, don't you?"

"What's the worst that could happen?"

"Loss of job. Loss of lives…"

"Exactly. Come on."

"How I'd love a job that permitted such spontaneity." There's a flash of disappointment, a longing for simpler days. She downs the last of her coffee.

The good-looking doctor across the way looks up from his bleeping pager and gives Holly a theatrical wink. "No rest for the wicked," he says.

"Right behind you," she replies, a statement that injects a spring into his step.

Why does this bloke bother me? Of course people look at Holly. It never used to fuss me. When I could detect a whiff of jealousy aimed at me—I *loved* that. Why not now?

"Who's that?" I ask.

"A colleague," Holly says. "I've got lots of them."

"Do they all spend their tea break gawping at you, though?"

"Are we really doing this? Again?"

"He's clearly into you."

"He's into everything in a skirt. Year one nurses a speciality."

"You sound disappointed." I mean it as banter. But there are edges on the words.

"I need to get back," Holly says. She doesn't meet my eye.

"Sorry," I say. "I'm a dick. Sorry."

"I *do* have to go."

"Of course." I stand, my T-shirt covered in crumbs. "I can still see you tonight?"

She shrugs. "Sure. I'll call you when I get off."

"Can't wait."

We hug. Her embrace is loose, dutiful. She smells like heaven. It takes every fiber of my pathetic self-control not to refuse to let go.

"Love you," she says.

"Love you too," I tell her. If she notices the crack in my voice, she doesn't say.

We are *in love*. Yet I'm not celebrating. Right now, perhaps we do love each other equally. But something in our respective tones gives away a truth: I love her a little more each time I think of her; she loves me a little less.

I watch as she breezes across the cafeteria, through the doors into a world where she is *somebody*. So professional, so smart.

So completely out of my league.

Closing Time

The address on my driving license has led me home. It's a terraced house in Balham that I share with Loz and three other
lads. We all, it appears, have the same attitude toward washing
up and mowing the lawn. They gather in the kitchen, a couple
of them in suits from day jobs, smoking and drinking Strong-
bow and talking about the eclipse.

Loz, having made it home this afternoon from the flat I woke
in, debriefs everyone on his night of passion. He says how he
wondered if I was *finally* going to "go over the side" last night.
I find myself apologizing.

Taking a tinnie with me, I locate the bedroom that contains
holiday snaps of Holly. I shave, scrub myself raw in the tub, iron
the Ralph Lauren shirt I find, shine loafers. I upend the bottle of
Joop in the bathroom, steeping myself like a Christmas pudding.
If I'd managed to put my newfound career out of my mind, I'm
reminded by a call on the mobile: my boss telling me I'm late

for my shift at the Blue Moon, that they're already a grill chef down. I feign illness and hang up.

Two hours to kill till Holly gets off shift, so I walk into town with the guys. The Queen's Head is what Loz calls a *grunter pub*—all cigar smoke and dogs asleep at the bar. We play pool, sink a few beers and Smirnoff Ices. My cash is gone but my Switch card works a treat.

We move on, to the high street. I keep thinking I see Blake Benfield in the crowds. Certain I hear that well-spoken voice.

Check my phone. Nearly ten. No word from her.

Glass-fronted pub now, DJ on the decks. Shots of Aftershock to chase.

In the toilets, looking at my reflection in the mirror. Thoughts of those many polished men who share Holly's days. Is it any wonder she hasn't called? Look at me. How embarrassed must she have been, me turning up at her work?

Back in the bar, girls looking over at Loz and me. Older than us. Work in *accounts*, one of their birthdays. I get a round in, light a match and pretend it's a candle she can blow out. Singing. Loz gets a number and a quick snog.

No call. Who am I fucking kidding?

Blake Benfield, over by the pinball machines. I'm sure of it.

False alarm, looks nothing like him.

Another round. Talk of a club.

In the toliets again. A mate of a housemate rakes me out a line of something. Bad idea probably. Split-second decision. It's like crushed glass up my nose and it's done now. More drinks and we're dancing and talking shit with the girls and they're saying to come on to this place with them and another tray of shots and bottles of Reef to suck down and the music's pumping now and it's dark and there's no way I can see Holly like this and anyway no way she wants to see me or she'd have called hours ago.

Another line up me and we're outside and I'm in the road and nearly getting myself run over and Loz is calling me a nutter and it's like old times and let's get a cab up west and fuck there's

Blake Benfield and I'm in the mood to take him now but it's someone else and we're waiting for a taxi and some arsehole's pushing so Loz shoves him back and there's shouting and I'm yelling calm it down you pair of wankers and he's not worth it and there's limp handshakes and our cab turns up and we're off toward the bright lights and it's like the pressure's off now because once you've fucked everything up there's no chance anymore of you fucking up anything and now I see it, why it was that last night I was taking the easy way and wingman-ing this guy when I should have been with *her*.

Not because of the promise of more fun, not a fear of missing out. Easier. *Safer.*

In the club, shit-faced. Triple vision.

Focus.

2 Missed Calls. Holly.

Can hardly go now, can I? Relief.

Why am I *relieved*?

What is wrong with me?

Where's Loz? Long gone.

Hit the bar again.

God, I love her. I could've been with her, right now.

Another drink.

Well, that's done it. Won't want to know me. What else did I expect?

Drink.

Fucking loser.

"Maybe you've had enough now, mate."

"I'm fine. You worry about yourself."

Just one more.

I love her so much.

One for the road.

Make it a large one.

Quick one before home.

Is that the world fading out?

Or is it me?

JUNE 4, 2012 | AGE 36

Born to Die

Rain falls in sheets from the coffee shop awning we shelter beneath. It is the shop front that was once a wine bar, later a chocolatier. The opposite bank of the Thames is near-invisible, a gray mist at the surface as if the storm clouds have squeezed the life from between the sky and the ground.

Jazz, the kid who bought me a hot chocolate the last time I saw him, sits opposite me and funks on my guitar. His chord shapes come slow, but he's nailed the busker's expression—all pouty lips and winks into fresh air. He's filled out, bum fluff given way to precision sideburns. Sixteen now apparently, though he was surprised I had to ask.

"Queen's gonna love this, man," Jazz says.

"Reckon she's got an umbrella." I catch the eye of the barista who glares at us through the glass; at some point we'll have to order something or face the weather.

"Still, cheers for the day off school, your majesty," he says. "What's a *flotilla*, anyway?"

"Some boats. Exciting stuff. You'll see for yourself if you hang about long enough."

It was the lead story when I checked a newspaper for the date: the Queen's diamond jubilee. Police in hi-vis line the river, together with hardy onlookers, oblivious to the rain as they wait on a glimpse of the royals, still hours away. Even if I hadn't got thoroughly pissed off with the rain, I couldn't busk if I wanted to now; a patrol car parked in the middle of the concourse paints the puddles electric blue. The memorial I got bollocked for sitting on last time I was here is nowhere to be seen—a fixture that the future is left to deliver.

"It's an A7 chord," I tell Jazz, moving his third finger into position on the fretboard. He's managing a clunky rendition of "Wonderwall." "You need to loosen up, *feel* it."

"That's what you always say. Maybe I'm just not *groovy*."

"Sure you are. Need a better teacher, that's all."

"Yeah, old cuz, that's it."

I woke this morning in that squalid bedsit above the shop, out east. The place was much as I last left it—untouched by ambition or fresh paint. The hangover, and the half hour spent staring down the toilet pan, though deserved after *yesterday's* misadventures, is of course evidence of a night I have no knowledge of. I know that much about how *this* works. Once again, there was cheap sherry in my kitchen cupboard. Without it, even getting dressed would've been a stretch. The morning light brought no cash. I now have seven quid to show for two hours spent crooning in the pissing rain.

Maybe I'm glad of the reason to do something. To not spend the day staring at mold multiplying on a ceiling, dwelling on last night. I can't think about it. It's killing me.

There is a point to all this—to my predicament. This is the certainty that I've come to as I've played this morning, invigorated by hair of the dog and heavy weather. If I can understand *why*, I can escape its grip, surely? There is a way out. There has to be.

I need to talk with my strange new friend—Dr. Paul H. Defrates. I may have seen him yesterday, but he saw me *thirteen years ago*. That's a lot of time for research. What does he know now?

"You hanging about?" Jazz asks. "Give the old Queen a wave?"

"Not gonna make any dough round here, mate. Need to take a wander. Pitch up somewhere else." Rain slaps the material above us harder than ever. Twenty quid, that's the aim. Enough to get out to Dr. Defrates's home in the suburbs, with a bit left over for *provisions*. Why does the thought of not being able to get hold of something to drink leave me so utterly terrified?

"Yeah, gonna get moving as well." Jazz lays the guitar in its case like it's a precious artefact. There's a shift in his demeanor, a deflation.

It occurs to me that the last time I saw him he was on his way home from school. But there's no school today. "What brought you down here? Sunbathing?"

"Shopping." He raises his rucksack, half-unzipped with bananas and a bottle of cordial visible. "Should be getting home, man."

"Where's home?"

"Old cuz, haven't I told you where I live before? Your memory ain't so good."

"Don't I know it."

"You should get, like, checked out or something."

"I'm on the case."

"Serious," he says. There's worry is his eyes.

"Don't sweat it, mate. So…home?"

"Sefton Hills, innit."

"Jazz, that's miles away."

"Two miles. And a bit." He shuffles to his feet and pulls up his hood.

"There's gotta be a hundred shops between Sefton Hills and here."

"Yeah, yeah. I know. Hope you make some decent money, cuz." He dodges a deluge of water off the awning. "Catch you later." His eyes dart, bird-like, across the concourse and along the riverfront.

"You okay?"

"I'm cool, man." He gives me a thumbs-up, hands jittery.

Why does he come here? Spend time with me, a washed-up old busker with a face like a lunar landscape?

He's frightened of something, that's for sure. I spent my own teens shit-scared of the next corner; the signs are clear enough.

His hunched back fades into the rain. I need to find somewhere sheltered to play, make a few quid. My selfish instincts are like a chain that I have to strain against till they let me go.

I hurry to catch up with my guitar in one hand, towing my amp trolley with the other. "No need to take off so fast," I tell him.

"Gotta get back. Been gone too long already."

"You're not so keen on being home?"

"It's okay. You know…"

His pace slows and we walk side by side, his hood angled toward the pavement, though he never stops throwing glances down side alleys. He needn't worry; I've seldom seen these streets so quiet.

I ask Jazz why he doesn't ride the bus back to Sefton Hills, but he's evasive.

"Can I level with you?" I ask. "Things aren't *right* with me."

"You're not ill or nothing?" His tone is careworn, too used to bad news.

"Nah. Just an…issue."

"Get a tissue," he mumbles.

I gently shove his arm. "I forget stuff. Things aren't quite in the right order."

Jazz doesn't look surprised.

"So sometimes I need to be reminded of stuff. Don't take it personally. Doesn't mean I don't care, yeah?"

"Not your job to care, old cuz."

"How long we known each other?"

"Couple years, maybe."

"Well, that makes us mates, doesn't it?"

"Guess so." It saddens me how that simple statement seems to touch him. "I just like watching you play, innit. Like chatting to you. You're cool. Interesting."

"I'm *interesting*, that's for sure. So I've never walked home with you, like this?"

He shakes his head, and I'm for once pleased with myself. It seems I'm capable of outplaying my *in-order* self. After last night, it's reassuring that I'm capable of any basic human decency.

"Start from the beginning," I say. "Tell me about you. Gimme the Jazz 101."

We've walked a mile by the time I've broken down his resistance to talking about himself. He tells me how he and his granddad left Iraq when he was six years old. How they left their home on the outskirts of Mosul just weeks before the combat began. I nod along at this lesson in history I've not lived through, context to that sticker on my guitar case that shouts *Stop the War in Iraq*. He tells me how they lived in a hostel for their first year and a half in the UK, forbidden even to venture out without asking permission. His parents were supposed to follow on after. Jazz hurries over this detail and I think better of prying; all I know is it's been just him and his granddad ever since they came here.

We're on the Sefton Hills estate now. We walk alongside a long row of garage doors, rain stripping paint and oxidizing metal before our eyes. Jazz, distracted for a while, is alive with nerves again.

"How's home?" I ask. "Your granddad, he's cool?" I think of

Dad, of how returning from school felt when life wasn't going his way.

"S'fine. All good."

"Sure?"

"My grandfather. He's a bit unwell. That's all."

I glance at his rucksack. "Doing the shopping. Good man."

"Couldn't get everything."

"What you short of?"

"Nothing much. Just put a couple of bits back."

"Jazz, what couldn't you get?"

"Dunno, just like…bread, breakfast stuff."

My seven quid of change slaps my leg as we walk. *Easy come, easy go*, says a voice in my head, and I feel for once like the man I once was. "Where's the nearest shop, Jazz?"

"It's okay. Doesn't matter, man."

"It bloody does matter."

"I don't need help. We're okay."

"Pay me back next time, mate. A loan, yeah?" I stare at him till he cracks.

"There's a SquareDeal up that way." He points along a path that cuts between two low-rise blocks on its way up to the main road. "I don't go there, though."

Doing his shopping miles from home, hanging down at the river, the hypervigilance. I get it. It's not home he's scared of, it's getting there.

"Who's picking on you, mate?"

He stares at the ground, ashamed. "Don't matter."

I crouch, stare into the tunnel of his parka. "I've been there, mate. *Boy*, have I been there." Even now, thinking of the hold that just the idea of Blake Benfield had over me—has over me—makes me unwell. "We're gonna get the rest of your shopping, Jazz." Who better to have your back than someone with nothing left to lose?

"I ain't a pussy," Jazz says. We keep close to the building, the walkway above us providing shelter. "But if anything happens to me and I can't get back for…"

"I don't think you're a pussy. Besides, who's gonna be out on a day like this?" Water streams from cracks above us.

"What else would anyone be doing?"

With the convenience store in sight, ganja smoke hangs low in the air. Three kids, Jazz's age at most, huddle in a doorway. I'm glared at, but that's all they've got. A lug of gob splats on the ground in our wake. A shout of *dirty gayboy* comes once we've passed.

"Don't say anything," Jazz hisses at me.

"You got it." To react would be to condemn him next time he's alone, I know that.

We negotiate the narrow aisles of the store. I pick up bread and cheese and veggies and the staples that, according to my kitchen cupboard, I don't buy myself. I'm doing the maths as I shop, holding back exactly enough for one tinnie; tonight I'll have that and no more. Jazz is adamant he'll pay me back, but it's him doing me the favor. I feel *necessary*. And I have something to tell Holly about.

"You don't need to hang about, man," he tells me.

"It's cool." We walk the perimeter of Sefton Hills, which I guess isn't the quickest way to his. "Any idea why these little shits pick on you?" I ask.

He shrugs. "Just kinda started at school. While ago."

"You do okay at school?"

"Used to. *Too* well, I guess."

"Not anymore?"

"Helps not to look too…smart."

"So they leave you alone now you've stopped trying?"

He laughs. "No chance."

"Keep being clever, then."

"Cos it's that simple."

I smile at him. He makes more sense than he realizes. Letting people see that you're clever means daring to stand out. That's not for everyone. Like him, I acted dumb for years at school; dodged the attention. It was only in sixth form, when life was sparking, that I was content to be *seen*. Is that what happened with Cambridge? Did that beating I took from Blake Benfield make me want to fade into the crowd again? Did I trade my future for the safety of anonymity?

"Get along—that's all I wanna do," Jazz says. "I ain't interested in making enemies."

"What's your subject?" I ask him. "What lights a fire under you?"

"Science is kinda cool."

"Now we're talking."

"Few years back, we did this sleepover at the Science Museum. Wanted to spend a week there, man. Couldn't get enough of it."

"Gotta love the Science Museum. So what you gonna do with your life?"

"See what my GCSE results look like. Got my last few this week. Ain't expecting much."

"You'll be fine. What'll it be, nuclear physicist?"

Jazz shrugs. "My grandfather reckons I'll be a politician."

"You fancy that?"

"Nah, cuz. But he reckons that's the key—reckons the only people who make good politicians are the ones who don't want the job."

"Think I like your granddad."

"It's all bullshit, though, innit? Like, *countries* and *my god's better than your god* and all that."

"Yup."

"Some people are dicks."

"They are, mate. You know what, though? You take away countries, and imaginary friends in the sky and whatever, but people'll still fight. They'll find something, like where people are putting their genitals behind closed doors, or football, or over where you can park your car."

"Man, you're negative!"

"Life grinds you down." I return his grin. "Time's a right bastard!"

Jazz crouches. Surrounded by cigarette ends, a shock of giant daisies has busted through a jagged joint in the ground. The white petals shiver, sparkling with beads of the clearest water. He takes a moment to enjoy their glow, before pinching off three at their stems. "Look good at home," he says, trying to feed them into his rucksack.

I take the small bunch from him. "There's loads. Have the lot."

"Nah. I take them all, no one else gets to see them."

We continue our stroll, Jazz a half step ahead of me. "Your granddad's right, you know," I tell him.

"What?"

"You should be a politician."

"No chance." Jazz points to a row of ground-floor flats. "Fourth one along, red door. That's me."

Let Her Go

Jazz and I take a shoulder each and lift the old man from the bathroom doorway. We prop him against the wall in the corridor. I order myself not to react to the smell, to keep my gaze away from the dark patch on the guy's trousers. He's dazed, like his head's too heavy for him. Deep brown eyes that can't find anything to settle on.

I reach for the mobile phone in my coat. "Shall I call an ambulance?"

Jazz shakes his head. "Nah. Don't worry." He strokes his granddad's hair, and they converse quietly in Arabic.

"Has this happened before?" I ask.

"Shouldn't have been gone so long," Jazz says. "He falls sometimes. Should've been here."

The old man grunts at me and holds Jazz close; his instinct is to protect in spite of everything. Jazz whispers something to him, and his expression softens.

There are wet bedsheets piled high in the bathtub. The curtains are closed in the living room. A small dining table is stacked with textbooks and ring binders. But that is the extent of the mess: carpets are spotless, kitchen clean. The place is sparse, few furnishings and nothing hanging on the walls. They've been here years, but it has the feel of somewhere temporary.

Jazz helps his granddad with his trousers. My instinct is to look away, breath through my mouth. But my instincts, I'm learning, are sometimes ugly.

"You got tea?" I ask Jazz.

"One thing we have got."

"Stick us one on, yeah?" I usher him away, look his granddad in the eye. "Let me give you a hand, mate."

"You don't need to do that, man," Jazz says.

"Two sugars," I tell him.

The thought of cleaning up someone else's shit is worse than actually doing it, it turns out. Holly must see this sort of thing every day at the hospital. Would she be impressed if she could see me now? I rinse the guy's underwear and imagine casually telling her about this, like it's nothing.

"You need to get some help," I tell Jazz later in the kitchen.

"No," he says, voice like steel. "I can look after him."

I put the first load of washing in the ancient top-loader and set it on a boil wash. "I'm sure, but—"

"He's always looked after me."

"Jazz—"

"He's just having a bad day. Bad *few* days. It's okay."

"What's wrong with him?"

"Dementia. Lewy bodies. It's where there's protein deposits in the brain that interrupt normal cell function." He speaks with a medic's authority, and it occurs to me that he's his granddad's interpreter, in addition to everything else he does. "He's okay."

I sort through a batch of sodden clothes. "You're doing a great job, mate. But you gotta ask for help when stuff gets on top of you."

"I'm fine. You don't need to worry about it."

I begin clearing the counters. "How many exams you got left?"

"Only three."

I look out the window at the rain that's backing off. I'm nigh on skint and it's late afternoon; is there any point going looking for Dr. Defrates now? "Your granddad's having a nap. I've got everything here. Go and do an hour or two on the books, yeah?"

"He'll want to eat soon and—"

"Jazz, I've got it covered, mate."

"It's my home. I can—"

"Mate, for once, let someone lend you a hand."

With some persuasion he eventually leaves me to it. I work my way through the washing, and I fold the stuff that's draped over cold storage heaters. I even show Jazz's school shirts the iron, although I add more creases than I remove. From a recipe of Mum's I remember, I start making a potato soup, and I butter a stack of bread.

It's a basic meal by someone who's no cook, but when we eat together, both Jazz and his granddad come back for seconds, giant daisies beaming at us from the center of the table. I grab a couple of his textbooks and quiz Jazz. The old guy puts the telly on: highlights of the Queen in the pissing rain on the Thames and an absurdly long clip of her boat being parallel parked.

I slip outside the front door and light my last ciggie. Perched on the railings, I scroll through the numbers in my phone. There's a *Holly Home* and a *Holly Mobile*.

I've not forgiven myself over *last night*—not even close. But I feel good enough to speak to her, in a way I couldn't have imagined this morning. Funny how a simple act of decency makes me feel worth something. Who have I *really* helped this afternoon? We are what we do, it seems.

"Don't think my phone's working," I say to Jazz when he wanders out to bring me another tea. "Got any clues?"

"Not much of an antique expert," he says, smirking at my battered Nokia. He taps a few keys. "Out of credit, cuz."

"Right. I can fix that?"

Jazz looks like he's about to take the piss, but he knows about my memory. "You gotta buy some. Go to a newsagent's. Or maybe you've set up your debit card?"

"Got it."

"You gotta make a call now?"

"Kind of."

He dashes inside and returns with a cordless home phone; at last, some technology I'm familiar with.

"I'll pay for the call. Promise."

"Shut up," Jazz says, leaving me alone.

The receiver shakes as I tap the number in. What am I going to say to her? *Sorry*—that's a good start.

Three times I try her mobile, met with the same recorded message: this number is not in service.

What are the chances she's home? Where *is* home? It has to be worth a try. I dial the landline.

The male voice is familiar: Holly's dad. He's softly spoken and friendly, but the sound transports me to that night in his house when he threw me out. It takes me a moment to do the mental arithmetic: that was late 2010. A year and a half ago. It seems safe to assume he hasn't had a change of heart toward me, whatever it is he thinks I've done.

"Hello, hello?" he says again.

Would he recognize me, just from my voice? He detests me— of course he would.

"Hi," I say, when it's clear he's about to hang up. There's silence again.

"Hello? Who is it?"

"Might I…" Why am I so nervous? "Might I be able to speak with Holly, please?" I ask as politely as I can, the very voice that's kept in reserve for love interests' parents.

Silence. It's an eternity before he speaks. "I'm afraid you can't." There's no aggression; voice softer than ever.

"Might you be able to tell me where I could find her?" I sound like a ten-year-old addressing their teacher.

The line is quiet again. "Who is it calling?"

"It's...Colin." God knows why I settle on my own father's name. "I'm a friend. An old friend. Just trying to...catch up."

"Colin," Holly's dad says warmly. "Did you know her well, Colin?"

"Yes," I say too eagerly. "We were at university together. At Imperial." A detail to give the lie some color.

"I see." So sorrowful.

I'm compelled to fabricate more detail. It comes so easily. "I was on her floor in halls. I'm in town, wanted to look her—" I freeze.

Did. That's what he said. *Did* you know her well?

"I'm very sorry, Colin," Holly's dad says, reading the silence. "I'm so sorry you should find out this way."

"What?" I shake my head. "Find out what?"

"Colin, Holly..."

"No." I don't think a sound leaves my mouth.

"Holly...she... She passed away."

Blood roaring in my ears. "Please?"

"I'm so sorry, Colin. We lost her...some time ago. But it is, still, very raw. She touched a great many lives."

I'm standing on the very crack along which my world breaks apart. "What?" I whisper.

"It was nearly five years now."

My voice is nowhere.

"Are you still there?" he asks. "Colin?"

"No."

"It's hard to—"

"You're wrong."

"I wish—"

"Why would you say something like that?"

"I'm so—"

"No. No way. Don't say it again."

"Colin, please try and be calm."

The phone slips from my grip, plastic shards and batteries exploding across the path. I snatch it back up.

"Hello?" I shout into the shattered receiver. "Hello? Hello? Mr. Chan?"

The gray day fades as I stamp through the streets of London. Tunnel vision, like I might outrun the racket in my head.

He's lying?

How?

Fucking how?

No way that happened.

When?

Sorry, but *how*?

It's bullshit. No chance.

Why? Fucking *why*?

A devil of my own making takes control. He knows what I need. Knows I don't want answers. I want to be free of the questions. Want there to be no need for them.

Like gold treasure in the streetlamp's glow, pound coins stacked in the center console of a VW. It takes three strikes with a stone to put the window through.

With my liter of vodka, I walk no further than the alleyway next to the shop I bought it from.

And I long for the silence.

MAY 1, 1997 | AGE 21

Lovefool

Midafternoon in the park. Trees bursting with blossom so dense it muffles the shouts of kids and the chiming call of an ice-cream van on the warm wind. The bluebells are out, spring so vibrant it could be unreal.

I unroll the blanket and set out the haphazard sandwiches I made. My hands are still shaking. Two kids nearby are flying a kite. It's painted like a phoenix. It hovers and swoops above our spot, and it reminds me to feel free. The sickness that's dogged me all day backs off; I might eat a little.

"About eight hours left," Holly says, smirking as she checks her watch. She lies back, hands behind head. Reflected in her vintage sunnies, sky and hurried clouds. "Till the Tory reign of terror is over."

"I should've got some champagne, really." I stop myself short of admitting that I have no money to my name. Instead, I slop generous measures from the half bottle of Pimm's I found at home into plastic cups, adding a token of lemonade.

"Oh, this is celebration enough! Cheers, baby."

I knock mine back and refill.

"Well, this is a first," she says. "Haven't been on a picnic since I was, I dunno, *tiny*."

The image of her as a child stabs my heart, and I force it from my mind. "It's not much, I know," I say, assembling discounted Scotch eggs and a giant pork pie on a plate and slicing them into delicate bite-size pieces.

"Nonsense. We're eating like royalty."

"Not sure about royalty. But it's possible we're living in a…" I start to snigger.

Holly grins. "Living in a?"

"We're living in a…Ginster's Paradise."

"Christ, you're a dick," Holly says through giggles. "That's more like it, baby. You've been kinda *elsewhere* today."

"I'm cool." The laughter loosens me.

"You've haven't seemed in celebratory mood."

Beyond the park, a car passes with a loudspeaker begging the undecided to vote Conservative. "Sure I am."

"Come on, what's on your mind?"

"It's nothing." I smile at the kids twenty feet away as their kite snaps at the line. "Your dad, what does he think of me?"

"Gosh, baby. Where did that come from?"

"He must think you could do better for yourself?"

"Not at all. No way. Hasn't he always been cool with you?"

"I guess. Dunno, just a vibe."

"He loves you, baby. Stupid as it sounds, he trusts his darling daughter's judgment." She ruffles my hair.

"You're a doctor, man. I'm a bloody pub manager. *Trainee* pub manager."

"What does that matter? Besides, it's a stopgap, innit? You'll find your calling."

"Yeah, sure." So what that I already know I'm stuck in that career for years to come?

"Baby, you charm parents with the very best. What's got you worried about Dad?"

"Ah, nothing." It's a theory I've dared to contemplate a few times today: Could her dad have been lying to me on the phone? Did he somehow know it was me calling, hate me enough to concoct my worst nightmare? Is he, despite appearances, a nasty piece of work? It's close to impossible, I know it. "Being silly. I'll behave myself," I tell Holly.

I woke this morning in the Balham bachelor pad I share with Loz and three others. Holly's body, warm and naked, was spooned into mine. Awake before her, I dashed to the bathroom, hyperventilating, cold with sweat, guts explosive. I paced and I taught myself how to breathe. In the cool calm after panic, I made my resolution: this is a day not to be wasted. No Dr. Defrates, no sadness about Mum, no fretting about Blake Benfield. Me and Holly, that's all.

With no money in my account and just coinage in my room, I managed to assemble a half-decent picnic from discounted Spar produce and the few edible contents of our fridge. We cast our votes at the town hall, both of us struck by an irrational need to retrieve our ballots to make absolutely certain we hadn't accidentally ticked the box for the Tory. The self-doubt was with us most of the morning.

My soup-orange Mini was slumped grubbily at the curb, evidently having dodged being sold to fund uni as was my intention. Rustier than before and low on fuel, it carried us away to this park in the suburbs. London is buzzing today with an urgent lust for change; perhaps I'm the only person with a wish to hold on to everything exactly as it is.

"What?" Holly says, stuffing a cheese-and-pickle sandwich into her mouth whole.

I grin in reply. We're lying on the blanket, barely a foot apart. The sun flits in and out, threatening clouds rolling in.

"You keep looking at me funny," she says. "What gives?"

"You're perfect. I tell you that every day, right?"

"Shut up," she says, butter smeared across her cheek. She's dressed in an oversize lumberjack shirt, gathered at the waist. She self-consciously tugs at the short hem.

"You can't imagine how perfect you are. You've got no idea how much I love you." My cheeks burn but I don't care.

"Wowzer!" She fans her own face. "What's with the outpouring? Not that I mind or anything…"

It's less than two years since our date, since the river. I've yet to begin ruining this relationship. "You ever worry about the future?"

"Hardly at all. Three or four times an hour, maybe."

"You ever shit yourself that everything's just right, and you wanna hang on to it, cos it might just fucking disappear?"

"*We*, baby, are going nowhere."

"I wish that—" My voice cracks unexpectedly.

"Oh, stop your worrying, mister!" Holly says. She shoves aside the food between us and rolls into me. I hold her so long and so tight it's like we overlap. No concerns about what might be coming, just a gratitude to this cruel system that we're granted this moment.

"Give us a leg up," a child's voice demands.

"Please!" adds her male companion. The pair of them, ten years old maybe, tower over us where we lie. "Gotta get our kite back."

I sit up. The wind is whipping up, sky darkening. "Sure thing. What you done?"

"Got tangled up in the branches," the girl tells me.

"Bad luck." They're rough sort of kids with no apparent adults in tow. That they've chosen to spend their afternoon flying a kite makes me instantly warm to them. It's wedged in the horse chestnut tree behind us. "Let's see what we can do."

"Don't be ridiculous," Holly shouts. "That is a *long* way up. How did it get *there*?"

The girl tuts. "Line broke, innit," she shouts back, as though Holly's an idiot.

"Yeah, line broke," I repeat at Holly. "Obviously." She rocks with laughter and gives me the finger.

Up close to the tree, the kite is way higher than I thought, a lurid fiery phoenix some forty feet up.

"Look, maybe it'll blow itself down," I offer.

"Just a leg up," the girl calls, leaping toward a fat branch at the trunk. The boy does his best but can't find the strength.

"No way," Holly shouts over from the picnic blanket. "Don't even think about it. If something happens to them, Alex…"

I scan up the dark center of the tree. It's built for climbing, though it'll need the stride of a six-foot adult. My jeans are hanging halfway down my arse as I scramble onto a stout branch. The first stage of the climb is easy enough, but the gaps between boughs is ever increasing. I'm at rooftop height and having to bear-hug each new limb to make it up. My arms are leaden and shaking. The higher I go, the greener the bark. It's slippery as ice, and my Reeboks lose all purchase, vanishing from under me. My flailing hands find a hold and for a moment I lie bent double, looking down at the kids below.

The rain comes. At first a pitter-pattering on the high leaves, but soon great dollops are scything toward me. This is ludicrously dangerous. For a *kite*, of all things! No chance of aborting the mission, though. What better judge of character than children? If they think you a lightweight, that is what you are.

Crawling along a high branch. Weight evenly distributed, but still the timber sags and creaks. Out of the green canopy, into the weather. A choppy sea of clouds from here to the murky city skyline. Christ, I'm high up. The park below is fast emptying, just Holly standing alone looking up, hair turned wild by the downpour.

The kite is four feet from my reach. I'm swayed to and fro by the wind. The lurid orange phoenix dares me. An inch closer would be suicide. I snag an adjacent branch and snap a length free. It's long enough; I tease the kite free and watch the tail corkscrew as it cartwheels to earth.

"That was *ridiculous*," Holly says, shaking her head as my feet meet solid ground.

"Yeah," I say, grinning. I feel unreasonably satisfied. "Where are the kids?"

"Said they'd be back later for it."

"You are kidding me?"

"Nope." She giggles. The more she looks at my crestfallen expression, the more it becomes a belly laugh.

"Did they even say thanks?"

She leans on my shoulder. "No."

"Bloody hell. *Back later for it*, indeed."

The park is ours alone now. We sit in the shelter close to the trunk, and Holly rolls us a smoke to share. "Play something," she says, eyeing my guitar case that she rescued from the rain.

"Why did I bring that thing?"

"Because you're a cool dude?"

"There's a definite *type* of guy who brings a guitar to a picnic, don't you think?"

"Yeah, maybe."

"It's not a great look."

"I'm glad it's here. What happened, you forgot to be all cynical and sneery when you were packing to come out?"

I pop the latches. "You might be spot-on there."

It takes me no more than thirty seconds to find my groove. Holly's head rests on my shoulder. I play the Buddy Holly standards: "Everyday," "Peggy Sue," "True Love Ways."

Evening brings with it clear skies. With soaked grass beneath our bare feet, we fly the kite we won.

"What do you want to do tonight?" I ask her.

"I'm afraid it's a night in," Holly says, letting out the last of the line. "We have election results to watch."

"Of course we do."

"I reckon I'll be glued to the telly till at least three. You can keep me in cups of tea and snacks."

We shield our eyes as we look up, watch the kite reaching for the sunset.

I put my arms around her waist. "Sounds like absolute perfection."

OCTOBER 28, 2008 | AGE 33

Mr. Rock & Roll

Don't cry. Today has been a crash course in the rules of this place, and this is surely one of them. Don't fucking cry. Besides, if I start, how would I stop?

Mum sits opposite me. Pale as a ghost. It's a decade or more till the cancer will come for her. No—the only thing making her ill is me. She smiles and looks around this big room with an expression that suggests she's finding plenty of positives. There's an absurd nod of approval, but still we don't begin a conversation. All about us, there's a hubbub of people chatting.

Did I ever *talk* to my parents? We coexisted in a house for twenty years or more; information was passed between us as required. Is that conversation, though? Do we know how?

"Are they feeding you okay?" Mum eventually asks. Her tone is bouncy; only one answer she wants to hear.

"Really good." I ate a sandwich and an apple for lunch, whilst perched on a skidded toilet pan with a missing seat. That's the limit of my knowledge of the catering here. Were this a hotel, I'd probably complain.

"You *look* well."

"Cheers." I don't. My complexion might be consistent with an enforced break from the sauce, but everything about me is colored with defeat. "You look lovely, Mum."

"Just a bit of lippie," she says. "Remind me to wipe it off before I…well, you know."

"It's…really nice to see you." Weak words, but they ache in my throat. I want to be honest, to hug her and tell her how desperately I need her. But I'd lose control.

"There's a machine," Mum says. "Shall I get us a hot drink?" Again, the ludicrously upbeat tone. "I've got a little change."

"I'm fine, Mum."

She tries to disguise her disappointment at not being able to busy herself, squirming on her chair. It is, like all the furniture in here, bolted to the floor.

"How's Dad?" I ask.

"Oh, Dad's…Dad."

"He didn't fancy coming? I mean, I'm not sure I'm terribly fussed either way."

"He's outside. In the car."

"As he wishes."

Mum looks at the low table between us. "He's never keen on me…visiting."

"Nice gaff like this?"

"All these *men*. Not the sort of place…"

I look around at the officers patrolling the room, and those guarding the two entrances—one for visitors, one for *us*. "Reckon you're probably safe, Mum."

"I don't think I'll be able to come again."

"You're visiting to tell me you won't be visiting?"

"You know how it is, Alex."

"Yeah, I suppose I do."

"I've been desperate to come, though. Even with all the rows it caused."

"I'm okay."

"My son. My *boy*. In…here. You have no idea."

Is this what Dad meant when he blamed me for her cancer? Is this the *stress* he was banging on about?

I grab her hand, look her in the eye. "I'm okay, Mum. Please, I'm fine." A necessary lie, and I deliver it well. "Don't you go worrying about me."

Waking this morning brought no pain; no poison rotting my bones, no immediate need to vomit. I should have been suspicious. Instead, I floated in the middle ground between sleep and waking, hearing without listening to the creaking pipes and distant footsteps of this vast building. Not even the stench of boiled-to-buggery vegetables brought me to my senses. For a blissful moment unaware I was anything other than a young man with a glowing future. With the six a.m. alarm call came the realization that I was in a bunk bed in a twelve-foot-square room, HMP Meadway embroidered on the sweatshirt I'd slept in.

My cellmate is a six-foot-three beanpole with a scar across his shaved head. I mistook his silence for an attitude, but when he made us both a coffee and passed a tray of cereal up to my bunk, it was clear enough it's just that he knows little English. As though it's an unremarkable part of our morning routine, he dropped his pants and sat on the toilet in the corner of our cell. A thin curtain hid him from sight, but offered no such barrier to smell, or noise.

My morning was spent painting walls in an unused cellblock. I worked meticulously, took some satisfaction as the blockwork took on its uniform gray sheen. It's a job I'm told pays a couple of quid a day and seemingly keeps me in rollies. Telly has taught me to be petrified of the men in here, but no one seems to want to do more than get on with their day in peace. Sure, there's clearly a hierarchy to be preserved, and there are staff who are too keen to be popular with those at the top of the pecking order. To anyone who went to an all-boys school, it's a familiar system.

How long have I been banged up here? Long enough for everyone to regard me as part of the scenery, that much is clear. I've no clue how long I'm serving. It was late 2010 when I woke in that shitty bedsit out east. The girl, Kenzie, told me I'd been there five months. That's two years from now; was that straight after my release? No wonder I couldn't find somewhere plusher to live. Ex-cons: no one's favored tenant.

Every day, I'm living effects of *causes* I can scarcely believe. But *this*? This is batshit crazy. I'm no criminal.

I've thought a lot today about what Dr. Defrates said: how my life already exists in its entirety. Past, present and future, all sealed in a block, just as everyone's is.

We are eternally haunted by our own past and our own future.

So what, I just put up with *this*? Trust to my luck, hope that each morning takes me to a date before my world fell apart? Can I live like that?

How did Blake Benfield do all this? Where is he now? I wonder. A free man while I serve time for a crime I've no knowledge of?

Mum chatters about the workplace politics at her fire station, how there are threats of cutbacks. "What if they're out on a call all day?" she's saying. "How can they possibly be expected to feed themselves? I mean, half of them can't boil an egg. Well, it's not their business to, is it? They'll just end up going hungry. Or they'll be eating junk..."

Her eyes flit back and forth between me and the fluorescent tubes above us whilst she delivers a monologue. I listen intently, each word a gift now I know there's a time when her voice will not be there for the hearing.

It's fifteen minutes before she runs dry, having seamlessly segued on to the subject of the *marvelous* Carpenters tribute act she saw last week, and from there to my golden brother, Ross, and his new massive house in the suburbs of Adelaide.

"What did I do, Mum?" I shoot the words into the lull. Who else do I ask?

"When do you mean?"

"To end up here. What do they think I did?"

Her eyes are heavy, pulled to the floor. "Alex. Please."

"I shouldn't be here. I'm not a criminal." I gaze around the visiting room, compelled to look for confirmation that these other men are a breed apart. But no one here looks like any more or less of a deviant than I do.

"Let's not talk about it, love. Not again."

"Mum, I really need to know this."

"Alex, I do know you think this is terribly unfair." She looks at me fleetingly. So sad. "It *is* unfair."

"So why the hell am I here?" Mum balks at my tone, and I apologize.

She goes to hold my hands but stops herself. "Someone..."

I lean forward so we're almost touching. "What, Mum?"

"A person is dead, Alex."

"What, because of *me*?"

She shrugs and nods at the same time.

"You don't seem very sure," I snap, earning myself a glance from a warder.

"Alex, please. Let's not do this."

I shudder with disbelief. "Mum," I whisper. "Mum, there's no way on God's earth I've killed somebody. No way."

A tiny nod, no eye contact.

"Mum, look at me. Please. Do I *look* like someone capable of killing a person?"

"No. No," she mumbles. "Of course not, love."

"This is nuts. Fucking nuts." I grab at my temples.

"The court made their decision, Alex. And we've all learned

to live with it. Please let's not waste the time we have. It's not long before I have to go."

"So I said I was innocent? I pleaded not guilty to this crime?"

Mum takes a deep breath. "A couple more years, love. Then we can all put this behind us."

"Did you believe me, Mum? When I denied whatever I'm… accused of? In *court*?"

"No mother wants to think ill of their son. Heartbreaking, Alex. You have no idea."

"So you believed me?"

"I was on your side."

"*Was?* Mum, has Dad been in your ear?" I slap a heavy palm on my thigh. "I can imagine *he* had me hung, drawn and quartered from the start?"

"It's been hard for him too."

I grab her hands in mine. I want to tell her: how this life isn't mine, how I should be heading off to Cambridge right now, how I know nothing of this alleged crime. "This, Mum, is a stitch-up. A massive stitch-up."

"I know it doesn't seem fair." Mum lets go of my hands. She turns her head so there's no danger of catching my eye. "Think what it's like for the poor girl's family, though, Alex."

"*Poor girl?*"

"Holly." Mum can barely utter the name. "Dear Holly."

"Holly? My girlfriend Holly?"

"Please, Alex."

I throw myself back in my plastic seat. Slap my hands against the armrests. Another admonishing glare from a screw.

"No chance," I eventually say. Face on fire. "No chance whatsoever."

"Please calm down," she says. "You look…crazy."

"I didn't do it, did I, Mum?" I hiss.

"I've always given you the benefit of the doubt," she whispers.

"Fucksake."

"Are you okay? You don't look..."

A cold tear slices down my cheek. "I'm all right."

"Darling, I can't bear seeing you this upset."

A guy walks past us on his way back to the wing. I recognize him from work this morning. I try to cover my face with my arm but I'm too late. He gives a sad smile, eyes that understand.

"You don't need to worry about me, Mum," I tell her. She doesn't.

Because I get it. This is why I'm here. I'm certain of it.

There is absolutely no possible chance I killed Holly. Insane suggestion. It is an impossibility. The sun going round the moon. Camel through the eye of a needle.

This is my proof.

This is a stitch-up.

What else about this miserable, failed life I'm visiting is a setup too? A great deal, I'd wager.

"Thank you for your faith in me, Mum," I say, voice cracking. The room around us is emptying now. "I will prove you right. I swear to you I'm an innocent man."

She passes me a tissue. "I should be making a move."

"I'll clear my name, Mum. You watch. Please, don't be ashamed of me a moment longer."

"Not ashamed, love." She shuffles to her feet. Checking herself in a pocket mirror, she starts to wipe away her lipstick.

"I'm the victim here. I swear to God. You wait and see." I recall Dr. Defrates's exact words when I asked him why this was happening:

You'll have your reasons.

What better reason than proving my innocence? Justice being done? Saving my own future?

"I'll tell Dad you said hi," Mum says, makeup deleted, scrunching her reddened tissue into a ball.

"If you like."

"Well, see you...anon."

"Please, could I have a hug, Mum?"

"Is that allowed?"

The warder chuckles as he passes, playing a tongue across the fringes of his silver beard. "No tearing each other's clothes off. Other than that, you're fine."

She's awkward in my arms, but I hold on to her till I feel her loosen. The last time I hugged her there was nothing to her; so close to the end. Eventually she squeezes me back. It feels like she's longed for this as I have.

When will I hug her next? Will this all be over by then?

"I love you, Mum," I whisper into her ear.

She gently pulls away, and we hold each other at arm's length.

I think of the times I've told her I love her since *this* began, the reply she's always given me.

"I know, I know," I tell her. "You can't remember when I last said it."

She grins. "I do remember, as it happens."

"Yeah, well, I'm gonna fix it. What was I, like five years old?"

"You rang me once, totally out of the blue. Just to tell me you loved me."

I let go of her hands. "When, Mum?"

"I was taken aback. Wondered what on earth had got into you!"

"When was that? Do you remember? Tell me you remember."

"Would you believe it if I said I know *exactly* when it was?"

"Go on."

"Not that a demonstration of affection from you is unusual or anything."

The guard passes us again, tapping an invisible watch on his wrist. The room is almost empty. "Going right now," Mum says.

"When, Mum?" I'm doing my best to ask casually.

"A good few years back. It was the day of that eclipse. You remember that? Remember phoning me up? Just because..."

"I do."

"I was sitting at the table afterward and having a gasper, and thinking—what's got into Alex? What's he done now that he's softening me up for? Has he been drinking?"

"I hadn't."

"I was touched." She squeezes my hand and turns for the exit. "Do it more often!" She doesn't look back, nor tell me she loves me too.

Rooted to the spot, I watch her go. When I clapped eyes on her this afternoon, I was in the grip of defeat. Is it possible she leaves me as a man in control of his own destiny?

How long till lights out? I can only pray that sleep carries me outside of these walls.

Because there's someone I have to talk to tomorrow.

JANUARY 23, 2023 | AGE 47

Running Out of Time

I collapse into the low chair. I've walked two hundred meters from where the cab dropped me, and I'm hopelessly out of breath. Sweat pours down beetroot calves, so shinily swollen I couldn't get a pair of trousers over them and had to settle on a pair of Scoutmaster shorts. The receptionist considers me with suspicion above the rim of her glasses and tries the phone again. I urge myself not to panic at this struggle to get oxygen into my lungs. This body is destroyed.

A couple of kids snigger as they pass. I hear the word *pedo* uttered, for the second time since I set foot on site ten minutes ago.

You're not going to die here, I tell myself. My heartbeat wobbles in my neck. I clutch the vinyl chair with sausage fingers. In an attempt to distract myself, I watch the notices scrolling by on the LED display above the door. Block capitals inform me that Beekenside Secondary operates a zero-tolerance policy to the possession of weapons.

The receptionist passes me a visitor's lanyard. "Paul—Dr. De-frates, rather—will be down when he's finished with his class."

"Thanks." My voice is a gurgle, but no amount of clearing my throat has made it sound any more human. I am a man, barely of middle age, broken by booze.

She backs away sharply. I don't *think* I smell, but I do have the look of someone who you'd play it safe in proximity to—breathe in through the mouth and do so as little as possible.

The bell sounds and the building comes alive, a thousand pupils making a dash for the gates. I had begun to doubt I'd make it here before the end of the day, but with my pulse rate slowing, I enjoy a moment of private celebration.

I awoke some hours before dawn arrived this morning, sleeping in my family home for the first time since this nightmare began. I was reminded of being sick as a kid, as I flitted from feeling close to death, to terror-filled sleep, and back awake in time for several lurching staggers to the bathroom. Only by daylight did I register that I was not in my own room, but in what had once been my parents' bed.

A black-and-white portrait of Mum in a gilt frame was among the empty cans and full ashtrays on the mantelpiece. Unmistakably early 1970s, it's a picture from before she met Dad—all cheekbones and ruler center-parting like her idol Karen Carpenter. I was hollow as I stared at that photo: not so much grieving for the person no longer here, but for the one I never knew.

There was no clear evidence as to how long I've been living alone there. Unopened bills in red envelopes were tossed about the place. Dad's answerphone blinked urgently at me in a way it never had when he used to insist it was essential for his work. Eight messages, all from Ross. My brother's ever more frustrated voice fluttered and slurred on the worn tape. "When are we getting the house on the market, Alex?" "Stop ignoring me. I can't afford to pay another month of Dad's fees at the home, Alex. Too many obligations here." "Are you there, Alex?" "Have you found somewhere else to live yet, Alex?" "Call me." "Christ's sake, Alex. If I have to fly back I will." "What is wrong with you, Alex?" "Will you just call me already?"

I didn't call him back. It would have been easier to write the day off, sleep off the agony of this body. But I can't risk waiting for a better day *tomorrow*. Today I am a free man, at least.

Finding Dr. Defrates meant finding some cash. I tore through the house: not even pennies under sofa cushions or in clothes pockets; I'd swept the place already, it would seem. I remembered the fireproof lockbox Dad kept in the base of his wardrobe, home to valuables including his gold watch. It was where he always kept Mum's Midland Bank passbook, which she'd occasionally be allowed before having to check it back in again.

I'd beaten myself to it: lock already smashed open, metalwork buckled and torn. Just some insurance paperwork remained.

Among the mess, I did find some receipts from a pawnshop on the high street called The Cash Angels. Instantly the missing television and hi-fi made sense. Nothing of value left in the house: Dad's cufflinks and bracelets missing, no power tools in the shed, even the cake mixer gone. Self-preservation stopped me dwelling on this too long; safest to think of the perpetrator of these acts as a stranger to me. But it made searching out Dr. Defrates all the more pressing.

At the pawnshop, I was greeted like a minor celebrity by the girls behind the safety glass. "That old thing again?" one asked as I waited for them to value my guitar. "How many times you bought that back from us?" Even the other customers laughed when I said I couldn't remember. "We'll keep it to one side," the girl told me as she counted out thirty-eight quid. Parting with it seemed no great loss; going busking with it today is out of the question. I'd tried a few chords back at the house, but my fingers, swollen and numb, made playing infuriating—like using a typewriter whilst wearing boxing gloves.

Despite the brain fog, I could still remember the address

Dr. Defrates gave me, and I was soon in a cab. The mid-terrace cottage in the suburbs looked alarmingly disheveled. I peered through a filthy bay window at books stacked to waist height and at a fireplace that had avalanched ash past the hearth and onto the many overlapping rugs. Back in 1999, he'd been so insistent that I'd *always* find him here. What—twenty-four years ago? I rapped on the door a fifth time. My heart sank and my hangover gripped harder.

"Excuse me," I said to a neighbor as she emerged from her own front door. "Is there another way in?" I gestured to the stack of catalogs and newspapers in the porch, blocking the doorway.

"God, no!" she said with a smirk. "Paul just steps over them. Always has. Not sure he even notices such things. Mind on far *bigger* things."

"Paul? Paul Defrates? He still lives here?"

"Never lived anywhere else, I don't think. But he's at work now." And she gave the address of the same inner-London school that Dr. Defrates himself had given me nearly a quarter of a century ago. Furious with myself for the wasted jaunt out to the suburbs, all but the last quid of the guitar proceeds were gone by the time I arrived outside this building.

"Aha! Alex Dean!" Dr. Defrates booms as he strides through reception. "Long time no see."

Bizarrely, it feels a lifetime since we last spoke, though it's only been four days—for me. He limply shakes my hand, and I'm forced to grab on to him in order to extract myself from the seat. I'm short of breath again by the time I'm on my feet. "I never imagined you'd still be working at the same school," I tell him as we weave through corridors. "I'd have been here much earlier today if I'd known."

"I'm something of a *lifer*. That's what the staff here call me." He chuckles, as if the joke is on them. "Thirty-two years and counting."

"I'm impressed," I tell him. "Tough job, I'm sure."

He laughs again, walking such that he leads with his chin. When I met him that day of the eclipse and we strolled beside the river, he'd seemed so much older, as though he could have been my own schoolteacher. But the years have been far kinder to him than to me. He's still the egg-shaped giant he was, the pounds he's packing keeping him wrinkle-free—face and bald head so taut they have a sheen to them.

Dr. Defrates's office is no more than a storeroom attached to his classroom, and it's in the same disarray as his house. I move a tower of files and some plates to uncover a stool to sit on. He pours himself a glass of tomato juice and takes a deep swig. It leaves a red moustache which he wipes away on his sleeve. "Alex?" he says, holding the carton aloft.

I hold up a palm. If he had a shot of vodka and Tabasco to go with it, I'd accept the offer in a flash.

"Good for the intellect," he mutters as he squeezes behind his desk. Not a square inch of the surface is visible.

I glance around the place, but nothing among the squalor gives anything of value away about this man. I know nothing of him, other than that he's my only hope.

"What is it you teach?" I ask.

"All sorts. History to the younger years. Economics and philosophy at A-level. Latin on the rare occasions when the interest's there."

"Wow."

"We live in an era of *specialists*, Alex. Modern life says that to be successful one must know one subject, inside out. But I find it's far more interesting to know one thing about everything, than to know everything about one thing. Don't you think?"

"Sure."

He browses through an exercise book before groaning and scribbling with a red Biro. "Tell me—to what do I owe the pleasure?" he asks.

"I don't have anyone else I can talk to. About *this*. Sorry. You don't mind me…showing up?"

"I'm delighted you have. Touched, even."

"Something has…come to light. I think so, anyway."

"Tell me more," Dr. Defrates says.

"I think maybe I can *change things*. Can I change things?"

"Let's start with what's happened to bring you here."

"It's nothing terribly scientific," I say, suddenly embarrassed about what I've come to discuss.

"Pleased to hear it," he says. "Science is a wonderful discipline—the best, perhaps—but it does rather get in the way of new ideas, what with its incessant belief that everything it already knows is correct." He gives a deranged tomato juice smile. "Go on."

"So, a while back, I met my mum in 2019. She was…*dying*." The horror of the word assaults me.

"Oh, I am sorry."

"I told her I loved her. It was weird, like it was really hard to say it to her. And she said I'd never told her that before. That was 2019, right?"

"I *am* listening," Defrates says, one eye still on his marking.

"Then the next day, for me anyway, was that day I met you. In 1999. The eclipse day. I rang her up, just to—you know—say hi. And I told her again. I said I loved her. And she—again—said I'd never told her that before."

"Understood."

"But this is where it gets interesting. I saw her again yesterday. *My* yesterday."

"Year?"

"2008. I was in…prison."

"How awful," Defrates says in passing, like I'm describing a nasty common cold.

"And I told her I love her, again. And I'm ready for her to say how I've never said it before. But she doesn't."

"She remembered you saying it in '99?"

"Yes!"

"What's your point? You said it and she remembered."

"Don't you see? In 2019 she told me I'd never said it before. So when I turned up in '99 after that, I changed something. I changed...*history*." It sounds silly to say out loud, and Defrates emits the snigger the statement perhaps deserves.

"Steady on. A minor detail of history. Not the sort of event on which civilization hinges."

"But maybe *my* civilization hinges on it."

"Well, perhaps."

"So, am I right? Can I change things?"

"We can *all* change things, Alex."

"Look, you said that my life already exists in its entirety. I'm just visiting it in the wrong order. So if it's all already *happened*, how is it that I can do something in an earlier year, and it have an effect at a later time?"

Defrates stares at me with excited eyes. "The great mystery of *agency*!"

"Is it a great mystery?"

"The greatest. You may also recall that I told you how *everybody's* life already exists. Before your accident and your trip into the Thames, Alex, you'd have assumed your actions had the ability to change your future?"

"Of course. Basic cause and effect."

"So we accept that something can already exist, yet be *unfixed*?"

"I don't know."

"No one *knows*, Alex. But you're a highly intelligent man, a fellow Cambridge alumnus, but for circumstances beyond..."

I nod, glad of the recognition.

"*Your* life," Defrates continues, "just like mine and everyone's, *exists*. But only when a day is lived, does it become *observed*."

"Right."

"I want you to imagine a body of water. A lake, let's say. Picture it if you will?"

"Looking at it right now."

"You are, say, fifty meters from the water. Now tell me, Alex, how deep is it?"

"How would I know that?"

"Well, of course you *can't* know, can you?"

"I can only guess."

"So, that water could be anywhere from, what—a meter deep, to maybe a thousand meters deep. Agreed?"

"Sure."

"And if you were to jump in and swim to the middle, say, only then, once you've left the shore, once you've actually ventured in, would you be able to find the true depth. So here's the question. Before you jump in and measure the depth, how deep is it?"

"Interesting."

"You understand me?"

"Maybe I do," I tell him.

"Until you measure it, it is both a meter deep, *and* a thousand meters deep. And every possible increment in between."

"The depth only becomes a fact when it's observed."

"Oh, I do love it when a student of mine *gets it*," he says, grinning.

"You think that's how it works? How my life works?"

"If it is, it's how *everybody's* life works. The future already exists, and yet there is free will. As I say, the great mystery of agency. What exactly *do* we have control over?" He grabs a fistful of exercise books and continues to mark them at speed, big looping *Well Done*s and *See Me*s and *11/10*s in red pen. "They keep telling me I should let my students submit their work *electronically*," he mutters. "Over my dead body."

"So, let's get this straight," I say. "I'm visiting a life that's already been lived. But if I do something different to what was done before, if I *change* something, I'll see the consequence of that the next time I'm in a later year. My life will *update*."

"That seems a safe enough bet. Do something different, and there will likely be an *effect* down the line."

"So I can change this...life..." I'm short of breath again, and a sweat breaks. It's my only hope.

"Within reason." He says it like it's obvious.

"What does that mean?"

"None of us can change the world to suit us. We can only change ourselves."

"But this life. I can make it better? Fix the things that have landed me...*here*?"

Defrates rocks back in his seat and smiles at his own thoughts for a moment. "I told you, I'm sure, how we are surrounded by our own past and own future?"

"*Haunted* by it, was how you put it."

"Lovely turn of phrase. We are indeed haunted by our past and future. We are wont to repeat our own habits, our worst mistakes."

"But are we *destined* to repeat them?"

"Aha! That's the question! No, I don't believe we are."

"Go on."

"Change will require a conscious *effort*. You'll be pushing against the weight of your own history."

"What does that mean?"

"Like walking against the wind. When you begin to do something different, there is a resistance. It is easier to walk on a path already there than it is to cut a new one."

"Right."

"Unless you fight, you'll be following the exact route already laid out."

I think of that day I went back to Jazz's, how it took such an effort to accompany him back home even though he was so clearly scared. A battle to do what I knew was the right thing. I was, it seems, breaking new ground. Making a change.

And I think of that night out when I got wrecked with Loz

instead of seeing Holly like I'd agreed. So easy. Path of least resistance. Own worst enemy.

"I shouldn't have been in prison," I tell Defrates. "Yesterday, when I was banged up. There's no way I did what they say I did."

He mutters exasperated words into his marking.

"They say I killed someone. That I killed...this girl." It's useful to say it aloud, appreciate how absurd it sounds. "Holly. The girl I'm in love with."

"Awful," he mumbles, although it's hard to tell if he's replying to me or commenting on some kid's essay on the Great Depression.

"I didn't do it. It's impossible that I did it."

"I believe you, Alex."

Such a simple statement, but it's exactly what I need to hear.

"Last time we met," I say, "you said there'd be a reason for this...*weirdness* happening to me."

"Of that I have no doubt."

"Is this it, do you think? Clear my name, get justice?" Racing pulse, again like I'm teetering on the brink of a cardiac arrest. "Get back the life that should be mine?"

Defrates looks me full in the face. There's a flash of something in his expression: Is it annoyance? Or pity, perhaps? "You can but try," he eventually says, in the tone an adult uses to tell a kid they can be anything they want to be.

"If I do clear my name, can I escape this, do you reckon? Go back to the start?"

"I'm only learning, Alex. Just as you are."

"Well, you seem to know a lot more than I do." I don't mean it to sound as aggressive as it does. "Sorry, but I still don't understand how is it that you know about this?"

"I'm sure we covered this when we met before. I'm an *interested party*."

"That was the exact phrase you used. You have a great memory. That was a long time ago, for you."

Momentarily, he's lost for words in a way I've not seen him before. "Understanding this is my life's work," he says. "Well, along with *this*..." He gestures to indicate the building around us.

"Understanding what?"

"Time. Our perception of it. Our *consciousness*."

"And I'm what—some sort of case study?"

He makes a show of being offended, which seems too theatrical to be genuine. "I only want to help you, Alex, that's all. But if you can help me, tell me of your experiences, that in turn may help me a little."

Nothing he says seems like much of an *answer*. But I have what I came for: I can change my fate, it would appear.

I decline his offer to stay and help clear his marking backlog. Whatever our thoughts on the matter of free will, I have no say in this thirst that grips me. I'll allow myself just the one, but this is a headwind that this wretched body can't walk against.

We part without a handshake, but with a promise not to be strangers. Outside, I drift into the frozen January night. So much to think about, but one thing only on my mind.

The Loneliest

For the first time today, there is feeling in my hands. These swollen fingers ache with the cold. I'm shaking so violently it's difficult to speak. A couple passes close to where I sit.

Steam plumes as I call out to them: "Can you spare any change, please?"

Like so many before them, they pass by as if I'm a ghost they aren't attuned to.

"I just need enough for a bed for the night," I say as a man in a camel coat draws near. It's a lie that makes me loathe myself, but those words earned me the first and only whole quid I've made in the hour I've been here. Alligator skin shoes that likely cost more than a month in a hotel scribe a wide semicircle around me.

The mile-and-a-half walk from the school to my busking spot by the river was like a marathon, but no use asking people for money where there's no passing trade. If I thought playing music here was hard work, it's nothing against trying to make a few quid without laying on a performance in return. But these hands are wrecked, and my guitar, for all I know, has found a new home. Only once will I do this. This is the last day I'll allow myself to be out of options.

"I'm hungry and I'm cold," I say to a group of teenagers. One looks like she might stop and give me something, but then she looks at the uneaten sandwich next to me and she's on her way. It's still in its box, and I tuck it out of sight; it was bought for me by a lady in a headscarf who spoke no English. But food is the last thing I feel like.

I look across the concourse at the shop front that was once the wine bar Holly and I sat outside the night this all began. The chocolatier that occupies the place now is still open; beyond the glass, people who look so sharp you'd swear they were European pick treats from iron platters. On two occasions I've met Jazz down here. Where is he now? It's 2023—he'd be twenty-six, twenty-seven, maybe? What sort of man has he grown into? Did he dare to stand up and be clever? Was he brave enough to shine? Be *someone*? God, I hope so.

Cramp grips and I stagger to my feet. I cling to the granite plinth, central in the concourse, that I've been sitting against as I've begged. Only, here in the later years I've visited, it's the memorial that I got bollocked for busking on in 2019. Three doves sculpted in thin metal soar from the center on delicate stalks. Polished to a shine last time I saw them, their wings are matte with frost tonight. On the plinth lies a modest bunch of flowers. Pearls of ice stick to red and white petals. It reminds me of the bouquet I bought Holly that perfect afternoon. I cringe at my crass attempt to frame myself as someone with *charm*. Where did that guy go?

On the other side of the memorial now, I see that the granite has been daubed with spray paint. I shake my head and drop onto by backside as three men—city types—approach. I don't have to ask for change or offer one of my untruths to attract their attention. "Get off the street," one says as he passes, tan briefcase swinging wildly past my head. "Dirty little waste of oxygen."

A curious mix of panic and defeat begins to settle. I stop asking for money. The cold paralyzes me. I reassure myself with another pathetic lie: that someone will come looking for me. Who would, though?

Two young guys pass nearby. Early twenties, cool in a gawky way, they can't keep their hands off each other. They are so clearly high on the thrill of falling in love. The taller of the two nods at me. He reaches in his back pocket and passes me a tenner. I can't find any words to thank him but he seems able to read my wet eyes. "Anytime, pal," he says, on his way again.

I make the short walk to a late newsagent's, donating my sandwich en route to a rough-sleeper. Outside the shop, I clutch the bottle of cheap Scotch to my chest. These are the precious moments when I am free: not pissed, nor desperately seeking booze. Fleetingly, I am both sober and content.

Half the bottle down and my mission is in clear focus: I find out what happened to Holly. I find out who framed me. And I get my life back.

MAY 28, 2005 | AGE 29

Trouble

A tapping at the door snatches me from sleep. Sunlight slices between the curtains. This bed is massive and mine alone, plump cushions scattered around my head like I've been packed for transit. I kick the duvet aside and prod the curtains of the nearest window apart with my foot. A glorious morning spills in and fills this big room to the brim.

There's a chaise longue beside the bed with an open suitcase on it. Clothes lie tossed over the back. The other half of the room contains a writing bureau and various antique-looking armchairs around a slim telly. I smirk at my good fortune at finding myself not just in a room of a nice hotel, but a suite no less. I've woken in worse places, after all.

Again, there comes a friendly sounding knock. I plant my feet on the carpet. My head throbs. I'm tempted to smile in response to the pain and the swimming sickness; this is a young man's hangover, not a body rotted by the sauce.

"Yeah, yeah, keep your tits on," I shout in reply to another tap.

"Come on now, Alex my man," a man says, crisply spoken and jovial. "Big day. No use hiding."

I snatch the hotel dressing gown draped over the bedhead. It's white and fluffy as a cloud.

"Brother!" says a man who is not my brother when I open the door. "How you feeling?" He's taller than me and exudes a certain vintage cool as he stands, head to one side, back arched, thumbs slung in the pockets of loose chinos.

"Could use a coffee," I tell him as he swaggers in and flings all the curtains open.

"Sure thing," he says, grabbing the phone and ordering room service with the efficiency of someone who does so regularly. "I've been in touch with Laura already," he tells me. "Everything's tickety-boo their end."

"Laura?"

"Chief bridesmaid reports that your beloved is already in phase one of hair and makeup."

I scan the room again, take in the details I should have noticed already: the gray morning suit hung in cellophane on the wardrobe, the silk cravat, the drum-shaped box open on the bureau containing a top hat.

"Safe and sound, fear not," the guy says, snapping open a velvet-lined case in which nestle two dazzling gold rings. He pulls out the larger band and squints to admire it. "All engraved nicely." He passes it to me and I almost drop it from my vibrating fingertips.

Elouise and Alex XXVIII V MMV, it reads in looping copperplate on the inside surface. My aching brain takes longer than it should to translate the date.

"Today, I am your humble servant," the guy says, tucking the rings safely away. "And I shall try to banish from my mind the repulsive idea of you spending the rest of your life…*riding* my sister."

A silver tray is delivered and set down by an equally silver old man.

"Looks like you need this," says the guy who's apparently soon to be my brother-in-law, as he pours the coffee.

"I'm getting married." I manage to avoid phrasing it as a question.

"Bit late to repent now." He reclines on the chaise and drags on an upward-pointed Silk Cut. He waffles about the many branches of his family, and the corners of the British Isles from which they've traveled for this.

I excuse myself to the bathroom. The morning air that breezes in when I open the window is so green and so warm it ventilates my brain. The outside is a landscape by Hornby, absurdly bright-colored fields stretching to infinity dotted with meandering sheep and cows. In the far distance, a church spire rises from the haze.

What the fuck am I doing here?

Who is this *Elouise* I'm marrying?

Should I be excited? I'm terrified.

There's one person, and one alone, who I'd gladly commit to spending the rest of my days with.

Where is Holly? Is she still...alive? I drop onto the toilet seat and concentrate. When Holly's dad told me over the phone that she'd died, he said it'd been five years. That was 2012—the day I was at Jazz's flat. This is 2005. She must still be here, be *around*. The discovery of that fact is like an iron yoke being lifted from my back.

"All right in there?" my unfamiliar best man shouts. "Haven't escaped out the window, I trust?"

"There's an idea," I mumble as I take a much-needed leak.

"Lads are downstairs. We should grab some brekka," he tells me as I return to the room and accept his offer of a ciggie.

"And the...girls?" I ask sheepishly.

He glances at a watch with more dials than an aircraft cockpit. "Right now, they'll be on their third bottle of Bolly. Primer applied and ready for some Dulux non-drip gloss."

"They're at...?" I prompt him as casually as I can.

"They're all at Mum and Dad's still." He grins at me. "She's not going to leave you at the altar! I promise. Don't look so worried."

I force a smile. "I'm not worried about that." I'm really not.

Downstairs, we are last to arrive at a table laid for twelve. It's men only, all my age give or take, except for a sixtysomething bloke with a demented twinkle in his eye that hints at a thousand scarcely believable anecdotes desperate to be told. He is, I'm told, my bride's disgraced uncle Mike, who is not welcome in the family home. I give him a nod, sensing a kindred spirit in this room of strangers.

By the time the full English breakfasts are landing on the white tablecloth, I have established a few facts.

The woman I'm due to marry today—Elouise—is a corporate lawyer, working for a Magic Circle London firm. I don't know how long she and I have been together, although the term *whirlwind romance* was uttered at one point. Her folks have a property in a place called Christchurch, a few miles from this hotel in the New Forest. Her brother—my best man—is called Christopher. Not Chris. Christopher. There was a stag do some weeks ago in the family villa in San Sebastian, where from the baying banter it would seem that each of us established our credentials as *legends*.

These people are my ushers, my wedding party. Why is no one I recognize here? Where is Loz? Where are those guys I shared a house with? My actual brother, Ross? The people I was so close with in sixth form? Instead, from the way he holds court with them, this circle appears to belong to Christopher. Have I become a part of it purely because of my relationship with his sister? Have I binned my old pals for them? Is that me—am I one of those people with a high friend turnover?

The grandfather clock in the dining room is striking ten when

Uncle Mike returns victorious to our table, holding aloft a bottle of Cognac he's procured from the bar. Indiscriminate shots are slopped into our coffee cups. The volume ramps as we drink and mingle, yolky plates repurposed as ashtrays.

"You missed out last night," says a guy who goes by the name of Dommy. He's standing too close to me and wearing a conspiratorial expression as his gaze flits around the room. He blows a ring of cigar smoke.

"How so?"

He reacts like I've told a great gag. "Turning down my kind offer, Dean!" He's nearly a foot shorter than me and a personal-space invader, closing the gap every time I move away. I look around the room, trying to catch Christopher's eye in the hope he'll come and rescue me. Dommy's elbows clash into me as he jitters on the spot, forcing me by his proximity to look down my nose at him. "You boring old bastard! Missed *right* out. You wanna hear all about mine?"

I've no idea what he's talking about, other than the fact made clear from his body language: this isn't for public discussion. "Yeah, I suppose…"

"Course you do! She was fucking great!" He bares his teeth, face alive with enthusiasm and aggression. "Snorted a load of charlie out of her snatch."

"Lovely," I say with a smirk.

"Your last night of freedom, Dean. Should've taken me up on it. Could've been you."

"That's very kind." I rake a hand across my scalp, my hair cut shorter than it's been since I was ten and prickly at the edges; no lank tar-stained fringe today.

He squeezes my arse. "Never let it be said your old mate Dommy doesn't know how to treat you. Thought you'd be all over it."

I've no wish to be the sort of man who'd be entertained by

a prostitute the night before his wedding. Why, then, am I uneasy with this Dommy's disappointment in me?

"Gave it to mine proper hard," Dommy's telling me. He's
chewing his bottom lip, eyes full of hate, involuntary small thrusts
at the hips. "Didn't like it, did she? She's all like, 'Take it easy,'
and I'm like, 'You'll take whatever I give you, love.' After all,
who's paying the bill?"

I don't reply to this vile little man, instead looking down at my
hands. I've never seen a wedding ring on these fingers. In prison
in 2008, the first day of this in 2010, with Jazz and his granddad
in 2012, in 2019 when Mum was dying, yesterday when it was
2023. Not married. This is a marriage that is destined to fail.

"You two!" Christopher says, strutting over to us, swilling
brandy and smoking flamboyantly. "Pair of miscreants! Joined
at the hip again, I see."

I shuffle away from Dommy, but it's as useless a maneuver
as ever.

"Reliving the stag?" Christopher asks. "Pair of you did well
to live through it."

"Yeah, yeah. That's it," Dommy says, jabbing the small of my
back out of sight. "Reminiscing!"

"Looks like I'm going to have to keep you two apart today,"
Christopher says, enjoying his own voice even more now he's
had a drink.

I nod along and pretend it's not news, as Dommy takes too
much enjoyment in reminding Christopher what we got up to
in Spain a few weeks ago. It seems Dommy and I were inseparable; the two-night cocaine bender comes as no great surprise.
I'm more bemused by reports of the swim the pair of us took in
a murky canal that turned out to be contaminated; dysentery
during a coach journey and on a delayed flight home was surely
not as hilarious as Dommy makes out. And I struggle to laugh
when he describes the massive over-order of tapas one evening,

providing ammo for the mother of all food fights and our group being banned from several seafront restaurants.

"Bloody love a wedding," Dommy says when we're alone again, topping up our brandies.

"Wish I shared your enthusiasm," I reply.

"Ah, you'll be fine, Dean. Once you see your bird, looking a million dollars."

"She's all right? Elouise—she's...nice, you reckon?" I cringe at the adjective I've chosen.

Dommy screws his face up in a show of mock arousal. "She's fit, mate."

It gives me an odd buzz—that hint of envy in his tone. I've no desire to marry this stranger, but the fact that other men perhaps *would* want to spurs me on.

"Want some marriage advice?" he asks.

"Not from you," I reply.

He bends double in the belief that I'm joking. "It's just a *deal*, this marriage thing. That's what you have to understand. You've got to act like you're a one-woman man. Dote on her, buy shit for her, look like you're house-trained in front of her friends, pretend like you worship her more than her mates' husbands do. Do all that, yeah?"

"I'll bear that in mind." I hold my cup out as Uncle Mike passes with the brandy, instruct him with my eyes to *fill 'er right up*.

"Even she knows it's bullshit, Dean," Dommy goes on. "All women do. They know we're dogs, that we're off sticking our cocks up anything that gives us a second look—younger than her, prettier than her, dirtier than her, whatever. She *knows* it, Dean. They all know it. Deep down. They know they aren't going to change us."

"It's a theory, I suppose."

"Abso-fucking-lutely it is! But you've got to let them have their show. Don't embarrass her, that's the key, mate."

"Right." I smile and nod in the way I do when cornered by

an amiable drunkard outside a pub: enough to be polite, not so much that they are encouraged.

"Seriously, old pal. As long as you never show her up, you can do what you damned well please *from this day forth*. Even if she suspects you've been at it, she won't sweat it. As long as no one else knows. As long as the veneer of perfection remains intact. Simple creatures, women. You getting me?"

A welcome distraction is provided by Uncle Mike, who has begun a rendition of "Get Me to the Church on Time," arms outstretched as he strolls around the bar. His enthusiasm is un-damped by the fact he doesn't know half the words, filling the voids with tuneless *da-da-da*s.

Cool air whips in from the doors which have been opened onto a terrace. The most distant fields are a deep green, dark clouds above them threatening to steal this bright morning.

What if I ran now? Didn't look back? How would my life update in later days?

It's so tempting, yet I can feel the invisible bonds holding me back. The weight of history. I *could* strain against it, leave this behind.

But what would I achieve? What if I made my future life worse? Is this wedding a bad choice? How could I possibly know? It terrifies me, but that alone is no reason to run.

The breakfast crowd thins as the lads return to their rooms to get dressed up, the order given to reconvene in the bar for a pre-church drink in an hour. I let Christopher guide me through the hotel. I allow the current of fate to draw me along.

Dry Your Eyes

I wish I could stop shaking. A gale blows and branches clatter against the arched window. Shadows sway this way and that against these dark vestry walls. I face the corner. Plaster powdering to the floor like dandruff. Mushroomy smell of timbers being consumed by rot. A couple of remaining blue choir gowns with frilly ruffs hang on a rail—although no outfit for this nonsensical show is as absurd as what I'm wearing. I look like that person at every fancy-dress party whose commitment doesn't match their costume.

The door to the church itself is ajar, candlelight flickering in response to the gathering storm. I can hear people filing in, squeaks of shoes over hushed pipe organ—music so painfully somber it's as if only the organist and I are in on the secret. I glance down at my watch: 12:33. My bride is officially late. No hurry, darling.

The small line of coke I let Dommy serve me in the car over has worn off, my brief belief that everything would be okay replaced now by jittering anxiety and a rough throat. I should be beside Christopher right now, waiting at the altar. There's a photographer in a Hawaiian shirt round here somewhere who, from our brief introduction outside, appears to regard this entire event as a stage for his art. He'll be furious at my absence; no long-lens reportage of nervous groom.

But I need to be here. If only I knew what to say. Why can't I even bring myself to look at her?

She clears her throat behind me. "We really don't have long, Alex," Holly says.

"This is bullshit," I mumble.

"Language!" she whispers, mock disapproval. "This is the House of the Lord." Her humor is unconvincing.

There's a break in the organist's repertoire of wrist-slitting anthems. Christopher's voice echoes through the space next door as he entertains the waiting congregation.

"Why are you here?" I ask.

"Charming."

"Sorry. I don't mean it like that. *How come* you're here?"

"Because we're grown-ups, Alex. If you're cool inviting me, then I'm cool coming. I thought it was a good idea, actually. Not so sure…now."

I bury my shaking hands in my pockets and turn to face her. Why does it *hurt*—just looking at her? I want her so badly it's like being punched. I don't care who's soon to walk down that aisle. There's no way that person can do this to me. This feeling is indivisible.

"Very much a standard sort of wedding for me," Holly says. "Always like to start proceedings with a private audience with the groom in the vestry." She rearranges a stack of gold bangles on her arm.

"Sorry. For dragging you in here." I'm not sorry. I'd been

with Christopher and my four ushers doing a meet-and-greet at the church entrance when she turned up. Bizarrely, given that I think about her perpetually, it took a moment to place her as she strode toward us across the churchyard, long enough for my best man to ogle her and say, "Look out, boys, incoming." Like seeing a famous face in the supermarket, there was a delay in computing these two colliding worlds. Among guests in backless dresses with Louis Vuitton handbags and red-soled Louboutins, Holly's tie-dyed dress which was once a T-shirt and her mirror-polished Doc Martens effortlessly demonstrate the difference between fashionable and *stylish*. My groomsmen, as one, cheered as the two of us disappeared in search of a little privacy, when eventually I was able to utter a word to her and ask if we might talk for a moment.

"Drink?" Holly says, raising a silver chalice and bottle of communion wine.

I catch a wet single-malt burp behind pursed lips. "Think I'm okay for a min."

"As you wish."

"What happened to us, Holly?"

"Is this really the time, Alex?"

I shrug. "Sure it is. If I'm about to make a massive fucking mistake."

"Last-minute nerves, mate. You're good together. Elouise is cool."

"You know her?"

"Well…no. Looking forward to getting to. Not like you've been together long enough for the whole let's-meet-our-exes thing."

What a depressing word that is. Ex. *My ex*. Two lives, hopes and dreams intertwined—reduced to two letters.

"Whirlwind!" Holly says, and I wonder if I detect just a hint of hurt. Maybe I'm hoping it's there.

"Everyone keeps saying that."

"Nowt wrong with being decisive. Unless of course…?" Holly mimes a bump over her tummy.

"Jesus Christ, I hope not." Maybe I can deal with this marriage being short-lived, but walking out on a kid? "You reckon she might be…pregnant?"

"No, Alex. I'm being facetious."

"Well, don't."

"You look petrified. Everything'll be fine. Promise."

"Sure it will."

"This is the start of a great new chapter for you."

"Maybe it's not the chapter I want."

Holly rolls her eyes. "Nice new house. Great job with her dad. No more gigging and pub jobs to get by."

"I like playing. More than anything."

"It's you who keeps saying it's time to get serious."

"What a bore."

"You'll be grand. You've got it made with this one." Again, a touch of irritation, I'm sure of it.

I look at her properly for the first time since we've been in this small room. She sweeps a heavy handful of curls from her face and smiles at me. If I'd allowed myself to forget it for a minute, the knowledge hits me full force now: this woman is going to die. This beautiful young person of little over thirty has maybe two years to live. And whatever it is that's going to happen to her, it'll be me who gets the blame. Can I stop it, change our fate?

"You know I'd never do anything to hurt you, don't you?" I say. It's all I can do not to burst into tears.

"I know that. Of course I know that."

"I could never ever…harm you. Promise me you believe me."

"Don't be ridiculous," Holly says. "Deep breaths, Alex. Come on, mate, calm down."

I hold my hand to my mouth as my guts convulse. My cheeks puff out and boozy acid floods my throat, but I keep it in. Bells peal above us, crescendo building. "I wish this was you and me, today," I tell her.

"A nostalgic moment, I think. That's all."

"What happened with us?"

"Too young, I guess."

"That's bullshit."

"We wanted different things, didn't we?"

"Did we?"

"We were both ready to move on, I think."

"Really?"

"Come on, mate. I was buried in my career, wanting to get a place. You wanted to have it large with your mates. Different things."

"Fucksake."

"What was it we agreed? Right person, wrong time?"

"You're just *right person*."

"Let's not do this, Alex."

"So I fucked it all up between us, basically."

"Alex, we agreed—"

"I'm an idiot, you know that? Best thing that ever happened to me, and I have to ruin it."

"It's a decision we made together, ba… *Alex*."

"Right person, wrong time. We really said that?"

"Too often," Holly says. She peeks around the door into the church. "We really should be getting in there, you know."

I shoot a look at my wrist. "She's only fifteen minutes late."

"Maybe *she's* having second thoughts."

"We can hope."

"Come on," Holly says. Raindrops like fists are hitting the small window now. "Best I walk round the outside, avoid any awkward questions."

I back into the wall, stand firm. "Why have I fucked up so bad?"

"I'm sorry?"

"Why didn't I go to Cambridge? Get my degree, get a great job? Make a life with you? *Be* someone. Achieve *something.* Why didn't I do that?" The wobble in my voice makes me pity myself even more.

"You're not a failure. You've done…your own thing."

"Where did I go so wrong? Why won't I let myself do something good? Why do I destroy everything?"

"Stop it."

"What happened that night, in '95, on the Thames?"

"A decade ago, Alex. Let's not rake over it."

"Why's everything been shit since then?"

"Has it? We still had good times. And I told you a million times—I loved you for *you*, I didn't stop just because you didn't have this prestigious degree and this…dazzling future."

"I reckon you loved me a bit less."

"Enough, Alex."

"What did he do to me?"

"Who?"

"Fucking Blake Benfield. That fight destroyed everything."

"Yes, the mysterious Blake Benfield."

"What do you know about him?" I snap.

"Very little. Not for the want of asking. Not something you've ever confided in me, dearest."

"You know the name, though?"

"I know that's who you were fighting that night. I know you have 'unfinished business.'"

"Yup." My hands shake harder.

"That's all I know. Maybe time to let that one go."

"Maybe." I go to hug her, to tell her how sorry I am. But we are interrupted by the heavy door to the main church swinging open.

"Here he is!" says the vicar, eyes that have seen it all. "We really must be taking up our positions. Your beloved will be with us very shortly."

"Last-minute pep talk," Holly says, more embarrassed than she has any reason to be.

He smears his hand against the gold-threaded cross on his cassock, taking my hand in his. His head is bald and unusually large, which, coupled with his prominent bearded chin, gives him the outline of someone wearing a crash helmet. "This is meant to be, Alex. It will be wondrous." He lays a big hand on my head, and I'm amazed how reassuring it feels. "This will be *stupendous*."

"Those are the exact words I keep telling him," Holly says, not fully disguising the chuckle in her voice.

"Thank you," he says to her. "For supporting a friend in his moment of doubt."

"Thought we might have a quick drink," she says, pointing at the tray of wine and silver paraphernalia.

"You wouldn't want to drink that." The vicar laughs. "Awful muck! Wouldn't even cook with it. Heaven forbid the Church of England could supply us a nice rioja. Maybe a fruity Bourgogne, even. But alas, no."

"How disappointing," Holly says.

"Oh, it is, dear." He grins and lays a hand on each of our forearms. "Before each communion, I have to bless an ample quantity of this awful wine to see me through proceedings. One tends to play it safe—it wouldn't do to have the cup run dry. Unfortunately, regulation dictates that whatever's left after communion, the presiding minister must drink in full. Sometimes half a liter of the dreadful stuff!"

"Wow," Holly mumbles.

He sweeps his cassock, inviting us to follow. "I get home to the wife for Sunday lunch, and very often I'm pissed as a fart!" He laughs raucously and steps through the door ahead of us.

"Thanks," I whisper to Holly, stopping on the threshold. A step further and I'll be in view of the waiting congregation. "Where would I be without you?"

"You'll be just fine, Alex." She turns to walk back around the church.

"Really appreciate you coming today."

"We are grown adults. This is what we do."

"Hope you don't get lonely. I'll introduce you to some people at the reception." I will, if there's anyone there I actually know.

"I'm cool. I didn't come alone. Got my—what did the invitation say?—my *plus one.*"

"Anyone I know?"

"I hope you'll get to know each other. You'll like him, Alex. I do."

"Boyfriend?" Why is a wave of panic lifting me clear of the floor?

She has the coy smile of a woman in love. I can't bear it. "Sure, yeah."

The vicar leans round the door. "Alex!" he hisses. "Look lively. Car's here at last."

"Coming," I snap.

"Go," Holly orders.

I let the vicar return to his post. "Serious?" I ask her. "Is it…"

She fiddles with her left hand, worrying at her jewelry. "Yeah."

I stare at the ring on her fourth finger. Gold band, trio of diamonds.

"I've been meaning to tell you."

"Congratulations." I'm surprised that I manage to get the entire word out.

"Thank you." The way she says it, all swoony and screwed-up-faced, makes me want to die.

The bells are silent now. The organ too.

"What's his name?"

"Let's talk later, yeah? You gotta move."

"His name?"

"Maxim."

"Maxim?"

"What of it?"

"What sort of name is *Maxim?*"

"It's my fiancé's name, Alex."

"Christ. Maxim. Sounds like a...brand of tampon."

"Don't be a twat, Alex."

"Where d'you meet him? Gladiator fight?"

"I'm big enough to be pleased for you, yeah? I'm here, aren't I? Wishing every happiness to the guy who I thought might be my one and only."

"Shouldn't have bothered."

"Just piss off and get married, yeah?"

"Sorry. I'm sorry, Holly. God, I'm such an arsehole."

"Maybe lose the self-indulgence, yeah?"

"I'm so sorry."

She turns and opens the door to outside, raising her clutch bag over her head, ready to do battle with the weather. "We'll all have a drink later, maybe. When you're a bit less...stressed."

My legs want to buckle beneath me. But I know if I drop, I'll never get up.

Applause ripples through the guests as I join a grinning Christopher at the altar. I wipe my tears on the sleeve of my tailcoat. And I wait to meet my wife.

Smile Like You Mean It

Elouise picks a piece of confetti from my forehead with a long, precise nail. I chuckle and she smiles, wriggling into the back seat of the Maybach limousine that's apparently carrying us to a reception, content, it seems, with how this day is playing out. As the vicar said not ten minutes ago: "I'm pleased to report the ceremony has gone with precisely the *one* hitch," to no one's amusement greater than his own. My misery did nothing to derail proceedings, nor did Dommy's *hilarious* loud coughing in response to the *speak now or forever hold your peace* invitation.

We come to a stop at the end of the golf club's long drive-way. Two flutes of champagne are passed to us in the car. The worst of the weather has lifted for now, and the grounds roll out in every direction, brochure-perfect striped lawns under a crazed sky. I let myself look properly at her for the first time. She's blonde, delicate, with perfect teeth and high cheekbones.

But I can't look into those blue eyes for long. I feel a strange claustrophobia, as if the air is too hot in close proximity to her.

"Love you, husband," she says. Bouncily, quick smile. She puckers her lips, and they squidge against mine as I move in clunkily. She checks her lip gloss in a pocket mirror that comes effortlessly to hand.

"Bottoms up," I say, gulping three quarters of my glass down in one. It is only lightly fizzy and has a burnt caramel sweetness; regular champagne would seem unrefined in comparison. I eject the strawberry from the rim out of the open door because it's in the way of my nose.

"Christ, Alex!" Elouise laughs. "Can't take you anywhere! Can you just *wait*?"

Our loud-shirted photographer laughs as he kneels on the front passenger seat, lens aimed back at us. "Sorry," she says to him. He calls over to the staff, and I am topped up by a man with a white apron and an air of condescension.

"Like this," she tells me, interlinking our arms and then raising her glass to her lips.

"Lovely, lovely," the photographer says, shutter rattling, as we switch our smiling eyes between each other's and the camera. The booze taunts me by spritzing against my nostrils, and it's all I can do not to order this guy to get a bloody move on.

"I guess this is the way all the best couples drink," I say behind grinning teeth. "You reckon this'll be us, down the local, me with my pint and you with your half, conjoined at the elbow?"

Elouise emits a small grunt that is somehow harsher than being told to shut up.

"It'll look a treat in the album, or on a nice canvas," the photographer reassures us.

We are led to a series of locations around the grounds, where we are directed into poses of varying absurdity. The distant clubhouse, meanwhile, is alive with chattering guests, the sound of clinking glass making me as impatient as a child hearing a fun-fair from the queue outside.

"Look at us," Elouise says, as we hold each other in an arm's-length embrace beneath a heart-shaped arch of ivory roses. "Imagine if someone had told us, that night we met, that this is where we'd be in a year." She's silent as she waits for the flash gun to stop firing. "Would we have believed it?"

"Maybe we would," I say. It seems safest to give some illusion of keenness. Her slender body is tight against mine now, just a wafer of silk and some hired trousers separating us. My hand is half on her arse. Tradition dictates we sleep together tonight, zero effort required. The thought doesn't excite me in the least. All I want to do is find Holly, new boyfriend or not.

"You knew? Straightaway? This was *it*?"

"Think so." My voice rings with insincerity. I'm anxious as the photographer leads us into a miniature maze—somewhere from which the bar is not visible. We assume the positions of her leading me joyfully by the hand through the hedges. There's no danger of our personalities being visible in these pictures.

"I think I did too," she tells me. "Not that you had much competition that particular night."

"Did I not?"

"I can safely say you were the only one I could possibly have fallen for!"

"The only...one?" I mumble it more to myself than to her, in no mood for trying to excuse my amnesia.

"I've seen my share of ropy speed-dating crowds," Elouise says, as we assemble into a damsel-in-distress aesthetic. She smiles, and I get the vibe we've reminisced about this a hundred times already.

Speed-dating. Meeting women was never a problem for me, not since I started playing music in the Blue Moon. Catching someone's eye in a crowded audience was such a thrill, espe-cially under the gaze of other blokes. And Elouise—she's a very attractive woman, regardless of whether or not I'm attracted to her. What the hell were either of us doing speed-dating?

The photographer promises he'll not be much longer as he leads us to an ornamental garden, not that Elouise seems in any hurry to get away. He ticks off this last location on a typed list that he and she drew up after a recce of the site. I am manipulated into a ballroom dancer's hold, *my wife* arching dramatically from me.

"Hope you're a bit looser than this tonight," Elouise tells me.

"Oo-er," the photographer coos, relishing the innuendo.

"On the *dance floor*," Elouise laughs.

"I'll have had a few by then," I say.

"Not too many to forget your moves, thank you very much," she says.

The photographer lights up with excitement. "You're doing a routine?"

"That's the plan," Elouise says. "We've been having lessons with a national champion."

"I love a choreographed first dance," he says. "Always blows the guests away. And does it make for some excellent photos…"

I can't be bothered to break the news to them; they'll find out soon enough. Excessive drunkenness—either real or feigned—seems the easy way out.

"This one took some convincing," Elouise says.

"I bloody hate first dances," I say, with accidental honesty.

"So you've mentioned once or twice."

"You'll knock 'em dead," the photographer says.

I'm getting a cramp in my calf from holding this pose, and I'm listening to the distant merriness of people draining our free bar. "Funny, isn't it? I mean, when the dancing starts, that's like the end of the formalities." I sound more riled than I mean to. "All the buttoned-down ceremonial stuff, done. Time to throw some shapes. Get pissed. Let your hair down."

"Don't be a bore, Alex," Elouise says.

"Don't you think it's like a euphemism…or something?" It's an attempt at wit, one that would surely amuse Holly. They're looking at me disappointed and not faintly amused. "*The choreographed first dance.* Here's the bit where married life gets spontaneous and…oh, no, no it doesn't. Best not leave even this bit of free expression to chance."

"Sorry about my husband," she says to the photographer. "Sometimes he likes to try and sound smart. It doesn't suit him."

The rain falls once more. The two of us run, hand in hand, for the clubhouse. Elouise trails me, dress billowing as lightning sheets across the sky. I shoot a look behind us and see that we've left our friend far behind, hastily packing away his camera and lenses.

There's barely time to neck a pint in the deserted bar before we are introduced as a married couple to our guests. We are seated at the top table, along with my parents, my in-laws, Christopher and the chief bridesmaid, Laura. All sat in a line, we face into this room of people having more fun than us. I take minutes to drain the bottle of white and start work on the red. Next to me, Elouise's mum makes conversation with Dad, keeping a rigid distance like the Queen meeting the public.

My new father-in-law leans close to Mum and makes her giggle, demeanor that of a boss seducing his new secretary. I shimmy along behind the chairs and tap her on the shoulder. The buzz of drinking fast is at its peak, and I'm briefly confident. "Love you, Mummy," I tell her, arms outstretched.

There's a disapproving edge to her grin, but she climbs to her feet all the same. She looks a million dollars—hair professionally styled and heavy on the blue eye shadow. It seems that the rules on her appearance have been relaxed for this occasion; either that or she's straight-up defied Dad. She looks like that young woman she was in the photo I found on the mantelpiece long after she'd…gone. This hugging me business is still alien to her, judging by her awkwardness, but hopefully we'll get the chance to get better at it. I put out of my mind that frail ghost of herself she was, close to the end in 2019. Instead I squeeze her tight and tell her again that I love her and that I'm so happy she's here, and eventually she loosens as if slow-cooked. So what that all she can say in reply is that she's having a lovely day? With her here, a part of who I really am is here, a fact I can only appreciate now I've lived days where she isn't.

"How's my boy shaping up for you, Derek?" Dad calls along the table to Elouise's father as starters are served. "Promoted him to the board yet?" Dad winks at me. As he takes a sip, his wineglass shakes on his lips. His suit sits on him differently to these people's: too high on the shoulders, too long in the sleeve. His gold watch, deliberately slack so it hangs over the back of his hand, is too shiny.

"There's an old trick in business, Colin," Elouise's father says. "Keep your best people at arm's length." He fires a charming grin at me. "Promote this guy too fast, and he'll be in my job before I know it. I'm not that silly!" He has the tone of a primary teacher praising a no-hoper.

Dad nods at me, gives a look that suggests he and I are on the same team. "Always knew this one was going places." It's the closest to a compliment he's ever paid me, however misplaced.

A smirk seeps onto Elouise's face. Whatever I do for her father, I suspect it entails little more than tea-making.

"What is it your business does?" Mum asks Elouise's father. "Alex never really explains…"

"Private equity," my dad interjects matter-of-factly, as though he is intimately familiar with the profession.

"We are troubleshooters, first and foremost," Elouise's father says.

"Or vultures," Elouise's mother says. Her tone is not chiding; she says it with an illicit pride.

Dad laughs unnaturally hard, fumbling for a top-up of wine the moment everyone's eyes are off him.

"We buy ailing businesses. We talk to the staff, to the customers. Find out what works and what doesn't. Negotiate with anyone who's owed money. Make the thing work."

I nod along, almost catch myself believing it's as noble a pursuit as he makes it sound.

"Alex is a fine asset to the team," he continues, as if my appointment has nothing to do with marrying his daughter.

Elouise and her mother, I've noticed, are talking among themselves, paying us no interest as we carry out a near-shouted conversation along the table. Christopher, now brother-in-law as well as best man, has left in pursuit of more fun.

"It's about being good with people, most of all," her father says.

"Same with what I do," Dad says.

"Right, right."

I wonder for a moment where Dad's professional life has taken him in the ten years that have passed since *this* began. But as he talks too lengthily about relationships forged with drivers and his covering for their misdemeanors, it's clear he's still managing the same courier fleet. I'm willing him to be quiet as he tells a nonecdote about a diesel van being filled accidentally with petrol; behind the polite expressions of my in-laws, he is clearly being dismissed as a crashing bore.

Sometimes my dad is so easy to hate. God knows he's been shitty enough: the times he threw me out for no good reason; the punishment of waking me all night by repeatedly switching on the bedroom light; the birthday checks that had stops put on due to insufficient gratitude. So why, now, do I feel so sorry for the guy? I can't think ill of someone so vulnerable, so eager to be accepted. He glows red at the earlobes, lubricates with regular slurps of wine and keeps absently supping long after the glass is empty, eyes reaching for interested faces as he waffles. This man, I have to accept, is very much my father.

In the gents I find Dommy, along with a couple of guys from

the hotel earlier who ooze the same us-and-them confidence as my new family. Dommy racks up lines of gear atop a cistern, cubicle door wide open.

"Why not just do it off the top table, mate?" I say to him over my shoulder whilst I pee. "It'd be less obvious."

"Am I sorting you one out, Deano?" he calls back.

"Maybe I'll wait till after dessert. Keep my appetite."

"Don't be a boring wanker." He passes the rolled fifty to another of my new best friends—Will or Willy or Mark or something. Face-to-face with me now, Dommy looks totally cooked, eyes that had been mischievous this morning flaring with rage. "Come on, come on," he says, so close his body's on mine. "Just a morsel." He pinches powder between his fingers and holds them under my nose.

I snort it up. "Reckon the missus will notice?" I ask.

"She won't give a shit, Dean. You're her bit of rough."

"Does someone *marry* their bit of rough?"

"Right place, right time, old chap." He inhales deeply through his nose, snot gargling down his throat. His two companions finish at the cistern, arranging yet another serious rail for Dommy.

"Her, or me?"

"You, Dean! Of course you. You're *punching*, mate. Well above your weight."

"Am I?"

All three of them roar with laughter. It takes me a moment to realize they're not being deliberately mean—they think I'm kidding. "Way out of your league," says Ben or Dick or whatever.

"Sure," I say. "That's why we got married." I'm fast becoming restless, my mood getting darker by the second. The cocaine— heavy on speed, it seems—was an error.

"Like musical chairs, Deano. She gets to thirty and the music stops. You're her *chair*." All three of them fall about at this, Dommy repeating the word *chair* at ever-increasing volume. "Deano, you met at a dating agency!"

"Speed-dating," I correct him, for all the difference it makes.

"Nothing says 'I'm gonna marry the first wanker who I've got a couple of things in common with' more than using a dating agency."

"I should get back," I say, turning for the door.

"Oh, come on, Deano," Dommy says. "You look like you're surprised. You're a *barman*! Hardly with you for the scintillating conversation, is she?"

"Fuck off, Dommy," I mumble through numb lips. Who is this prick who thinks he can sneer at my intelligence? Did *he* land a place at Cambridge, the only person from his school to get even close?

"Chill, man," Dommy says, blocking my path. "No need to get salty."

"Catch you later."

"Sorry, man. Sorry." Dommy hugs me, walloping me on the back. "Am I forgiven?"

"Yeah, yeah," I say.

As I approach the door, it swings open from outside. A guy I don't recognize walks in. He's taller and broader than me. "Alex!" he says, South African twang in his voice. He holds out a big hand, leather bracelets round his wrist. "Congratulations, fella! It's a total pleasure to be here."

"Thanks for coming," I say.

"You boys up to the naughty stuff?" he asks. He's model good-looking with an easiness of manner that makes friends on first sight.

"Line, good sir?" Dommy asks.

"I think I'm good. Maybe I'll take you up on the kind offer later." He grins at me. "Holly warned me about you. Party animal. Man after my own heart."

"You're...Maxim?"

"Maxim. *Max*. Pleasure, mate." He shakes my hand again.

He's unquestionably the coolest guy at this wedding. And he's here, rightly enough, with the coolest woman.

I make my exit, certain that if I loiter near the urinal I'll be treated to the sight of him unfurling a knob twice the size of mine.

The drugs have served to turn my overriding mood up to eleven. I am more miserable than I've been all day. As I weave between the tables back to my seat, I burn with anger and dislike toward these noisy people. At the top table, Elouise demands to know where I've been, complains that she's had to do the rounds of our guests without her new husband on her arm.

A realization strikes me: this isn't a marriage, it's a *wedding*. I slump into my chair. To either side of me, Mum and Dad look bored as they watch the room; this new circle of mine has tired of making conversation with them.

Holly's in the far corner of the room. She looks to be enjoying herself. How is this not killing her? The way it's killing me.

A trio of desserts lands in front of me, and I push them round their giant plate whilst everyone else eats. I'm so done with this day. I haven't the will to speak to another person, to pretend any of this is okay.

A man in a red coat with a red nose stands in front of the top table and chimes a wineglass. He tells everyone this is the part of the day they've all been waiting for. There's a joke or two and much drunken laughter—something about the day being so emotional even the cake's in tears.

"You will shortly be hearing from our venerable host and father of the bride, Mr. Derek Knight-Baker," he announces to cheers from the room. "And then, if you can bear the anticipation, from the very best of best men, Christopher Knight-Baker." There are whoops and fists hammering on tables. "But first," he says, turning and winking in vaguely my direction, "we must hear from the warm-up act."

The laughter peters out and the room is quiet. "Ladies and gentlemen!" he booms. "I give you...the groom! Alex Dean!"

Ordinary People

"Thank the bridesmaids," Mum whispers to me. The room is so silent I'm sure everyone can hear her.

My standing here, mute, got some sniggers to begin with. But as a painful minute has ticked by, faces have fallen blank.

"Thank them all for coming," my father-in-law says. "That's all you need to do." I give him half a nod, and he slumps back in his seat. "How many has he had this time?" he mumbles.

I knock back the champagne that's been poured for the toast. Whether through nerves or the cocaine, my mouth is far too dry to speak.

There's a faint cheer and some giggling from Dommy's table. "Speak up, old chap!" Uncle Mike heckles.

A rustle of restlessness replaces the silence. A few hushed conversations begin. The toastmaster begins his walk from the doorway where he and the serving staff stand. I raise a shaky palm.

"This is… This is nonsense." My voice, through the radio-mike, sounds alien and awful, its tremor amplified dispropor-tionately. "All of *this*."

The quiet is back in abundance: syrupy, noisy silence. The man in red is a statue.

"This is all just for show." My eyes find Holly's near the back. She gives me a sad smile. I make a point of casting my gaze around the room, but always I return to her.

"This isn't *love*. This is a *party*."

"Nowt wrong with a party!" Dommy calls out. No one laughs.

"You're right," I say. "Nothing wrong with a party at all. But love—love isn't a party." I glance at Elouise. My *wife*. She listens intently, chin propped on fist, intrigue and wariness in equal measure.

"Love doesn't lessen with each guest that leaves. It doesn't end with the last one out the door. Love is what's left when every-thing and every*one*—all of this—is stripped away."

At the fringes of my vision, I see a smile bloom on Elouise. But my gaze, like a compass to magnetic north, swings to the back of the room. "Here's something I've learned. Your world can be torn to pieces, everything back to front, inside out. Wrecked. You can be living day to day, hour to hour. Every-thing you thought you could rely on, everything you thought was real—gone. Everything gone, except love. Because, believe me, love is *indestructible*. It's like the framework of a building that stands after a fire. Not only is it still there, but it's clearer than ever for having everything else, all that is comfortable and reli-able, burned away."

My heart thumps. The nerves have faded, but my anger hasn't.

"Love isn't something that you put on an agenda. How could you? It turns up when it feels like it, and immediately it eclipses all other plans. There's no *right time*. No wrong time. When love shows up, it *is* time. Whoever coined the phrase *right person, wrong time* can go to hell. Alone.

"Love isn't about shared interests, is it?" I'm ranting now. Face burning. Flecks of spittle. "Why would you want someone with the same interests? Isn't love about showing someone your world, and they theirs?"

I take a deep breath. Mouth arid. "Love isn't something on a list of things to be done. Not a box to tick. It isn't a crown, a cherry on the top, a penthouse, a finishing touch."

Elouise's nodding serves only to spur me on. "Love isn't the ability to wake up next to someone every day. It is the unbearableness of *not* waking up next to that person, every single day."

Holly plays it cool, acts like she's not aware of my stare that's unwavering now.

"Love is not about saying *this is where I belong*." My voice is quieter now. "It's about being completely, hopelessly, profoundly unable to belong anywhere else."

The room is silent as they, and I, realize that my speech has run its course. I raise my empty champagne flute. "Anyway... To the bridesmaids!"

A lukewarm toast is made. The room floats somewhere between confusion and relief.

Except Maxim, who claps hard. "Well said, sir!" he shouts— thoroughly decent bastard that he is.

JANUARY 22, 1998 | AGE 22

Lucky Man

A gift. A day to take for ourselves, before everything is laid to ruin.

"I'm not exactly an old romantic, I'm afraid," I say. "Could've come up with something better."

"Nonsense," Holly says, snuggling tight against me. "I've almost managed to forget how badly I've cocked everything up."

We sit on the coarse carpet in close to darkness, gazing up at the model of Earth and the twinkling universe surrounding it. A PA announcement tells us that the Science Museum will be closing in ten minutes.

"Stop your worrying," I tell her.

"Six months off qualifying and I drop the ball. Way to go, Holly."

"I promise you you've passed."

"I'm touched by your faith, baby. However misplaced…"

I picture the eclipse day in '99, the swanky hospital, my insecurities over her success. Eighteen months from here. "Mark my words, darling."

She was awake before me this morning. Tearful and agitated, she'd slept little, fretting over a disastrous exam yesterday. Cheering her up was the only possible thing on my agenda. Bank account and car running on empty, a trip on foot to my favorite museum was all I could offer. I'd imagined we'd hang about for a couple of hours, but all day has slipped past us, and we've barely looked at a third of the exhibits.

"Do you find it makes you feel pathetically insignificant?" Holly asks, staring at the constellations. "So...vast."

"Sure. And yet, would you believe there are more possible moves in a game of chess than there are atoms in the known universe?"

"That's not true."

"I swear it is."

"Sounds bonkers."

"Numbers are bonkers things." A twinge of sorrow as I say it, that I left my studies behind.

"Gimme another one," Holly says. "I love your facts."

"Six billion people in the world, give or take, right?"

"Yup."

"Now, if you were to count to six billion, counting one number every second, and never stopping to sleep or take a dump, how long would it take you?"

"No idea. A month? Twelve millennia?"

"About one hundred and eighty years, actually."

"I was close."

"Now, imagine there's a global rock-paper-scissors competition," I say. "Everyone in the world plays the person nearest them. Winners stay in—they play the nearest winner. So on and so forth till the last two people on Earth are left. They play off to be champion."

"Got it."

"Tell me, *Dr.* Chan, given a six billion population, how many games has the global rock-paper-scissors champion had to play?"

"Just tell me. Don't want to look a dick."

"Thirty-two."

"You're full of crap."

"I'm telling you, man, numbers are bonkers!"

A security guard ushers us along to the exits. Holly and I walk arm in arm through the deserted Space Hall that had been full of school groups when we arrived.

"Thank you," she says. "I've almost managed to forget."

"Cool." I too have been saved from dwelling on my yesterday—an evening that ended with me matching Uncle Mike shot for shot at the bar.

"Everything's all kinda *here and now* when I'm with you," Holly says.

"Same." We peck each other on the lips. "Although *here and now* is something of a debatable concept."

"Here we go."

"Well, in Einstein's model of the universe, all of space exists, as does all of time. So much as *here* means different things to different people, so indeed does *now*."

"It's possible that I might be scienced out," she says.

I stop at the exit and look guiltily at the box that invites donations. "Get you next time," I mumble.

"You really dig this place, don't you?" Holly says.

"Silly, innit? Used to come here a lot as a kid."

"With school?"

I flush with embarrassment. "By myself, mostly. Hour or two, here and there."

She squeezes my hand. "That's kinda…sad."

"What a weirdo!"

"Stop it. I think there's a lot about your childhood I'd be fascinated to know."

"Not at all."

"You're never keen to chat about it."

"Nonsense. Nowt to tell."

"Hmm."

"All very gray and unexciting."

"Whatever."

Stepping out onto Exhibition Road, we are assaulted by sharpened road salt on a frozen gale. "Shitting hell!" Holly shouts.

I hold her face to my coat and clench my jaw, grateful for the change of subject.

AUGUST 8, 2011 | AGE 35

Read All About It

London burns. Jazz and I sit on a rooftop, eight stories up. It's the late morning after the night before, and it's peaceful here in the warm wind which carries a tang of toxic plastics. This is the uneasy calm of a ceasefire, though; not the end of hostilities. I can feel it. Last night was the third of the riots, Jazz has explained. The roughest yet. Black smoke billows diagonally into the blue sky: dead ahead, left and behind us.

I like it. This solid home of mine has turned on itself, fucked itself up. It's shown itself to be vulnerable. I feel somehow less out of place today.

"Another?" Jazz says, relieving me of my plastic cup. I give him a thumbs-up, and he pours me more supersweet coffee from the thermos he brought along. We're close enough mates, it seems, for him to spot my hangovers on first sight and, without judging, to know what's good for me. Who cares that my only friend is a fifteen-year-old schoolboy?

This morning found me on the floor of the shitty bedsit in East London. Bedroom door wide open to the hallway. Jeans wringing wet from the crotch outward. No possessions to speak of bar a mobile phone with a chipped screen. Zero cash. Empty bottles. I awoke to the laughter from another tenant: "At least you haven't shat yourself this time—that's something," he observed from outside my room.

This is a day I can't afford to waste. I forced myself into the shower, let the hot water sear my skin as my stomach pumped out the last of the poison. Shaking too much to play guitar, and bemused by the trilling alarms and crystalized glass everywhere, I came here to the Sefton Hills estate. As if still a teenager myself, I knocked for Jazz.

He told me how the police shot a man last week, and everything kicked off after that. But he reckons it's been brewing awhile. "Happy people don't riot," his granddad told him. I agree.

"Man, I need to get my shit in order," I tell him as he mills about on the rooftop behind me.

"Right now, old cuz, we need to stay well away from everything." He scatters some scraps of food from a carrier bag. Pigeons circle and flap like newspapers in the wind.

"I don't have the luxury of waiting this out."

Jazz makes cooing noises in reply to the assembled flock. Some he greets like old friends. "You're too hard on yourself, man." He says it like I imagine a counselor might—supportive yet tired of my whining. God knows what crap he normally has to put up with from me when he seeks me out down at the river.

I glance at my naked ring finger. It's six years since I walked down the aisle. "How long did that last, I wonder?" I mumble. "Be surprised if we made it to the end of the honeymoon. What happened to that bright new career with her old man? I excelled at that, clearly."

Jazz perches against the railings next to me. I take my eyes from the smoke belching silently from London, look into his worried eyes. "Sorry, man. You keep feeding your birds. I'm moaning."

"You never said you'd been married," he says. "What went wrong?"

I'm about to tell him I don't know, but that's not true. "Wrong person."

He nods, hand-feeding toast crusts to a brace of tame birds. Before we came up here, I watched him gather food waste from a communal bin store. He freezes, raising a hand to silence me, listening for anyone coming up the stairs. "False alarm," he says. "Some lads come up here in the evenings. Usually have the place to myself at this time." This is the only high-rise on the estate, and it's derelict. Supposed to have been demolished years ago, Jazz explained earlier, as he led us up a metal fire escape with the casual confidence of someone who comes here daily. The security door between the stairs and the roof hangs open, long since wrenched from its frame. There are rusted tinnies and shredded train tickets about the place. No square foot of wall has escaped the wet end of an aerosol can.

"I went to prison," I tell him. "For a while."

"No biggie," Jazz says.

"Have I not told you that before?"

He shakes his head. "I kinda know you got…secrets, man. Shit you don't wanna chat about."

"What *do* we talk about, usually?"

"Music. You teach me guitar, innit. You help with school stuff. Politics and… I don't know, everything."

"You're not surprised, that I was inside?"

"What d'you do?" he asks.

"I was stitched up, mate. Banged up for a crime that I am utterly incapable of. That's the truth, I swear it. No way on God's earth I did what they say I did."

"Don't have to convince me," Jazz says.

"They say I…say I killed this woman. She's called Holly. I was…*am*…in love with her."

"Shit, man."

"There's no way, Jazz. Zero chance."

"Of course."

"I need to know what happened to her." Despite the agony and the poison coursing through me this morning, I knew I had to make this day work for me. Any date after Holly's death is a chance to find out what happened to her. An opportunity to discover why I got the blame. Who knows how many chances I'll get to find out? Once I know, I can stop it happening. Force myself into the *headwind*, make the difference. Let our lives update. Save her. Save myself. Change the cause of these effects.

"You've checked online?" Jazz asks.

"Not really sure what—"

Jazz smirks, retrieving a small mobile phone from his pocket. "What's her name?"

"Holly."

"Surname?"

"Chan. Holly Chan."

"And she...died when?"

"I don't know exactly," I tell him. "2007, I think."

"Four years ago," Jazz mumbles as he taps keys. "Shouldn't be a problem."

"Who you calling?"

"Cuz, you crack me up sometimes. Worse than my grandfather. This her?" He passes me the phone. A color headshot of Holly fills the screen.

"Fuck. Where did you get that?"

"Facebook. Memorial group. Got like a thousand members."

"Right. Everyone loves her. Loved her, I guess."

"You're right," Jazz says. "Was 2007. Thirty-three years old. Sad, man."

My heart pounds. "How did she die? I need to know."

Jazz scans the screen whilst I take deep, slow breaths, fight the urge to throw up.

"No sign of a how," he tells me. "Lots of *taken from us too soon* and that."

"Jesus."

"And you're saying people think it was your fault?" Jazz asks.

"I know they do. I went to prison for it."

He navigates his phone once more. "Old cuz, nothing on Google."

"What does that mean?"

"Look, there's stuff about Holly—memorial groups, official notice about her funeral."

"Funeral."

"But that's it," Jazz says. "If she'd been killed, it would be all over everywhere. That would be news, wouldn't it?"

"Definitely."

"I can't find nothing. She was probably like ill or something."

I shake my head. "That's crazy. If it was my fault, we'd know, right?"

"Hundred percent."

"So how do I find out what happened to her?" I ask. "Library, or something? Hospital?"

"Reckon I'd just ask someone who knew her."

I think about her dad, him ejecting me into the winter night in 2010. "Don't really know anyone."

Jazz passes me the phone. "Here's a list of a thousand people who might help."

"What is this?"

"People who've joined the memorial group. Maybe one or two might know how she died, don't you think? Shall we message someone?"

"Jazz, you absolute..." I scroll through scores of unfamiliar names. Choosing someone is like sticking a pin in a map. What do I say to them, anyway?

"Anyone you know?" Jazz says. "Someone who'd help you out?"

I'm about to tell him *no* when, among the list of randoms, a name jumps out. Maxim Masondo. "I met this guy. He was… cool."

"Let's send him a message."

"Say what?"

"That you knew this Holly. Ask how she died."

I stare into the distance at smoke that is no more than wisps now, like a bonfire ready for more fuel.

"Come on," Jazz says, "I'm writing it right now. *Hi, Maxim…*"

"Let me, yeah? My problem, man, not yours." I take the phone from him. This guy was Holly's fiancé. Were they still together at the end, two years after my wedding to Elouise? It's likely. Twice I try asking the question, only to delete what I've typed. I need to tread carefully; if he's good enough to give me one chance, that's all I'll need.

"Could you ask him if we might be able to meet up?" I say, passing the phone back to Jazz. "Please, mate. Tell him it's Alex Dean. He'll know who I am." He'll know all right, but I have to find out what happened to her.

"Result!" Jazz says. "Maxim is online."

"Which means?"

"He'll get this message straightaway."

"Tell him I'd like to buy him a pint." No matter that I have no cash; I'll deal with that later. "It has to be today."

"You sure, old cuz? Reckon it's gonna get a bit sketchy out there later."

"Has to be today. Tell him I don't need much of his time. Just need to talk."

"You got it."

"Mate, I need this to work."

"Sent," Jazz says, propping the phone against the base of the low parapet wall such that we can both see the screen.

"That's a nifty gadget," I say.

"Nifty!" Jazz laughs. "It's hardly an iPhone, old cuz. It's my grandfather's, really. We share it. He's cool like that."

"How is he? He still works?"

"Like a dog. Says he won't have me wanting for nothing. Works too hard."

I smile at him and hope he doesn't read the sadness. It's still a year in the future: that day I went back to their flat and his granddad had fallen in the bathroom, dementia advancing fast. "He's a good man."

"The best," Jazz says. This kid is kind and decent in a way that can so easily be taken for weakness.

"Tell me what this baby does," I say, pointing at the phone, no choice but to change the subject.

Blaming my spell in prison and my ropy memory, I'm able to get Jazz to bring me slightly up to date with technology: the explosion of the internet since '95; the ubiquity of email; the iPhone, finally putting a name to that handheld that has everyone transfixed in the later dates; text messaging, which even my own battered mobile, it turns out, is capable of.

"We're in business," Jazz says. He grabs his phone from the ground, screen glowing.

I buzz with nerves. "What does he say?"

"He wants to know where to meet."

Blind Faith

I walk through a city that is near-deserted. No bars spilling punters onto pavements this evening. The sun has dipped behind the buildings now, leaving these streets a bizarre no-man's-land. Half an hour ago there were commuters dashing here and there, heads down. Now occasional groups of mostly young lads huddle in doorways and railway bridges. Are they waiting for the dark, or for someone else to kick things off?

I'm still ten minutes from the Blue Moon when the sound of sirens and burglar alarms begins to fill every distant corner of the warm evening. Jazz reckoned things have been quieter out west the past night or so, and it's a pub I know well enough in case it turns out this guy wants to kill me. I daydream about the gigs I played there saving for Cambridge, about the night I first set eyes on Holly.

The ground shimmies with a distant explosion. From somewhere there is the noise of a crowd shouting; no words or voices cut through, just the howl of a collective primal rage that I don't so much hear with my ears as feel in my chest.

I pick up my pace, adrenaline pumping. For once, I am in control. I need nothing from Maxim other than the knowledge of exactly what happened to Holly in 2007. This is where I start fighting back.

The pub is quiet, mostly lone drinkers. In the stale boozy air, this place seems insulated—the feel of an air-raid shelter. It's not seen a refurb since my heyday here; still the same low-ceilinged, darkly furnished hole it always was. The names of rock and roll royalty who've played this legendary establishment still cover the walls, but there's no band or open mike tonight.

I know I worked here as assistant manager for some time after my spill into the Thames, but the guy who serves me at the bar shows no hint that he recognizes me. I order a pint, armed with the fifteen quid I got for my phone from perhaps the only used electronics store in London that hadn't bolted its shutters down.

Was my positivity on the way over simply because I knew this was the destination? I watch the tilted glass trickling full with foamy beer, and I'm at peace with myself, wanting for nothing at all in this brief instant. Neither pissed, nor driven by the pursuit of drink. What it would be to be able to live feeling like this always.

I look around at each table in turn. No sign of Maxim, although I am ten minutes early.

A broad-shouldered man bowls along the walkway behind the bar, duty manager. He places a hand in the way of the barman's as he rings up my beer on the till. "Pull the cash drawers," he tells him. "Sorry, pal," he says to me. He rings the time bell. "Gentlemen! I'm afraid, on orders of the police, we have to close early. If you wouldn't mind finishing up and making your way out ASAP."

"Am I good for five minutes?" I ask. "I'm waiting on someone."

He shakes his head, and I watch in horror as he grabs the

Stella that never reached my hand, emptying it into the drip tray. "Locking up right now," he says, swinging a set of keys with the authority of a jailer.

I wait on the pavement, not ten meters from the pub's entrance. Groups of lads walk past me with the purpose of people who know where they're going. Half an hour passes with no sign of Maxim. Public transport must be a nightmare; of course he's running late.

I lap the outside of the building, check he's not at another door. People are running up the road now. The night is stained orange by fire a few streets away, sparks like flies soaring into the sky. Glass breaks and voices shout, so close now. A helicopter passes so low I feel the gush of warm air.

Where is Maxim? I need just a minute of his time. Where the fuck is he?

I search down nearby streets, never letting the Blue Moon out of my sight for long. He *must* be coming. An hour late almost, but the streets are treacherous. He's got to be round here somewhere.

Two roads from the pub and I find myself among it. A small hatchback burns, tongues of flame licking from kicked-in windows. Some stand and watch, as entertained as if it were bonfire night. Minutes pass and there are no approaching sirens. That chopper nearby looks to be a news crew, nothing more. No one pays me the slightest attention as I glance desperately down side alleys in search of a familiar face.

It's clear enough to everyone here that the police aren't coming. A group of kids barely in their teens set a wheelie bin alight and roll it into the middle of the road. Two blokes wrench the shutters open on a convenience store and put the window through. There's a cheer and a dash for goods. A newsagent's gets the same treatment. A carpet outlet too. Some bloke kicks unabashedly at the door to a shop selling hearing aids.

It's dark in the convenience store as I weave between the other *shoppers*. The booze aisle is almost stripped already, but I lay my hands on a couple of bottles rolling around on the lowest shelf.

When did we decide it was okay to behave badly just because no one's here stopping us? Did this happen when everyone was told they were an individual? Everyone out for themselves. Fuck *society*. I wonder what Maggie thinks of these riots. What does she make of me and all these people, helping ourselves? Righteous indignation? Or swollen with pride that her ethos still endures, all these years on?

Who'd have thought it—Alex Dean, child of Thatcher.

A hit of neat white rum and my search for Maxim is reinvigorated. I *will* find him.

I duck into a narrow side street that leads toward the tube, which as far as I know is still running. Surely this is the way he'd be coming in?

The streetlights are out, and all these small shops and the boutique offices above are locked down. I take a left turn into a degree of darkness I've never known in this town. People scurry like rats through these alleys, dodging the mob. Not until an approaching person is right on me am I able to look them in the face. Panic grips tighter with each mumbled apology to someone who is not Maxim.

A door between two shops opens in front of me, and I have to pull up sharply to avoid walking into a suited man as he steps into my path.

"Whoa!" he says, holding a leather briefcase as a shield between us. "Easy, mate."

"Yeah, yeah, sorry." I edge past him, but it's tight; he's one of those blokes who needlessly stands ground. I glance at his face and then back along the alley. It takes a second to process what I've seen. Already my body has reacted: red alert, fight or flight.

I look again, have it confirmed. His expression shifts as he realizes who I am.

"Jesus fucking Christ," he says. A shake of head, half a smirk.

He's gained a few stone, lost half his hair since we fought on the banks of the river. But I'd know Blake Benfield anywhere.

Mad World

"What is wrong with you?" Blake says. "You gonna get out of my way or what?" His voice is unchanged, a sound that transports me to being that teenager who was perpetually terrified of this guy.

It's easy enough to block his path in this narrow walkway. He's two inches taller than me, feels like two feet. "What did you do?" It infuriates me that my mouth wobbles as I say it. Why am I on the verge of tears?

"Jog on, yeah," he says. "I got a home to go to."

I instinctively swig from the bottle of rum. It's like drinking neat aftershave. "What the fuck did you do to me?"

"Are we really doing this?"

I yell it in his face: "What did you do?"

"You're a bit of a fucking weirdo, aren't you? Don't push me. I'll knock you silly."

"That night? By the river? In '95?"

"Do one, yeah?" He pushes up against me.

The feel of his firm body. Smell of burned-out house in my nostrils. Danger I might vomit.

"Got a family to get back to," he says. "I reckon you *don't*."

"Tell me what you did!"

"Look at you. Fucking peasant." He tries to shove me aside. I resist with all my weight. He could turn and go the other way. Not in his nature.

"You nearly fucking killed me." Somehow the statement doesn't do justice to the life I've been left with after that night.

"Nearly killed you? Whatever, mate."

"Jumped in, did I?"

"Fucking years ago. Let it go."

"No chance."

"You got lairy. You got the kicking you deserved. Get over it."

"You ruined my life. You ruined everything." I look at the ground, expensive pattern brogues toe to toe with my shitty trainers. How different things might be without this man. I take another hit of rum, so much it dribbles out of my mouth, standing firm in his path. "You owe me," I hiss, bold with the booze.

I wasn't yet ten years old when I first met Blake Benfield. March 1985. Still there is a certain sort of spring evening—damp and richly blue following a promising day—that never fails to remind me of our early encounters. Even as an adult, such evenings have brought with them a sense of immediate threat, unspeakable evil—the devil himself—lurking just beyond sight.

I was cycling along the path that ran parallel with the railway, tracks to one side, graffiti-covered rear ends of buildings on the other. The surface was chalky and rutted and booby-trapped with white dog turds.

It paid to be out of the house on Sundays—Mum would be working and Dad would be lying on the sofa watching *Sunday*

Grandstand, his mood darkening as the day wore on and the tinnies went down until inevitably something, anything, would
be my fault.

Blake was with another guy who I would come to know as
Stuart. I stopped fifty feet short of them and watched. They
were standing in the overgrown brush and taking it in turns
to throw stones at the windows of the Scout headquarters. The
glass would resist at first, then begin to spall, before eventually
giving way into the blackness inside when a rock landed on target. They were fourteen, and they looked to me like teenage
boys always do to a nine-year-old: strong, cool, dangerous, like
they knew everything.

"Nice bike!" Blake called out to me. It wasn't a nice bike and
we both knew it. I wanted a BMX so badly I doodled them all
over my schoolbooks and would stare longingly at the one in
the Argos catalog. What I actually rode was a three-speeder that
had once been Mum's. I'd removed the basket, rattle-canned the
frame in matte black, kitted it out with some clattery Spokey
Dokeys, but its origins were clear.

"What you looking at?" Stuart asked. He was the sort of kid
who could shout the odds but was near-incapable of ordinary
conversation.

"Just…watching," I told them. Shy.

"Wanna go?" Blake asked. So I joined them. My aim was off
to start with, but the sound of a successful hit and eventual surrender of each pane was addictive. I threw rocks till my shoulders ached. Whenever a train came by, we'd give middle-finger
salutes to the passengers and enjoy their impotent fury. One train
driver sounded his horn and gave us a wanker gesture out of his
open window; we were overjoyed.

The pair of them lived in Great Pines, an estate a mile from
mine where the houses had steps to their front doors and there
were islands with trees in the middle of the road. But after that
first meeting, if I cycled beside the tracks or through the park, I

tended to find them out and about somewhere. Blake was quick to identify how I might be of use. He and Stuart had earned a reputation among local shopkeepers. With me in tow, their notoriety became an advantage. They'd stand idly near the counter, where their every move would be watched. Sometimes there'd be a row when the owner asked them to leave. Either way, I'd be free to sneak in and fill my rucksack and sleeves without being bothered. When they heard the trill of bicycle bell from outside, they'd know the job was done. I don't think they wanted most of what we nicked: crisps and sweets and fizzy drinks— certainly they let me keep what I wanted. It was the outsmarting that these guys got off on.

There was a house near mine that had burned down a few months earlier. Local legend had it the man who lived there did it deliberately and his wife had died as she'd slept. I'd been past only once shortly after it happened; the blackened glass and tongues of soot licking round the front door had given me the creeps.

"Wonder if she's still in there," Stuart said as we stopped on the street outside one Sunday evening. "Lying in bed, covered in maggots." I jumped as he tickled my face with his Marlboro-stained fingers.

I kept a pace back as Blake jumped the front wall and cupped his hand to look inside. We squeezed down an overgrown alley to the rear of the house. The back garden was a mess, brambles and a heap of scorched furniture tossed out by the fire brigade. The back door was splintered where it had been axed open. A poor attempt had been made to secure it with a piece of ply. It put up little resistance.

We took it in turns to stand on the threshold. Even I was pretty certain the lady wasn't in here; the older boys must have known. But it was the first time I'd seen them look unsure of themselves. When pushing on and exploring seemed the obvious next step, they lit ciggies, became unusually pensive. There was some shoving of each other into the kitchen, with its plastic cupboard fronts that had run like paintings in the rain and its sink brimmed with black water.

"Dare you, Al," Blake said. "Get in and nick something."

"No chance," Stuart said. "Kid's a pussy."

There was a sparkle in their expressions as I pigeon-stepped inside. It was, I suppose, something close to respect. It felt great.

My feet squelched on the wet carpets and bouncy floorboards, but when I stopped moving, the house was so quiet I could hear my own breathing. The washing machine had sunk in on itself, its door twisted into a hideous white plastic smile. It taunted me as I sidled past. The stench—sour and toxic—stuck to my nostrils for days. The living room was a crazy sight. One side lay consumed by fire: table and chairs whittled to skeletons, timbers etched with charred cubes, ceiling hanging down. And then just feet away there were books still readable but for water damage and mold, floral curtains barely dusted with smoke, photographs of schoolchildren wrinkled with damp inside their frames. It was the memory of this room that visited me at night for some time after. Annihilation and life in such proximity. Like a face with half the skull shot away.

Yet I pushed on. I was petrified to the point of nausea. But I'd rather have risked death than lose face with these guys.

Upstairs I found a bathroom so wrecked I could see clean through the floor. And beyond a closed door, an almost untouched bedroom bar the filthy water that had run down the walls and slackened the paper as it went. The bed was stripped; if she really had snuffed it here, her body was long gone. A teddy bear lay facedown on the damp carpet; I sat him on the windowsill facing into the room, a draft at his back that might dry his fur. I picked through a few drawers and found a brooch and necklace, both gold, both green in places. Not interested in their value, I wanted only proof I'd been here.

For the rest of that evening, I was one of *them*, no matter that I was five years their junior. We commandeered the prefab garage at the end of the garden, cleared ourselves some space and unfolded the garden furniture. They shared their ciggies and taught me how to smoke properly. At graphic length, they told me about the things they'd done with girls.

It wasn't long after that day when Blake found a mountain bike of my size outside the train station—a Peugeot with five gears, no less. I knew, even as I pedaled furiously from the scene, that it belonged to another kid, and this wasn't fair. But guilt, in front of these lads, would be weakness. I couldn't place the hollowness I felt as a freight train mangled my old bike, thrown on the line by a hysterical Stuart. I'd hated the thing really—why did it hurt to see it go?

That garage behind the burned-out house became a hideout for Blake and Stuart, and on Sundays I'd join them. There was the time when they had a porno mag. Blake thumbed through each glossy page in turn and talked me through everything in detail. "These are lesbians," he explained as we studied a zoomed-in image of two vaginas grinding together. My heart pounded. "Look, look," he kept saying, even though I *was* looking, as he held the magazine close to my face. "You got a stiffy?" he asked.

I blushed, looked down as if to confirm it to myself. "Maybe."

"Good boy," he said, red in the face himself. Stuart meanwhile stared furiously at the pictures, hissing insults at the naked and prone women.

Those lurid images etched themselves onto my brain; all week afterward I was seeing them in their every detail. I was perpetually nervous and guilty and repulsed, and keen to see them again.

Blake was alone in the garage the next week. He told me Stuart had got himself grounded. My worries that the porn was a one-off were unfounded; he had a fistful of the stuff. These were a different league, though—Spanish or Italian and explicit to the point I felt ill. An hour or two passed, Blake close to my ear as he whispered me through the positions on display. He passed me each of his cigarettes when there were a couple of pulls left.

"Got a stiffy?" he asked, just as he had before. Only now he seemed nervous.

I nodded and smiled.

"Me too," he said, "look." I watched as he made the bulge in his jeans pulse up and down. "Wanna see it?" I'm not sure how I replied, but his trousers and pants were round his knees in a flash. "Hold the magazine," he said, starting to stroke himself. I held it at my chest, wide open for him to see. For thirty seconds at a time he'd be content before changing his mind about which picture he wanted or how I should be holding it. "Look at my dick," he hissed when I shifted my gaze anywhere other than him.

"Fuck off, you little shit," he said moments after he'd finished, whilst stuffing himself hastily into his pants. He had, the instant he was done, switched into the meanest version of himself.

I was off my food that week and quieter than usual. I thought of nothing else. It was like I was in receipt of a secret, one that I wouldn't know who to share with even had I wanted to. Both at school and home, I'd become separated from everyone else. This drew me to Blake, somehow the only person I felt I was now on a level with.

Again the next Sunday, he was alone in the garage. The anger from last week's closing moments gone. More ciggies, more porn. Things happened as they had before. He was red at the ears, too smiley, shaky. I held the pictures, obeyed the order to find a different one every minute or so. Here and there he'd whisper instructions like: "Tell me it's big. Like you're amazed by it. Say *wow*." The rampant fury the second he was done was almost expected, something that was barely upsetting.

Why did I keep going back, week after week? It was automatic. Was it the threat of what he'd do if I didn't show? Maybe. But there was something else. It seemed easier to let it carry on than not to: when stopping would mean finding a compartment in which to file it.

I don't remember the date, only that it was raining. It had started as usual: a Sunday afternoon, new porn, Blake's quiet-voiced arousal and eventual undressing. He was even sweatier, wilder, redder than usual. So crazed he could barely maintain a rhythm. He stopped, grinned.

The frog-leap of his Adam's apple as he went to speak. "You do it." He was breathless with nerves. "Do it for me."

I was bad at it and he said so. But not bad enough to be excused. I listened to his barking instructions. It can't possibly have been so, I'm sure it was only a minute or two, but in my memory I was there for hours.

No words after. A shove out of the door. A long walk home with my stolen bike. Any thought about what had happened in there killed on first sight. Think about *something else*.

Still, I tried to go back. Blake was never in that garage again. It took weeks to find him. Told me I'd die if he ever saw me again. After that, we only ran into each other through bad luck. Once I told him I was sorry. I was. The years passed, but the fear of encountering him never did. It was at its worst when it'd been a while, as if seeing him was inevitable, and therefore overdue.

"What's the point of you?" Blake says. A toothy grimace an inch from my face. Rank coffee breath. "What are you on this Earth for?" He's towering over me and I'm off balance. I stumble against the wall. "Dirty, stinking scum."

There's an explosion not far away, followed by a cheer. The night sky glows brighter than ever. The sirens are coming now, swelling in volume from all directions. "You know what you did," I say.

"You're a wrong'un, Dean." He backs up enough to look me up and down. "The state of you. I'm going home to my family now." He smirks, and I'm more aware than ever of my ill-fitting trousers, my T-shirt with its frayed Reebok stripes, my nicotine hair, my blotched face. "You should go back to yours," he says. "I'm sure loads of people are missing you." He could turn, leave any other way, but he chooses to push past me. The shoulder of his suit grazes past my chin.

This guy haunted my childhood. He beat me and left me to die in the Thames. He turned my life into this disordered wreck. I am a pathetic, failed *effect*. How much of the *cause* is down to him?

There's heat in my eyes. A tingling on my nose. I'm allegedly thirty-five years old; why does it feel like I'm about to cry? Why is my reaction to this guy just as it was in my teens?

I take a hit of booze.

No way. No fucking way.

The half-full rum bottle slips out of my hand and shatters on the ground. Blake turns.

"Don't you dare walk away from me," I shout.

He stops dead, scowls at me over his shoulder.

"How dare you imagine you can just walk away, after everything you've done."

He's back in my face again, chest against mine, but I stand firm.

"You should've died in the river, waster," Blake says.

"You fucked everything." Why do I sound so weak?

"Who'd care?" Blake spits. "Who'd care if you were dead?"

I glare at him. I don't know. Who would care?

"You're an evil bastard, you know that?" I hiss, forehead against his.

There's a shout from behind us. Two heavy palms land on my shoulder. Another hand slams into Blake. We are wrenched apart.

I stagger backward against the wall and lose my footing. Blake goes over on his back, sprawled like an upturned beetle. There's the squawk of sheared fabric: his trousers bust open at the seam.

Two police officers stand over us. "Get up, you pair of pricks!" the stockier of the two says. He grabs his baton and extends it with a flourish.

"You think we haven't got better things to do than deal with stupid fuckers like you?" The policeman, short and square-headed, looks at me like I'm dog shit on his shoe. He's holding the tip of his baton an inch from my front teeth. Like a million other coppers, he exudes the air of someone who shouldn't be anywhere near the job.

"I'm going," I mumble.

"You're right there," he snaps. He barrels into me, and I am swept along the alley in front of him. Blake, meanwhile, suited and spewing well-spoken apologies, makes his exit in the opposite direction.

"Don't let me see you again," the officer shouts, shoving me out onto a pavement thirty meters from where we started.

"Yeah, yeah," I mumble as he takes off.

These streets flicker with blue light and fire. A moment's panic is stilled when I find the fifteen quid I got for my phone still in my pocket. All thoughts of finding Maxim, all hopes of knowing what happened to Holly, are overridden now.

There has to be somewhere in this crazy city I can get a drink.

DECEMBER 24, 1996 | AGE 21

A Long December

"You're absolutely certain I can trust you not to take a dip, yeah?" Holly says.

I shudder. "As long as no one throws me in, we'll be just dandy."

"Am I being insensitive? You're sure you wanna be here? There are other bars in London—you know that, right?"

A waiter brings our order: two massive hot chocolates with cream and marshmallows, and a snowball cocktail each on Holly's insistence. "I like it here," I say, spearing a morello cherry with my cocktail umbrella and popping it in her mouth.

"Nothing says Christmas like the taste of fizzy custard," she says, slurping noisily. She pulls her scarf tighter. There are no tables free inside, and despite the propane heater above us, the cold gnaws at my toes, and our breath plumes in the small space between our faces. The bookies are giving evens on a white Christmas.

I gaze toward the Thames. The afternoon sun is sinking toward the water fast. Holly grooves to the unfamiliar pop song on the bar's sound system, making eyes at me and lip-synching the words *Come a little bit closer, baby, get it on, get it on...*

This is the place she and I came in '95. It's where I took my spill into the river. There will, in years to come, be a coffee outlet here instead of this bar, later a chocolatier. I will ply my trade as a busker on this concourse. But right now, it is how it once was. There is nowhere I'd rather be.

"Get everything you wanted?" Holly asks, whipped cream on her nose.

"Too late if I haven't." My rucksack beside me looks barely half-full with hastily bought presents, a few rolls of street-market wrapping paper poking out. Holly sits surrounded by shiny boutique bags with rope handles. I've seen enough films; I know I'm supposed to buy her a first edition of some treasured book or an antique music box or something, but having been gifted this day, I wasn't about to waste it with her not at my side for any longer than I had to. I've got her some gloves with a leopard print lining that'll look a treat with the afghan coat she's wearing, and an umbrella with rainbows on. If I've cocked this up, at least I'm unlikely to be watching her unwrap them anytime soon.

"So tempted to fuck my placement off tomorrow," Holly says. "All this training for the pleasure of giving up my Christmas Day."

I spark up a Marlboro Light. Much as the image of her is with me always, it's the tiny mannerisms that are the greatest pleasure to be reminded of; like the way she gently plucks my cigarette from me, the balk of the occasional smoker as she takes it down, the sparkle in her big eyes as she exhales into my face. "Do it," I say, knowing well she won't.

"Seven a.m. start, no less," she says. "What time you due in?"

"Me?"

"Putting it out of mind? Enjoying the moment? Quite right."

"Am I working? *Tomorrow?*"

Holly chuckles, assumes I'm joking around.

"Seriously, though?"

She scrunches her face, like I'm setting her up. "Christmas lunch at the Blue Moon. What did you say—seventy covers booked?"

"Seventy turkey dinners," I say, as if marveling at the fact. "Don't these wankpots have homes to go to?"

"You said it yourself, baby—lots of people with a story when they book their table. An empty chair the family can't bear to look at. I think it's a nice thing, giving up your Christmas Day. And if *I* have to…"

"Yeah, yeah." My career at the Blue Moon has well and truly begun, then; a few years from now I'll be reaching the dizzying heights of assistant manager. A spell working for Elouise's old man, then living out my best years busking on almost this very spot. What a way to make a living.

"Do you reckon I could still go to Cambridge?" I ask her.

"Wow. Where did that come from?"

"It's only been, what, a year and a bit since I was supposed to start."

"Sure. You've not mentioned it, though. Not since…"

"I should've gone. Shouldn't I?"

"Go easy on yourself," Holly says. "You weren't in great shape. Not for a while after…"

"I could've deferred, right? Gone this September instead?"

"How come you're only saying this now? I thought you liked it at the pub?"

"It's a waste, surely?"

"I've…sometimes thought that." She rolls her eyes as though she's been chastised for airing this opinion in the past.

"Look at you. Going places. Flying…"

"Don't make this about me, Alex. I love you whatever. Cambridge undergrad or pub…person." She's embarrassed at her inability to articulate my job title.

"Maybe you won't always. Might get boring."

"You gotta do what makes you happy. It's that simple." She squeezes my hand and borrows my ciggie again. "Remember when we first met, how you used to say that you wanted people to look up to you? That you didn't care how, but you wanted people to look at you and see success."

"Yup. What a twat."

"A touch unspecific, maybe. Shallow, if I'm harsh."

"Fair."

"So what *do* you want?" Holly asks, shuffling in close. "God, we never talk about this stuff anymore. What do you want, Alex? Where do you see yourself?"

"Dunno. Being respected still kind of appeals. Be a welcome change."

Holly jabs my arm. "Dick."

"Nah, bollocks to all that. You know what I want? I want to be married to you. Family, maybe. Don't care if we're rich. Not poor, though—bored of that. But yeah, that's it. Married to you. Not interested in anything else."

Holly grins. "Righto."

"Serious."

Her face flushes pink. "This is a weird sort of proposal."

"Yeah, fuck it, let's get married."

"You mean, *right* now?"

"Should be good availability, very quiet time of year for the church."

"Indeed," Holly says. "Excuse me, Rev, any chance of some quick vows between evensong and midnight mass?"

"I'm not kidding, you know. I want to marry you."

"Well, that's sorted, then."

"Let's go ring shopping," I say, scalding my mouth as I sink half my hot chocolate in one.

"Yeah," Holly says. "Let's do that."

We both know we're kidding about, but there's a shift between us as well—a greater separation from the world beyond our bubble. Locked together, we stroll up the boulevard away from the river with a million colored lights twinkling above us. In the square, the Salvation Army band plays "Once in Royal David's City" beneath a sky fast turning dark blue. We kiss and I tell her I love her.

I have the satisfying sense of pushing against something: a gentle headwind, the weight of history. Small perhaps, but I'm making a change from the life I once lived on this day. Telling Holly what she means to me, how deeply she's loved—it is, I suspect, new. Might this update my later life?

Even if we were genuinely in the market, the pieces in Hyman's Jewellers would be way off-limits. But still, we lean close to the glass cabinets and argue between the two-carat diamond solitaire and the emerald ring with cluster. Holly's obvious breeding outweighs my clear lack of it: the shop assistant soon has a velvet pillow out, and various rings are being slid on and off Holly's slender finger. "We'll have a think," I say after half an hour of dreaming.

Outside, a homeless man sits begging below the jeweler's window. Shoppers crane over him to look at ten-grand Rolexes. His face is red with sores, eyeballs yellow, breath steaming as he asks in vain for spare change. He's like a mirror—me twenty years from now. Or maybe tomorrow. I say to Holly I'll catch her up.

He tells me his name is Keith. Two years living rough, give or take. Had a house and family. Lost his young daughter three Christmases ago. Forgot how to *be*. Found solace where he could—bottom of a bottle, sharp end of a steel needle. Can't see himself doing this much longer.

Keith tells me he's sorry when I wipe a tear on my sleeve. "It's this band," he jokes. "Silent Night" rolling warmly from the French horns now. He says it's eighteen quid for a night in the hostel. I give him all I have: thirty-five quid left, having rushed my shopping. Who gives a toss if he blows the lot on booze or smack instead? He'll find some peace and warmth either way. He doesn't smell so great when I hug him. I'm not enough of an arsehole to wish him a merry Christmas, so I tell him he's doing just fine instead.

I find Holly's looking on from the other side of the square. "I said I'd catch you up," I say.

"You told me you wanted people to look up to you," she says as we leave the crowds behind. "I do. I look up to you more than you can imagine."

We go back to my parents' place and hole up in my room. Snuggled on my single bed, we watch *The Muppet Christmas Carol* and *It's a Wonderful Life*. Christmas pop songs play quietly as we make love, slowly, too intimate to even consider a change of position. Holly falls asleep near instantly, her ear against my thumping chest. A few distant fireworks ring in Christmas Day. I've never known a bed so soft, a room so safe. Joni Mitchell's "River" plays on the radio, volume fading to a whisper. I skate away.

JULY 29, 2007 | AGE 31

Foundations

"The man at the barbecue is king!" says a guy in maroon shorts and Ray-Bans. He holds a bottle aloft. "Bubbles?" His name, I have gleaned, is Terry. He lives two doors down from Elouise and me. He's here with his wife, along with some other neighbors— ten of them altogether.

I hold my glass out and take a swig to chase the cider I've got on the go.

"Magnificent space," he says, gazing in exaggerated admiration at our new kitchen extension. This gathering, according to Elouise, is a *topping-out ceremony*, in honor of the completed building works. "Bifold doors," he adds, "what a marvel they are..."

"Had to sell a kidney for them, mind," Elouise says, wafting over with a tray of gazpacho soup in shot glasses. There are Parmesan tuiles standing in each—I was awoken before six this morning to the frenzied sound of these being made. "It was

that or move, though," she tells our neighbor, whose bonhomie appears momentarily shaken. I catch myself joining them as
they gaze at the back of our house. All three-bed semidetacheds
originally, the rows of neighboring houses have all tumored to
varying degrees, incongruous tile-hung boxes and glass panes
plunging upward and rearward.

"Turn those steaks," Elouise hisses once Terry is distracted.
"They're not supermarket crap." I prod them around the grill,
only too happy to have this job when the alternative is min-
gling. She shakes my Bulmers can: empty. "Jesus, Alex. Think
maybe you could rein it in before you make a fool of yourself?"
I don't reply, and she is soon smiling and circulating once again.

Two years since our wedding day and we are, in the middle-
class sense, *doing all right.* This is a West London road with grass
verges and parking restrictions. On the drive there's a Honda
SUV and a silver Porsche Boxster, both nearly new. Telly is fifty
inches. Kitchen worktops in granite. Chalky white en suite with
his and hers basins. I daren't explore the garage for fear of finding golf clubs.

I put some stuffed chicken breasts on a low heat. It's been
sunny all day as I've run around following Elouise's orders, but
the dark clouds are stealing the early evening light. My wife
delivers salads that look like abstract artworks to the two round
tables I assembled from flat-pack before breakfast. I glance at
my wedding ring, gleaming platinum as out of place as the Tag
Heuer on my wrist.

It appears that yesterday with Holly achieved nothing. Making my feelings known, my desire to marry her, hasn't suc-
ceeded in updating anything to my advantage. What more can
I do than be honest? What possible cause can I instigate that'll
have a real effect? I'm overdue an audience with Dr. Paul Defrates, I know that much.

The first drops of rain fall just as I'm flashing the stuffed sardines. "Abandon ship!" Terry cries. There's a scramble to get everything indoors.

"It's cool," I tell Elouise in the kitchen. "I think everyone's having a good time, still." She polishes beads of water from cutlery. It takes me by surprise how sorry I feel for her. I go to put my hand on hers, but she snatches it away.

"Just have a drink, yeah?" I say.

"That's not the answer to everything," she retorts, quiet so our guests can't overhear.

Today, it's been the only answer. I've been drinking discreetly since midmorning; it's kept the sense of claustrophobia, and the sickness that accompanied it, at bay. I slop a decent-looking white into her glass. "Let's enjoy ourselves."

"I *was* enjoying myself, till this." She shakes her head, looking through our glazed back wall at a garden that's dark as night. "Jesus, Alex."

"I'll say this for bifolds—they give a cracking view of the rain."

"Oh, piss off."

"I'm not sure the weather is my fault." I say it like a man who's not sure of it at all.

I'm astonished when, minutes later, we're taking our seats to eat and Elouise sits just inches from my side. "Cheers, husband," she says, chinking my glass and squeezing my thigh. She smiles widely with newly touched-up red lips, although there's something twitchy, squirrel-ish, to her movements.

"Calm down," I whisper. "Tuck in."

She doesn't register that I've spoken, looking on approvingly as our neighbors fill their plates and dish up compliments.

"Beautifully cooked steak," Terry's wife says.

"All my wife's work, really," I say. "Just the lackey, me."

"Too modest," Elouise says, leaning her head against my arm. "He's quite the chef."

I'm oddly elated that I've impressed her. Why, I don't know.

"I spent a fair bit of a time in a grill kitchen in my pub management years," I tell the table, wearing a wanker's winking smile. "Must have paid off." So what that I've not lived a single one of those shifts, that I only know of this career because I've been told about it?

"Long time ago," Elouise says, stroking my hand.

"Gone up in the world since then," Terry observes. "How is work treating you, Alex?"

"Oh, you know..." I feign chewing on my mouthful, even though the meat melts away in moments.

"Remind me, what is it you do?" another neighbor asks.

"I work for Elouise's father." It's the only truth I can lay my hands on. "He's in private equity." I repeat, as best I can remember, the summary Elouise's dad gave at our wedding of his business activities.

"Alex looks after compliance," Elouise says, pride in her tone. Everyone nods, and I'm praying they won't ask what *compliance* means. No one does; they either know perfectly well or daren't admit they haven't a clue.

The attention leaves me soon enough, Elouise quizzed instead about recently making partner at her city law firm. "You'll be a kept man, Alex," Terry jokes. I spend the next few minutes looking for an opening in conversation where I can mention how I landed a place at Cambridge; thankfully the urge wears off before the chance arises. We eat delicious food and invite our neighbors in turn to talk about themselves. We are, it appears, good hosts. Elouise holds my hand and gives me a twinkly smile. Again, I'm warmed by reassurance. I'm not sure I like this woman very much, and yet I crave her approval.

There are photos of the two of us dotted about the room. This morning, when the house was alien to me, they were the first things to catch my attention. My wife was shouting at me from the kitchen like I'm a persistent nuisance, whilst I was surrounded by framed snaps from Caribbean holidays and the

Goodwood Revival and Royal Ascot in which we don't just look happy—we look glowingly, perfectly, *irritatingly* in love. On this evidence alone, I'd never suspect that here are two people who simply came into each other's lives at the optimum moment: any port in a thirtysomething storm.

"Music!" Elouise says, leaping off her chair like she's been electrocuted. She faffs with a bizarre-looking stereo, all black and shaped like a gherkin tipped on its side. The volume is sufficient to be intrusive.

"Really?" I say as she retakes her seat. "Not the Rat Pack! Anything but that." Elouise glares at me.

"Not a Sinatra man?" Terry asks. He's shimmying in his seat along to "The Lady Is a Tramp."

"God, no," I tell him. Stone-cold sober, maybe I'd have taken a second to realize how no one else is fussed by the music choice. But I've had a few, and I'm aware I've been almost mute as we've eaten. This is the first subject to arise all day that I'm comfortable talking about.

"Icon of his time," Terry says.

"Yeah, but it's just music for people who don't like music, isn't it?" I reply, nothing more than small talk.

I can feel Elouise's stare burning into me. "My husband would have us banging our heads to something," she says, smiling but with a tone that doesn't match.

"Easy listening," I say. "That's what they call this sort of thing. I mean, who chooses music on the basis of how easy it is to listen to? It's like—I don't know—choosing food because it's easy to chew." I intend it as a witty observation, but I'm aware I sound boorish.

"Be very dull if we all liked the same things," Terry says. "What's your bag?"

"Don't ask, Terry," Elouise says. "There's a risk he'll get his guitar out."

"I'm not sure there's much chance of that," I say with a chuckle.

"My good lady wife likes to keep it buried under all her junk." I spied my guitar's hard case in a spare room earlier today, beneath several bags of clothes.

Elouise and I retreat to the kitchen with cleared plates. "Going good, don't you think?" I ask.

She turns slowly, her features and small frame oddly angular, like she's been carved from rock. "No, Alex. No, I don't."

I upend a wine bottle over my glass only to realize I've already drained it. Instead I settle for a beer from our bank safe of a fridge. "Everyone's having a good time." Foam splatters on the floor as I ping the cap. I dive for a cloth in the hope I can wipe it up before Elouise sees.

"Do you set out to embarrass me?"

"I don't know what—"

"Is it *deliberate*, Alex? *Oh, look, Elouise has got everything just so. Let me piss all over her fire.* Is that it?"

"What the hell are you talking about?" I'm halfway through swigging my beer and it catches in my throat, sounds like a snigger.

"You're an arsehole," she hisses, checking behind her for any of our guests. They sound to be enjoying themselves in the dining room, the volume of "Mr. Bojangles" turned up.

"I was just kidding around, that's all. Don't take yourself so seriously."

"Fuck you!" she snaps. "Don't take myself seriously? We can't all be a joke like you. Someone's got to take some responsibility, you know."

"Yeah, all right. Keep your hair on." I reach in the fridge for the desserts. "Perhaps let's get on with entertaining, yeah?" I withdraw the tray of individual banoffees set in crystal coupes. It's heavier than I'm expecting, and I watch in horror as they wobble off balance. I manage to right the tray, but one of the beautiful puddings slips off the side and explodes on the floor. I'm dashed with whipped cream nearly to the crotch. Elouise looks like she's been informed of a close relative's death.

"It's okay, it's okay," I say. "It's just one. I'll go without. I'll make sure no one notices."

"I can't believe you," she says. Terry pops his head round the door to check all is well. Elouise sends him away to enjoy himself with a freakish smile. "You have to ruin everything."

"It's just a pud. I'm sorry."

"You don't think you're enough of an embarrassment already? Have to get pissed, belittle me in front of friends, fuck everything up as well?"

"Don't call me an embarrassment."

"What would you prefer? Waste of space? Thick-as-shit simpleton?"

"Steady."

"So I'm wrong, am I?"

I bite my tongue. It's against my instincts to not argue back. But I want to do better. I'm *trying* to be better.

I sweep the pieces of broken glass into a corner and rinse a cloth in the sink, aware that she's glaring at my back but doing what I can to ignore her.

"You're so fucking ungrateful. That's the thing that gets me."

I turn toward her and shrug my shoulders, determined not to be provoked.

She's boiling over with rage. "Everything you've got is thanks to me. Absolutely *everything*."

"I've no doubt."

"You're *nobody*. A total nobody. You know that?" Her eyes bore into to me, craving a reaction. It seems this attack is made regularly.

"Don't be a…" I stop myself short.

She waits on the rest of the sentence, mouth hanging open.

I begin a lap of the kitchen, checking drawers and cupboards.

"What the hell are you looking for?" Elouise asks.

"There's gotta be some cigs round here," I mumble. I've been busy enough all day to go without, but I'm dying for one now.

"You quit! You promised. We had an agreement, Alex."

"Did we? Or did you just *tell* me that we'd agreed? I am *nobody*, after all."

"You are not smoking."

"I'm afraid I am."

She's in my face now. "You're so weak, Alex. Call yourself a man?"

"Leave me to it, please."

My search unearths nothing.

"Don't you dare do a disappearing act," she says as I make for the hallway. "Not now. No fucking way, Alex. I swear, if you walk away right now…"

"I'm gonna find a gas station. I'll be back in ten."

I've no idea which of the two cars on the driveway is mine, but I grab the key for the Porsche Boxster. Fifty meters from our house I pull over, engine idling. The wipers sweep away what is barely drizzle now. Streetlamps glare from the glossy road surface. For the first time all day, I can breathe.

I pull my mobile phone from my pocket. I've scanned through it in quiet corners a few times, but this is the first chance I've had to properly scrutinize it. I scroll through the list of contacts, though I know from earlier that Holly's name isn't there.

It's 2007. This, to the best of my knowledge, is the year she… *it* happens.

Not only is Holly not on this phone, nor is any other female name other than Elouise's. Just a long list of guys, mostly unfamiliar. The few text messages are all businesslike. All from men. Why don't I know any women at all?

I read through the phone book again. One name jumps out at me.

It can't be. Can it? Maybe. It has to be.

I'm suddenly lighter. I hit the green button. It's ringing. Heart racing.

Surely there's no way I know someone called *Buddy*.

To Build a Home

"You do realize you're not *actually* James Dean?" Holly says.

"I'm close enough." We're finally free of the city traffic, and a cool wind batters my forehead. "Top down, little silver sports car. Just you, me and the open road." I offer her a drag on my cigarette but she declines. I'm pushing my luck when I lean back in my seat and put my left arm around her, my right stretched out to the top of the steering wheel.

"None of that, thanks very much," Holly says, manhandling my arm back where it belongs. "You're giving me a lift, remember? Any other taxi driver tried something like that, and I'd be macing the bastard."

"All right, all right." I slow for a roundabout. "Where now?"

"Third exit. Follow the signs for Dagenham."

"You got it." It's absurd how happy I am simply driving her somewhere. When I got through to her an hour ago, she was adamant we couldn't meet. There was irritation in her tone, a hint that me making such requests is not unusual. She told me how she was visiting her aunt this evening, out Essex way. I said I could be with her in ten minutes, save her the train fare.

"Maxim says you're a lucky bastard," Holly says, looking up from the glowing phone in her lap. "He wants to know how you can afford a Porsche."

"He doesn't mind?"

"What, you and me? In the same car? Scandal!"

"I guess."

"He's cool, Alex. Not a jealous bone in his body."

"He *is* cool. Where is he tonight?" It's funny, her talking about her fiancé doesn't bother me. It's enough her just being here.

"Soup kitchen. For the homeless. And injured pussycats."

"Right."

"You're such a twat. He's out with the lads."

"Good man." The road opens up into a dual carriageway. I drop a couple of gears and gun it up the outside lane.

"So, where's your beloved tonight?" Holly asks, raising her voice over the gale that whips across the cabin.

"Sitting right beside me."

She gives me the middle finger. "Elouise."

"Oh yeah, *that* beloved. She's...at a dinner party."

"And no one invited you? *Bless.*"

"Erm, no, I was invited."

"You didn't fancy it?"

"We were sort of...hosting it. It was our dinner party."

"My word, Alex. Wow! You really are quite something, aren't you?"

"Don't. I feel bad about it, believe it or not. I think maybe me and her are...incompatible."

"You reckon?" she says in a tone that suggests we've discussed this a great deal.

"Does this sort of thing happen a lot—her and me?"

"More than it should, wouldn't you say?"

"Why can't we…get along?"

"Well, you don't exactly help yourself."

"You reckon it's my fault?"

"You've literally just walked out on a dinner party. And I bet everything was *just so*."

"Total perfection."

"Oh, Alex, Alex, Alex…"

"She's fucking horrible to me."

"And I've no doubt you drive her nuts, baby."

I grin at her. *"Baby?"*

"Old habits," she says, not meeting my gaze. "Eyes on the road, yeah." She takes my ciggies from the center console and lights one, handing it to me after she's taken a couple of puffs. Even the wet filter in my mouth feels like the best of times.

"What the hell was I doing? Why did I marry her?" I ask.

"She's not so bad."

"She's a total control freak, Holly."

"Well, there is that."

"And a bully," I add. "Surely I could see the signs, before I said *I do*?"

"Yeah, I suspect you could."

"I'm a fool."

"Such a mystery," Holly says, rifling through CDs from the glove box. She feeds REM's *Automatic for the People* into the stereo.

"Go on. I'm missing something here, aren't I?" I say.

"Choosing to live with someone who never thinks you're good enough, who you can't impress even when you can be arsed to try, who holds your entire sense of self in their hands."

"Why don't I just leave her?"

"Yeah, I don't reckon you'll do that."

I stop myself mentioning that I know perfectly well this marriage is destined to end, and to end very soon. Although it may, of course, be Elouise who does the leaving.

"What's it all about, Holly?"

"Come on, Alex. You're an intelligent man." Her hair flails across her face as we top eighty.

"That I am. Did I ever mention I got a place at Cambridge?"

She punches my arm.

"Tell me," I say.

"Elouise is exactly what you're used to, Alex. She's home from home. Someone whose expectations you want to live up to. But even when you do your best, it's not even close to good enough."

"Jesus."

"Ringing any bells?"

I nod. "Why would I marry someone who's like my dad?"

"Dunno, baby. People do these things. Pursuit of validation, I guess. Ask a psychologist."

"I really should."

Holly points left, and I join the slip lane off the main road. "How's the dinner party going, do you reckon?" she asks.

"Bloody hell. Better than if I was still there, I suspect."

"You don't do yourself many favors," Holly says.

We're on a B-road now. Out here the rain has only recently stopped; it is especially dark and smells of fresh earth. Holly turns the stereo up: the piano intro to "Nightswimming" fills the car.

"Is she what I deserve, do you reckon?"

Holly laughs.

"She is, isn't she?"

"I don't think that, Alex." Holly puts her hand on mine where it rests on the gear lever.

I try to lace my fingers into hers but she pulls away. "Let's go somewhere," I say. "I'll take you to your aunt's another time. Literally *any*time. There's gotta be a nice country pub round here."

"Those were the days," she says. "I think we're a bit old for all that."

"Live a little."

"No, Alex. We've gotta stop this, really. *You've* gotta stop it."

"Stop what?"

"I'm not your marriage counselor. And I won't be your crutch. You can't keep calling me up every time you and Elouise have a bust-up."

"I do this too often?"

She nods. "You've gotta work through this stuff yourself. Me and you—we're ancient history."

My eyes settle on her engagement ring. "Not to me we're not."

"There comes a time to be grown-ups. You can't keep escaping your married life, taking a girl for a late-night spin in your Porsche with the roof down."

"It is pretty cool."

"Maybe it's not as cool as you think."

"What happened to us, Holly?"

"You always ask that."

"Because I'd give everything in the world to have you back." I turn and look her in the face, close to tears and unashamed of it. How do I tell her that there are all these things I've done to fuck my future up, but I have no knowledge of doing a single one of them?

"Remember that Christmas Eve?" I ask. "When we said we'd get married. And we looked at rings we couldn't afford?"

"That was a good day."

My yesterday; nearly eleven years ago for her.

"The best," I say, glad that at least this—this bizarre system— still works as I've come to believe it does.

"You're happy, yeah?" I ask.

A slow smile spreads across her face. "I am, Alex. I'm really happy. It's taken a while. Long while. But yeah, I am."

I smile back. It takes me by surprise—it doesn't hurt. I *think* I'm happy for her. Incredible.

"It's not what you want to hear," she says. "I'm sorry."

The first car I've seen in five minutes hammers toward us, lights dazzling me. It passes, purple ghosts of its headlamps etched on my eyes. In its wake, this country road is darker and damper and quieter than ever.

"I will never stop loving you," I tell her. For the first time today, I feel it: the making of a change, if only slight.

"One of these days you will."

"I really won't. Even after you've forgotten all about me."

She tuts. "No one forgets their first love."

I look her in the face. "What an idiot I am."

"Alex," she says. I shake my head, wearing the smile of the defeated.

"Alex!" She's shouting this time and pointing ahead of us. I focus on the road ahead.

A car is pulling out of a side turning. We're doing sixty-five miles per hour. Oblivious to me approaching, it pulls into the middle of the road, its silver flank glowing in my headlamps. We're closing on it fast.

"Alex!" Holly shouts again. "Fucksake!"

I hit the brakes. We're almost on it.

Adrenaline surges as I stamp harder on the pedal. Holly is flung against her belt. I'm not wearing mine; I brace with arms locked against the wheel.

Speed comes off fast—sixty, fifty… Nearly on it now but we might almost stop in time.

"Fucking hell!" Holly screams, jamming herself back in her seat.

Like having a carpet yanked from underneath us. Perhaps something slippery on the road. Maybe I overcorrected the steering. The car slews to the left. Still going fast, sideways now. Black trees race past the windshield. A jolt as we clip the curb. My reactions are off; I steer too much into the skid. The car flings around to the right, so violent my brain can't keep up; vision a blur like a camera panning too fast. My and Holly's heads smack together. Sliding. Sawing at the wheel, back end fishtailing. Left. Right. Left. Right. Still at speed we're aimed at this other car.

There's a gap between it and the bank. Maybe wide enough. I try to correct our trajectory. Reflexes blunted—limbs half a second behind my brain. It's no good. We're going to crash.

Everything slows. Must be barely a second from impact. Yet I can think. How strangely time behaves.

I understand. I've changed nothing. Nothing that matters anyway.

This crash that's about to happen is not an accident. Not in the eyes of the law. Sure, someone's pulled in front of me. But I've been drinking all day; I'm way over the alcohol limit. And I wasn't paying attention.

Holly's arms are over her face. Knees in the air. Petrified. Last few instants of this world.

One last attempt: off the brake and back on. Yank the wheel right.

Something miraculous happens. Tires bite just enough. We chink to the side. Instead of T-boning the car in our path, we scythe past it, skim the bank instead. The rear of our car bucks into the air before crashing back down again. We spin around, bounce one side of the road to the other. Sound of buckling metal as we ricochet between curbs. Our momentum, which had threatened to slam us into another car, is dissipated instead.

We're at hardly more than walking pace. Out of danger.

"What the fuck?" I mumble. "What the actual fuck!"

Holly stares dead ahead, a trickle of blood on her forehead from where we came together. "You're an idiot," she's saying, voice shaking. "Fucking idiot."

How did I beat this? Did my last-minute realization buy me enough time to save us? Or was it plain luck?

We're stranded across the middle of the road at the mouth of a sharp bend. Engine running, REM still blasting, though this Porsche is clearly going nowhere fast.

I look to my left, watch as the car we've just avoided drives off obliviously in the direction we've come from.

"Jesus Christ," I say, shaking my head. I start laughing—I can't help it.

"Fuck!" Holly shouts. "No!" Pure panic.

Yellow light blooms on the trees around us.

I spin around. Brighter and brighter. A pair of racing head-lights explodes out of the blind curve. Bearing down on us. Eyes of a monster.

We are blocking the road. Nowhere for the van to go. No time for it to brake.

Three tons of steel. Fifty miles per hour. Aimed at Holly's side of this already damaged car.

The force is staggering. Vision turned to red. A bang so loud my eardrums tear. Our car blasted down the road as if fired from a cannon. I'm tossed onto Holly, no seat belt keeping me in place. Her small body cushions mine. Bones crack like firewood.

We are still at last. Ears howling. Cubes of glass falling silently to the ground. Thirty meters away, the van lies on its side, steam rising in the glare of one headlamp.

I am sprawled over the passenger seat. Holly's legs are against the crushed-in door, seat belt still bound around her waist. She is bent over the window ledge, head and shoulders hanging outside of the car.

An attempt to free myself. I can't, foot jammed in the twisted footwell. I want to see her, to hold her head in my hands.

Sirens. Blue light everywhere. Green jumpsuits with hi-vis cuffs. Oxygen mask. Jaws slicing steel.

Back of an ambulance, doors open.

A police officer. A plastic tube thrust near my mouth. "Blow into this, please."

Glance toward that stretcher in the road. Little activity. Face covered.

I'm so sorry.

I'm so *envious*.

Something for the pain. Fading out.

Please.

Please let me go with her.

MARCH 1, 2017 | AGE 41

Bitter End

Sky gray. A freezing wind rushes toward the river, polishing the white salt that's dried into the concourse. Not the faintest hint of spring.

Another hit of cheap cider that smells like a cleaning product. Two liters down. What is it, lunchtime? I've never felt more remote from these people who mill around with warm coats and takeout salads and reasons to exist; a different species, really.

There's another glance fired in my direction, a look that doesn't linger but asks, *What has the world come to?* Maybe it's me they're so disapproving of. Maybe it's this memorial I'm slumping against as I drink. It is, once again, vandalized. Not just spray paint today; those soaring silver doves have been twisted and bent double on their slim stalks, nose-diving, beaks smashing down into the granite plinth.

I shouldn't be sitting here—disrespectful, I know. But I'm

barely feet from where Holly and I sat that Christmas Eve, just two days ago. It feels as distant as the two decades that have officially passed. Besides, this place seems appropriate: a shrine to the wasting of human life.

Not even my fire-and-brimstone preacher friend has persuaded me to move. He breaks occasionally from his mike, looks over with sorrow in his eyes. When I gaze clean through him, he seems to understand. He knows a lost cause when he sees one, knows when the devil's got there first.

I woke in my car this morning. Frozen. Trousers soaked from yet another of my *little accidents*. My only pair, I'm still wearing them now. Guitar case present and correct, but no music in my soul; instead I begged with eyes to the ground till I could get my hands on these couple of bottles, plus a Coke can to use as a decoy.

The Thames is inviting. I've fantasized all day about loading my stinking clothes with rocks. Let the water do the job it so nearly did when Blake Benfield sent me in. But things like that take strength.

Easy way out, isn't that what people say? Bullshit.

It's one final act of taking back control, in a life that's left you with no control over anything else.

Everything I've ever done has been an attempt to be in control. And I've lost. Even that one last option, of choosing my own exit, I am too weak for right now.

I take a hit of booze, and another after that. It won't bring the courage I need.

OCTOBER 23, 2008 | AGE 33

We'll Live and Die in These Towns

Whoever it is ringing the doorbell won't take the hint. I roll over in bed and drop my knees onto the floor. I've been lying awake for an hour, staring at the ceiling of this small room I've never seen before. I had no plans to get up.

"All right, all right!" I shout, unhooking a toweling dressing gown from the door. It's new and pleasantly scratchy. The living room of this flat is even smaller than the bedroom, barely big enough for the two-seater sofa. The outline of someone short and wide is visible through the frosted front door that leads straight into this room.

"Thank God for that," the lady says, wiping a theatrical palm across her forehead as I answer on her twentieth press of the bell. Broad smile, red cheeks: the look of the cheerfully overworked. "Leave me waiting much longer and I'd have to mark you as missing." She raises the lanyard round her neck. "Bernadette Delaney. With the Probation Service. Alex Dean, yes?"

I nod. "Do you…need to come in?"

"Better than doing it on the doorstep, don't you think, dar-ling?" She sidles past me, huffing as she dumps a rucksack on the small square of floor. "Went to the caff on the way up." She produces two Styrofoam cups. "Tea or coffee? I'm easy, I'll have what you don't."

"That's really kind," I say. This is a rare morning when I don't have a hangover. My mouth is moist and doesn't taste like shit. "Tea. Lovely. Thank you."

"How you settling back into the swing of things?" she asks, pulling forms from a plastic sleeve.

I try to keep a gap between us as I wedge myself into the other side of the sofa. "Yeah. All good." Surely that's the right answer.

"Great. So in the week since your release on license, what have you been up to?" She scribbles to revive her Biro.

"Oh…this and that," I tell her. I notice the gray band around my ankle, like an eighties Casio watch. An electronic tag, I imagine.

"Nice place you've landed yourself," she says, looking at the tiny kitchen and the grass area outside the window. "Trust me, I see some absolute tips doing this job."

"I can well imagine." I think of that bedsit over a shop out east that I've woken up in three times; the black mold, the com-munal kitchen with padlocked cupboards, the landlord and his minder demanding rent. I always thought that was where I ended up immediately after my release from prison. This flat is a palace by comparison.

"Have you made any progress with looking for a job?" Ber-nadette asks.

"Yeah. I'm not really… I've been sort of…keeping an eye out, you know? Been looking in the paper," I add, almost shouting the point as it pops to mind.

"Relax, darling. There's no right or wrong answers here. We're not going to send you back to prison for not having a job inside a week of release. I'm not here to hassle you. I'm here to support you as you get back to a new sort of normality."

"No, sure." I take a slurp of scalding tea and smile at her. "Thank you."

"I do appreciate that your life has changed dramatically since you offended." She thumbs through a ring binder.

"How do you mean?"

"Well, I understand you and your wife divorced whilst you were serving your sentence."

"Right! Yes, of course. I thought you meant *bad* dramatic changes."

Bernadette laughs. "Yes. Been there, got the T-shirt!" She makes a show of studying her own naked ring finger. "And there's of course the matter of losing your job."

"Sort of came with the wife."

She appears unsure if I'm joking or not. "What sort of employment do you envisage yourself looking for?"

I shrug, at a loss.

"What—if any—qualifications do you have?"

I'm silent; I don't mention my four As at A-level. Nor do I tell her about Cambridge. Does it count for anything if you don't actually go?

"Any particular fields of expertise? Experience?"

My guitar case is wedged between the kitchen and bathroom doors. In here it looks as big as a cello. "I'm a bit of a musician."

"Hmm." Her manner suggests she's not unused to her ex-cons imagining they'd have been the fifth Beatle if only they'd been dealt a better hand.

"I busk a bit," I tell her.

"Maybe we should be looking for something with a little... security?"

"I was in the pub management game, a while back." I'm unable to attach any enthusiasm to the statement.

"Unlikely to be compatible with the terms of your curfew." She smiles warmly. "That's useful info, though. Lots of transferable skills. Let's work on that." She begins filling out a form. "What is it, the twenty-third?" she mumbles.

I watch as she dates the paper: *23-10-2008*. "Is that…right?" I ask.

She double-checks her phone. "Yup. Where *is* this year going?"

I look at her glowing screen, confirm it for myself. This doesn't make sense. How can it be 2008?

When Mum visited me in prison it was October 28 of this year. Five days from now. Am I going to do something that lands me back inside? Surely Mum would've said something, if I'd already been released and sent back.

Has something changed? Something updated?

"Are you okay, my darling?" Bernadette asks.

"Seems…it seems a short sentence. For…"

"Death by dangerous driving?" she says.

"Yeah. Only, what, a year?"

"What was the sentence?" she says, more to herself than me as she flicks through a file. "Thirty months. You were released on license after twelve. Not unusual. Taking into account your guilty plea, that you cooperated totally with the police investigation, that you've shown remorse. Nothing but glowing reports from the staff at Lydd."

"Lydd?" But Mum visited at HMP Meadway.

"You started a rather well-subscribed book club there, I see."

"This *Lydd*—is that the same as Meadway?"

Bernadette looks at me like I'm mad. "No, darling. They're about a hundred miles apart. And Meadway's a Category B—tight security. Not an open prison like Lydd."

A year in an open prison. And now this flat, instead of that squalid bedsit I was released to after a much longer sentence.

Bernadette is waffling something about the Job Center and the allowances I can claim.

"Guilty plea," I mumble.

"Sorry?"

"I pleaded guilty?"

Again, the funny look from her. She double-checks my file. "Absolutely."

I think back to Mum visiting me in prison. She talked about a trial, how she'd given me the benefit of the doubt when I'd protested my innocence. "Let's say I had decided to plead not guilty back then," I ask. "I'd have got a longer sentence, yeah?"

"Assuming the court *found* you guilty, yes. They'd likely have been a good deal harder on you. There's no need to rake over it now."

I wave the point away as if it's nothing. But that must be it: the first time round, I fought the case. And it seems I got a longer sentence for my efforts, in a much tougher jail.

Bernadette checks I have money for food and that I'm taking care of myself. She runs me through the services I can call on if I'm struggling. "Anything else I can help with before I go, darling?" she asks, breathlessly packing her files away.

"I'm cool," I tell her, my mind too occupied to pay her much attention. "Actually!" I snap as she reaches the front door. "Are you…driving?"

She nods. "Parked around the corner."

"I almost forgot to say. I've got an interview today. For a job. I mean, it's probably pointless, but…"

She eyes me with a hint of suspicion. "You'd like a lift."

"Only if it's not…"

"Where do you need to be?"

"You know Beekenside Secondary? I know a teacher there. He's put in a word for me."

"What's the job?" she asks.

"Just…maintenance."

"Excellent. But you can hardly go dressed like that."

"Give me one minute max," I reply, dashing into the bedroom.

With Every Heartbeat

Dr. Defrates wears a smile that's a touch inappropriate given that I'm telling him about the death of the woman I love. He faces across the playground as I regale him with the details of these past few days.

A game of twenty-a-side football takes place on the asphalt around us. "The joys of lunch duty," Defrates had said when, ten minutes ago, a young chaperone provided by reception brought me to him. We are surrounded on all sides by the dull concrete school building. A chip-fat waft idles by from the canteen extractors. In the corners are those kids disinterested in the game—the small groups and the loners. Kindred spirits: those who'd never give away free time to sport.

"Careful!" Defrates shouts as a ball narrowly misses us and slams into the wire fence behind. "You were saying...?" He resumes his grinning into space, hands back in pockets, spreading his cord trousers wide like poles in a marquee. His posture is as ever: excessively leaned back, bulging tummy exaggerated.

"Do you mind me coming?" I ask him. "Sorry. There's nobody else I can talk to about any of...this."

"Don't be silly. I'm delighted you've sought me out." And he actually sounds delighted, just like last time.

Who the hell is this guy? I might get to the bottom of it, if only I didn't have a thousand more pressing questions for him.

"Carry on," he says. "Please."

I bring him up to date: Holly, the accident, how originally I was in prison for much longer but now I'm free early. "What do you think changed?" I ask him. "Why is my life running differently? Why has it updated?"

"Updated," Dr. Defrates says. "Very good turn of phrase. Like it!" I'd managed to forget how cryptic this bloke insists on being.

"I don't know what I did to make the change."

"Does it matter?" Defrates asks.

"I want to understand. I *need* to."

"Up! Up! Up!" he shouts at a heap of kids, before a bundling has the chance to catch on. "I imagine," he says, attention back with me, "you will have assumed a different attitude to something or other. Taken a new approach."

"So what of that day when my mum visited me in prison? It's supposed to happen in a few days' time. But I'm not there. I lived that day."

"It has—to use your term—*updated.*"

"So it's gone? And what about those days when I woke up in that horrible bedsit? Are they gone too?"

"Nothing's *gone.* Modified, perhaps. Adjusted to allow for changes you've made. Introduce a cause..."

I nod. "Get an effect."

"Quite. Have we talked about how nothing is real until it is observed?"

"Yeah."

"I can stand here and tell you exactly where that football is at any given moment. But if I turn my back, does it mean the ball can't move somewhere else?"

"I get it."

"My last sight of the ball is only that—its position when I was observing it. Whilst I'm not looking, it can roll away, explode, turn into a golden eagle. The fact that I was previously observing the ball is relevant only to me—it makes no odds to the ball itself."

I smile. "This is like the great mystery of agency, isn't it?"

"Oh, yes, agency! That slippery little customer!"

"All of time already exists, and yet we have free will. We can change things."

"You've been listening. Jolly good!"

"So why," I ask him, "do you reckon my prison sentence changed? Updated? Why did I plead not guilty when originally I pleaded guilty? I don't get it."

"A shift in attitude, I'd wager."

"How so?"

"Tell me how you felt. After the accident?"

"What sort of question is that? I felt like I wanted to die. I couldn't bear it."

"So you felt...*guilty*?" His eyes glow with the word.

"Obviously."

"Like it was all your fault? Like you'd make amends if only you could?" He moistens his smile with the tip of his tongue.

"Exactly that. But times it by a million."

"Well, it seems to me that a man who felt like that would probably do all he could to atone for his sins. Would you not agree?"

"Sure. But—"

"I'm hypothesizing, of course," he says. "But let's say that this time around, in the aftermath of this tragic accident, you are full of remorse, where originally your response had been anger, an insistence on placing blame on other people involved in the collision. And this new attitude of contrition colors your every interaction with the police, the courts, et cetera."

"Interesting. You think that's it?"

"It takes a certain maturity, it takes *strength*, Alex, to own up to one's mistakes. To surrender control."

There's a shout of "Sir! Sir!" from twenty meters away. A football is rocketing toward us at chest height. Dr. Defrates raises his right leg behind him. At the last instant he turns on his left heel. His stained suede Hush Puppy meets the incoming ball, which leaves his toe in a curling arc. It's a piece of one-touch play worthy of a pro. At the far end of the playground the goalie is as surprised as I am, the net bulging hard behind him within a half second of the ball leaving Defrates's foot. An almighty cheer goes up from both teams, scores of kids running past and high-fiving this thoroughly unathletic-looking man.

"I think you will have made a series of better choices," he says, unmoved.

"Erm, that was quite a goal, mate."

He nods as if he's already forgotten about it. "You understand me?" he asks.

I smile at a bunch of nearby kids who laugh as they reenact Defrates's star turn. "I guess so." The last time I met this guy, I'd recently learned of Holly's death. I was racing to clear my name, to have someone to blame. Desperate to be *in control*. Was it that sort of attitude that landed me a long jail sentence? Can a change in perspective have such profound effects?

"There's something you need to understand," he says. "You're asking me what it is that you've done to make this change. What were you expecting the answer to be, I wonder? That you'd done something minutely different? Walked a different way, crossed someone's path, triggered a change in time's trajectory from an inconsequential act?"

"Maybe. I don't know."

"You've seen too many movies, young man." Trademark patronizing grin. "Time doesn't hinge on the small details. Change is not effected by a misplaced foot here, a flap of a bird's wing there."

"I guess."

"You're heard of the butterfly effect?"

"Sure. The theory that a tiny movement of a butterfly's wing in the past can have a massive effect on future events."

"Precisely. And I believe that theory to be utter cobblers."

"Okay."

"Change, Alex, comes about from a commitment to making a difference. To deviating from the path of history."

"Walking into the headwind."

"Exactly!"

The playground deflates as the bell sounds for the end of lunch. I nod at Defrates. "Life doesn't hang on the small stuff."

"Indeed. And this life you are leading—it has the potential to update further. Make a change for the better, you see the difference. Just as you have with this early release from prison. Make more good changes, you might reap more benefit. Commit to making real difference, those changes may begin to add up."

"To a life better lived?"

"You can but hope." He traps an errant football beneath his foot as the kids file past us. "It's perhaps not as much effort as it sounds."

"Constantly pushing against the weight of history? It sounds like effort."

"Good decisions lead to good decisions, just as bad decisions beget more bad decisions. Worth bearing in mind."

I can only hope he's right. Because I may have made this one small improvement, but I've achieved little else. Still, on the day I experienced immediately after the crash, I was living in my car, skint, boozing, fucked. My shortened prison sentence, my more comfortable flat—they are something. If a change in at-titude yields a result—a real, tangible result...

"What the fuck is this all about?"

Defrates gives me the same admonishing look he no doubt reserves for students' bad language. "It'll come to make sense, I dare say." He turns on his heel, begins a slow walk toward the building.

"Will you just tell me everything you know?"

He wears a look of hurt. "I am helping you at every step of the way. I don't have all the answers."

"You've got a lot of them."

"And that is why you came to find me today."

"It was you who came looking for me the first time. Eclipse day '99—remember?"

"Aren't you glad I did?"

"Who are you, Dr. Defrates? Who are you, really? Things don't...add up with you. You know too much about me, about what's happening."

He raises a palm. "One thing at a time," he whispers. "Please."

My pulse is quickening, but I stop myself being any firmer with him. He's right: I came here because I need him. Without him, who do I have? I don't know who this bloke is and what he's withholding, but I believe every word he has told me.

"Look, I totally appreciate your help," I say, in sight of the gates now. "But I want my life back."

"This *is* your life, Alex," he replies.

"You know what I mean."

He sways his head side to side, like it's me who doesn't un-derstand.

"I want to go back. To before all this...shit started."

"You show me any man, Alex, and I'll show you someone who wants to go back to when they were twenty and falling in love."

"Okay." I'm tiring of the discussion.

"Perhaps you're luckier than you realize," he tells me.

"Lucky? Yeah, all right. How do you figure that?"

"Oh, we'll see," he says, patting me amiably on the back at the gate. "So long, old friend."

Back on London's streets, I can't possibly be far from a pub. I've a thirst-on for sure. But it feels like habit today, not a raging need that's capable of dragging me against my better judgment. And I've no hangover to feed; a year inside has at least served to keep me away from the sauce. There's twenty quid in my wallet, from where I don't know. But I have no clue where more will come from once that's gone.

I pick up my pace, almost jogging. I reckon I'm half an hour from my new flat at this pace. I'll grab my guitar. On a day like this, I might make forty quid, and still make it back indoors for my curfew.

Good decisions, after all, lead to good decisions.

SEPTEMBER 6, 2013 | AGE 38

Hey Brother

Friday evening, crowds drinking outside bars on the sunny side of the street. The clink and burble, the air easy with blue cigarette smoke and forgotten stresses. My forehead is warm where I've caught the sun. I walk with the pleasant exhaustion of someone who's given themselves fully to their work. My guitar case is heavy with over a hundred quid in coins and fivers.

I can scarcely remember enjoying playing as much as I have today. With a steady audience generous with their hard-earned, I was vibing like the performer I once was. So what that my repertoire includes nothing from the past eighteen years? Fleetwood Mac and the Smiths and Nirvana felt as fresh today as the Thames that glittered alongside me. It was a four-hour stint that kept my mind away from my crime and what is lost, even if playing Buddy Holly was out of the question.

Home, I order myself. Never mind stopping for *just the one*.

I pick up my pace. People talk about the devil on their shoulder, but my demon lives right in the middle of me. Give him an inch and he'll take a mile. But I'm showing enough resolve for him to shut up. Not that he's beaten, merely clever enough to save his energy for when I'm weaker.

Home is the same small flat as yesterday, albeit more cluttered; it's been five years since my release, and finding myself in the place gives something close to comfort, something like hope. An hour's walk from here; I wonder if I can be the sort of man who gets in and cooks himself dinner, watches a chat show.

I turn a corner, a street where it's mostly shops and not hostelries, no longer listening to other people enjoying themselves. Outside a Marks & Spencer, two store detectives wrestle with a shoplifter, pinning him against plate glass. I'm drawing level on the far side of the street when I recognize their prey.

"Jazz! Mate!" I shout, weaving across the road with my amp trolley rattling behind me. "What the hell's going on?"

The burly man holding him loosens his grip, suddenly giving consideration to what is *reasonable force*.

"I done fuck all," Jazz says, trying to prize an arm away from his chest.

The other guard rifles through Jazz's sports bag, producing a couple of family-sized shepherd's pies, a fistful of tikka wraps, biscuits, a four-pack of beers.

"I paid, you dick. Go ask, yeah?"

"In a bit of a hurry for someone with nothing to hide," the guard says.

Jazz kisses his teeth. The duty manager joins us on the pavement and bags up the goods. "Police have been called," she says.

Jazz glares at me with wide eyes. *It's okay*, I mouth. I'm struggling to believe how much he's changed. His features are recognizable enough: same razor-sharp sideburns framing his round face. A little over a year has passed since the day I ate dinner with him and his poorly granddad, when he was studying for the last of his GCSEs. He's seventeen now. Sure he's filled out a little, grown into those gangly limbs, but that's not why he seems like a different person. It radiates from him: he's angry, life-hardened. Those eyes that had sparked with energy are a door into the dark now.

"Keep your shit, then," Jazz says, huffing through his nose. "Just put it all back. I don't care. Go on, get your dirty hands off me."

"Don't work like that, kiddo," the guard who unpacked his bag says. He moves close behind his colleague.

"How much?" I ask. "For these bits?"

"Don't get involved," the guard tells me.

"How much?" I repeat, louder this time.

"You get on with your own evening, sir. If you *do* want to buy something…" He gestures toward the open doors where shoppers pretend they aren't watching this unfold.

Jazz stares at me. For a moment, the defiance and the bluster is gone, replaced by the fear that I've seen too many times. Panic, almost. No longer resisting the efforts to restrain him, his hand falls to his side. His fingers fumble around his waistband. The guard glances downward, and Jazz freezes.

"If I pay," I snap, grabbing hold of the guard's arm, "no crime has been committed. Everyone can go back to their evening. Hardly a police matter, is it?"

I'm ignored, my hand firmly removed. But Jazz has seized the brief distraction, hand slipped behind his belt. Metal glints for an instant. My and his eyes meet. I understand why he's going for that knife.

I barge between the two guards. "I'm paying!" I shout. "Come on, take my money! What's wrong with my money?" The restraining I receive is ham-fisted, no more than a few slaps to the arm whilst they focus on not letting Jazz loose in the scrum.

"Sir, please!" one shouts.

I raise a hand. Hold the other low and lean into Jazz. A strip of warm steel is palmed to me. "All right, all right," I say, stepping clear. "Keep your tits on." I give Jazz a stealthy nod, knowing he had no intention of attacking when he reached for the knife, just needed it off his person before a search.

Bursts of distant siren fill the London air as they always do, but forty minutes pass before an acceptance settles over these two guards and their manager that the police have better things to do. I try not to look smug when eventually they accept my offer. I take Jazz's bounty to the checkout, grabbing us a couple of Cornetto ice creams while I'm there.

"Nowhere to do your shopping nearer home?" I say as we walk together in the direction of the Sefton Hills estate.

Jazz smirks. "I like Marks & Spencer, old cuz. Going up in the world."

"Aspirational. I like it!" Time was when he came down to the river because he was too afraid to be seen on the estate. This new demeanor of his suggests that's no longer the problem.

"Been caught a few too many times up my way, man," he says. "Too many eyes on me." He moves closer to my side. He's got to be six-two now; next to him I feel small. "Thank you. For back there. I owe you, man."

"It's really nothing," I say, unsure if he means for paying or for pocketing the knife. There's shame in his expression, and I know better than to give lectures—what right do I have, anyway? "You can carry this, though." I pass him my guitar, leaving me a hand free for my ice cream.

"Where you headed?" he asks.

"Homeward bound." He looks on incredulously as I break briefly into song. "Near your neck of the woods," I add. In truth, my flat is a good mile from Sefton Hills. "You back at school, yeah?" I ask, breezily as I can. I brace, surprised at how fearful I am of the wrong answer.

"Term started this week."

"Cool. What, upper-sixth now?"

Jazz nods.

"Glad to hear it. You doing okay?"

"I'm still there, innit. Just about."

"That bad?" This is the guy who, by his own admission, was doing too well at school. "You gotta hang in there, man."

"Yeah, yeah. I'm back after summer, aren't I? One more strike and I'm out, they reckon." He grins at me.

"What you been getting up to?"

"Nothing interesting. Missing lessons, no homework, couple of rows…"

"How were those GCSE results of yours?" I ask.

"Old cuz, we've chatted about this a hundred times."

"You know me, mate."

Jazz laughs. "That memory of yours, man! Killed off too many brain cells." He reaches into his shopping and retrieves the four-pack of Stellas. "Want one?"

"More than you can imagine." My devil stirs. The aliveness that exists in the narrow window after the promise of a drink and before the consumption. "But I'm good. Laying off it."

"Shit, man," Jazz says. "Well played."

"You did okay? In your exams?"

"Six As, cuz. A-star in history. Did a bit shit in English."

"Wow. You beaut!"

"You always say that."

"I'm proud of you, mate. You can't imagine how proud."

"Shut up, man."

"Look, I know I'm a total nobody. I'm the bloke who plays guitar and sings out of tune for a quid here and there."

"You ain't never out of tune."

"Whatever. I'm a skint, ex-con, boozing, divorced, no-hope busker with some pretty profound memory issues. But, believe me, I know potential when I see it. Don't wank your life away like I did, Jazz. Please. You're far too…good for that."

"Yeah, you're always saying shit like that too."

"I'm wiser than I look."

By the warm light of a September evening, even Sefton Hills manages to look attractive, unmown communal spaces richly green and bolting with meadow flowers. In the shadow of a long block of flats, a group of teens are gathered around a bench. Jazz walks a step ahead of me. He slows. A guy of the same age locks eyes with him. The rest of the group—two girls, two guys— look on in silence. I hang back as Jazz walks a slow arc past the bench. The guy he's in a staring contest with jerks forward on his seat. "Look at you, man," the guy says. "Dirty cunt."

Jazz kisses his teeth. "Fucking pussy," he mutters. We're ten meters past them before Jazz breaks his stare and resumes a nor- mal walking pace. Even then he keeps shooting looks back, ex- aggerated aggression drawn on his face.

"I have something of yours," I say as we turn a corner and leave them behind. "You know, this ain't the best idea." I'm try- ing to sound younger and cooler than I am.

He takes the knife out of my hand down at my side. "Don't stress yourself, old cuz." There's insolence in his tone which I've no business reacting to.

This is the guy who would come to the river and watch me play, rather than risk running into the kids on this estate; who would act dim at school to lie low from the bullies; who picked giant daisies, raided the food bins to feed the pigeons. I can scarcely believe what fifteen months has done to him.

A realization strikes me: that the worst our enemies can do is turn us into them. That, surely, is the greatest victory they can ever score.

"Your granddad," I say, the dull red front door of Jazz's flat in sight. "He's...?"

"Home now," Jazz says. "They kept him for a few days. Docs reckon he's okay now."

It neatly answers my curiosity as to whether he's still *with us.* "And is he? Okay, I mean?"

"Fell over, didn't he. Out by the main road. Cracked his head open. Fifteen stitches. Bad concussion."

"Because of the...dementia?"

"I'm an idiot. Wasn't looking out for him. He went off wan- dering."

"Hardly your fault, mate."

He puts his key in the door. "Have to keep him locked in. Feel like a jailer, man."

The last time I followed Jazz into this flat, I was immediately met with the sight of an old man collapsed in the corridor and the stench of shit. I leave my shoes at the door, set foot on the pristine carpet. The curtains are drawn, the flat in cool twilight. It smells only of tumble-dried linen, as sparsely filled as it was before. His granddad is in an armchair in front of the telly, snoring loudly. He slumps with his arms and chin tucked to his chest like a sleeping child. There's a dressing taped to the left side of his head. At his feet is a dinner plate and a bowl, polished clean.

"You're getting help, right?" I say, watching as Jazz unloads the shopping into a near-empty fridge. There's a baffling array of medications on the worktop.

"I don't need help," he snaps.

"Jazz, he's unwell. There are people who can... I mean, there must be..." It's clear he can tell I've got no idea what I'm talking about.

"It's cool. Man of the house, innit. All good."

"You hungry?" I ask.

"Nah, man. I ate at school."

"You could eat again? I could get us something in—your granddad too? I've done okay today..."

"Gonna let him sleep. You done enough, man. I got this."

"Sure you have."

"Do *you* want something to eat? I can heat something up," he says.

"You're doing a blinding job, you know that?"

Jazz shrugs. He whispers something in Arabic to his granddad, covers him with a blanket and kisses him on the forehead. Grabbing a sweater, he leads me back outside.

"Gonna catch up with a few mates," he tells me.

"Cool. What's the crack?"

He gives me a look, like I'm deranged.

"What you...got planned?"

"Old cuz, not sure they're really your scene, you know?"

"Mate, I'm not about to impose. Got a home to go to, believe it or not. Just good to hear you're..."

"Not Billy No-Mates?"

"No. I mean...well, yeah. That."

"Man, am I that tragic? Just some guys from school."

"And they're a...*sound* bunch?"

Jazz chuckles. "You're worried I've fallen in with a bad crowd?" He says it in the voice of an old git, and it's a fair point.

"Cool. Sorry." I think of my own teens, about that social reshuffle when I started sixth form. Like Jazz, I'd been a loner till then.

"Friday night, innit," Jazz says. "Have a smoke, maybe. Chill the fuck out."

"Amen to that." I walk with him as far as the abandoned block where he and I watched London burn two years ago. "If there's anything I can do," I say as he shoves demolition fencing aside at the foot of the staircase.

"Bruv, I'm gonna pay you back, yeah? Every penny you spent out today. Interest too."

"You don't need—"

"I'll do it. I swear. I've got a job. Soon as I get paid..."

I shake my head. "Jazz, please—"

"Just give me a few days, yeah?"

I nod, recognize the futility of argument. "Sure. Take as long as you need. Have a good night."

Jazz smiles. "Sorry. I'm keeping you out of the pub, aren't I?"

It's fast getting dark. I'm still a mile from home. I no longer have an evening to kill. "You really are."

He pounds up the metal stairs. I wave to him as he disappears onto the rooftop—the only friend I have in this world.

AUGUST 20, 2019 | AGE 43

Before You Go

My dad and my brother sit opposite me. The limo slows from its already sedentary pace, and we pass through iron gates onto the long driveway. Lawns to either side are garishly green on this glorious summer day. Air-conditioning runs full blast; it's so synthetically cool in here it makes the world beyond the windows seem hazily unreal, like looking up at the sun from just beneath the surface of the sea.

I recognize a few old faces as we draw near the chapel and begin a bizarre ballet with the hearse in front, driving in circles round the courtyard. There are three people in fire service finery, the neighbors, relatives from Dad's side. Heads are bowed, sad glances fired our way; they seem sheepish, like everyone was having a good laugh among themselves till we loomed into view.

Dad looks around, makes grunting noises as he acknowledges who's here. Ross moves closer and lays a big hand on his shoulder.

"Tie," Dad says to me.

"What about it, Dad?" I ask, tugging at my collar. My ill-fitting black suit has a strong smell of steam cleaning and mustiness—unmistakably a charity shop purchase.

"Looks scruffy," Dad says. "Wants to be a half Windsor. Or a full, if you like." He prods a thumb against his own tie. "Nice and symmetrical, like mine."

"Let's not worry about it now," I say. It feels like a parole board meeting, the two of them opposite me like this.

"Sort it out," Dad says flatly. The crunch of gravel beneath tires falls quiet as we come to a halt.

I yank the knot undone, inexpensive material scrunched and worn thin. Why has he picked on this detail of my attire? My trouser seams are screaming under the pressure of swollen thighs. The bulk at my ankles has left me with no choice but to leave my shoes unlaced. Despite the effort I have made in recent days, the fact clearly remains: I still *drink*. My brown fingers shake as I try to remember an alternative to the school knot.

"Let me," Ross says. There's a strong flavor of Aussie to his accent from the decade he's spent down under. He loops it round his own neck, passing it back to me in seconds ready for tightening. He doesn't appear to be dressed for a funeral: open-neck shirt, gray herringbone jacket with funky lining, flamboyantly fluffed black pocket square, trousers tight enough to reveal his lack of socks. His haircut—high and tight—belongs to someone twenty years younger.

We are a minute or two early. Mourners shuffle around from the rear of the building and gaze at floral tributes on the lawn. I have the sense of being in a queue. 12:15, 1:00, 1:45—a never-ending procession of parties that leave one body lighter than they arrived, move on to the pub to begin the forgetting.

The order of service is on the seat beside me. It's not easy—seeing the words and the dates. Here and there, I can think to myself, *This is Mum's funeral*, and it is just a simple, digestible fact. But then the statement comes alive. This is it. She's gone. How much of me went with her?

I stroke the glossy paper with my thumb.

Don't cry. Fucking hell, don't cry.

I've come so close so many times today.

Barbara Katherine Dean 1st March 1953–30th July 2019. The power of it dissolves in time; it is just a cold statement again.

The picture chosen for the front is all wrong. It's Mum with Dad, taken back when Ross and I were young. She is, already, fading. They should've used that photo from the mantelpiece at home: black-and-white, late teens, Karen Carpenter hair, everything still an option; when you've made no choices, none of them have had the chance to be wrong. She sparkles with life in that picture. When my time's up, I'll be wanting a picture of that afternoon on the Thames in '95 to be remembered by. Before the lengthy business of dying began. When I was all cause, no effect.

I browse through the running order. It seems unlikely that I'm expected to say anything, but after being caught out at my wedding, it feels prudent to check. The music is, unsurprisingly, dominated by the Carpenters.

"I'm not…playing anything, am I?"

"Let's not go through that again," Dad says.

"Look, I'm not asking to play. Just wondering if…you know…"

He rolls his eyes. "It's not all about you, Alex," he mumbles. "Just today."

I watch as our mourners file inside. There's a group of lads I recognize as Ross's mates from his school days. There are a couple of colleagues of Dad's. People who knew Mum only a little but have turned out to support their friend. No one, as far as I can see, is here for me. No sign of Loz or the others from sixth form. Why am I longing to see Jazz's friendly face? He'd be twenty-three.

An undertaker opens the car door. The humid air we step

into feels foreign. Flowers are moved from the coffin in the vehicle in front.

"At least she's no longer suffering," Ross says, giving me a lopsided smile.

"So you keep saying," I reply.

Those were his first words to me this morning. I woke— backache, pins and needles in both legs—on the sofa of the family home. The front room in which, as far as I know, Mum must have died. The hospital bed that had looked so big in there, so harrowing, gone. A collection of equipment remained huddled in the corner ready for return: drip stands and oxygen cylinders, et cetera. A bulky plastic toilet seat unnecessarily haunted the bathroom; I slung it in the wheelie bin. Ross was asleep in his childhood room, mine still piled to the ceiling with junk. He came alone, four kids and a heavily pregnant wife left behind in Adelaide. I should probably be grateful; if he'd turned up with his brood, I don't imagine there'd have been room for me as well. God alone knows where I call home right now.

Dad was in his suit and Brylcreemed to perfection by half past eight, a clear four hours early. He meandered about the house, picking up ornaments and things off the kitchen worktop and considering them as if they were new to him, inspecting and dusting and rearranging them slightly. I have mostly only seen his back today.

I do want to buy in to the idea my brother keeps airing—of this being relief. *For the best.* But the house, as imperfect as its history is, had a certain energy that has gone. A stillness has descended that I can't imagine will pass when the grieving is done. Maybe the reason I can't see this as a blessing is because my bizarre predicament means I've not experienced so much of her suffering. But then, nor has Ross, given that he's only been in the country two days, and he won't shut up about what a fine development this is.

We're standing at the rear of the hearse when I catch sight

of a latecomer dashing toward the chapel. He turns to look at me as he reaches the doors. *Sorry, sorry*, he mouths, shaking his head and tapping an imaginary watch. I raise a hand to him—it's fine. Although I have no clue what on earth Dr. Paul Defrates is doing here. *You okay?* he mouths.

I give him a thumbs-up, willing him to move inside before Dad or Ross asks who he is.

Am I okay? He's the first person to care. His concern makes me suddenly sadder; heat in my eyes.

No. Don't cry.

His ample frame disappears through the arched doorway, trousers so baggy they've frayed at his heels. He is the only person capable of looking worse in a suit than me.

"Tallest two at the back," the undertaker tells us as the coffin glides rearward on small rollers. Ross and our longtime neighbor Adrian—both six foot three—crouch beneath it.

"Now, walk slowly and in time with each other," the undertaker goes on, guiding Dad and me into position at the front. My hands shake as I link arms with him.

We rise to standing, and for a moment we are not level. I am bearing at least half of the weight alone, daylight over Dad's and Ross's shoulders. Yet this box is so light. It feels empty. Is she even in there? Has that wretched illness taken that much of her, hollowed her out?

"Sorry," I snap, folding at the knees.

The other three lower their corners, and the undertaker guides the coffin back down. "Take a moment," he tells me.

"Sorry. I wasn't...ready. Not quite." It's the truth. I am hopelessly unready for this. I'm a man of forty-three, apparently. At what point is someone ready for this?

"Let's just get this nailed," Ross says. Again the lopsided smile, his philosophical face. He pats a palm on the polished timber. "One last journey, Mum."

Maybe it's okay for him. Even if it was mostly from a distance, he had time with her—years of phone calls and birthdays and Christmases. Since '95 I've only had a few days. And there is a circle of life for Ross: he has a family of his own, a new baby due any moment. His world gives, and it takes away. It is in balance. Love already redistributed.

I gaze across these lawns that surround us, at the thousands of small granite markers and the splashes of colored flowers. Is this where Holly came? Somewhere like this, I guess? How different things could be right now. With her, I could face this. Face anything. How I've destroyed it all.

Who am I to shirk this job, this one small responsibility?

"Come on now," mumbles Dad. "Please." Our eyes meet over my mother's coffin. He's unable to look at me for more than a second, but in that instant, his expression says everything: how this is my fault, how the stress and disappointment of *me* made her ill. Killed her. "Pull yourself together, boy."

I drag my sleeve across by blazing face. "Sure, yeah."

"You're good?" the undertaker says.

I assume my position.

It rang through the house every Sunday morning of my childhood, yet Karen Carpenter's voice has never sounded so haunting, so certain of its own tragedy. "The End of the World" plays in this softly carpeted room, somehow too quiet and too loud at the same time.

We deliver the coffin in what feels like barely three strides, a blur.

The ceremony seems so hurried. Why this sprint to commit her body? Why won't they slow down? A runaway train, out of my control.

A reading. A poem. Another song. This could be for anyone.

The celebrant takes to the lectern. She checks her notes. "A good woman," she says. "When I asked Colin to tell me about Barbara, those were his first words—she was a good woman." There are murmurs of agreement. There follows a eulogy that only Dad could have provided. Her life, it appears, began only when she met him. Her defining moments being the things she liked to bake, her enjoyment of fish and chips in Wetherspoons, the hotel in Tenerife she always insisted they return to, the pride she took in her home. No mention of that young woman photographed on the mantelpiece. The person who left school at fifteen and worked two jobs till she'd saved enough to be free; who flew to Spain and worked bars and sang with a band; the girl who then spent three years on cruise ships, chambermaiding till she worked her way into the cabaret; who returned home and put herself through college. Who then met my father—an event which trumped all that had come before.

Still, she was a *Good Woman*. On that, all agree.

We are invited to take a moment for quiet contemplation. I fight the desperation to stop time here. This, I know from the celebrant's tone, is the end.

"Yesterday Once More." It's the perfect choice. Mum got to choose the music, at least.

She would sing Ross and me to sleep with this song. I see her now, in the half dark of a bedroom with closed curtains on a summer evening. Eyes focused somewhere far beyond the walls. Her voice carrying me away, a song that I never knew to end. A single tear attempts to break free.

I pull myself back into the moment. Shoot a look toward Ross, wonder if the same memory has struck him. His lopsided smile is back: philosophical Ross, at peace with this. *Such is life*, his expression reads. The other side of him, Dad. Rigid, tight-lipped. Stoic. His eyes dart to me, and back again.

Another memory strikes: London Zoo, biblical rain, snuggled inside her raincoat beneath an awning, sharing an ice cream, furry toy elephant more fascinating than the real ones whose persistent toileting we are finding hilarious.

Stop it. I swipe a finger across my cheek. Can't risk him seeing. I can well imagine what he'll think of me if he sees. What right do I have to grieve, anyway?

I focus on the carpet. What's it made of, I wonder. Wool, I guess. Or maybe…*think*…

School. Not first day, but early. Autumn. Walking. Frosty spider's webs. Looking for the biggest, best orange leaves—

No. My shoes. Where are they from? Secondhand surely, someone older than me, kind of boxy, aren't they…

Slow-walking in the shallows…

Interesting place, when was it built, I wonder? I'd guess at maybe…

Long grass, salmon paste sandwiches, sodding wasps…

Got to be quite a big oven, how hot, though? How long does it take…?

A and E, gashed-open leg, she arrives so panicked, smile so fake even to a five-year-old but the pain is gone…

I think this is the last chorus, not a long song really…

Snowman in streetlights, hot chocolate…

Yes, they're fading it now.

Shallow blue curtains whirr to life, slide on their rails.

A few more seconds and I'll have made it. Held it together.

Last glimpses of that wooden box. Going, going.

Gone.

Don't think about it. Don't you dare.

People file out and we follow. It is done.

Now You're Gone

We are last to arrive at the social club. Ross bids our driver good-bye with a pat on the back and a scrunched twenty in his palm. It's busy inside—touchingly so. The warm air smells pleasantly of old lady perfume and buffet. An unrequested white wine is passed into my hand by a cousin. Any thoughts of not drinking today are washed away. There's a twinge of excitement, a brief visit to the sweet spot where sobriety meets the certainty of booze. I knock the glass back in one.

I'll have a couple, no more. Adrian the neighbor calls from the bar, asking if anyone wants anything. I raise a hand. "Whatever you're having, not fussed," I shout back.

I find Dr. Defrates alone in a corner, watching the room with what could be interpreted as mild amusement. "Very sorry for your loss," he says.

"Cheers. So everyone keeps saying."

"What else is there to say?" He dabs his mouth with a napkin, removing only a third of the mayonnaise on his top lip. His plate is piled high, held close under his chin. Usual posture: leaned slightly backward, height and girth exaggerated. His black tie is absurdly long, following the hill of his gut up and back down again before tucking into his trousers.

"Thank you. For coming along."

"Not at all. Pay my respects."

"I'm guessing you never met my mother?"

"No, no." He sways where he stands. His foot is unintentionally smearing an errant finger sandwich into the carpet. "Saw the announcement in...now, where was it? The *Gazette*, perhaps. Thought you'd perhaps appreciate a friendly face."

"I do."

Dr. Defrates gives me that smile that suggests something is always being withheld. "Cancer, yes? Awful bloody illness."

"Yup."

"Still, it's their loss really," he says, casting his gaze across the mourners around us. "Don't you think?"

I frown at him, stretching out my arm to receive a welcome pint being delivered.

"Not quite the same for you," he goes on. "I mean, who knows what *tomorrow* will bring?"

"Yeah. It's not really any...comfort." It has of course occurred to me that perhaps I'll see Mum again, have the great privilege of spending more time with her. But it feels like no more than the promise of being able to see video footage or look at photos. The outcome remains unchanged: this tragedy has been set. There's no taking that away. Unless of course Dad is right, that it really was me that did for her, killed her with the worry and the disappointment.

"Insensitive of me," Defrates says. More statement than apology.

"You reckon something like this could be...changed?" I ask.

"By *you*?" He looks at me like I'm a half-wit. "How would you do that?"

"Yeah. Sure."

"Very little of this world exists at our own behest. So little over which we have control."

"You don't think an illness like hers could be...you know... caused by—"

"A person?"

"Yeah."

He snorts into the glass of squash he's gulping. "No, I don't! I'm not about to offer false hope here, Alex. This is way beyond...*you*."

"Right."

"Disabuse yourself of any ideas of having any ability to... right this."

"Got it."

"I'm sorry, but—"

"No, it's fine. I think that's the answer I wanted."

He nods, like he gets it, and for a moment I have no suspicions about his motives. Is he really here just because he cares about me? Why would he?

"How are you bearing up?" he asks.

"I've not had much time to get used to the idea. Am I doing okay? I don't know."

"Since we last met. You've been getting on all right?"

"Doing my best."

"Of course you are."

"Trying to live the right way. Am I making any difference? Hard to believe I am."

"You'd be surprised."

"Why do you say that?"

"Oh, a little friendly encouragement, that's all. Good decisions—"

"Lead to good decisions," I say, finishing his sentence.

"Just as bad decisions beget bad decisions," he says, grinning at his own wisdom.

He begins another scan of the buffet table and—affable fellow that he is—is soon embroiled in conversation with a cheerfully senile great uncle.

I'm loitering at the bar, in receipt of a third pint, when Ross beckons me over to join the couple he's talking to.

"Alex?" the lady asks. She's late sixties perhaps, stylish black dress and asymmetrical hairdo. She smiles nervously at me. "My word, it's lovely to see you." I lean toward her embrace, and she kisses me on the cheek before studying me up close. There's a delightful smell about her: expensive perfume and cosmetics, delicate cigars, and a little too much white wine. "You don't recognize me," she says.

"Maybe I..." There's something familiar about her, more a feeling than a recognition.

"It's fine, darling."

"Aunty Liv," Ross says, patting her on the shoulder. "Mum's sister." Introduction made, he seizes his opportunity to escape.

"Right! Yes, sorry," I say. It's a name I know from birthday and Christmas cards as a kid, usually complete with a very welcome fiver or tenner. Her resemblance to Mum is clear enough, if some way from uncanny. "Of course. Don't think we've ever met in person."

She looks suddenly sorrowful, and I'm worried I've cocked up; not recalling meeting her does not mean *she's* not met *me*. I should be aware of that by now.

"Many, many moons ago. You'd have been too young to remember," she says to my relief.

"Brian," a man says, a step behind her. He shakes my hand with vigor. "*Uncle* Brian, if you like, which I suspect you don't." He's slight and dapper, pristine white beard on a genial face; perhaps I would like to call him Uncle.

"So lovely to see you," his wife says again, with a look of not quite believing she and I are being reacquainted.

"You've come back from…" I say, leading her to finish the sentence for me. "I remember Mum saying you lived a long way away. Sorry, I forget where."

"Yes, yes," she—Aunty Liv—says. "If you consider Kent to be a foreign country." Roll of eyes.

"Don't bother the poor chap with the politics," Brian says.

"Thanks for coming," I say.

She clutches my wrist. "Poor old Barbara. Gosh, I'm so sad."

"She'd be touched that you're here." It's an empty sentiment, but safe.

"How are you bearing up, darling?"

"Getting there." I shrug. These are the generic responses I've been offering all who've asked, but it seems not to wash with Aunty Liv.

"I can't thank you enough," she says. "For being with her. At the end."

I nod.

"Ross was telling us. How you were holding her hand when she went. She would've known you were there. She'd have been at peace with you at her side."

I've gleaned from stilted conversations earlier today that it was four a.m. when Mum passed, but the fact that I—and I alone—was present is news to me. How unusual to encounter a fact about myself of which I can be proud.

"You were everything to your mother," she says.

I nod, too embarrassed to disagree, although my eyes find Ross on the other side of the room. Golden boy, success story.

"So, tell me about you," Aunty Liv says. "What are doing with yourself these days?"

I feel a spritz of panic, for once not because I don't know the answer. If I had the nerve I'd run now; better than witnessing their disappointment at the truth. "This and that," I say. It has the opposite effect that I was hoping for; they are intrigued, think I'm being coy. "I play a bit of music."

"Like Barb!" Aunty Liv says. "She had such a voice. Like an angel. Where do you play?"

"Pubs, clubs. That sort of thing." I'm looking clean past them. Strictly speaking it's not a lie, just twenty-five years out of date.

"Alex! I never knew... Never knew you were such a talent." She says it gushily. It turns out there is something worse than failing to impress someone: watching as they force themselves to enthuse over modest achievement.

"Kind of a hobby, that's all." There's a silence; they're waiting for more. "I got a place at Cambridge," I say, and instantly hate myself for it.

Aunty Liv looks at her husband. "Didn't I always say?" she says.

"Which college?" Brian asks, eyes alight with interest.

"Christ's."

"Excellent! Of course, it is a second-rate dive of a university..."

Aunty Liv slaps his arm. "Brian's an Oxford man," she tells me.

"Right. Great," I say, desperate to reroute this conversation.

"Baliol," he says. "Classics. You?"

"Sorry?"

"Your course?"

"Yes! Maths. Mathematics. With chemistry."

"Blimey! Next you'll be telling us you got a first."

Tempting though it is to continue this charade, I can't bear to lap up this respect I've not earned. "I did get a place," I tell them, eyes to the floor. "But I...didn't take it up."

"Whyever not?" Brian asks.

It feels as though, if only I'd had the chance growing up, I'd have been close to these two. Till now, there never seemed to be anyone in my family who were *my people*.

"I had an accident," I tell him. "Couple of weeks before term started. Kind of derailed things."

"Oh, I am sorry. Could you not have deferred? They'd have had you still, I'm sure of it. You must have tried?"

Aunty Liv glares at him, and he lets the subject lie. What is it she's sensed from me?

We talk about Mum instead, anecdotes from her childhood which I've never seen photographs of.

"Did she talk about me much?" Aunty Liv asks, when inevitably we reach the point in her history when she married Dad.

"Let's not dwell," Brian says.

"Sure," I say, unconvincingly. "Sometimes. Quite a bit, really."

"Did she *ever* talk about me, Alex? About *us*?"

"Erm, I think…"

"Bloody hell. Erased from history, were we?"

"Come on, Liv, lovey," Brian says. "This really—"

"God knows why I'm surprised…" Her eyes find Dad, his back to us across the room.

"We should draw a veil—" Brian begins to say.

"Brian!" She dispatches her husband to get us all a drink. "Do you smoke, Alex?" she asks.

Outside on the patio, I accept her offer of a Café Crème. She squints toward the blazing afternoon sun and smokes deeply and silently for a minute, red lips puckered round her cigar.

"He's a piece of work, your father," she says, not looking at me. "Sorry, but he is."

"I guess." I feel a bizarre compulsion to defend him. "Has his moments."

"What the hell did she ever see in him? Bloody hell, Barb!" She gives me a resigned smile. "She sure knew how to pick 'em."

"You and Dad never got along?"

"Something like that. Sorry, Alex, this is your mother's funeral. Don't mind me."

"It's cool. Tell me what happened. I think I'd like to know."

"We were really close, Barb and I. I used to spend weeks at a time with her when she was out in Spain. She never told you that?"

I shake my head.

"The signs were there with *him*," she goes on. "Right from the start. Telling her what to wear, how to have her hair, who she could see. Why didn't we do something?"

Brian emerges from inside. The brandy I requested is a decent double.

"I'm surprised we even got an invite to the wedding," she says. "*His* sister as bridesmaid, though."

"Must we, Liv?" Brian says.

She cuts him with her stare. "I think one domineering husband is enough for this gathering, don't you?"

"As you were," he mumbles into his Scotch.

"We kept up with them, here and there," Aunty Liv tells me. "But it was when you came along—that's when things really changed."

"How so?"

"He couldn't bear it, Alex. Not having her full attention. Having to *share* her affections. Her loving something—someone—else."

"You reckon?"

"It was New Year. You would have been three years old."

Brian exhales noisily into his glass, eyes flickering like he's braced for a punch.

"You came to ours. The three of you, maybe Barb was pregnant with Ross, not sure. Just a little gathering, few drinks, bit of a spread. You weren't misbehaving, not really. You were just being a kid—into everything. You wanted to *know things*, that's my abiding memory of you. Far too bright to sit still, to do what you were told all the time. Not naughty, hardly at all, just…busy. He hated it, Alex. *Hated* it. Your mother, doting over you, everyone saying how clever you were. You see, I think he took it to mean that people thought you were brighter than him. Jealous of a sodding toddler! Have you ever heard anything like it?"

"I dunno." The suggestion is both ridiculous and unsurprising.

"We were all talking about something or other. And you had this book you'd picked up. A DIY manual, of all things— you liked the pictures. You could read a few of the words, and you were getting frustrated, wanting help. Your dad had been on your back all afternoon, telling you to belt up, to go away. You were interrupting us a bit, I suppose. And your dad, he just snapped."

"Yeah. He does that."

"Not a word from him. Stood up, grabbed you rough as anything. He carried you straight out the front door. Your mum— she looked miserable, but she didn't do anything. Knew better, I suppose, just kept whispering that she was sorry. A minute later and he's back inside, pouring himself a drink and acting like nothing's happened. You were *three*, Alex. Do you remember?"

"Don't think so."

"An hour went by. Barb was distraught, I could tell, but she didn't say a dicky-bird. Why didn't I speak up? There was something about him, Alex. He frightened people. We all sat there, laughing at his jokes, pretending nothing had happened. Only when it was getting dark did I slip out and look for you. There you were, down the road, in the back of the car. You know the most heartbreaking thing of all? You weren't crying or anything. Just staring dead ahead out through the windshield. You were used to it!"

I nod. I've no memory of this particular incident, but there was nothing unusual about being locked in the car.

"Not even upset," Aunty Liv goes on. "There was a big wet patch on your trousers, poor thing."

"Spare him the details," Brian says.

She shushes him. "When I got back inside, I did speak up. I

told him to go and get you, that you'd been punished enough. I'll never forget the look on Barb's face—she, I'm sure, was going to pay for me interfering. She looked so scared. But he did as he was told, went to get you. And your dad sat there till it was time for you all to leave, absolutely silent, totally blank. So uncomfortable."

"I know that expression." I've seen it a hundred times. Like a firework, after the fuse has burned down, when all is briefly quiet.

"And that was the last time we were considered to be a part of the family. That was my punishment for disrespecting him. Barb wasn't allowed a relationship with me. I'd call, but she'd fob me off. I wrote, Alex, for a while. No reply. I was, quite clearly, persona non grata."

She isn't really telling anything I don't already know. This story is unremarkable against my memories of my father. But it's strange how hearing his behavior being laid out by someone else makes me see it differently.

"He made both your lives a misery, Alex," Aunty Liv says. "As for Ross, well, they look like they get along…"

"The son he wanted, I think," I say, irritated at how riled I sound.

"Probably not bright enough to upstage his pathetic father."

I catch sight of Ross inside, no sense of inferiority for once.

"I am sorry to bang on about this," she says, lighting another smoke. "Why couldn't she bloody leave him, for God's sake?"

I think of the safe box in Dad's wardrobe: where he kept Mum's bank books. Not that I ever had the sense she wanted to escape.

"These things cast a long shadow, Alex," Aunty Liv says. "Being treated so poorly by a parent."

"Steady, Liv," Brian says. He gives me a conspiring glance— as if to say, *Don't worry about her.*

She holds my hand. "A child needs to be loved without condition. It's not…your fault, if things haven't always…gone to plan. When home isn't a place of safety, where do you build a life from?"

"All right, now," her husband says.

"I've said my piece," she replies.

Why does Blake Benfield spring immediately to mind? I befriended those older boys because I was rattling around the town on my own like a nine-year-old vagrant. Looking for kinship where I could.

"Sometimes I wish we'd tried harder with Barb. And with you," Aunty Liv says.

"Not your fault."

"I'm annoyed with myself sometimes, Alex. I allowed myself to be upset, to be offended at my being exiled. And because of it, I've missed out on a relationship with my sister."

"Please don't blame yourself. It's okay, I get it."

She tuts and shakes her head. "Perhaps you never stood a chance, Alex. Screwed right from the start."

"Enough," Brian says.

"It's okay," I say. "I'm…okay." Why does my voice crack as I say it?

Aunty Liv stares into my eyes, which I know are reddening by the second. She has a stoop about her now, a good two inches shorter than she was before she polished off a bottle of white. "I *am* sorry," she says, looking laboriously pained and holding both my hands.

It's funny: it's not the likelihood that I've been wronged that's upsetting me. No. It's her sympathy that's crushing me. I can't bear it.

"Must just…" I begin to say. My throat aches, voice nowhere. I point inside, in the direction of the gents. "Won't be a…" I raise my index finger—*one minute*.

Locked in a cubicle, away from her pity, my composure creeps back. I am soon back under my own control.

Maybe It's Time

"Easy, tiger!" Ross says. "Am I gonna be carrying you home?"

"Everyone drinks at a funeral," I reply. The server sets down another Stella and a brandy chaser on the bar.

It's early evening now. My long-lost aunty and uncle have said their goodbyes. For a couple of hours I've been mostly sitting in the sun and drinking, courtesy of the card my father left with the bar.

"Join us, yeah," Ross says, guiding me by the shoulder to his and Dad's table. "Come on."

"Cheers, boys," Dad says. He raises his glass, first to us, then heavenward. "Cheers, love."

"To Mum," Ross and I say.

"Well, that went as well as can be expected," Dad says. He surveys the buffet table that looks like it's been mauled by a fox, and the towers of used pint glasses. Two distinct groups of guests remain: one propping up the bar and the other crowded round a smoking table outside. And nursing a lime and soda whilst watching cricket on the big screen, Dr. Defrates is yet to leave.

"Did her proud, Dad," Ross says.

Dad slips his glasses off and massages the bridge of his nose. "She'll be ready to collect tomorrow, they say. From the crem. Need to take all the flowers away too. You're around for that?" I'm about to reply when he raises his head and looks at Ross. "Reckon you can spare a hand?"

"No sweat. Got another two days before I fly out," he says.

Dad's nod oozes gratitude. "Any thoughts about the urn for the ashes?"

"I kind of liked the polished cherrywood one they showed us," Ross says.

"She liked cherries," Dad says. "Still, at their prices it should be lined with bloody gold. Tempted to knock something up myself. Christ, there can't be much more than a matchbox full of her." He and Ross chuckle privately at the gallows humor.

"The walnut with maple inlay was pretty smart too," Ross adds. "A plaque in brushed silver would set it off a treat. Modern, stylish."

No opinion of mine is sought; it's safe to assume I wasn't present at this meeting with the undertakers. Who the hell am I, after all? I'm just the guy who was by her side all night when she was dying. Whilst others slept. Whilst others went about their new life on the other side of the world.

"Have we reached a decision on where she...goes?" Ross asks.

Dad shrugs. "Take her home with me, I think." He winks. "Keep an eye on the old girl. Make sure she stays out of trouble."

"Sounds about right," I say, light as air.

He nods at me and takes a long draft of his beer. "I suppose you'll be in need of a bed tonight, yes?" he asks.

"As opposed to the sofa, you mean?"

"I mean, I take it you're coming back with us tonight?" He has the tone of someone enjoying their own magnanimity.

"I can take the sofa tonight," Ross says.

"You're jet-lagged," Dad says, waving him quiet.

"It's cool," I say. "Not sure where I'm headed just yet."

Dad raises his eyebrows at me. "Right. Okay. Where else did you have in mind, on a day like this? Other than being with your family?"

"Dunno. Not sure I'm ready to turn it in just yet."

"We're probably staying here for another," Ross says.

"Yeah," I reply. "Think I'll see where the night takes me."

Dad glares at me. He's expecting a reaction, a capitulation, which doesn't come. "So, what?" he says. "A night on the tiles, is it? Get shit-faced?"

"Maybe." I've no plan to hit the town, no money even if I wanted to. But no wish to spend the evening with him.

"You're incredible."

"Oh, stop it, you two," Ross says, big grin. "You're always bickering."

"*Bickering*'s not really the word," I say. "Suggests someone's arguing back, doesn't it?"

"What would your mother think?" Dad says.

"Whatever you told her to think, I suppose." I sound like an insolent teen. But rarely before have I dared challenge him. Why? I guess that as soon as I'd learned to talk, I'd learned not to talk back.

It's silent round our table. I stroke my beer glass, watch tiny bubbles gather at the bottom, rise and burst free.

"You broke your mother's heart," he eventually says.

"Yeah, you've said."

"I don't know why you even came here today. Not after everything."

I'm not angry; his words aren't spearing me like they always have done. I am not looking at him and longing for his approval; I am seeing the bitter man that Aunty Liv knew.

"Because Mum would've wanted me here, Dad."

"She'd probably still be here..." he mumbles.

I don't take the bait. Sure, I could shout, tell him he's a bully. Tell him he wrecked Mum's life by controlling all that she did. Blame *him* for her passing. Suggest he locks her ashes in the safe box in his wardrobe so no other man can look at her. But I can't find the passion to make the point.

"You wasted your own life," he hisses, voice low so no one other than Ross can overhear. "You killed your ex-girlfriend. And you made your mother ill."

"Yes," I reply.

He glares at me. His eyes are wild, but there's something else. Primal: the look of the fighter, with the fear he might lose.

"I'm sorry you think that way," I say. I lower my gaze, no wish to come across argumentative.

Dad shakes away the hand Ross puts on his shoulder as he urges him to calm down.

I can see it now. Every time I've let this man make me angry; every time I've boiled with fury for hours and days after his attacks; every time I punched myself in the head till I was bleeding and seeing double; or worse, the times when nothing could stop the tears coming, hating myself with a white-hot fury for my weakness—when I was only letting him win.

The worst our enemies can ever do is to turn us into them.

His anger isn't producing anger in another. He doesn't know what to do.

I slowly stand. Dad and Ross watch my every move. I have become *unpredictable*.

"I'm going now," I say. "And I've no wish to see you again."

Ross raises a palm. "Now, let's take it..."

"Safe trip, brother," I say, leaning over the table and shaking his hand. "Go well, yeah?"

If only I'd known it years ago: that the only way to deal with a control freak is to remove yourself from their control.

"Bye, Dad. Thank you." I hold my hand out six inches from him.

His expression hovers somewhere between confusion and being utterly incensed. His hand meets mine. A little limp, but it's a handshake all right. Because he has no clue what else to do.

And I turn my back on them.

Outside, I draw heavily on a scrounged cigarette. The sun is low and hotter than ever as I lean on the fence—consider the world beyond here.

"You're okay," Dr. Defrates says, approaching behind me. It's an observation more than a question.

"You're still here?" I'm surprised how glad I am of him.

"Sure. Summer holidays. My time is my own. Of a fashion."

"Thanks."

"Keeping an eye on a friend. Least I can do."

"Appreciate it."

"Beautiful evening," he says, standing alongside me like we're both watching the same distant spectacle. "Something about a nice view that makes one glad to be alive, don't you think?"

"I guess..."

"I find it bowls me clean over sometimes. The sheer gratitude of being alive. So much beauty."

I smile. Perhaps I feel it too.

"It's been a tough day for you," he says. There's a knowing glance, like he means more than just laying Mum to rest.

"Think maybe I just spoke to my dad for the last time."

"You've done very well, I think," he says, same tone as he'd use to appraise a student's work.

"How do you mean?"

He focuses somewhere beyond those dark trees on the horizon. "Do you perhaps feel as though you're standing at the very fulcrum about which your life might pivot?"

"Don't know. Maybe. Am I?"

"It's a question for you."

"Why are you here?" I ask. "What is it about me that interests you? Really?" I don't mean to sound as blunt as I do.

Defrates turns to face me. "I think you're ready now," he says.

"Ready for what?"

"Perhaps it's time you knew everything."

When the Party's Over

"Have I told you about this place?" I ask Dr. Defrates.

"I gather it has importance, Alex," he replies.

"Always with the cryptic answers."

"Shall we see what we can do about that?"

We sit inches from each other, our legs dangling over the edge of the concrete. Two meters below us, the Thames slops lazily against the wall, the same deep blue as this night. Behind us the concourse is still busy; my usual busking spot is occupied by a gregarious juggler of dangerous things who exudes prodigious talent and misery. It's taken twice as long as it should to get here from the crematorium, Dr. Defrates never exceeding twenty miles per hour in his crap-filled Toyota Prius.

"Five years from now," he says. "2024."

"What about it?"

"This is the place you choose to take your own life."

"I'm sorry?"

"Drunk as a skunk. Liquid courage, I suppose. Coat full of rocks. Dead of night. No question of it being an accident. Suicide."

"How the hell would you know that?" I'm staring at him, but he gazes over the river with a calm smile.

"Interesting that you should choose *here*," he says.

Is it hard to believe I'd do such a thing? I think of that morning when I awoke in my car to find a hosepipe on the seat. God knows how many times I've tried to end this wretched life.

"Why, do you think?" he asks. "At this spot?"

"Dunno. I had a fight here. In '95. Got my arse kicked."

"Oh, I know all about that. That is, of course, when all this... *silliness* began."

"Sure."

"But imagine if life had continued in its correct order for you after that incident. As we've discussed ad nauseam, Alex, your life already exists in full. So if you had experienced your life in its rightful chronology, what would lead you to end it here?"

I shake my head. "I don't really know." And yet that isn't true. I can't put my finger on the precise reasons, but I *do* get it. Everything was perfect that day with Holly; my life vibrated with possibility. And that ended right on this spot, when I ran into Blake Benfield.

Why is it that people have their ashes scattered on the football pitch where they scored a hat trick? On quads of their Oxbridge colleges? Is it to lay themselves to rest at the very peak of their glories, where they had the world at their feet? To mark the exact point at which they took their first missteps toward failure?

"I believe you," I tell Defrates. "Rings true."

"I'm sorry."

"So I've got five years left, then?"

"Well, you in fact have every day that you haven't yet experienced left to live. I'm pretty sure that's how it works."

"Ages, then."

"I think so."

I look down at the water. "So you don't think I'll be escaping... *this* anytime soon?"

"I never like to give false hope," he says. "I'm still learning, though. You know that."

"So, what else do you know?"

He returns my stare, and I'm suddenly nervous. Excitement, or dread? I'm not sure.

"You are not the first, Alex," he says. "This is not...unique. Not entirely."

"My situation?"

"*Atemporal consciousness*, as the few scholars of the subject have dubbed it. The business of one's human experience being de-tethered from the ordinary passage of time."

"This has happened to other people?"

Dr. Defrates rocks his head side to side. "No cast-iron proof, perhaps. But I'm certain. I *know* it to be the case."

"There's...evidence?"

"Does the name Frank McVie mean anything to you?"

"Doesn't ring a bell."

"No reason that it should. On the face of it, he was a wealthy man from Lancaster, Pennsylvania, who was considered to have a few mental health issues. He died in 1969 at the age of forty-one, following an unfortunate run-in with a flatbed truck. Un-remarkable, in the grand scheme of things."

"Sure."

"Do a little digging, though, and it gets interesting. He was from a poor background. Eight siblings, father was a laborer who squandered most of what he earned. Frank was working on building sites from age fourteen. Hand-to-mouth existence. You'll find all this on the net if you care to look."

"I'll take your word for it."

"Aged eighteen, and Frank's laboring on a build in the cen-ter of town. Three stories up and he trips on the scaffold, falls onto the street twelve meters below." Defrates slams his palms together in an enthusiastic reenactment. "This was 1946. No care given to workers' safety."

"Of course."

"Frank McVie nearly died right there. Long recovery. But he *did* survive. And he went on to become very well-off indeed, a series of exceptionally prudent investments in the stock market. Bought a mansion on the outskirts of town. Renowned for his generosity. It was a bit of a local joke—that his bang on the head was responsible for this carefree attitude he had to his money."

Defrates is a natural storyteller, and he's finding his stride.

"But something was driving him mad, Alex. Driving him *nuts*. Someone of lesser means would have ended up having themselves committed, most probably. But Frank had other ideas. He employed the services of a Lucien Watts-Cook, a psychiatrist with a reputation for being somewhat unorthodox. In other words, someone open-minded enough to not have his patient banged up. Watts-Cook moved into Frank's house. Was there for years. He knew exactly what was going on with Frank. He studied him, wrote reports, tried various medications—sedatives, LSD, Largactil, you name it. To see if it would make a difference.

"Now, as I've already told you, Frank died young. How he died—*that* is interesting! He was walking into town. Perhaps he was a touch dozy on one of his psychiatrist's libations, maybe it was a simple accident—who knows. He tripped at the curb, stumbled into the path of a lorry. He passed away instantly."

"You think he was in the same situation as me?" I ask. "He was…atemporal?"

"His live-in psychiatrist, this Watts-Cook fellow, was certain of it. Wrote thousands of pages about his time with Frank McVie—how disorientated his patient often was, how his memory was not linear, how he knew things that hadn't happened yet. There's little doubt about it, this was a case of atemporal consciousness."

"Fascinating."

"It gets much better, Alex." There's glee in Defrates's voice. "It was Frank McVie's untimely death that brought with it a few clues. You see, he died in the same place where he'd suffered the earlier accident on the scaffold, the point at which his atemporal consciousness began. In fact, it's likely the two injuries occurred in the *exact* same position. An interesting coincidence, don't you think?"

"Seems pretty unlikely."

"Coincidences *are* unlikely, Alex. It's rather their defining characteristic."

"Point taken. Go on."

"Lucien Watts-Cook formed a hypothesis. He proposed that if someone were to suffer a particular brain injury twice, some time apart, leading in both cases to a drop in brain activity to a certain level of subconsciousness, and if these two injuries were to occur in the exact same geographical location, this might lead to a form of *temporal confusion*. A slipping from the grid, if you like. The time frames of the two injuries becoming muddled."

"You think this is it?" I ask him.

"Science leads us to believe that all of time, and all of space, exist in a preexisting block—everything that is to happen has already happened. Our memories, our lived experiences, they are indexed against this passing time. Cause then effect, cause then effect, ad infinitum. But if an error occurred—a person's consciousness jammed between two points on the map of time— where might that leave them?"

I nod, take it on board. What else do I have to explain this?

"From the perspective of the victim," Defrates continues, "life would appear to become disordered following the first injury. Which, in the case of our Frank McVie, made him a lot of money, but it cost him his sanity."

"I'm exactly halfway there," I say.

Defrates laughs heartily.

"Why isn't this widely known about, this atemporal consciousness?" I ask.

"Lucien Watts-Cook published his findings, only to be shunned by the medical community. Written off as a crank. Or worse, a charlatan—a little too keen to relieve poor old Frank McVie of his cash."

"I can't imagine medicine and metaphysics are terribly compatible."

"Indeed. But there are other cases too, Alex. Tito Raminhos, for example. Portuguese bare-knuckle fighter. In his case, less than a year between the initial injury and the last—a fatal blow in the same ring as the first. A year lived in random order, if his reports are to be believed."

"Incredible."

"And it's not just him, Alex. In every single case, the one uniting factor is the two traumatic brain injuries, both at the precise same location."

"So when I top myself here, when I throw myself into the water, I'll suffer the exact same brain injury I did when Blake Benfield sent me in?"

"To the best of my knowledge, yes."

I think back to the things Dr. Defrates has told me previously. They make a curious sort of sense now: his claims that I already *have* escaped, that I have my reasons for being in this situation, that I'm luckier than I think. I will—or did, rather—end a life of misery by jumping into the Thames as a forty-eight-year-old man. And this is, what—a chance to right that failed life?

"A lot to get your head around, yes?" he asks.

"You could say that."

"It's reassuring, no? Having a reason? Knowing there have been other cases?"

"I suppose. Need to let it sink in, make sense of it."

"I'll help you wherever I can." He says it in that glib way of his that I've previously thought to be insincerity; perhaps it's actually him playing down his efforts, how much he cares.

"So you're my Lucien Watts-Cook, I guess?"

Defrates laughs. "Hardly! Psychiatry is a long way from my field."

"I'm a sort of case study for you, though? That's it, right?"

He huffs, fumbles with his words. "No. I wouldn't say that. This is merely a subject in which I am…interested. I've given a fair share of my life to its study, I suppose."

"You're being cryptic again. I'm sure you said you'd tell me everything."

"Yes, yes."

"How did you find me?" The question blurts out of me the moment I think of it.

He gives a resigned chuckle. "Well, there is that."

"How would you know that I have this atemporal consciousness thing?"

He's silent for a minute, gently nodding. "There will come a time when you will do your own research into this phenomenon. You will, by then, be a little more proficient with the internet and the wisdom it holds. You will discover eventually the same cases I've told you about. And in the course of your research, you'll discover me."

"How so?"

"Simply because I've written a few articles on the subject. Not in what you might call *mainstream* publications, mind, but I am perhaps the closest thing to an authority you're likely to find. Certainly in this neck of the woods, anyway. You will contact me. You shall want to discuss your condition."

"But I already know you." It's a stupid comment, but I'm not understanding him at all.

"Let's put it another way—you've already looked me up online. You've already made contact. Some time ago."

I wrestle with my confusion for a moment. "No. Sorry. That's not how this works."

"I appreciate that," he says apologetically. "February 2015—that's when you'll get in touch. Or when you *did* get in touch, depending on how you prefer to look at things."

"I haven't been to February 2015, though. I've not lived a day there."

"Well, no, not yet."

"Sorry, but we've discussed all this," I tell him. I'm trying to piece together how to articulate that what he's saying is impossible. It *is* impossible. "It was *you* who found *me*. When you turned up on the day of the eclipse in '99. If I'd contacted you first, since all this began, I'd know about it. I'd *remember* doing it."

"Yes. Exactly right."

"So if I haven't done it yet, if I haven't yet done my research and sought you out, if I haven't *experienced* that February day in 2015, how do you know me? How did you know to come and find me?"

"There you have me." He gives me a half smile.

"Give me a clue here, mate."

"Everything I'm telling you is true, Alex. I know you are atemporal, because you contacted me for advice."

"This doesn't...*work*. What is it I don't know? I'd have to have already been atemporal to have a reason to look you up. So unless I was so blind drunk at some point that I've forgotten living an entire day..."

"The answer is far simpler than that."

I shake my head.

"Let's put it another way—how could I have experienced something that, as far as you are aware, is yet to happen?"

"I'm tempted to say it's impossible, but that word's kinda redundant these days."

Defrates chuckles. "You're an intelligent man, Alex. Think about it."

It takes no more than a minute for it to dawn on me. I turn and meet his stare. Yes.

"You've worked it out, haven't you?" he asks.

"Maybe I have."

"Go on," he says, enjoying the suspense.

"What happened to you?" I ask.

He winks at me. "Very good, Alex."

"Traumatic brain injury?"

Dr. Defrates nods. "Unfortunate incident on a steep railway embankment. If the train had been moving any faster I'd be a goner. Nasty accident, from which I have a classic case of atemporal consciousness." He grins. "My name's Paul Defrates, and I'm atemporal!"

"Welcome to the club. It's kinda shit."

"I've been at it much longer than you, young man. Unlike you, though, I don't have anyone to tell me how it ends."

"I reckon I know where it ends."

"Yes, indeed! My least favorite stretch of railway track."

The humor burns out. We sit in silence, consider our mutual tragedy. "I'm sorry, mate," I eventually say. "How long's it been?"

"I was thirty. November 1990. And the latest days I've seen are 2028, so I guess things end round there."

"How much of it have you lived?"

"Most, I'd say."

"Christ. You must be sick of it."

He shrugs. "The days can be very long, but the years short."

"You think we're missing a trick?" I ask. "Reckon we should take a leaf out of Frank McVie's book—make a load of cash?"

"To be granted this unique perspective, and to squander it on simply accruing money? Not for me. Nor you. Money's not your god, Alex."

"I don't know…"

"People who pursue money are those with nothing better to pursue," Defrates says, enjoying his own wisdom.

"I guess."

"So now you finally have your answer," he says, smiling again, "as to why I'm so damned interested in this subject!"

"Thanks. For coming to find me that day."

"Like I say, it was you who found me, really."

"Whatever. So what is this, an atemporal consciousness support group?"

"I hope we can do a little better than that," he tells me.

"What's the plan?"

"I've given a lot of my life to researching this. To understanding it. You're a great help."

"Cool."

"So much still to know," he says.

"Like?"

"Like how random is it?"

"The order we get the days in?"

"Exactly. Is there a *reason*? A logic to it? I've looked for patterns, for an algorithm, but I'm drawing blanks."

"Interesting. I've got a question."

"Only the one?"

"Can we escape? Get back? Have a *normal* life?"

"Gosh, you do like asking that question, don't you? Another answer I one day hope to have. Trouble is, Alex, it's not always easy to keep focused on my research. You know what it's like—the time that gets wasted orientating ourselves every day. Then I have my students, names to remember, syllabuses to keep abreast of." He says it with a smirk.

"You enjoy it, don't you? Being kept on your toes. Why else would you do it, the teaching as well as everything else?"

"It's rather good for the intellect, yes. Life is rarely dull!"

The night is still warm when eventually we rise from the side of the river. People milling about on the concourse are noisy, loosened by booze and August. It's impossible not to recall the terrace bar that was once here, stretching to the river's edge. Where I drank with Holly. Where I fought with Blake Benfield.

"Thought I might treat us to a few overpriced confections," Dr. Defrates says, pointing toward the artisanal chocolatier in the building the bar once occupied. The shop is in the process of closing for the night.

"Sure, why not."

We pause a moment by the memorial in the middle of the concourse: granite plinth, soaring chrome doves. Unvandalized for once.

"Nasty business," Defrates says, gazing down at a single bunch of flowers. "I despair of the human race sometimes."

I scuff my shoe on the ground. "What a day. Can't believe I buried my mum. Well, cremated her. Crazy."

He gives me a sympathetic smile. "You did well. She'd be proud of you."

"Dunno about that. A booze-addled failure with nothing to his name, in a charity shop suit? Hardly an achiever. Cheers for coming, though. Means a lot."

He waves it away, no worries. "Who knows what tomorrow will bring?" he says.

"Sure."

"Just keep living well, Alex."

"I am trying. I think."

"Keep it up. Strain at the weight of your history."

"Keep running into the headwind," I add.

"Real change is possible, Alex." His eyes burn into me. "Take the initiative," he says firmly. "Whilst you know change is possible."

"You think the opportunity passes?"

"Rot sets in," he says. "You live a life you're not happy with for long enough, and it's possible to forget that things could be different."

"Sounds like my life in a nutshell."

"You know the life you want," he says.

"Sure I do."

"You've already done good things, Alex. Strike whilst the iron's hot."

"Do you...*know* something? What is it you know?"

His trademark self-satisfied smile returns. "Just friendly advice, no more."

"All right."

"But I'll tell you this—you may be nearer to the cusp than you think. A step or two in the right direction, and who knows what might happen?"

"Understood." I nod and think better of quizzing him further.

He stares again at the base of the memorial and shakes his head. "Terrible."

We're standing side by side. He has the appearance of someone paying their respects: head bowed, silent contemplation. I wait on him, glancing down myself at the brass plate with its inscription.

OMAR JASSIM, WHO FELL HERE JULY 4, 2014.
MAY HE REST IN PEACE.

"So it goes," Defrates says.

He turns on his heel, a sudden shift in mode. I follow as he struts toward the chocolatier. "Cognac truffles, I think," he says. "Yummy, yummy."

APRIL 23, 2000 | AGE 24

Rise

It is the sort of spring morning that is capable of making me smug that I'm up when the rest of the world is yet to wake. I crack open the Venetian blind, and stripes of sunlight fan across the kitchen, revealing the aftermath of a poker night: grease-steeped pizza boxes, drained tequila bottles, scattered playing cards—some of which have been partially incinerated in an act of comical sore-losing that I have to accept was probably me. This is the terraced bachelor pad in Balham I share with Loz and three other lads. Not that there's much chance of any of them rising anytime soon; 06:28 reads the clock on the microwave.

The instant coffee I fix myself is so strong the milk disappears without a trace. It scours the taste of booze from my throat. My head is woolly, but I've no plans to sleep it off. I know from the radio alarm that woke me at six that it's Easter Sunday and, according to the highlighted schedule in my bedroom, I'm supposed to be working at the Blue Moon today, early start.

I take a seat on the back doorstep. The garden is dotted with crumpled cans, bulging bin bags at its perimeter. Yet in defiance of the neglect, it bursts with new life—shocks of bright green grass, scores of daffodils proud beside the crumbling path. In the distance, a mist hovers over London, bronzed by the rising sun. The air is green with the smell of a landscape awakening after winter.

I'm smiling as I think of Dr. Defrates outside the wake yesterday—what he said about a nice view making him grateful he's alive. Perhaps this isn't much of a view, but the beauty is unmissable.

Warming my cheek against my coffee, I fiddle with the Nokia that was charging by my bed. I hit the call button again. Is three attempted calls before breakfast too many? Probably. Again, my heartbeat pounds in my skull. And again, the foreign dial tone times out. No answer from Holly.

My disappointment evaporates in seconds. It is enough to know she exists. To know she and I are under this same sky, wherever she may be.

And Mum, she's here too. Probably awake already. In her kitchen, having her coffee. A few miles away.

Perhaps that's one of the great joys of being young: that everyone you've ever loved is still alive.

I scroll to the number marked *Work*. My call is answered by Mick, the same manager as back in '95. His tone is matey; we were drinking buddies back then despite his seniority, and it appears that's not changed. I'm due on shift in fifteen minutes, he tells me, sounding harassed. I'm a little off-color, I explain, a lie that's surely given away by my bright tone. He begs me not to do this, not today. It seems I have form for skiving. Over two hundred booked for lunch, he reminds me. Easter menu, three courses. I'm supposed to be filling in in the kitchen. They're counting on me. Bet it's just a hangover, he says, getting irate now. You can't keep doing this, Alex.

I lower the phone from my ear, though I can still hear the

frantic clankings of food prep in the background. Can I justify giving a chunk of this day to my job?

Can I justify letting people down? As this guy half expects me to do? Take the easy way out?

"Gonna struggle to be there for seven," I tell him. "More like half past."

"Put your foot down," he says.

"Nah, gotta walk over." Even with the coffee I can't shake the taste of alcohol.

"What's up, car trouble?"

I'm not in the mood to lie. "Might be a touch over the limit still."

"Since when's that bothered you?"

"I'll be good to work after the fresh air, don't worry."

"Get moving, yeah? I'll have a hair of the dog waiting."

I tell him that a coffee will do just fine, and it seems he thinks I'm joking.

I pause after he hangs up and take in my surroundings again. Though I can hardly spare the time, I decide to give the kitchen a speedy tidy-up after last night's obvious revelry. And for good measure, I do a lap of the garden and bag all the empties. The journey to work is made at a semi-jog.

The Blue Moon still wears its music pub ancestry on its sleeve, though it's clear from the polished wineglasses on tables that it has repositioned itself as a gastropub since my heyday here. I haven't a clue what I'm doing in the kitchen, but I work at a pace all the same, help where I can with slicing joints of beef, plating salads, deep-frying stuff till it looks like something I'm used to eating. Beyond the open fire door, a perfect spring day blooms. The heat and the pace inside are like nothing I've experienced: invigorating and comically hellish simultaneously. Familiar as I am with the unruly nature of time, I'm still shocked when a six-hour shift flies by in an instant.

"What's this?" manager Mick asks as I hand him a folded note over the bar. "A while since I had a love letter."

It's midafternoon. The lunch rush thinned. I decline his offer of a Stella, instead sinking ice water so fast my skull seizes. "Sorry. Happy to work a bit of notice," I say in response to his shaking head as he reads. "Don't want to let anyone down."

"What's brought this on, Alex?"

"Nothing personal. Just been doing a bit of thinking."

"Ah, man. You're part of the furniture."

"Yup, I know it."

"Is this about money? Might be able to juice some lemons…"

"It's not the money." It's really not. The decision was made on my brisk three-mile walk over and, as contented as I feel after a session of manual labor, I'm not going back on it.

"So, come on, what you gonna do instead?" he asks.

"No plans."

"Seriously? Everyone's got plans. Even me, Alex! One of these days I'll be getting myself a nice little boozer down on the South Coast."

"You've said before." I don't point out that he was talking about this idea when I was working here saving for uni: *years* ago.

"So this is voluntary unemployment?"

"Mick, I'm twenty-four years old. In this great city."

He smiles. "Yeah, you'll be fine." He mimes spitting into his palm, and we shake. "Now, where am I gonna find myself a new assistant manager, eh?"

It's a small change. But it's a shift in attitude, an application of pressure on myself. I know I was working this job right up till I met Elouise—that's another five years. Instead, tomorrow the comfort of routine will be gone; might ambition fill the void?

Out on the street, I try Holly's number again. Still the foreign ringing tone, still no answer. It takes me five minutes to compose a short text asking—begging—her to get in touch. As I type, a message lands from Loz:

Fucking hanging. Need to get back on it asap. Bull's Head my man?

Glorious

"What's wrong with you, dude?" he asks as I slide him a beer across the table and take a swig of my Coke. "First you start tidying the house—thanks for that, by the way—and now you're off your booze?"

"Just thirsty," I say.

"Not as thirsty as I am," he says, sinking most of his beer in one draft.

This place is an old haunt from our sixth form days. It reeks gloriously of the classic pub smell that's nowhere in later years: stale bitter, chips, lashings and lashings of fag smoke. "I can't get hold of Holly," I tell him.

He's not looking at me, instead staring at the rear view of two women at the bar. "Is that a surprise?" he asks distractedly.

"Tried her, I don't know, five or six times. No answer."

"Five or six times?" He sniggers. "You stalking her?"

"Need to talk to her, man."

He is caught out by the subject of his gawping and snaps his attention back to me. "Really? Can't leave that alone, can you?"

"Where is she?"

"Why you asking me?"

"Sorry. Just having a bit of a…day of it. Got confused."

"You daft old pisshead," Loz says.

"I'm right in thinking she's away, yeah?"

"Bloody hell, you're not kidding, are you? The last I heard on the matter, she was in the States. Working out there for a year. That's right, yeah?"

I nod, a flush in the cheeks hopefully not revealing my disappointment that I definitely won't be seeing her today. "Why's she not answering her phone, though?"

Loz exhales noisily. "Women, dude! You think *I* understand what goes through their heads? She's probably realized what's good for her."

"You think she's ignoring me?"

He laughs and slaps the table. "Shit, Dean! I think that's a racing certainty. What's got into you?"

"Don't rip the piss, man." I hide behind my glass, gulping down its syrupy contents. "Me and Holly, we're not…*together*?"

Loz's expression softens. "Dude, it's hard to keep up with you two. On, off, on, off. Yeah, maybe you guys seem a bit more… done, this time. You know, what with the whole *leaving the country* business. I mean, as hints go…"

"Why am I such an idiot, Loz? Can you answer that?"

He looks again at the women by the bar, their group now increased to four. "Nothing idiotic about wanting to sample all of life's joys. There is fruit hanging ripe on the tree, my man. Don't you love these first hot days of the year? Skimpy little outfits. It's like we've forgotten what tits and legs look like. I'm a dog in heat, dude."

"I want *her*, mate. Nothing else. I *love* her." There's warmth in my eyes, tingling at the bridge of my nose. It's weirdly thrilling to say it: requited or not, it is a fact of which I am utterly proud. "I love her more than I thought I could love anybody."

Loz pats my forearm. "Maybe you should try telling her that."

My mobile spins circles after I toss it onto the table. "Yeah, why didn't I think of that?"

"You're a bit sober for the whole heartbroken routine," Loz says.

"Sorry. You bored of it?"

"Ah, it's okay. It is usually when you're shit-faced at two a.m., though."

"Sounds about right."

"What you having?" Loz asks, draining his glass.

"Dunno. Soda water, maybe. Reckon they do coffee here?"

"I don't know, Alex, I've never asked. Nor has anyone else."

"Don't really want to be getting on it," I tell him, feeling I'm letting the side down. "Need to head over to see my mum today. Can't be turning up pissed."

"Got the whole family thing to do?"

"Not if I can avoid it. Just wanna see my mum. While I have the chance."

"Sure," Loz says. "One won't hurt. Come on, have a beer, dude. It's my round."

I glance around the pub. Early evening now and the place has filled out. Someone's put Oasis on the jukebox. People are relaxed, enjoying themselves. I can be one of them, right? I don't have to drink till I'm the last man standing, till I lose control. I'll drink like they do: a cold lager or two.

Whilst Loz is at the bar, I message Holly again. There's no danger of an essay with my typing speed. Simply: I HOPE YOUR DREAMS COME TRUE I WILL LOVE YOU FOREVER.

If I had time, I'd add footnotes that I'm neither pissed nor being sarcastic, but instead rely on the right tone carrying over the Atlantic.

"Said they'll join us in a few minutes," Loz says, nodding toward the women at the bar.

Stella spritzes beneath the tip of my nose and there is, for an instant, nothing in the world that troubles me. "Think I'll let you handle them, old chap."

"We'll see," he says.

"Why are we not together?" I ask him. "Why am I not moving heaven and earth to be with Holly?"

Loz exhales noisily. "Complicated, innit, mate."

"I don't know. Why is it?"

"You want different things."

"Fucking hell, that old chestnut." It's exactly the reason Holly gave for our split when we were hiding in the vestry on my wedding day. "Right person, wrong time?"

Loz nods, ignoring the bile in my tone.

"What are these 'different things' that she and I want, Loz? Do you know the answer to that? Because I'm clueless."

"Come on, man. She's out in the States, cracking on."

"Could I not have gone with her? What's keeping me here?"

"None taken," Loz says, grinning. He flips open a deck of ciggies. I instinctively help myself. Half my beer already gone.

"If you'd wanted to go," he says, "you'd have done it, wouldn't you?"

"I'm a twat."

"Chill, dude. It's not your scene, is it? She's got her career. Ready to settle down. Get focused. And well, you..."

"Out of my depth? That's it, isn't it?"

"If you like. Not ready, I guess. No shame in that."

"So basically, I got scared that it was all going too well. Sabotaged me and Holly, because I was afraid of stepping up?"

"Mate, you need to lighten up."

"That's it, though, innit?"

"You're a young, good-looking man with the gift of the gab, dude. Why would you waste that being a one-woman man?"

"Why do we do it, Loz? Tell each other this sort of shit?"

"Take it easy."

"I don't mean just you and me. I mean...*guys*?" I drain my glass.

Loz is crestfallen as he spots the women now have company, their partners by the looks. "We do not want to be old and gray and wondering why we didn't have fun while we could."

"You'd be surprised," I say, snapping harder than I mean to, already on my feet and aiming for the bar and another round. "I'm not sure all regrets revolve around not doing enough shagging."

He gives me a wonky grin, as if to say, *Are you sure?*

By the time I'm being served, it's rowdy in here. I double up on the drinks to save queuing again; we'll have these, and then I'll get a cab over to Mum.

"You really reckon I want...other people?" I ask Loz, helping myself again to his cigs. "Have I said that?"

"Words to that effect. One of these days you might even stop dithering and actually get some action."

"Don't hold your breath," I say, relieved that it seems I've remained faithful at least, even if Holly and I are not necessarily an item anymore.

"Dude, you *loved* it. Back in the day. Getting around."

"Is that what we actually want?" I ask. "To seduce? To be seduced?"

"Dunno, dude," Loz says. "Probably. Sounds a bit deep for this time on a Sunday. You been at the charlie again?"

"Are we trying to prove something to ourselves all the time?"

"So you're seriously telling me you don't enjoy getting laid?"

I check my phone and toss it back on the table. No messages. "I don't enjoy fucking up the only good thing that's ever happened to me, because of some pathetic compulsion to put my shagging shoes back on."

"She'll come around, dude. Don't sweat it."

"You know something, Loz? When I used to play music at the Blue Moon, back before I met Holly, I used to...*get a bit*."

"I remember well. It wasn't that long ago. You're talking like this was in a past life."

"Funny that."

"You were something of a legend."

Even now, I feel a hint of pride as he says it.

"That's the thing," I tell him. "That's why I did it. I bloody loved it. *Men* seeing me being successful with a woman. The envy. The credibility."

"And you reckon that's what turns you on?"

"Pathetic, isn't it?"

Loz shrugs. "You're being harsh on yourself."

"Couple of times, I remember leaving the Blue Moon with a woman at closing time. Clear to everyone where our evening was headed. Mate, I used to feel like I was ten feet tall. And I don't think it was anything to do with the promise of sex. It was all about the guys I worked with and the guys I knew in there seeing me do it."

"Men competing with men, dude. I get it."

"Not even competing. Desperate for the respect of other blokes. What's that about?"

Loz raises an amused eyebrow at the two glasses I've nearly emptied as I've been ranting.

"It's ridiculous," I say. "Imagine meeting a woman, Loz, and being so crazy about her that even after knowing her five minutes, you're daydreaming about weddings, and what your kids might look like, and growing old together. Then imagine fucking all that up, because you won't dare step up and be someone. Wanking your life away instead, obsessing over the approval of other men."

"Shit, dude. Been doing some soul-searching here, haven't you?"

"Have you ever heard anything so tragic, though? Alex Dean—so keen to fit in he'll destroy his own life to do it."

"Come on, man, lighten up, yeah? Give her a bit of space. She'll have you back." He holds his pint glass aloft.

"Yeah, go on," I tell him. "I'll have *one* more."

Loz scrunches his empty cigarette packet. "Gotta be a machine round here," he says, craning his head over the crowds.

"There's a Co-op over the road," I reply. "You get the drinks in, I'll run over there."

I dart outside into a spring day that's ebbing away, air cooler and damp under a sky that's as clear blue as it's been all day. Everything is soft and hazy from the booze as I weave across the several lanes of the busy main road.

The shop has a shell-shocked look about it, alcohol and Easter egg shelves stripped almost bare. A single bunch of flowers remains among a cluster of emptied buckets. The small red and white heads are wrinkled and facing so glumly downward that I find myself pitying them. I grab them for Mum, hoping some love and a vase of water might revive them.

I join the queue, scan my phone again. Nothing. One more call: foreign tone, rings out. Who can blame her?

Two checkouts side by side. I go left, and the couple waiting behind me go right. Six feet away. The server's ringing up my fags on the till when I look idly to my side.

I snap back, dead ahead. *No.*

The server looks at me, a touch perplexed. She must be thinking: Where has that chilled man gone? Why are his hands shaking so viciously he can't hand over cash?

What is wrong with me?

Electricity in my veins. Too much oxygen in my chest. Suffocating me.

"Are you okay, sir?"

Fistful of money rolling over counter, onto the floor. Flowers slipping under my arm—two heads leaving their stems. People looking. Palm raised, shuddering, keep the change.

Mistimed exit. Alongside each other at the door. Shoulders barged. Not deliberate, not by me, anyway.

What now? What am I supposed to do now?

The Time Is Now

Blake Benfield stands six feet from me on the pavement. A case of beer is jammed under his arm higher than is necessary, broadening him out. The woman with him—blonde, big hair, petite—looks irritated, like she knows too well this shift in his mood. "Can we just go home?" she hisses at him.

Nothing's been said between us. His eyes bore into me. I don't meet his stare.

"Off you fuck," he says to me. His girlfriend attempts to lead him away, but he's a statue.

The cellophane round the flowers crackles as they shake in my hand. I glance at his furious face and the shock strikes through even the deepest, most private places inside me. Like looking at the devil himself. Every darkened room of my childhood comes back to me, where this face waited, closing in till it was inches from mine. The face that made nowhere safe, nowhere my own.

I can hear his voice in my brain. Can smell the smoky house. The smoky breath close to my ear.

This is how clapping eyes on him always felt. Funny how I'm able to forget.

"Yeah?" he snaps, lurching toward me. I stumble a half step back despite the distance between us.

Why is it always this way? Fight or flight. I'm paralyzed between the two. When I was a kid, I always chose flight. Fighting with him near killed me. It *did* end my life—my life as I knew it.

Why can't I turn my back, walk away? I'm so sick of it being this way.

"Get fucked," I say, scarcely raising my eyes higher than his dazzling white Nikes.

Why do I feel so small? He's got two inches on me at most, a touch broader at the shoulders. But he's a giant over me. I'm what—twenty-four? He's got to be close to thirty. Two adults. So why is it just like it was, when I was nine and he was fourteen?

Blake snatches the pathetic bunch of flowers from my grip. He snaps the stems in half and throws them into the road.

I watch with an unfathomable dread as first a car avoids them, before a bus howls over them.

"Jesus Christ, Blake," his girlfriend says.

He ignores her, hanging on my next move. Everyone knows an act of aggression requires a response.

I wring my hands together, so sick of seeing them shake. "No," I snap, looking him in the face. "Not doing this."

He closes in, barging his chest against mine. I'm propelled backward, one foot slipping down the curb. Blake closes the space, on me again. "Let's have it, cunt."

Never move backward. First rule of fighting.

I stop scanning the area for a weapon. Who cares there are bottles spilling from a bin ten feet away?

Who cares that I'm shaking?

Who cares that he's publicly disrespecting me?

That I'm backing away?

That I look weak? Small? A lesser man?

That I'm *losing face*?

I've spent a life risking anything in the world rather than losing face. It's what led me to Blake, made him take to me, led me into that burnt house, into that garage with him, made me eventually fight back, put me in the water.

I can feel the weight I'm pushing against. The tide of history. This takes so much *effort*. To resist this headwind.

But I am done. Too done with this bullshit.

I *am* fighting.

"How could you do it?" I say. It comes out whiny. I'm shoved backward again, my shoulder grazing a road sign.

"The fucking river?" he says.

His girlfriend grabs at his swinging arms, screams at him to stop and take them home.

I shake my head. "How could you do that to someone?" A tear slices down my cheek. I don't wipe it away.

"You're a smug cunt that got lairy and got put on his arse."

"Not that," I say, two palms raised.

"You got a hiding and you're still crying about it."

"The house in West Way. That house that burned down." I drag my palm over my face.

Maybe no one else would spot it, but he's up so close it's unmissable: the skipped beat, the flicker of a thought he never permits himself to think.

"The house, yeah?" I say. "Of course you remember it."

"Dunno what the fuck you're talking about." He bares his teeth like an ill-kept dog, flecks of spit on my forehead.

"You do, Blake." Each word an *effort*, forced past my juddering jaw. The tears fall fast now. "You *do* know. You know what you did."

Face touching mine. "Don't push me. Don't push me, you

piece of shit." But his eyes are at odds with the words. Wild— eyes of the attacked, not the aggressor.

"What you did. In that place. How do you live with it?"

Blake's girlfriend is still mouthing off to his side. He spins around and points a finger at her. "Fuck off, yeah?" he shouts at her. "Go. You wanna go home so much? Off you go."

She walks away, shouting every filthy word there is at him, threats through angry tears that *this is really it this time.*

I'm backed against a lamppost. We're separated from the busy road by a lay-by. A parked van screens us from the passing traffic and a hundred witnesses.

I keep my hands down low; whatever he does, I won't strike back. Whatever happens, happens. What more do I possibly have to lose?

"Does it not bother you, Blake? Knowing what happened that day?"

"You're chatting shit," he says. His gaze darts up and down, hyperaware. "Don't chat fucking shit."

"You hate me so badly, because I remind you. Is that it?"

He takes a step back, wags a finger at me. "You need to sort yourself out. Fucking…prick." For a second it seems he's ready to walk away, but he can't do it.

"That's it, isn't it? You try not to think about it, don't you? And that's why you can't deal with me."

He's quiet now, swaying on the spot. Torn, perhaps. Fight? Or flight?

"That day," I say. "When you…" Why can't I say the words? "When you—"

· His hand slams against my throat. The back of my head clangs against the lamppost. His face screws in on itself. He drives all his weight into my neck.

I can't breathe. My hands wrench at his forearm. It's like an iron bar.

Clenched teeth an inch from me. "Don't you ever, ever…"

I'm wrestling his arm. It's no good. My head feels like it's going to explode. Ringing in the ears. Blood in my neck, hammering against his grip.

Eyes like they'll burst out of my face. He glares back. He doesn't look like a murderer. Not even angry—not when I *really* look. He looks lost, panicked. More out of control than ever.

Vision swims. Sounds of traffic like they're coming down a long tunnel.

No strength left to battle with the arm that strangles me.

But still, I stare him out. Make him look at me. Make him remember why it is he can't cope with me.

He bends his elbow and thrusts me away from him. But he succeeds only in shoving me against the lamppost. The force, instead of pushing me over, unbalances him.

Time slows. It unfolds beat by beat. The unruliness of time shouldn't surprise me.

Blake stumbles backward. His foot finds the edge of the curb rather than flat ground. Disorientated by rage, he staggers off balance into the lay-by, past the front of the parked van. His hands flail but don't find a hold on the hood.

Each step with which he tries to right himself lands an instant too late.

My hands clutch my battered throat, knees so weak they are buckling under me.

In ultraslow motion, it becomes inevitable. The approaching car, at forty-plus, can't see him because of the parked van. As Blake veers, arse-first, into the road, they won't know he's there till he's on them.

His expression is fury, not fear. Unlike me, he can't see the fate that awaits.

This man would see me dead given half the chance. He's already had a good go at it.

From somewhere, I find the strength. I spring forward from

my crouching start. In one stride I'm off the pavement and into the gap in front of the parked van.

I grab Blake's shoulder. Throw my own weight backward. His trajectory is slowed. He sees the approaching car. Reflexes out a hand to grab my waist.

At the last instant the driver sees him, brakes and swerves. But they are too late.

The front wing strikes Blake's hip. The door mirror slams against his thigh, exploding into a thousand shards.

But it's clear as he clings to me: I've saved him from serious harm.

A blast of horn as the car drives away. A shout of *dozy tosser* from the open window.

I'm standing over him. He gazes up at me. Confused. He's silent, can't bring himself to ask the question. To ask why.

"I'm not like you, Blake," I tell him, inches from his face.

The worst our enemies can do is turn us into them.

"It's done now," I tell him. "This never happens again."

His nod, at first imperceptible, gathers conviction.

"I don't want to hate you anymore," I say. He is totally vulnerable beneath me, but this power brings no satisfaction. I feel nothing other than crushingly sorry for him—for the tortured kid who grew up to be a tortured man; for the person in front of me who's spent a lifetime turning their fear into aggression, their confusion into hate. And suddenly I need to tell him: "I don't hate you." Because it's true.

"And you need to stop hating me," I tell him. "You understand me?" I care less than ever about my tears. They are no indicator of weakness.

Blake doesn't speak, but there's no argument in his expression.

"Maybe you need to stop hating yourself, yeah? We were kids, Blake. Just *kids*."

His eyes widen—could be anger, or fear.

I'm crying so hard I can barely speak. "I don't believe you set out to do what you did. I think it just…happened. I don't think you…meant for that."

Blake shakes his head. "I didn't," he says, a sharp whisper. "I never did."

"You didn't know what you were doing. Not really. I *get* that."

"I never meant for it…"

"I get it. What happened, happened. Maybe I'm starting to deal with that. Time for you to do the same, yeah? Take some responsibility for the shit you've done in your life." God knows I'm trying to.

He nods again and holds my gaze, and I can see that it's over now.

"If we see each other again," I tell him, "we walk on by, yeah? We're done."

"Yeah," he eventually says.

I help him to his feet. He grimaces as he dusts shards of mirror from the bloodied graze on his hip.

"Looks nasty. Might be an idea to get it checked out," I tell him as I turn to walk away.

In a daze I wander across the road to where the pub is. I've been gone barely ten minutes. Inside, Loz probably isn't missing me yet.

I stand at the door. People walk past, do a double take at my scarlet face, bloodshot eyes, sheen of tears that still fall. The pub is uninviting now. My unopened ciggies have been battered and scrunched by the brawl. I toss them into a bin.

Slumped in a side alley, I call the only person I can bear to speak to. There's a moment's reluctance when I ask Mum if she can come and pick me up, and a suggestion she might need to run it past Dad. But then she seems to glean something from my tone and lowers her voice, says she'll be right here.

Her old Fiesta still smells like the 1980s. A cassette of the Carpenters plays, worn and warbly. She stiffly pats my knee as we drive slowly through a twilit London and I sob in the passenger seat.

"Yesterday Once More" comes on. The song she sang me to sleep with. The song that—yesterday—we laid her to rest to.

"Can you stop the car please, Mum?" I ask.

She pulls over and shuts off the engine. I clamp my arms around her and bury my face against her hair. Over and over, I tell her I love her, and that I'm sorry.

At first stiff, she softens soon enough, hugging me back and stroking my hair and begging to know what's wrong.

"I need help," I'm eventually able to tell her. "Please help me, Mum."

"Anything," she says. "Absolutely anything."

"I think I need to see someone. Talk to someone. Somebody who can help me work through a few things."

"A professional?" she says. "A...counselor?"

"I think so."

She nods. "Okay. We can do that, I'm sure."

"I was... I was..."

Mum squeezes my hand between both of hers.

"I was...abused. A long time ago. But I think I need some... help."

She hugs me again, harder than she ever has before.

At the uttering of those words, I sense something shift. Like a basement in my soul being opened up to the air and the sunlight; no difference to the damp and the rot right now, but the ventilation and the warming beginning.

Dr. Defrates's words are in my mind, reminding me that change has to be made whilst you still know change is possible.

"And I need help with the drinking," I tell her.

I can feel her nodding against my head. Her tears meet mine.

"Even tonight," I say, "I told myself I could have one or two, like normal people do. And I can't. And you know the worst thing, Mum? I don't even enjoy it. I do it because I can't *not*.

I've got an addiction, Mum. There's no point trying to deny it. I can't be bothered to be ashamed of it. I'm an alcoholic, Mum."

"I'll help you get everything you need," she says. "I promise you."

"I'm sorry. I just don't think I can do it on my own."

"It's okay, Alex."

"I know I can't, actually."

"Don't worry," she whispers, over and over.

We sit in her car, listening to the Carpenters, till well after dark. "It's going to be all right," she tells me.

And I dare to believe her.

APRIL 2, 2020 | AGE 44

Panic Room

I'm in hell. Where else could this be?

Huge room with no windows. Dazzling yellow lights. Much too bright. Head pounds, brain bursting out of skull.

Everywhere, frantic movement. And also, abject inactivity. People run, head to foot in blue plastic, no faces. And some lie facedown on beds. Plastic trunking plumbed to their heads like they're components in a machine. Screens, cables, cylinders. Not a square inch of floor visible. Bleeps, hisses, ringing phones. Stench of disinfectant. But something else too. Like meat, and waste. Death, I suppose.

No strength to raise myself from this chair. Arms won't respond, bouncing limply on my thighs. Gushing mask strapped to my face. Mist beneath my eyes. What are they making me breathe? Can't be air—so short on oxygen I'm panting. I find the strength, wrestle the mask aside, elastic tangling round my ears.

Straightaway, one of the plastic-clad people is on me. "Please…"

a voice says behind a plastic face shield and a 3M dust mask. Looks at bracelet on my wrist. "Please, Alex. For your own good. Don't keep pulling it off."

Again, the tarpaulin over the entrance is swept aside. Huge letters on the wall outside, handwritten, black marker pen:

COVID-19 PATIENTS ONLY.

Another bed in, at speed. Two more wheelchairs too. There's no room. Why do they keep coming?

Where the fuck am I? What is this place? What the hell is going on?

A display near my head. Figures in red. Heart 144 BPM. Sats 81%. BP 90/45.

Today so far is a mess. Drifting in and out of consciousness. Where did I wake up? A bed somewhere, no idea where. A place I've been before, or not? I don't know.

Ambulance in the street. Did I call them? No clue.

Next thing I'm here. Don't remember the journey. Like magic. I've been in hospitals before. They are nothing like this.

Flurry of activity at the bed nearest to me. Body turned faceup. Crowd gathers round. One of them jumps onto the bed, thumps ribs. Pumps at chest. There are other people here like me, conscious enough to watch. Faces of horror. How close are we to being on those beds? To having someone try to beat us back to life? Or finish us off.

They pump slower now. Defeat seeping through the crowd. Hand on the have-a-go hero's shoulder. *Enough now.* Tubes unplugged. Bed on the move. Space taken within the minute.

Next to me, a man. Sixty perhaps, no more. An iPhone is held in front of him by staff. There's a face on the screen, a younger woman. He's been crying all the time I've been here, but he stops now. Smiles, convincing. Draws enough breath for a short sentence. Says he'll be fine. Promises. Needs some help breathing, that's all. *Sedation*, the woman in the plastic interjects. *Ven-*

tilator. Be right as rain. Don't worry. But I love you. You make me proud every day of my life. Never ever forget that. Promise me you'll remember what I've said. But I'll be fine.

Her response, whispered, drowned out by the screams of a woman four beds away. "Leave me alone." "Get away from me." "Fucking cunts." Takes four staff to restrain her.

Tarpaulin swept open again. Another bed, a walking wounded this time. More space will come clear soon enough, I guess.

How long have I been here? Ten minutes? Three hours? Something like that.

Rest my heavy eyes. Open them. Someone is crouching in front of me, shrouded head to toe. Have they been there long? Head level with mine. Must be *news.*

It's a man. Bright eyes, dark skin. Points at a sign stuck to his apron, written in pink highlighter:

HELLO MY NAME IS SAMUEL, CONSULTANT, CRITICAL CARE.

Big, smiley self-portrait.

Heavy latex hand on my shoulder. "How are you feeling, Alex, my man?" Focused on me alone, ignoring the chaos. How?

Go to say I'm okay. No sound makes it past the mask, keeping me honest.

"I think you need a little more help," he tells me. "You feel a bit confused, yes? Anxious?"

I nod. Understatement.

"You are still quite hypoxic. We need to fight this virus a little harder. We need to get you on a bed. Need to rest you down on your front."

Stare into his face. Can't look at the beds, the million pipes. That's soon to be me.

"We'll give you something to make you sleep, Alex. You'll be very comfortable."

"Okay," I whisper. No choice here. I'm floating again, slackening my grip on the room.

Another staff member joins Samuel. They talk between themselves.

I'm weightless.

Samuel moves aside, his colleague taking his place in front of me. A gloved hand is laid on mine. I can feel shaking, and I don't think it's me. Maybe my imagination. The fingers wrap around, squeeze mine. Something familiar in the touch. Distant, another life.

My own reflection looks back at me from their face shield. I focus on the eyes beyond.

I am even sicker than I thought. This is a hallucination.

This is so cruel. So *comforting*. Beautiful, perfect Holly. I'm losing my mind.

"Alex," she says. Voice raised over the racket in here. The sweetest sound in the world.

On the inch of bare flesh between her gown and purple gloves, a hummingbird tattoo. Familiar. So pretty.

Everything soft now. I let the dream carry me.

"You'll be okay, Alex," she says.

I'm old, forties at least. She's long…gone. Been gone a long time.

"Holly?" I whisper. "Is that you, Holly?"

She nods, squeezes tighter. "We'll look after you. I promise."

So calm. All out of focus.

Samuel crouches next to her. "You know my man Alex?" he asks.

"We go way back," she says. Eyes lock on mine. "Don't we, Alex? What were we? Old flames. Soul mates of a sort, perhaps? Once upon a time."

She softens. Fades out. Back in. She's not real. Can't be.

"Who can we call for him?" Samuel asks. "A wife? Partner?"

She shakes her head. "He's not married. Lives on his own."

Looks at me, thumb stroked on palm. "Is there anyone you'd like to speak to, ba... Alex?"

I'm silent. There's no one else I want. Whatever's brought about this stupor, I've no wish to snap out of it. Like a warm duvet around me.

"Can I let anyone know you're here?" she asks.

I lower my head. Her name badge is smaller than Samuel's handwritten sign, a standard NHS lanyard. *Dr. Holly Masondo-Chan*, it reads.

Masondo is Maxim's name. What a strange detail for my subconscious to embellish this fantasy with. She never married him. They were engaged when she died. When I...

She shakes my arm. "You're gonna be fine, Alex. Keep fighting the fight, yeah?"

Samuel lays a hand on her shoulder. "Get yourself back up to ICU," he tells her. "We got this all under control."

Fading out again. Bright lights. On a bed now. How did I get here?

I want Holly. Where did she go? Why can't I fantasize her back here?

Turned on my front.

She was so *real*. Was she here?

Anesthetic in my veins.

She can't have been here, no way. She's been gone years. A decade or more.

Slipping.

Unless.

Twilight, between waking and sleep.

Unless...something...

I'm floating off on a river. Cool sky. Calm waters.

Has there been... Has something changed?

Drifting away.

An update? Where Holly survived? Me and her not together, but still...

My thoughts like ghosts in the misty dark.

Could it be? Is that it?

Memory and fantasy and dreams and reality swirl together.
Become one, indistinguishable from each other, inseparable.

The chemicals coursing through me wash everything away.

Bliss.

And I'm gone.

JULY 4, 2014 | AGE 38

Changing

It's like I've been asleep for a month. A charging iPhone vibrates inches from my head and I flap leaden arms, eventually silencing the bloody thing. It's gone eleven, it tells me, in addition to serving me the date.

I'm alone in this double bed. I roll out onto the floor, begin a lap of this place. Third-floor flat. Cozy but clean. Leather sofa, quite big telly, coffee machine. This is *my place*, it seems. No evidence of anyone cohabiting. This is the third different abode where I've found myself in this period of my life: there was the shitty bedsit out east, erased by updates, replaced by the little gaff where I met my probation officer. And now this, the best iteration yet, if some way from palatial.

Beyond the Juliet balcony, it's a glorious summer day. There's a three-sixty-degree hum of traffic, the fringes of a view I'd know anywhere. Still a Londoner.

I feel rested. Restored. I'm thirty-eight and—incredibly—I *look* it. No jaundiced eyeballs, no burning bile, no lunar landscape cheeks or snooker-ball blue nose.

So why, when there's evidently no hangover, is there a black hole in my memory where yesterday should be? I remember Easter Sunday 2000: drinking with Loz, Blake Benfield, Mum's old Fiesta. So long ago. After which, a mess.

Think...

It's like trying to remember a dream, without the trigger that brings about the recall. There's so little. A glimmer of something. Being very unwell. So scared. Was there a hospital? Maybe?

Come on, man!

A fleeting glimpse of a room. People dying. A nightmare, surely? The image is gone as quick as it arrived.

The harder I push to reassemble it, the more disorientated I am.

Fevered fantasies of Holly. Wonderful Holly. Who else would I be dreaming of?

What happened to me?

Where have I been?

No good. My mind's blank. What on earth happened to leave me so lost?

A quick search and this unfamiliar flat gives up what it knows about me. Guitar and amp on their trolley, over a hundred quid in polythene change bags: I still cut my living as a busker. But drawers of paperwork reveal that I have more in the bank than I'm used to. Christ, even having an account is an update in itself. Filed deeper, a decree absolute: my and Elouise's marriage reduced to a form from the county court.

I look again at the date: July 4, 2014. Why does that mean something to me? Why is the shape of it familiar?

Scrolling through my phone, I find three missed calls in the early hours. All from the same person. And a text at going on four a.m.

Will get you your money. Sorry—keep saying it. Promise this time. Give me till weekend. Won't let you down.

I call him back straightaway. Try over and over, but his phone's off. Why is Jazz wanting to give me money?

The worry is a punch to the gut. Nearly a year's gone by since that night I saw him: angry, armed, clinging to his place at school. And beneath that hardened skin, the same kindhearted kid he'd always been.

A forty-five-minute walk in the glare of the midday sun and I'm on the Sefton Hills estate, rapping on his door. He answers on the fourth go.

"Thank fuck, man!" Jazz says, holding a hand to his chest. "Alex, don't do that to me, man!" The corridor is dark and stuffy. He looks lankier than ever, wearing only tight boxers and the glaze of a man who's catching up on sleep.

"Yeah, sorry. Tried calling. Missed you last night. A few times."

He beckons me in. I duck into the kitchen and flick the kettle on.

"Leccy's off, old cuz. Have to be a cold one." He reaches into the dark depths of the fridge and grabs two colas. "Warm one, maybe," he says, shuffling his feet away from the cascade of brown foam as he opens one.

Medications are still heaped on the worktops, but the day-labeled pillboxes are stacked and empty. I glance to the end of the corridor but the living room curtains are drawn, too dark to see if anyone's there. But it's quiet, too quiet.

The door to Jazz's bedroom is half-open. There's a dark suit hanging on it.

"Your granddad," I say, before I can stop myself. "He…"

Jazz shrugs. "Same old, same old, innit."

"He's still…? He's doing…okay?"

"Man, I don't know. Some days he knows who I am, have a bit of a chat and that. Some days I go there and…"

"Sorry, man," I say, disguising my relief that he's at least still with us. I lay a hand on his clammy shoulder. "They're looking after him okay? At the…hospital?"

"The home," he corrects me. "Guess so. Better than I did." His tone hardens as he says it.

"We'll be having none of that, thank you." I wag a comical finger at him. "What's with the whistle?" I ask, strolling over and examining the three-piece suit. On closer inspection it's navy with a pinstripe. "It's sharp, mate."

"Ain't mine, cuz. Borrowed it off a mate. His dad's in the rag trade."

"What you dressing up for?"

"Not gonna bother with it."

"Bother with what, Jazz?"

"Supposed to be prom night, innit."

"What, tonight?"

"Things I gotta do."

"You finished school, yeah?" I can't hide my glee.

"You know that, cuz."

I follow him round as he throws open curtains and aimlessly tidies things. "Mate, you can't miss your prom night. No way. Won't let you."

"Don't even fit me right," he says, brushing past the suit and slipping on a crumpled Adidas T-shirt from under his pillow.

"You still getting shit from people at school?"

"Nah, man. They're cool. Most of them."

"So what's the matter?" I ask, grinning. "Can't get a date? That's it, isn't it? Every girl's turned you down?"

He sniggers. "Cuz, I ain't got no trouble there. Definitely not the problem."

"So come on, who is it? This poor little thing you'll be letting down if you don't go?"

I detect the hint of a swoon, a man daring to dream. "Ain't so simple. Kinda need to be somewhere else tonight."

"No chance. Won't have it."

"Can't even have a shower," Jazz says, sniffing his own armpits in disgust.

"Let me put some money on the meter."

"No way, man," he says.

"It's cool, mate. I'm kind of…solvent. Got a few quid I can spare."

"Owe you way too much already, man."

"What is this bullshit, mate? That message last night? You don't need to be giving me money."

"I've ripped the piss out of you."

"Mate, don't worry about it."

"I'll get you your money," Jazz snaps. "I'm not a leech."

"It's fine. Don't even have a clue what you owe me anyway. Just forget it."

"You might not be counting, old cuz, but I am." His tone says this is an argument I won't win.

"Let me just sort this, yeah? Then I'll back off. Start calling my debts in. But today, I won't take no for an answer. You shall…" I stop myself going on.

"Were you about to say, *You shall go to the ball*?"

"No."

"You were, weren't you?"

"Maybe."

"Man, you crack me up." Our laughter is disproportionate, two lives that have been short on humor of late.

We walk together to the store on the far side of the estate. "That's two hundred and thirty-four quid I owe you now," Jazz says as I put twenty on his electric.

I try to disguise my surprise; it's more than I expected. "Yeah, well, whenever…"

"Got a few quid coming in. Have you square in a few days."

We take a seat on a bench in the sun. "Got yourself a job?" I ask him.

"I've always had a job, old cuz. Since I was like fifteen. Nights at Hill's the Fruiterers down on Commercial Way. Loading up the trucks. Swear I've told you that."

"Right. Of course."

"Fiver an hour, cuz. Can't get by on that."

"So what's the scheme?"

"It's nothing. Not really."

"Oh, come on, man. I'm a nosey git, me. Don't leave me hanging."

Jazz shakes his head. "This and that."

I tap his knee with my palm. "It's stressing you out, isn't it?"

"I'm cool." It's a poor lie.

"Talk to me, man. You want to, don't you? That's why you've mentioned it, right? Come on. I'm unshockable."

"Yeah, yeah. Just been doing a bit of…running around. That's all. Looking after a few things now and then."

"Looking after what, exactly?"

"I don't know. Just…stuff."

"Come on, Jazz. What *stuff*?"

"Seriously, old cuz, I actually don't know."

"What we talking—drugs? Stolen goods? Help me out here."

"Look, I don't open the packages, all right? They're taped up. And I don't go asking. Way above my pay grade. Kid drops something over. Wait for my instructions, deliver where it wants to go."

"You're not that naive, Jazz. You gotta have a clue what's in there?"

"I don't spend too long thinking about it. Easier that way, innit?"

"And you're keeping this shit in your flat?"

"I know it's stupid, man. Don't need a lecture."

I scratch in my pockets but there are no smokes. We're twenty meters from the shop, but I fight the tug of temptation. "Man, I get the money situation. But seriously…"

"You think I have a choice here, yeah?"

"You're playing with your life, man." I sound more preachy than I mean to. "Look, I get it. It's decent money."

"Not really, it ain't."

"Fuck it off, then. Let me lend you a bit more. I'm good for it." I'm beginning to hate myself for constantly trying to give him money; are there not better ways I can make myself of use to this kid? "Sounds like a load of risk for not a lot of bunce. Hardly worth getting yourself banged up over."

He wears the expression reserved for bollockings from out-of-touch teachers. "Reckon getting banged up's the least of my worries."

"Mate, there's other ways to make a few quid. I know I'm a washed-up old loser, but I'm not as dumb as I look."

"You think that's how it works? What, you reckon I went out looking for the dodgiest old white bloke in a Range Rover I could find, told him I'm looking for employment? That's it, you reckon?"

I shrug. "Look, I'm sorry. I'm not—"

"You got no idea how it is." Jazz stands and begins walking toward his flat.

I follow, a half step behind his shoulder, annoyed with myself. This guy needs a friend to talk to, and he's picked me. Judgment isn't a good look on me.

"Tell me how it is, yeah?"

"No one asks to do this sort of shit, cuz," he eventually replies.

"Things are desperate. I do understand."

"It's not even that. You get…*drawn* into it. Don't even notice it happen, not at first."

"Go on."

"Bet it's the same for anyone round here who's got themselves into something they shouldn't. No one chooses it."

"What happened to you?"

"People start to notice, when you're skint."

"The wrong people?"

"You know it. Was getting some bits at the twenty-four-hour Esso, two months ago, maybe. Like, three in the morning, just got out of work. I'm ordering through the little letterbox thing, and the old guy inside's running round getting my stuff, looking like he'd happily murder me if there wasn't a sheet of bullet-proof glass between us."

"That guy works in every late-night garage. Don't take it personally."

"He's ringing up my stuff, and it comes to more than what cash I got. So I do the maths, get it down to a tenner's worth. The old git's proper loving it by now."

"I can well imagine."

"Anyway, I'm walking away, about to cross into the estate, and some bloke stops me. Asks me my name, what I'm doing out and about this time of night."

"You tell him to piss off and mind his own business?"

"He ain't the sort of geezer you go disrespecting, if you know what I mean."

"You knew the guy?"

"I've seen him around Sefton Hills a few times before. Everyone calls him Stevo. Bald head, big ginger beard. He don't live here, though, that's for sure. He's old—older than you."

"Thanks a lot. What does he drive, a mobility scooter?"

Jazz ignores the joke. "Got a Jag, innit."

"So what happened at the garage?"

"Tells me he's seen me around. We chat for a bit, asks about my grandfather and school and work and stuff. Says he likes me, that I'm a good sort."

"And he asks you to look after his shit for him?"

"Cuz, like I say, it don't work like that. If it did, I wouldn't have got involved. Nah, he just gives me a score. Tells me to buy something nice."

I nod slowly. "Okay. I get it now."

"Tried to give it back, Alex. I swear I did. Trying to keep my hands off that money."

"But you felt like you were offending him?"

"Exactly. He's saying *let me help you out* and all that. And he ain't the sort of geezer people say no to."

"And then you're in his pocket?"

"Didn't stop there, cuz. Few days later there's a meat pack from the halal place on the doorstep at home. Don't get me wrong, it was welcome. And who do I send it back to anyway?"

"Devious bastard."

"There was things after that too—groceries, another twenty quid. A few weeks goes by. Then this kid on a BMX turns up at the flat. Says he's got something from Stevo. Tells me to keep it safe till I get texted an address. Says it's worth fifty quid to me."

"And you can't tell him no."

"I ain't stupid, cuz. I ain't got a choice. Got like five packages hidden round the place right now."

"Shit, man."

"It's a fucking stupid mess to get myself into. Right now, I ain't even got anything to show for the…enterprise. Still skint."

We're back inside his flat now. Jazz falls backward onto the sofa and buries his head under a cushion.

"Being skint's shitty, man," I say. "You must be getting help, right? Now your granddad's not…about?"

"Been trying to sort it," he says. "There's some benefits you can get. But it's all meetings, phone calls. It's *long*, man. Taking months."

"So there's no money coming in, other than what you…*earn*?"

"My grandfather, he used to get benefits when he couldn't work anymore. It weren't loads or anything. Enough to get a bit of shopping, pay the bills."

"It stopped?"

"He's in a home, innit."

"And you're supposed to run on thin air."

"They keep saying it's gonna get sorted."

"Mate, this is bollocks," I say. "We gotta sort this. It's one thing we *can* sort."

"You reckon? Cuz, it gets boring. Sitting on the phone, never getting through to no one. Run out of credit, can't buy no more. Then the leccy goes, can't even charge the phone till I get to school. Trying to do exams at the same time." He flings the cushion across the room and emits a growling noise, the way a kid whose frustrations are entirely trivial might.

With the electric back on, the kettle I flicked on nearly two hours ago has boiled. I fix us both a tea and open some windows, let the summer drift through.

"So, about this prom of yours," I say.

"Yeah, I dunno, man," Jazz says. "Like I said, things I should be doing."

"Like what? Sitting here, waiting for a text to land? Is that how it works? Don't sound like much of a life, man."

"I guess."

"Tell me about this hot date of yours."

There's the flash of a smirk, a puddling of the eyes. "Should go see my grandfather. You know, he's maybe expecting me."

"Bet you see him loads."

Jazz doesn't reply.

"Got a picture?" I ask him.

"Don't do this to me, man," he says, holding his phone face-down against his thigh, more childlike than ever.

"She's gotta be quite something."

His playful expression hardens. "Look, Alex, maybe it's better I leave this."

"You'll break a heart, man. Mark my words you will."

"People don't really know about…*us*. About me and…"

"You wanna keep it that way?"

"Maybe it ain't so simple."

I've removed his suit from its hanger, inspecting it on my lap. It's a nice piece of work: tightly tailored, lairy lining, doctor's cuffs with each button on a different color thread. "No one misses prom, mate."

"Tell me about yours," Jazz says, grinning.

"Jesus, man! What's to tell?"

"You ain't that boring, don't believe it."

"We called it a leaver's ball, back in the nineties."

"The 1890s?"

"Very good. I spent the evening—what I can remember of it—at the bar, ignoring my date. Got so shit-faced I ended up in A and E."

"Shit."

"Pathetic, isn't it? Had something of an obsession with being seen to drink more than anyone else."

"Why?"

"Now, there's an excellent question. I'll keep you posted if I work it out. I recall having this crazy idea that if I left a group of guys early, they'd start talking about me after I'd gone. Can't do that if you're the last man standing, can they?"

"So it weren't cos you were crazy nervous about your date?"

"Yeah, that too most likely."

Jazz smiles to himself.

I drop onto the sofa next to him and hook an arm round his shoulder. "Mate, you've just cold feet, haven't you?"

He giggles. "Nah, man."

"All bollocks, isn't it? All this *I've gotta work, got no money* caper."

"Those things are true as well."

"Tell me all about her, Jazz."

He taps at his phone with it close to his nose. A headshot

fills the screen as he passes it to me. Jazz shifts down the sofa, twisted away.

"Wow," I say.

"You don't need to say that," he mumbles.

"Mate, *wow*'s the word." I grin at him, and his own smile seeps back. "And this—tonight—is your first date?"

"If I go."

"Yeah, yeah. Many people know about you two?"

"Nah, not really."

"So come on, who asked who?"

Jazz is uncustomarily shy. "He did."

"You've liked him awhile?"

"Yeah, kind of. He's cool."

"His name?"

"Ty." There's a sparkle about him as he seizes the excuse to utter the word.

"He's gorgeous, mate," I say, taking a moment to appreciate again this square-jawed man staring from the screen and out to infinity. He exudes beauty and potential; I'm briefly envious till I remember how swiftly those joys are snatched away, how you only realize they were there as they disappear over the horizon.

"You really...think so?"

I pass his phone back. "Sure, man. Bet you two look cute together."

He shrugs. "Cheers, cuz." He's watery in the eyes. "Appreciate it."

"I'm really happy for you, mate. That you've found someone. Found something." My longing for Holly hits me like a kick in the guts. "It's a great thing—*wanting*. Maybe the best thing there is. Your granddad would be happy for you too."

"You think?"

"He loves you, doesn't he?"

Jazz gives a small nod. He turns away from me, stares out the window. I pass him a clean tissue from my pocket.

"Ty's going to uni," he eventually says. "Nottingham."

"You got the summer."

"Maybe."

"So go to uni as well."

Jazz smirks. "Not on the cards right now, is it?"

"How are the A-level results shaping up, do you reckon?"

"Cuz, how many times we talked about this?"

"Dunno. Once or twice?"

"When I get my results in six weeks, you'll be the first to know. Promise. If they're the same as I've predicted, we'll both be happy."

"Which was what?"

"Come on, man, you know this. Amount you bang on about it."

"Remind me."

"Two As and two Bs, innit."

I do my best to hide my surprise. Last year he was hanging on to his place at school by his fingertips. "Bloody hell, mate."

"Yeah, well, I ain't actually *got* them yet."

"That's insane, Jazz. You're a clever bastard, you know that, right?"

"It's thanks to you, innit, old cuz?"

"How do you figure that?"

"Come on, we both know I'd have been kicked out, like two terms ago."

"What saved you?"

"Shut up."

"What the hell's you being a bona fide genius got to do with me?"

"I do appreciate it, man. Even if I don't always tell you it. I do know that without you giving up all those evenings, tutoring me for nothing more than a cup of tea, I'd be in the shit right now."

"Jazz, mate…"

"I owe you, man. I'll never forget it, you know that?"

"I've been *tutoring* you," I mumble, trying not to phrase it as a question. "How long's it been?" I ask, giving the impression of racking my brain.

"Was after that day, innit. When I got caught thieving and you…intervened."

"Ah, yes. Hide-the-knife day!"

"Yeah, man!"

I laugh at the memory, the victory we scored over authority. "I've been helping you, since then?" I ask. "What, like *often*?"

He looks at me uncertainly but then shakes it away, familiar enough with my funny moments. "Two nights a week, wasn't it. Sometimes three."

"Fuck." It's like an explosion in my guts. It is, I suppose, *pride*. For this guy, and for myself too. Totally alien feeling. Booze wouldn't come close. Not even cocaine. "Thank you for letting me help you, man."

"What?"

"These results you're gonna get," I say, wagging a finger accidentally. "They're all down to you, yeah. Nothing to do with me. You gotta remember that. Letting me give you a hand, that's done more for me than it ever will for you. Understand that, yeah?"

"You chat some weird shit, old cuz."

"Yup, I know it." I'm light-headed, dry-mouthed. High as a kite. "Go to uni," I snap. "Whatever it takes, you gotta go. Jazz, don't waste this."

"Sound like my teachers, man. Might apply next year, if I can save a bit. And if my grandfather's sorted okay."

"Get on it. While you know you can. Good decisions—"

"Beget good decisions?" Jazz interrupts in a poor impression of my lecturing voice.

"I've said that before?"

"Once or twice."

"Just something a wise man once told me." I extract myself

from the sofa, too alive to sit still. "So where's this prom happening, then?"

"Party boat, innit, on the river."

"Christ, sounds dangerous. Sounds amazing!"

"Maybe."

"Jazz, mate, don't flannel me here, yeah? You were never gonna miss this, were you? A man in love isn't gonna pass up an opportunity like this."

He smirks. "Guess so."

"How long we got, till you're supposed to be there?"

"Dunno. Two and a half hours, maybe."

I wander into the bathroom and set a bath running, whipping up a handful of shower gel into a mountain of bubbles. "Not only are you going to *the ball*, my boy," I shout into the corridor. "But you are going without a care in this whole miserable world. Because you've worked very bloody hard for this."

"Give it a rest, old cuz," Jazz says.

"Because if you don't go," I tell him, "you're robbing this very proud old man of the chance to wave you off and shed a tear for the fine man you've become."

"Can't have that, I suppose," he says.

My back is already turned, Jazz's shoes in my hand as I prowl the flat in search of some polish.

"Make no mistake," I tell him. "This'll be the night of your life."

Iron Sky

The sun dissolves into the river. This familiar concourse is steeped in pink light. I've not played a note yet, but already a few couples gather at a distance around me.

I'm standing on the very spot which will, sometime soon, sprout that memorial with the granite plinth and the soaring silver doves that are catnip to vandals. But today, no such obstacle. This space is mine. I open my guitar case, let its red lining invite donations.

The light dims further. I tap out a groove on the sound box, come in with a two-chord riff. My small audience taps feet and smiles like they've heard this a hundred times. The lyrics of Dusty Springfield's "Spooky" float out into this tacky, holiday-warm night.

I saw Jazz off a couple of hours ago, half a mile along the bank from here. We hugged and he joined the crowd of bright, beautiful people as they filed onto a disco-lit deck, disappeared into a haze of smoke and carefree energy and too much fragrance. I promised him I'll be here when he gets back. With an evening to kill, every overflowing pub has called out to me, or more accurately, the sight of those relaxed drinkers has. But I am not one of them; I can't drink the way they can. Instead, as I've walked on by, I've felt the headwind hard: I am living this day differently, pushing against the weight of my history. A swift trip made back home for my gear. Right here, doing what I love most, is how I shall instead spend these hours till Jazz returns.

Why would I need booze, anyway? I'm high on the thrill of having done the decent thing for someone. If indeed we are what we do, I am for once not a disappointment.

I don't know a single song from the last nineteen years, but this growing audience don't seem to care. "Blackbird" by The Beatles now. The phone in my pocket vibrates. With barely a breath, into "There Is a Light that Never Goes Out." Again it rings. It's not mine; that's stuffed in my amp trolley. Who'd want to call me, anyway?

I snatch the phone for a few seconds between songs, keen not to lose my momentum with this crowd. It's Jazz's war-torn Samsung: I made him surrender it as we said our goodbyes. You can't let yourself go with the weight of all your troubles in your pocket. Two missed calls from the same unsaved number.

Jazz agreed: if any *jobs* land for him tonight, we can take care of them together later.

An hour rolls by. My audience evolves, but never shrinks. There's a fine take in the guitar case, pound coins like a mound of gold beneath the sodium light, a good few notes too. The phone against my thigh is quiet.

Why, then, am I feeling uneasy? I play on, but I can't shake it. I'm not lost in the music anymore. Things gnawing at my brain.

Am I messing with the wrong people here? Is Jazz so far in he's not even allowed a few hours to himself?

But it's not just that worrying me. It's like I'm pushing harder against history than I ever have, racing into the headwind. Without moving an inch. Like I'm holding back the tide.

Is this some sort of stage fright? I feel exposed all of a sudden. Panicked.

What is wrong with me?

The audience thins, the circle expanding away from me, less engaged. The few that danced are stilled. Play as I might—Clapton's "Let It Grow" now—I've lost the vim. These people perhaps haven't noticed the shift, only that they're no longer entertained.

I'm scanning the concourse. Hyperaware. Unshakeable sense of impending doom.

Why? What can I sense?

There's a group of men, four or five. Walking with purpose close to the water's edge. Well-dressed thirtysomethings with swagger. Are they looking for someone? They look like they're looking for someone. I roll around my chord progression over and over, forget the words I should be singing. They disappear into the distance, my stare following their backs. Just lads on a night out, perhaps.

Sort yourself out, man.

I try to lose myself in my work. Bash out the songs, one after another. My performance is square, unfree. Greasy hands slipping on fretboard. Vibrato in my voice. Playing music has always been my sanctuary; what, tonight, is different?

A man steps closer to me. Too close. Bald, short and wide. Beetroot face. He tries to sing along to "The Boxer," six inches from my mike. His breath is flammable. He's probably half an hour from passing out and pissing himself. I should know. I edge backward, pulse hammering. He has the familiar eyes of someone both content and one wrong move from fury.

He bumps against my guitar as he attempts to dance. I force myself to give him a wink; I've no right to this indignation I'm feeling.

A couple of police officers prowl the concourse thirty meters away, hands tucked behind stab vests. Do I call over to them? And say what? I'm *scared*?

In any case, their presence doesn't make me feel safer. It never has. As likely to be a source of danger as a defense against it. They move along without even a glance this way.

My drunken friend tires soon enough, staggers into the night.

I've said it to Jazz: how busking is like standing naked and letting people laugh at you. Often that's true, but it's never frightened me, not like it does now.

Short on breath, sick to the stomach, I force myself to go on. What else can I do?

This'll pass. Don't give in to it.

A boat meanders by. Deck flashing in green and magenta lights. Two hundred party animals tearing it up, time of their lives—Jazz's prom. Why am I so glad to see it? It'll soon be docking up the river where I saw him off four hours ago. In my pause between songs, a thumping bassline from their dance floor fills the night.

"Alex, you old git!" Jazz yells from the deck. There's a murmur of laughter from what remains of my audience. His voice is like a drug, calming me instantly.

In jest, I give him a two-fingered salute.

"Wait there, old cuz!" he shouts, the boat passing level. "Got people who want to meet you. We'll be there in ten. Don't go nowhere, yeah?"

I give him a thumbs-up. Another of their party has meanwhile climbed onto the vessel's roof. He drops his suit trousers and performs a flamboyant willy-copter for those of us on the bank.

"Kids today," I remark into my mike. My audience laughs, closes back in around me. The cool euphoria that follows panic washes over me.

What the fuck was that about?

Four breezy songs later and I catch sight of Jazz heading my

way. He walks along the very edge of the river. Hand in hand
with another young man. Even at this distance it's clear enough
from the way they carry themselves: tonight has been everything
they hoped it would be. I play a little harder, sing brighter. My
heart is full at the sight.

Thirty meters from me, they stop. They are alone, well ahead
of a group of their peers who are only now coming into sight,
heading this way.

I busy myself with my performance of "Hand in My Pocket,"
pretend I'm paying them no attention as they turn toward each
other, hands interlocked at their sides, and kiss. At first lightly,
tentatively. Their restraint is short-lived, surrendering to each
other. Letting go.

A cheer erupts from their friends in the distance, loud enough
that I can hear it over myself. The goodwill is infectious; there
are whistles from some of my own small audience as they follow my gaze along the bank.

If I was half as hypervigilant now as I was earlier, I'd have
spotted the people approaching from the opposite direction ages
ago. I'd have seen them long before they passed me and ap-
proached Jazz and Ty. Three lads. Early twenties, I'd say. Two
hanging back—wingmen—one leading the way. Barrel chest,
rugby shirt, stupid moustache. Arms that, although big, have
no reason to curve that far from torso.

In a world that belongs to them alone, Jazz and Ty separate
their lips by as much as they can bear to: a few inches, no more.
I can see Jazz's smiling face now. He gazes at Ty; no attention
spared.

This group of three are just meters off them. Is it my imagination, the way their front man, marching along the edge of the
river, seems on a collision course with them? Or is this a return
of the rabid paranoia?

I'm minded to drop the guitar, place myself between them
and this beautiful couple. But I hold myself back.

Why this sense of a headwind? There's a force, pushing me to act, which I'm defying. Staying here, playing on, is *hard*.

My suspicions are proven correct. Like a missile locked on target, the leader of this pack of three barges against Ty's shoulder.

Ty is spun around. His expression is utter confusion.

But it's the look on Jazz's face that breaks my heart. No shock there. No, this is a man caught out. Guilty. Of course this isn't okay; of course he's not allowed this triumph.

Jazz reflexes out an arm to steady Ty, stop him stumbling over the edge into the water.

"Ty!" someone yells from their group of school friends, a hundred meters away. "Omar! What the fuck?" They start running this way.

Omar. It takes a second to place it, no more. It slaps me round the head.

Omar. Omar Jassim. *Jazz.* A childish nickname, perhaps used only by me.

Today's date, that's been bugging me all day.

This very spot. Etched in brass. Bolted to granite. Soaring doves, petrol station flowers.

So lost in my own troubles, I've missed it. How the hell could I have missed it?

There's a boom through my amp as my guitar hits the ground. I take a stride in their direction, audience parting.

I can see the change of gear in Jazz's face; a switch from someone real to something he's been forced to learn. "Fuck you doing?" he says to the men facing him.

"Dirty faggots," their spokesman says. Face of the revolted. Stance of the righteous.

This attack is nothing to do with Jazz's debts. Or the man he's found himself accidentally in the employ of. Not a hangover from the days he was foul of the school bullies. No. Just plain old scum-of-the-earth homophobes.

"Fuck you!" Jazz says, slamming his palm against the bloke's toned bicep. He helps Ty to his feet.

The guy moves his face to within a few inches of Jazz's. He ejects a mouthful of spit that splatters across the bridge of Jazz's nose. "Filthy perverts."

"Please?" Ty says.

One of the wingmen steps forward, swings a kick into the back of Ty's leg. He crumples, staggering back a step before rolling onto his backside.

It takes every ounce of self-control I possess. I cling one hand to my mike stand, as though it might hold me back. Watching in shock and disgust, but I don't leave the spot.

My audience seems to be hanging on my move. They too look on, sickened, ready to act. If I get involved, some of them, I'm sure, will too.

It's like I'm dangling from a cliff's edge. Gravity pulls at me, tries to get me over. But I'm clinging on.

Things *have* to be different.

Maybe I have no way of changing this. Dr. Defrates's words in my brain, reminding me how little we have control over. Should I then wade in, do what I can to help?

The headwind hammers against me. Tries to blast me into this situation. History *demands* I involve myself.

If I let the path of fate decide the way, we're all screwed. So I stand. I watch this injustice, desperate to fight. But if I've learned one thing, it is that my instincts let me down.

Their group of friends races along the bank. They'll soon be with them.

Jazz and his aggressor face off. The lug of spit oozes down Jazz's cheek. The guy in the rugby shirt tells him he's dirt. That he should be dead.

Ty lies on the round, rolled in a ball. Gets called every name.

Their mates from prom, seven of them, stop a few meters

short. These people, they're not fighters. They say little, look on with panic. As impotent as I am.

I pray that Jazz won't look this way. Won't see me standing off like this, nothing more in my arsenal than this glare that bores toward the piece of shit in the rugby shirt. No sign of those police from earlier now they're needed.

I can see it, though. How this *could* be. How perhaps it was. Me, not resisting the draw of the pubs. Meeting Jazz here, well-oiled. Steaming straight in. Fighting for justice? Or fighting to be seen fighting? To look the part? Can see it: escalating the violence, fighting for Jazz so that he ends up fighting for me. An unlucky blow taken, or five. We are resilient, and we are fragile. So little between the two.

Could it be that involving myself condemns Jazz?

All I know: things *have* to be different.

"What you looking at, prick?" one of the wingmen shouts over to me.

I stand. The wind pushes but I don't move an inch. It's so unnatural to surrender my pride like this. I am giving away so much more of *me* than if I were to get stuck in, throw insults and punches. The man is yelling into a vacuum, wasting his own hateful energy. Not having it turned back on himself, amplified.

The worst our enemies can do is turn us into them.

Is that what's holding back this audience of mine too? Are they wise enough to know that intervening too soon might make this situation more volatile?

"Get fucked," Jazz shouts, barging a shoulder against his attacker. He reaches a hand out to Ty, helps him up.

The three guys block the way, not done. "Come on, then, walk past," one says. "I dare you, scum."

"You're the scum," a girl says, taking a step forward from their group of friends. She's five foot nothing in heels, wrapped in sky blue satin and coils of ginger hair. She doesn't shout, just states the fact. The rest of the group closes in, still a half step behind her.

"It's okay, Chels," Jazz says, holding up a palm.

"What are you so scared of?" the girl asks.

The bloke takes too long to reply. "Fuck off, fat slut" is all he eventually manages.

But it's clear: this situation is already less dangerous. Momentum lost. Diffused.

A woman in my audience, can of Pimm's in hand, edges close to me. "Don't stop for them," she says quietly. "Play something."

I'm unsure. But she's got a point: the mood on the concourse is tenser for this silence.

I step back, sling my guitar over my shoulders.

"You go wherever *you're* going," the girl says. "And we'll go where *we're* going."

It's an emergency song choice, the one that comes most naturally. No intro, straight into the vocal. "Everyday" rings across the concourse, out over the black water. The space is no longer claustrophobic.

I can't hear what's being said. A few sentences exchanged. Body language that talks of a confrontation done. Nowhere left for it to go.

My performance gathers confidence. The voice in my amp is more polished than I've known it in a long while.

At the river's edge, it's over. Shoulders are barged, a limp parting gesture as those three angry men fade into the night.

I'm sorry, I mouth to Jazz as he and Ty saunter over to this small crowd.

He shrugs. "No sweat, old cuz," he says, reaching past the mike and slapping my arm. He's a little red in the eyes, a touch shaky at the fingertips, but no worse.

Ty limps and he's tearful, but is soon comforted by this group of good people. More of their friends arrive along the bank.

These people are not even close to calling it a night. I switch up the tempo, belt out the songs.

Jazz and Ty tear it up with the best of them, an evening too perfect to be ruined.

Is that it? Is it done?

Disaster averted?

How can it possibly be so different?

Wasn't it Dr. Defrates who said how life doesn't hinge on the details? How change is born of committing to living differently?

And yet, with such a small shift in behavior, a tragedy has become—what—a blemish? On an otherwise joyous night?

Straight into "Shiny Happy People." Cheesy? Sure. But I'm washed clean of cynicism. The pubs have turned out, and this has become the biggest crowd I've ever entertained. People dance all the way from where I stand to the river's edge.

Was it such a small change? I wonder, barely half my mind on the question, as I hammer out the song. Would a small change take so much effort?

The final minutes of 4 July 2014 slip away as I play. And still, here he is: *Omar Jassim*. Having the time of his life.

SEPTEMBER 5, 1997 | AGE 22

Talk Tonight

"Did I save him?" I ask.

Dr. Defrates smiles. "How fascinating that you use the past tense, for something nearly two decades hence."

The waitress delivers my very expensive cappuccino, together with Defrates's very expensive frozen yogurt, to our small bistro table. He suggested Kensington High Street; he can settle the bill. "Think we're past the *mystery of time* stuff now," I say, slurping at the froth on my coffee.

"Perhaps it was he who saved you," he says. "*Will* save you, maybe I should say."

"Okay," I reply, not in the mood for unpicking his cryptic answers.

"Cause and effect," he says, like I should understand exactly what he's getting at.

It's late afternoon. I've spent all day trying to get hold of this guy, and the past half an hour sitting beside this packed street discussing the events of yesterday. Not that there's a better use of my time: Holly—*on* though our relationship appears to be— is abroad with old school friends for another fortnight. No option to text on my primitive mobile; not even the excitement of forensically studying her words to pass the time.

"So, that memorial," I say. "The one where I busk. It'll be gone?"

"We'll see," he says, ignoring a dollop of yogurt that plops onto his collar.

"Come on."

"Well, I think we can safely assume that," he says. "Not so much *gone*. Never to have been…"

"A life saved," I muse. A pang of joy at the thought of meeting Jazz in later years, seeing the man he becomes.

"A life *not wasted*."

"Is there a difference?"

"We'll see who is saved," Defrates says.

A shoulder sweeps against my ear, so packed on the pavement. My coffee slops into the saucer as another hip nudges our table. "This isn't annoying at all," I say.

"Fascinating, isn't it?" Defrates says. "I've been meaning to come up here all week. Not to pay my respects or anything. It's just…humans. Fascinating."

Most of the slow-moving throng carries bunches of flowers as they file toward Kensington Palace. Those who head away do so shining with tears. "This is a big deal, isn't it?" I saw the front pages on every newspaper stall on my way over; I know what's happened, that Princess Diana's funeral is tomorrow morning.

"Conspiracy by the florist companies," Defrates says. "That's my bet."

From here I can see where the tributes begin, the shallows of an ocean of flowers.

"Is this something we should try and...do something about?" I'm only thinking out loud.

"God, no!" he says, snorting with laughter.

"Understood."

"Let's worry about the things that exist at our own behest, Alex." Best teacher voice. "This is not our concern."

"You don't reckon there's something..."

Defrates sweeps away my point with the back of his hand. "Don't confuse the size of the grief with the magnitude of the loss. One life—all of *this*. There are greater tragedies every day, Alex."

"I guess." I picture the memorial by the river, how it tended to always bear just a single bunch of flowers: cheap, limp. It seems likely that it was me who was putting them there.

Defrates gestures toward the many passing mourners. "This, Alex, it's...over the top. Hysteria. And absolutely bloody enthralling, to anyone interested in people."

"I'm sure you're right."

"You know your trouble, young man? You're drunk on success!"

I smile at him. "Maybe."

"You're a young man. World at your feet."

"Whatever."

"You're positively *glowing*. It's lovely to see."

"Something about yesterday," I say. "It turns out I was tutoring this kid. Nothing in it for me, just helping him out."

"Good for you."

"And he's all set to ace his A-levels. A year before, he was likely to drop out."

"Satisfying, isn't it?" Defrates says, shuddering with brain freeze as he shovels in another mouthful.

"More than that. It was, I don't know, an actual *thrill*. Blew me away. Seeing a result like that."

"Inspiring another human."

"Yes! Exactly that!"

"So—do more of it." He chuckles as a couple passes by, crying hysterically.

"You know something, I've always thought that the one thing I wanted was to be looked up to. Maybe yesterday I saw what that actually *means*. Does that sound stupid?"

He shakes his head. "It doesn't look how you thought it would, does it?"

"I can't even describe it. How good it felt."

"It is quite something," he says.

My weighty Nokia tells me it's nearly five. "I'm gonna have to run," I say. "Leave you to your people-watching."

"Good decisions beget good decisions?"

"Maybe."

He winks before turning his back on me, gazing enthralled along Palace Avenue.

I'm heading against the flow of foot traffic as I march along the pavement. A few glance at me with distaste; I'm smiling whilst they sob. It's two miles' walk, give or take. Changes have to be made whilst I still know that change is possible. This is a rare opportunity: the gift of a day early in my life, before the rot.

I cover the distance in under twenty minutes, taking Battersea Bridge at a full sprint, headwind all the way. I'm puffing and glowing red as I stride through the doors of St. Christopher's College of Further Education. A few friends from sixth form went here; it's where Loz did his computer science course.

"Cutting it a touch fine," the woman on reception says when I ask about courses.

"Sorry. Got held up." I thumb a prospectus.

"No, I mean if you're hoping for entry this year. Term starts in a week."

"Is it totally hopeless?" I ask, sweat trickling from sideburns.

"Not necessarily," she says. "Sometimes we have spaces come free in the run-up."

"What do you need from me?"

She digs about behind her desk for some forms. From a small telly on the wall, a solemn Queen addresses the nation.

"Do you have any prior qualifications?" the woman asks.

"I got a place at Cambridge a couple of years ago," I reply.

"Okay," she says, nodding but not meeting my eye.

"Can we just forget I said that? I mean, it's not relevant, is it?" It's still automatic, my need to tell every and anyone. I don't know why. But I think this is the last time I'll be mentioning it.

"Well, if you—"

"Look, I got three As and a B at A-level. That was two years ago. I've been kind of…fannying about since then."

"Those are very good results."

"Do you need to see something? I've probably got my National Record of Achievement somewhere."

She makes no effort to disguise her laugh. "No, darling. We definitely don't need to see that. You could probably get rid of that."

"Right. Got it."

"Take a seat over there," she says, passing me a form. "I'll get it processed tonight. The admissions officer will be in touch after the weekend, fingers crossed."

I thank her excessively. In shaky handwriting, I fill out the application.

OCTOBER 18, 2008 | AGE 33

One Day Like This

Wide awake, jolting upright like I've been electrocuted. Heart pounding.

I've been dreaming of Holly. That apparition of her, cloaked in blue, masked face, purple gloves, hummingbird tattoo. Calm words, terrified eyes. Becoming a recurring nightmare. So real, though, so impeccably detailed.

I roll a sleeping bag down from my tacky torso.

What is this place?

This space is vast, pitch-black. There's a breathy hum of machinery, distant, but from all corners. A few red LEDs twinkling on the high ceiling. Small signs that glow neon green here and there on faraway walls. As my damp eyes come to life I can make out the words: *Fire Exit, Stairs, No Entry.*

Some sort of warehouse. Why am I kipping on the floor of a warehouse? There's a snivel not far from me. A gasping snore from somewhere else. A lengthy, low-frequency fart that ends on an uptick. Adjusting to the poor light, I realize I am far from alone. Haphazardly arranged, there are at least another forty sleeping bags on this scratchy carpeted floor.

I sit up, so stiff. God knows how old I am. There's a fog in my head and lead in my bones. This is no hangover, though. I recognize it: it's the feeling that comes with getting less than two hours sleep in uncomfortable surroundings; too familiar from teenage one-night stands.

Who are all these people?

I shuffle to my feet, take a walk. This building is enormous. A first suggestion of dawn turns a bank of skylights from black to blue. Light washes over a huge re-creation of planet Earth suspended fifteen meters in the air. A velvet rope prevents me leaving this room and crossing into the hall where a great model of the solar system is being slowly illuminated by the coming day, like this is the very beginning of time.

I know where I am. It is confirmed by the logos in the corners of posters on the wall. I've always loved this place. Although that fact offers no explanation as to what the hell I'm doing in the Science Museum at the crack of dawn.

In the fluorescent light of the toilets I take a long piss, stretch myself out whilst studying my reflection. Youngish, healthy. Hands pink, no tarred nails, no guitar string callouses. And that silver band on my ring finger. That's not been there for a while. A passing sickness at the memory of Elouise sliding it on.

The door swings open, almost catching me as I make to leave.

"Sorry, sorry," the kid says, flashing me a grin as he passes. He's barefoot, dressed in a Day-Glo tracksuit zipped to the neck.

I freeze, try not to stare at this prepubescent wisp of a boy as he uses the urinal. "Are you...okay?"

He turns. My suspicions are correct. Younger than I've ever seen him, eleven or twelve. But it *is* Jazz.

"I always wake up early," he tells me. "It's my grandfather,

see. He's up at like four in the morning every day. For work."
He scrubs his face with flat palms and hot water. So childlike.

"What does he do, your granddad?" I ask.

"Breakfast chef, innit. At a hotel."

Hearing his familiar voice unbroken is like listening to a recording of him on fast-forward. Why does the sound make me
want to hug him? Make me wonder if I might cry?

"Couldn't sleep either," I say. "Reckon anyone'll mind if we
take a look round? Not every day we get the Science Museum
to ourselves."

"Didn't they say about the alarms?" Jazz says. He does his
best impression of adenoidal authority, finger wagging: "The
motion sensors will be on till eight o'clock, don't leave this hall
under any circumstances."

"What's the time now?"

Jazz shrugs. "Nearly seven, maybe."

"Shame. Fancied a look round the Energy Hall. That's still
there, right?"

He laughs like I'm kidding. "Was last night!"

"Always bloody loved that. All the big old steam engines."

"Yes, we know!" Jazz says. "We were down there till, what
was it, midnight with you." He laughs and it soon spreads to me.
There's something radiating off him that I've never encountered
before: an easy happiness, a lust for fun.

What am I doing here, on a sleepover in a museum? Jazz
got to know me because he watched me busk. Because he was
hiding away from his bullies, needing a friend. That's how our
paths crossed.

Back in the main room, and Jazz's waking has had a dom-
ino effect, girls and boys rising and slipping from sleeping bags.
Mops of crazy bed hair and lurid dressing gowns flap energeti-
cally around the place. Jazz, a pace ahead of me, is relaxed—
clearly among friends. No bullies here. For a moment I feel out
of place, standing here, a grown man scruffy with sleep, in a

crumpled sweatshirt and trackie bottoms. But I am familiar to these children, it seems: smiles and nods and even a "Morning."

I dig in the rucksack next to my sleeping bag, withdraw what must be my phone. Stare at the date awhile.

Wow.

This is my third visit to October 2008. The first time, 28th of this month, I was in a high-security prison, HMP Meadway, Mum visiting. The second time, on the 23rd, my life had updated: I'd been released early, shorter sentence, nicer prison, meeting with my probation officer. Here I am, on the 18th, a free man.

This, then, is an update. A big, fat update.

Why am I here, though?

"Everything okay?" Jazz asks.

I shake my head, still looking at the date across the blue screen.

"Thought no one was allowed phones," he says. He grins cheekily down at me.

I shove it back in my bag. "Sorry, Jazz. Not ignoring you."

He sniggers awkwardly, reddens a little. *"Jazz,"* he repeats, like I've said something wrong.

"What is it?"

"Weird you calling me *Jazz*," he says. "Just sounds…funny."

"Well, it is your name!"

"Yeah, with mates…" He shrugs.

"Sorry, Omar!" I say, mocking voice. "There I was thinking I was one of your mates." Another kid passes by and laughs aloud at what I've just said.

"Course you are," he says, patting me on the shoulder, grin back full-width. "You're my very best mate, sir."

"What's that?"

He looks mildly panicked at my reaction. "Sorry, sir. Just saying—"

I hold a palm up. Try to reassure him nothing's wrong. But I can't speak.

"All right, sir," a girl with a foghorn voice says as she passes close by.

I nod, rabbit in headlights.

A group of lads heads my way as they leave the toilets. "Morning!" one sings at me. He lays out a hand for five, but I'm distracted and slow; he snatches it away before I'm even close. "Think you need a little more sleep, sir," he says, sauntering away.

I turn my back on the crowd and walk to the edge of this room, take a moment to gaze from the mezzanine into the next hall. The giant planetarium is glowing orange in the morning light. One small backwater in a beautiful universe. "Are you okay?" Jazz asks, a few steps behind me.

I drag my sleeve across my face. "You're a kind kid," I tell him. "It's a pleasure to know you. A real fu… A real damned pleasure. You know that?"

He looks a little weirded out. "You're a pretty cool teacher too," he says, looking at the floor.

I ruffle the back of his head, and immediately wonder if that's permissible. "Cheers, Jazz. Sorry—*Omar.*"

"Mr. Dean," comes a shout. I scan the chaos of the room, and find a woman with a mass of gray dreadlocks waving at me. "If you wouldn't mind, Mr. Dean." She is, it appears, the only other adult present. Helpfully she's wearing her Science Museum visitor lanyard.

I hurry over to her. "What can I do, Mrs. Linwood?"

She shakes her head at the sight of a ten-way pillow fight. "How did you sleep?" She clutches at her hip in pain.

"Dreadfully. You?"

"Yup. Still, that's the infamous Night at the Museum done for another year."

"How many's it been now?"

"What's this, my fifth? Not as many as you've done, I'm not as much of a fan of the hair shirt."

"They do seem to be enjoying themselves."

"Bully for them. The nocturnal farting, Mr. Dean! It's a wonder the whole place doesn't go up."

I rock with laughter.

"Best you feed the lions," she says. "Before they attack."

I dish out teas and juices, and breakfast cereals in variety boxes. The sound of more than forty Year Eights stuffing down cornflakes is quite something. No appetite myself, I sit awkwardly with my colleague, wonder what I possibly have to impart to these kids.

"Give us one of your quizzes, sir," a girl shouts. There are murmurs of agreement among the chomping and slurping.

Are they taking the piss? Am I being taken off here?

"Yeah, come on!" Jazz shouts from the back. There is a shuffling inward of bodies.

"I'll keep score," Mrs. Linwood says. "Let's have it, Mr. Dean, one of your legendary quick-fire rounds."

"On what?" I ask.

"Anything and everything, I believe," she says.

It takes me approximately thirty seconds to ease into the job, to slip into the mode of the performer. I fire questions at them: history, science, riddles, whatever. That I have no useful knowledge of events of the past thirteen years doesn't cause a problem. They shout answers over each other, celebrate their successes with abandon. They are perhaps the most thrilling audience I've ever held. Who, after all, is sharper, brighter, more cutting than a room of twelve-year-olds?

I'm not sure what I enjoy more: the sense of entertaining them, or the current of good-natured piss-taking that sweeps my way. I've never felt more looked up to, more like *somebody*.

Outside, we send the kids off to their weekends, some to waiting parents, others to their own devices. Embassy flags snap in the dusty autumn wind. Soot and the river on the air: my city.

"Mr. Dean," a man says, rich Middle Eastern accent. I meet his outstretched arm, and he cups both hands around mine as he shakes it. "So good to meet you." Jazz leans against the man.

"Likewise," I eventually say, playing the part of someone making his acquaintance for the first time. Not that I'd have recognized him at a glance. The first time we met, I was helping after a fall, dealing with his soiled clothes. The time after that, an empty shell of a man, unable to leave the house. But today, Jazz's granddad is a dark-haired, light-on-his-feet gentleman, looking far younger than his sixtysomething years. Although, up close, I see those same wise brown eyes. He's a remarkably good-looking man.

"Absolute pleasure," I add, disguising as best I can my sorrow. Only faced with him in good health do I fully appreciate the injustice ahead.

"My boy, and all his friends," he tells me. "They say very good things about you."

"Don't believe everything you hear."

Jazz's granddad slaps a palm against my shoulder and laughs. Clearly he's fresh from his early shift. His aftershave can't compete with that commercial kitchen smell, fryers and relentless toil. "You know what, Mr. Dean? My boy, he *loves* school! You ever hear such a thing?"

I smile. "No. Not sure I have."

"You keep it up, my friend. These kids, they're lucky and they know it."

"It's kind of you to say so, sir," I say, winking at an embarrassed-looking Jazz. "You must be very proud of the young man you've raised. Very proud indeed."

"Every day I am." He beams.

"You've done a fine job, Mr. Jassim. I mean it."

"My great pleasure," he says, batting away my words.

With everyone gone, I pace up and down Exhibition Road, flitting between elation and sadness at being alone again. I replay my conversation with Mrs. Linwood: how she said I'd been doing this annual museum trip for years. I've had, it appears, an unbroken career as a teacher. I've never been to prison, then. Have I, perhaps, committed no crime?

And if there's no crime... I almost won't let myself think about it.

I shake as I familiarize myself with this phone. There's a text waiting for me, sent by *The Wife*. I leave it unread for now, more pressing matters.

I read down my long list of contacts, slowly, as if to savor the hope.

No Holly.

I carry on down the alphabet, kid myself it might be lurking there. Two passes, then a third. Not even a *Buddy* this time. The hollowness of failure; too familiar.

BE DONE IN AN HOUR BABE, reads the message from *The Wife*. MEET AT ALLEGRA'S? XX

It takes a second to place the name. Allegra's—it's the coffee shop by the river. Later a chocolatier, artisanal no less. And also that terrace wine bar, once upon a time.

I toss my phone into my backpack, begin the walk. What else is there for me to do?

Dream Catch Me

"Your good lady joining you?" the waiter asks. I've seen this guy plenty of times, but never been a paying a customer of his. He perches on the edge of my outside table, as familiar as a mate.

"Should be here in a min," I reply, nervous swallow snapping the sentence in two.

"Large latte, extra shot?" he asks, like it's obvious.

I look up from my menu card. "Yeah, sure. Sounds fine." On the other side of the window there's a small selection of spirits on a high shelf. "You do a brandy?"

"Can do," he says. "Is everything okay, Alex?" He looks at me like I'm nuts.

"All good."

"So a brandy, then?"

I could murder something to quiet my mind. "Nah, just kidding about. I'm good."

"And a cappuccino?" He tips a nod to the empty chair.

"You got it."

There's a busker in my spot playing classical violin. The lady who collects for Christian Aid trying to catch people's eyes. This, perhaps, is no longer my world. Why then are Elouise and I regulars at this café?

The coffee arrives, strong and comforting. I study my phone again for clues, but it gives so little away. Barely a social life to speak of, it seems. I gaze out across the concourse to the river.

A fizz of adrenaline. Yearn for someone strongly enough and you'll swear you see them everywhere. Anyone with a comparable manner, or similar dress sense, or even of roughly the right size. Fifty meters away, incoming. Almost uncanny at this distance. I've been seeing Holly in every crowd since the first moment I met her, hanging on to hope till I'm close enough to accept that it's a stranger with a passing resemblance.

Aimed straight at me. It can't possibly be.

Heart thumping. I massage my eyeballs. They ache from lack of sleep.

Look again, refocus.

Her hair's all over the place, strands flailing in the wind. Woolly sweater pulled down over her hands, old trainers. She walks with purpose, expression blank, stressed.

It's her. It can only be Holly. No one else on earth compares.

Where is the feeling of triumph? Why am I not exploding with joy? She's alive. The one update that's kept me going. Instead I'm sick with nerves. Blood leaving my face. Hands shaking.

I'm paralyzed as she draws near. This close, I can't even look at her.

She must be here for someone else. That's it, isn't it?

I stare into my coffee, brown as mud. As I look back up, I'm expecting her to have disappeared. A hallucination. A ghost of the life I took.

She smiles at me. Weary. Slips her arms from her rucksack and lets it land in a heap next to the table. "Hey," she says. "Sorry. Got halfway out the ward and, well, you know..." She drops into the chair opposite me.

How had I forgotten the sound of her voice? Hearing it is like the sun rising on every memory of her, making them bright and real again.

"You life saver," Holly says, holding her coffee to her cheek before sinking a third of it in one draft. "How was the night at the museum, then?"

I force a nod, look up from my lap. She reaches a hand across the table. The hummingbird tattoo, modest stones on a stylish wedding ring, slender fingers reaching for mine.

I pull away. The table is vibrating, spoons jangling like an alarm.

"Alex? What is it, baby?"

My face folds in on itself. The tears come more readily than ever before. I try to speak but I'm incapable. Gasping for air. Our table rocks as my shoulders leap up and down, mind of their own.

"Please, baby," she's saying. "What's happened? Tell me what's happened." She's off her chair, crouching next to me. Her look of distress only makes me worse. I've no right to worry her. Why is this the saddest sight I've ever seen?

I try to resist the hand that reaches for my leg. "Sorry," I sob. It's inaudible. "I'm sorry."

She rubs my back. Her own eyes redden, tears welling. "What is it, Alex? Please?"

I thump a fist against the table, like a toddler unable to express themselves. Snot hangs like phone lines from my nose to my sleeve.

"I'm so sorry," I keep saying.

"I don't understand," she says softly, fingers through my hair.

No concern that people are looking, that I'm making a scene here. "Did something happen? On the school trip?"

I shake my head.

She passes me a fistful of tissues from her bag. I bury my face in them; they smell like her. "I love you," I tell her, as soon as I am able, words jerky. "I love you so much."

"I love *you*, baby," she says, nose against mine despite the hot, snotty mess that I am. "I can't bear seeing you like this. Tell me what's happened."

I take a minute to pull myself back together. "It's fine. Everything's fine."

Holly looks toward the Thames. "Is it being *here*?" she asks. "I guess I forget sometimes. We come here so often. And there's me only ever thinking of all the good times. I forget about your…"

"My…swim?" I smile shakily.

"Yeah. My bad."

"No, no. It's okay. Just got a bit…emotional. Seeing you. Remembering how…lucky…" It's no good. The tears are back in earnest.

Holly hugs my head tight into her sweater. For the first time in as long as I can remember, I have the feeling of not being on my guard. It's so long since I've been safe that I've forgotten how it feels.

"You want to go home?" she asks.

I shake my head. "It's fine," I say, words muffled by her clothes that I bury my face into. "Don't care…where we are. As long as you're there."

"It's okay now," she keeps saying. "Everything's going to be okay now."

Home

Nightfall brings with it clear skies and the clean-smelling chill of approaching winter. I arrange some kindling and a tower of logs in the grate. Using an old trick of my granddad's, I hold a sheet of newspaper over the fireplace, and there's soon a great suck of air as a blaze roars up the chimney, flashing this small sitting room orange. A brown cat of quite magical wiriness—named Oberon, I have discovered—weaves purringly about me before settling on the hearth so close she'll surely go up any second. I attempt to glide her away and she looks up at me with gemstone eyes, expression that says she knows how to take care of herself, thanks all the same.

"Indian, Turkish, Caribbean?" Holly asks from the doorway. She's fresh from the shower, hair tangled to her waist.

"Let me," I say, taking the fan of menus from her. "This ain't gonna be cheap, though." I can't remember the last time I had an appetite like this. Can't remember the last time I really ate anything. For the first time in weeks I'm actually hungry, famished really, and able to stop and think about food.

"You sure you wouldn't rather we went out? Saturday night…"

"Certain of it." She's asked the same question a few times this afternoon. Why on earth would we want to leave this home?

Our place is an end-of-terrace cottage, Victorian probably. The ceilings are low and it's packed out with an incongruous mix of stuff. There's a mantel clock that's been customized in the psychedelic color scheme of John Lennon's Rolls-Royce; a bottle green leather chesterfield worn to a shine; fluffy beanbags and a floral chaise; old books, fresh flowers. Holly and I sat in the garden a while earlier, paint flaking from a bench in the shade of an overgrown magnolia.

This could not be more different from that *property* I lived in with Elouise. It's a third of the size—no topping-out parties here for a white-walled, granite-floored extension, no bifolds for the neighbors to turn green over.

Memories line our walls: holidays with friends, days at the zoo, long walks on low tides. A life I've not lived, yet know intimately. As I've had to several times already, I step away from the display, check I'm not being overlooked. Dry my eyes. Tell myself this is *real*.

Just because I don't deserve it, doesn't mean I can't enjoy it, right?

There's a ten-by-eight of our wedding. Composition off, a little blurred, Holly bent double with laughter in a rock and roll wedding dress, me in a tweed three-piece looking at her like she's got a screw loose. Far too much captured for it to be a professional's shot.

I've pieced together what I can of my life since '95 in these few hours with Holly. I blitzed a degree course in the sciences in two years flat, after my timely enrollment at St. Christopher's College of Further Education. Lived at home all the way, paid my way with shifts at the Blue Moon. Followed it with a post-grad. I've been teaching at Copse Hill Secondary since.

No Elouise. No car crash. No prison.

We've been together every step of the way: no breakups, no *wanting different things*. Right person, right time.

What of the lonely busker's life, the body wrecked by booze, the shithole digs, homelessness? These things that once came after this date are surely banished.

Wedged behind the sofa is my Fender California. I extract it, no sign today of its sticker-covered case and trolley-mounted amp. I wipe away the veneer of dust, revealing a body free of chips and scratches, almost as sharp as the day I bought it when I was eighteen. It's way out of tune. I'm three lines into Buddy Holly's "True Love Ways" when I catch Holly watching in the doorway. I fall quiet, suddenly self-aware, as though I'm behaving like the charming busker of another life.

"It's been a while," she says, wide grin. She scoops up a bewildered Oberon. "Isn't Daddy clever?"

"Like riding a bike, I guess."

"You should get back to it. Those were the days. Miss them."

"Dunno. Maybe I've played enough guitar." Even as I say it, I know I don't mean it. This instrument has at times been my only companion, the only constant in an ever-evolving hell. A few days away from each other might be in order, but I can't imagine a life without the music.

"Keep playing," she says. "Please."

I play "Peggy Sue" and a few more numbers as Holly sits cross-legged by the fire, swaying and combing out her long hair. We are interrupted by the arrival of takeaway, an order big enough to see us through a week.

We get comfortable on the sofa and fill our plates. "You cool now?" Holly asks. "After...earlier?"

"Yeah, sorry," I reply through a mouth bulging with naan bread and saag aloo. "That was weird."

"Not weird, no apology necessary. You maybe think you should speak to Roni?"

"Roni?"

"Roni who you used to see."

"Right."

She nudges me in the ribs. "Therapist Roni, Alex."

"Yeah, of course," I say.

"You know, if you think you're struggling a bit, and maybe not wanting to talk to me about it."

"There's nothing I wouldn't talk to you about."

"But if things are still...bothering you, baby. No need to sweat it."

I feign racking my memory. "When did I last see...them?"

"What's it been? Three years?"

"Yeah, maybe I should sort something." I shovel in some lamb madras, wedge half a poppadom in its wake. Nothing has ever tasted so good.

"Us, being at the river today," Holly says. "Is it *him*? Is that what was getting to you?"

"Him?"

"I do understand, Alex. Had you run into him or something? I know how these things affect you. It is only natural. Never feel you can't say."

"Just a funny five minutes," I say, unconvincingly. "Kind of just got blown away by how...grateful I am for everything. For you."

"Well, I'm relieved to hear it." Holly squeezes my hand. "So not about Blake Benfield, then?" Her face hardens as she utters the name.

Food suddenly hard to swallow. "Blake Benfield?" Saying it brings a vision of his face into my mind's eye. Muscles that have been relaxed for the first time are taut once again. Even letting his name into this home feels wrong.

"It's okay. Say what's on your mind."

"It's...nothing."

She strokes my back. "It's okay for it to still bother you, Alex. These things don't just go away because life moves on." She shakes her head. "You were so young, Alex. Bloody hell."

Holly knows. Everything, it seems. Who else does, I wonder?

For an instant, I feel exposed, outed. But then, just like when I told Mum, there's the sense of a door being thrown open, breeze and light through a sealed room.

"It's cool," I say. "It really is." Cool calm replaces panic. Appetite returns full force. "Maybe I'll see this Roni again sometime. See how I go."

"If you say so."

She snuggles next to me and flicks on the telly. There's a chat show on, people I don't recognize talking about foreign lives. I'm perfectly entertained. Going through my phone earlier hinted at a slim social calendar, and now I understand. Why would I want to be anywhere other than here?

"You're happy, yeah?" I ask Holly.

"Utterly miserable," she says, forcing the last contents of a rice container into her mouth. We've been eating for an hour solid.

"Serious question."

"Bit deep, innit?" Her voice is muffled, flecks of food flying. "Sure I'm happy. You're not?"

"Everything's perfect."

"Jolly good."

"This is enough, though?" I needlessly wave my arms around, at this house, our stuff. "You're sure you don't want...more?"

"More of what?"

What *do* I mean? I'm thinking of that place I had with Elouise, and of that whopping residence Holly's parents own. There's nothing about those lives I desire. But what if that's what she wants?

"Guess I need to be sure, you know? That you're as...deliriously content with all this as I am."

"Is this about what you're earning again?"

"Again?"

"It's a staple twice-a-year wobble, wouldn't you say?"

"Sorry. What a boring subject."

She nudges my arm. "Your one, rather uncustomary insecurity, wouldn't you say? Baby, you work your arse off. And every kid in that place worships you. Well, nearly all of them, maybe."

"Yeah, all right."

She scowls at me, like I have form for rebuffing praise. "No one thinks any less of you because you don't go for promotions. In fact, I think more of you for it. Where on earth would you find the time?"

"I guess."

"I can well imagine how galling it is watching the PE teachers get the senior roles. Climbing the ranks faster than they can climb the sodding monkey bars..."

"Jesus. Infuriating. Must be."

"Like you say, they've got the time to go for the jobs, to do the networking."

"You really think...more of me?"

"For knuckling down? Getting on with being a damned fine teacher? Bloody right."

"All that matters, that is."

"We have everything we need, Alex. In abundance. And then some."

"Sure. Sorry, being a dick."

Holly rubs her belly and ejects an impressive belch. We've eaten the lot. "You're not gonna mention Cambridge, are you?"

"No regrets," I snap. "Not one."

"Really?"

"Sure. Even if I could go back and take my place, I wouldn't do it. Wouldn't risk a thing being different."

We lie on the sofa, watch a freakishly overproduced talent show and rip the piss out of the contestants.

"What happened to Maxim?" I ask, immediately worried I might not like the answer.

"Maxim?" she says, like she's struggling to place the name. "Are we talking the very smooth, very charming South African man?"

"Yup. Very tall."

She giggles. "That guy you hit it off with at my cousin's birthday, what, five years ago?"

I nod.

"What made you think of him?" Holly asks.

"Dunno. Wondering what he's up to."

"Isn't he on your Facebook?"

"Yeah, maybe."

"You were convinced he fancied me." She grins, face an inch from mine.

"Can hardly blame him."

"Do piss off. He was just a nice guy."

"He was a great guy." I snuggle against her a little tighter. Blur the line between us. Buzzing with gratitude for the web of causes, stretching down the years, that has brought about this effect.

Drowsily we watch the *News at Ten*. I can feel Holly's smirk as a story runs about the fallout from New Labour's years of careless spending, but I remain in smug silence. There's a piece about Princess Diana's legacy; Holly remarks how she can't believe it's been eleven years, and I can't stop myself saying how it feels like only yesterday.

We turn in early. Far too exhausted and stuffed for anything more, I spoon against Holly and she's off within a minute. There's a book of Salinger's short stories on my bedside table. In the dim orange light, listening to Holly's slow breathing, her hair on my cheek, I begin to read—desperate not to let go of this day. Oberon slips into a duvet divot, curled and purring in one move. I rest my palm on her rumbling fur. Outside the weather has turned: rain dashing the glass, the sash rattled by the wind. The lines in my book begin to swim, stack atop one another, smudge to gray. I resist, but it's no good.

I am carried away.

DECEMBER 26, 2018 | AGE 43

Perfect

Karen Carpenter sings "Merry Christmas, Darling" on the stereo. The TV's on too, but then it always was in this house; *It's
a Wonderful Life*, sound on mute. With one of Mum's legendary
buffets laid out—far too much for four—and the flashing colored
lights on the tree, this scene could be from any year of my life.

"Come on, have a drink," Dad says, for the third time. He's
looking at Holly and me on the sofa, but his armchair remains
aimed at the telly.

"I'm cool," I say. Again.

"It's Christmas."

"Sure. Gotta drive, though. Not much of a fan these days,
anyway."

"One won't hurt."

"I'm sure he knows his own mind," Mum chimes in. She
passes me a plate of cheese straws fresh from the oven—my
favorite.

Dad shudders faintly, a look that calls me a *boring bastard*. "Holly?" he asks. "Love?" His demeanor is immediately different. In the fifteen minutes since we arrived, he's been as deferential as a butler when addressing her.

Holly holds up a palm. "In a bit, maybe."

"You still off-color, dear?" Mum asks.

"We could go home," I say. Holly's been feeling rough most of the day. Should I have dragged her round here?

"I'm just gonna excuse myself for a moment," Holly says. She pauses at the foot of the stairs. There's something odd about the way she looks back at me. Pale and tired as she is, her eyes are bright and wary. Too nervy for the smile she gives me to seem genuine.

"I can wrap some food up for you," Mum says. "If you think you should go."

"No, Mum. I really want to be here," I tell her.

"If you're sure."

"Holly's a doctor," Dad says. "She knows if she's well enough to stay."

I nod, though I'm not sure it works like that.

The two of us woke up this morning in her parents' swanky residence, smoked salmon for breakfast and pastries baked in the range. Not that it was easy to relax with the memory of my last visit there; unable to shake the belief that her father would any second drop his utterly charming demeanor and set about me like he did *that* night. I drove us round here at lunchtime, ten miles per hour under the speed limit and checking thrice at every turning. Despite it being Holly who's out of sorts, she kept looking funnily at me at the wheel of our Golf GTI, asking me if I was feeling okay. We stopped en route at a seven-day chemist, and she insisted on darting in whilst I waited outside.

I fill myself a plate at the buffet. Dad waffles about Ross, how he and Mum had a video call with him and his wife and kids in Adelaide yesterday. "Always makes time, your brother,"

Dad is saying. He tells me how I should see Ross's house, see what a life he's made out there. His children, apparently, are all geniuses and love seeing their granddad. I'm not sure if they've ever met Dad in person, and I don't ask. "He's been promoted again," Dad tells me. "Head of global communications, would you believe?"

"Very impressive," I agree. "The whole globe…"

Dad cuts me a look. "Done us proud."

"You've both done us proud," Mum says, softly so as not to upset him.

Dad winks at me. "Yeah, yeah. You know what they say? Those who can *do*. Those who can't…"

I make out like I've never heard the expression. Mum tuts and mouths *ignore him* at me.

"Teach!" he says.

"Very good," I say, overly sincere.

"He knows I'm kidding," Dad says in response to Mum's disapproving glance.

I raise my can of lemonade in his direction, and he takes a self-conscious swig of beer. It comes as no surprise, yet still I'm strangely enlightened. Whatever I do, he'll find fault with it. He has long chosen his opinion of me, and no matter how well or otherwise I live this life, I will disappoint him. The only choice I have is whether to give a shit or not. How I wish I'd known that years ago.

Dad shuffles into the kitchen to seek out another drink, stopping on his way to check that I'm absolutely certain I wouldn't like one too.

"You two," Mum says, shaking her head. "Always been the same." She goes to stand and is suddenly rigid with pain. Her mouth twists into a grimace as she grabs the base of her spine.

I lurch off the sofa, kneeling in front of her and holding her other arm. "Mum?"

"It's fine," she says. Juddering jaw that proves it's not fine at all. She breathes deeply as I help her back into the chair and pack a couple of cushions around her.

"What is it?" I ask.

She checks behind her, makes sure Dad isn't returning. "Just happens every now and then. Don't worry yourself."

"How often?"

"It's nothing, Alex," she says.

"You need to be checked out, Mum."

She closes her eyes, sad smile.

"Mum, seriously."

"I have, darling." She talks in a whisper. "Been looked over."

"Well?"

She holds up a palm for silence. Dad returns, filling Mum's wineglass as he passes.

I stare at her, but she only smiles into thin air. Christmas lights of every color twinkle in her damp eyes. I squeeze her hand, and without looking at me, she squeezes back.

"Always loved doing Boxing Day," she says. "Really pleased you two could come. Look at me, always doing too much food. Eat up, make the most…"

I do as I'm told and fill my plate high. I sit close to her, try to get food down my aching throat. She and I both know it: today needs to be enjoyed. I think of that horrendous afternoon, when Mum's bed was in this room. Medication piled round the telly. Black gas cylinders where the Christmas tree and a few gifts now stand. Only a few months from this date.

She grins when inevitably the Carpenters album rolls around to "Yesterday Once More." We listen in silence, Dad engrossed by the telly. "Remember when I used to sing this? To you and Ross, when you were tiny?"

I nod, a rare perfect memory.

She leans close. "Was thinking maybe I'd like this song for, you know…"

"You have a merry Christmas, Mum," I whisper, a tear escaping unchecked. "A discussion for another day."

Just like that, I know that Dr. Defrates was right. There are things over which we have no control—most things, in fact. Mum is dying. Just as she always was. Next August, we'll say goodbye to her. Up till now, I've not been able to shake Dad's accusations: that the stress I caused made her ill, killed her. No logic could stop the guilt eating me. But I've lived a different life, and her fate remains.

My phone bleats in my pocket. A text from Holly:

UPSTAIRS XXX

There was a time when I'd assume such a message was an invitation to sneak off for a bunk-up. A second later, another:

I'M IN THE LOO! XXX

I roll my knuckles against the door. She opens it a crack, checks the landing.

"No one else is up here," I tell her.

Holly grins and ushers me in. She sits on the closed lid of the toilet, hunched and childlike.

"What's the matter?" I ask. "If you've done a massive shit and can't flush the bastard…"

"Shut up, you twat." She grins. There's color back in her cheeks now, in abundance. She stares at my face. "You been crying, baby?"

"No. Well, maybe a tiny bit. Tell you later."

"Sure." She wipes her face with a tissue.

"Have *you* been crying?"

She smiles, brighter than ever. "Yup. You bet."

"I don't get it."

"Alex," she says, passing me a white plastic stick from its hiding place behind the toilet. She's shaking as she hands it over.

I've never handled a pregnancy test before, but even I know what two blue lines means.

"Just when you've accepted it'll never ever happen," Holly says. Her face tells me everything: the years of trying and failing and soul-searching and giving up and the one-last-trying and the pain that have led us to this point.

"Fuck," I say. "Jesus Christ."

"You *do* still want this?" she asks.

"More than anything in the universe."

She nods, like she knew that would be my answer. "I just thought, maybe...when I was feeling all rough. And I wasn't expecting it to actually be...you know." She gulps in some air. "And then, like, pow!"

I rub her shoulders. "Nice deep breaths, yeah?"

"You don't think we're maybe...past it?"

"Nope. Do you?"

She shakes her head. "Never felt younger."

"I love you," I tell her, kneeling level with her, our wet faces touching.

"I know it's a long road," she says. "Lots of things might not be okay..."

"Stop it," I whisper. "It's gonna be fine."

"It just feels...different this time, you know?"

"Course it is." Her cheeks are boiling against my palms. "How long, you think?"

"Dunno. Head's a mess. Could be eight weeks already."

I do the maths: all being well, about the same time as Mum...

We hold each other tight. I cry for who is to come, and for who we are bound to lose.

This life gives, and it takes away. In balance. Love undying.

MAY 25, 2023 | AGE 47

Miracle

It's a warm evening, and the small bookshop is packed out. The place smells wonderfully of printed words and Pringles.

"Beer?" a well-spoken young man asks me. "Warm white wine maybe?"

"Thanks, but I don't drink, actually."

"Are you sure? It is free."

"No. I'm fine." I don't mean to snap.

Dr. Defrates stands at the front like a proud parent. He's dressed for the launch of his book the same way as every other time I've seen him: worn cords, Hush Puppies, overlong tie that rises and falls with his belly. In front of him, several hundred hardback books ready to sign, dedicate and sell. *Out of Time: Tales of Disorderly Lives*, it is titled.

He and I are both on half-term. Not that I've had anything close to a relaxed day. It has apparently fallen to me to ready my parents' house for sale now Dad's in a care home. On my last visit to 2023, I was squatting there, much to Ross's fury, but I have no such need now. Holly's with her own folks, down at the coast for a few days. She and *our child*. Just thinking those words gives me butterflies. They are due back this evening. At our home this morning, I couldn't possibly ignore the toys about the place and cute little bed, the mini toothbrush and hedgehog flannel. But I left in a hurry, forbade myself to look at the pictures on the walls. I want our first meeting to be in person.

"All right, sir!" says a familiar voice. "How's it hanging, old cuz?" A man stands in front of me, arms stretched out wide. He's late twenties, effortlessly sharp, million-watt smile.

"Jazz? Jazz! Bloody hell, man!"

"Told you I'd come," he says, hugging me tight. He smells divine. "Gotta make time for the best teacher a brother ever had."

"What you doing with yourself?" I ask, scarcely able to believe this voice is coming from this impressive man.

"Still a City banker wanker, I'm afraid. I'll jack it in one of these days, I promise. Get on with changing the world like you always said I would."

I look at his shoes, at his big watch. He glows with a cheeky pride. "Nah, man. Keep doing exactly what you're doing," I tell him.

"Remember Ty?" Jazz asks.

Jazz's boyfriend steps forward, and our handshake graduates into a hug.

"You look incredible together," I say, shaking my head in disbelief.

"Nearly nine years," Ty says. "Since that crazy prom boat."

I laugh along, remember that in their memory of events, I was doubtless *on* that boat. We talk about school and their careers that are flying, and I hold back the tears when they tell me an invitation is in the post for their wedding.

Dr. Defrates's literary agent, Harry, introduces himself to us.

He's a young beanpole of a man who is simultaneously shy and charming, as though he's constantly apologizing for the twinkle in his own eye. I ask him how well he thinks the book will sell.

"He's a fascinating man," Harry says.

"He's that all right."

"It's so interesting, this gray area he writes about. Not fiction, not quite fact either. It's up to the reader to decide what to make of his work."

"Interesting," I say. "You don't think everything is necessarily...true?"

"I can't wait to see how the public receive it," Harry replies, dodging the question.

A hush falls as Dr. Defrates gives a reading: an excerpt from the story he told me about Frank McVie—the American who became obscenely wealthy but lost his mind and invited a psychiatrist to live with him.

Afterward, the cash register rings and the books fly as quick as Defrates can sign them.

"Make it to Holly," I tell him, as he produces a copy which he insists is a gift.

When the party's done, he and I walk together through lanes of shops. The evening is still warm and light. Holly texts and says she's twenty minutes away; she suggests we meet for hot chocolates.

"Glad of this," I say, clutching the book in its paper bag to my chest. "Need to put my dear wife in the picture, I feel. This should help."

"Happy to be of service," Dr. Defrates says. He's bowling along in the way he always has, chin leading.

"So you've worked out all the answers, then?"

"Gosh, no. It's a collection of the case studies I've done. Some theories about the whys and wherefores. More questions than answers. I wish to start a conversation, lift the lid on it. That's all."

"Am I in there?"

"Do you want to be?"

"Not sure."

"I've not mentioned you by name. You're entitled to your anonymity. But you've been invaluable."

"You too, mate. Christ, just a bit."

Our pace slows as we reach the river. We turn left, head west along the bank into the setting sun. "Ah, the beauty," he mumbles.

"So why publish now?" I ask. "No more to discover?"

"What a thing for a science teacher to suggest." He laughs. "Most certainly not, young man."

"Not so young today."

"I have shared my findings with the world, Alex, for much more practical reasons."

"Go on."

"Because I am so very nearly *out of time* myself."

"How so?"

"You and I, regardless of the order in which they come, live each day of our life once. We are just like everyone else in that regard." His pace slows, and we meander close to the water's edge. "My first injury, the beginning of my atemporal consciousness, occurred when I was thirty. November 1990. The latest days I've seen are 2028."

"Ages away."

"Not for me, Alex. Since my injury, I've experienced something close to fourteen thousand days, give or take. Thirty-eight years, cumulatively, to put it another way."

"Shit."

"I can't be precise," he tells me, "but my number's nearly up. One of these days, I'm going to awake and it will be my last day."

"Is that…unavoidable?"

Dr. Defrates shrugs his shoulders and picks up the pace again.

"You told me how my second injury happens in 2024," I say. "That I'll be going into the Thames at the same spot as before. That's next year."

"Ah, but you've got so many days left, haven't you? Hardly experienced any at all, really."

There's a bloom of excitement in my gut. So much life to live. "Does feel like I've been at it ages already."

"Wait till you're where I am," he says. "Whilst your end day is next year, it is, for you, thousands and thousands of days away."

"I guess. So you don't think we can beat it? Live on beyond the date of our second traumatic injury?"

"It's a mystery I'll be uncovering soon enough," he replies, smirking at his own wit.

I wander into his path and force him to stop. "So in the four years between my end day and yours, 2024 to 2028, have you not seen me? Have you checked what happened to me? Surely that would give you your answer."

He shakes his head, that same self-assured expression that always made me wary. "It's inconclusive." A long stride, on the move again.

"What does that *mean*?"

"Read the book, Alex. I propose some theories."

It feels heavy in my hands all of a sudden. "Maybe I'll skip that bit. I don't know. Do I want to know?"

"It's the mysteries that make life exciting," Defrates says.

"Yeah. Maybe."

We reach the familiar concourse. A guitarist with a loop pedal plays, on the very spot where Jazz's memorial once stood. I bung the guy a twenty-pound note as we pass. The fire-and-brimstone preacher clearly has no idea who I am, but he tells me Jesus loves me all the same. The artisanal chocolatier has sprouted some tables outside where kids and parents drink from glasses piled high with cream and marshmallows.

"Look at us," I say to Dr. Defrates. "Both bloody teachers. How did that happen?"

He's unusually serious. "There's a better use of this life?"

"I don't think so, not for me. Were you always a teacher?" I ask. "Before the atemporal business? Before your first accident?"

He surveys the river—a lake of lava in the setting sun. "My life was a mess," he says. "I was thirty. Ruined marriage. Drink, cocaine, opiates, you name it. Career wrecked."

"You've never said."

"Why would I? I had the chance to start again, and I took it."

"It wasn't an accident, was it?"

Dr. Defrates smiles. "Me, headbutting a train? No, Alex, no accident."

"I'm glad you survived."

"So am I! *This*—our predicament—you could see it as a curse, forced to live life out of order, never knowing what comes next, what matters and what doesn't. But it can be a very fine gift as well. In the right hands…"

"Yeah, maybe I'm seeing that."

He looks around the concourse, and a grin spreads across his face. "Here they are, young man, that lovely wife and daughter of yours."

I fizz with nerves, look at my feet. "Daughter? We had a girl?" My nose tingles and it's all I can do not to burst into tears.

"Oh, my!" Dr. Defrates says, grabbing my shoulder. "Oh, what a thing! This is the first time? You've not met her yet?"

I shake my head.

"This is too perfect. You do know you *have* a daughter."

"A child, sure. No more than that." I'm shaking.

"It's okay to look, Alex."

I do as I'm told. Mother and child, hand in hand, a perfect silhouette.

"What's…her name?" I ask him.

"Peggy Sue, would you believe?"

"You're kidding me. Wow! *Peggy Sue.* That's so…cool."

"I must be getting on," he says. "This is all yours. Be sure to enjoy it."

"Thank you. For everything."

"Likewise."

"I'll see you around, I'm sure."

He pats my back.

I can see their faces now. She is Holly in exquisite miniature. She breaks free of her mother's hand. Makes a run for me.

"I don't deserve this," I tell Dr. Defrates. "No way do I deserve this."

"Stop attacking yourself," he says, a man tiring of me. "When will you see it? How that's precisely what's caused you so much of your trouble."

"You think?"

He turns on his heel. "So long, Alex," he says, walking briskly away, too decent to impose.

I crouch, hold my arms out wide.

She crashes into me full pelt, nearly sends my trembling frame clean over.

"Daddy!" she shouts. We hug each other tight. She's so tiny. How can a fully functioning human be so small? Little hot arms, strong enough that they're half strangling me.

I hold her at arm's length. She has Holly's crazy hair, her ever-fascinated hazel eyes. She wears a tracksuit covered with planets, and still-sandy jelly shoes. Already she's jabbering at a hundred miles per hour, about all the things they've been up to in the two days they've been away.

I give Holly a kiss. Sunscreen and sea salt.

Our little girl stands between us, and we take a hand each. We walk toward the chocolate shop. I'm struck by a yearning to know every last thing about her.

I shoot a glance over my shoulder. The river is dark as the coming night. Someday, I'll have to start worrying about the likelihood of my life ending here. But right now, I'm ready for it to begin.

EPILOGUE

"Are you okay?" whispers the vicar. She gives a bright-eyed chuckle.

"Never been better," I reply through a grin I couldn't lose even if I wanted to.

It's gone five, and the stained glass windows have turned to black. The church flickers in the light of a thousand candles.

"It's starting to snow, would you believe it?" Dad says gleefully from the pew behind where I stand. He winks at me. "You're a jammy swine, my boy!"

My best man, Paul, or Dr. Defrates to some, sniggers at my side. "What are the chances?" he says. "The man plans a winter wedding and the snow arrives right on cue."

"What are the chances..." I whisper back.

We smirk at each other. He's dressed in a sharp tweed suit which is an inch-perfect fit. Hired, obviously.

There are about fifty guests here. My brother and my good

friend Loz are on ushering duty, seating the last to arrive who sweep snow from overcoat shoulders and shoot well-wishing looks my way. Behind Mum and Dad sits Aunty Liv; she's already dabbing at a tear, much to Uncle Brian's amusement. I'm delighted they've come.

"It is time," the vicar says, squeezing my wrist.

My heart leaps.

The doors at the rear of the church clank open.

A rustle as best clothes turn rearward.

Beneath the great arch, Holly and her father. The snow swirls and squalls behind them.

Her father smiles at me. He takes a step forward, a patent Beatle boot pointing my way.

My and Holly's eyes meet. A half smile apiece, as nervous and as electric as the very first time we saw each other, all those years ago in the Blue Moon.

I knew I couldn't trust myself not to cry. They come fast, the proudest tears I've ever shed.

That familiar pitter-pattering intro plays through the church: Buddy Holly's "Everyday."

It is time.

★ ★ ★ ★ ★

ACKNOWLEDGMENTS

Thank you—

To my agent and friend Harry Illingworth, without whose passionate advocacy this book would not exist.

To Helen Edwards, for keeping the faith and finding the perfect home for *The Day Tripper.*

To Meredith Clark, editor extraordinaire and force of nature, and to all those brilliant people at MIRA.

To my brothers, Will and Sam, who respond to my constant requests for advice in good humor and continue to provide invaluable feedback on everything I write.

To my wife. As unpredictable and disorderly as life may be, when we face it together with the right person, we can do anything. Really, that's what the previous few hundred pages have been about. Thank you for everything, Vikki. The last words of this book belong to you.